APACHE DUNES

Also by G.D. Flashman

Justice Is Pronounced: Just Us

Every Man Must Die

Apache Dunes
2020 Colorado Independent Publishers Association EVVY Award Winner

What readers say about *Apache Dunes*

★★★★★ "A great read. You will feel as if you are watching the action REEL time!"

★★★★★ "Best read ever!!"

★★★★★ "Couldn't put it down."

★★★★★ "Extraordinary novel!"

★★★★★ "Superb Read"

★★★★★ "Tarantino meets Walter White"

★★★★★ "Warning: you can't put this one down"

★★★★★ "Great new read!"

APACHE DUNES

G.D. FLASHMAN

Originally published 2019 by Outskirts Press

This is a work of fiction. Names, characters, places, and incidents appearing in this work are the sole expression, opinion and product of the author's imagination only, are entirely fictitious and do not represent and are not based on any real life views of any character or event in any way whatsoever and any resemblance is strictly coincidental. Any and all references and depictions appearing in this work to real life persons, living or deceased, are based solely and entirely on the author's imagination and are in no way a representation of, or bear any resemblance to the actual views, events or opinions of such persons.

ISBN 978-0-578-88611-4 (print)

Also available in ebook

Cover and book design by Sue Campbell Book Design

Contact the author: magcltd@aol.com

For Susanna

Justice Is Pronounced Just Us

The Arizona Desert Just North of the Border with Mexico, Summer 2010

Del Kennedy, the senior DEA agent for the Arizona/Mexico border area, stopped at the Oasis, ten miles west of the town of Apache Dunes—the only gas station in the area. He filled his tank with gas and loaded up on bottled water, a vital commodity in the desert—particularly on days like today, when the digital thermometer in the car read 110, now 111 degrees.

He pulled out on the state road heading home to "the Dunes," as the locals called it, when his radio came alive.

"Batman One this is Cap Two Niner Niner, do you read me?" Del's moniker was Batman. His junior officer, Carl, was Robin.

"This is Batman One, Cap Two Niner Niner. I read you loud and clear."

"What's your twenty, Batman?"

"Just left the Oasis heading back to the Dunes. What's up, Snoopy?"

Snoopy was the affectionate moniker for Mike Connor, the self-appointed head of the local Civilian Air Patrol—comprised of only Mike. He was a decorated pilot from the Vietnam War who moved to the Dunes after retiring from the Air Force. He had a passion for flying, but was born sixty years too late. He yearned for the days when aerial warfare was conducted with a code of honor. The nickname came from his pride and joy, a replica of a Sopwith Camel WWI biplane. His favorite recreation was getting stoned and watching *The Blue Max* for the umpteen- thousandth time.

The locals speculated that Snoopy and the Red Baron were engaged in aerial combat every time they would look upward and see him doing his maneuvers. He had chosen the Arizona desert for its open skies and relatively laid-back attitudes. He was Harry Chapin's proverbial cab driver, but with a plane, not a cab. He liked to fly "high," thus enjoyed the solitude of the desert sky. The Dunes despite, or rather because of, the coexistence of so many smugglers and federal agents, was a "live and let live" kind of place.

Although Mike liked the Civil Air Patrol tag, it was rare to see any movement in the desert during the day. The smugglers could cause traffic jams after dark, but "only mad dogs and Englishmen ventured out in the midday sun" and there were neither in the Dunes. Hence, it was unusual for Del to get a call from Mike, or anyone, during Siesta time.

"Del, I took the Sopwith out for a spin and was just getting ready to head in, when I saw a dust cloud coming from north of the border at a high rate of speed. I circled around to check it out and it was a late-model car heading due north. I clocked her at over 100 miles per hour."

"Whoa, first of all, what are you doing up in this heat? I'm showing 111."

"Mother-in-law came for a visit."

"Roger that. Two things: was someone pursuing the car, and you said, her?

"My first thought was somebody must be chasing her, so I circled back, but if anybody was in pursuit, they stopped at the border. She just didn't know because of the trail of dust she was leaving."

"Again, her. How did you know it was a female?"

"I'm getting to that. Approximately eight clicks or so from the state road, the car died. Smoke was pouring out of the hood."

"No surprise there, in this heat and at those speeds."

"Roger that. When the dust settled I went in for a closer look and a lady exited the driver's side. And Del, if she isn't a movie star—she should be."

"Is she alone?"

"Roger that. I did a couple of turns and there is no cover for miles in any direction. She looked back to the south and realized that no one was in pursuit, then took out her cell and was trying to call somebody."

"Good luck with that."

"Roger that. She finally gave up and tossed the phone."

"How about water?"

"Del, she has on some type of sun dress and cowboy boots—nothing else. Not even a hat, and the dress doesn't cover much at all. She went to the trunk and retrieved a black duffel bag—one of those sport bags, but didn't open it. I haven't seen her with any water or anything."

"In this heat, that means she's gonna get sun stroke if she hasn't already. Can you put down?"

"That's a negative. I was heading in when I spotted the car. I'm real low on petrol."

"I'm doing a U-ey right now and heading west. Can you pick me up and guide me to her?"

"That's affirmative. Are you in the Batmobile?"

(The locals referred to Del's Range Rover with the bubble lights as the Batmobile.)

"Affirmative. I'll put the lights on."

Del headed west at full speed knowing that time was critical, intrigued by the situation.

"Del, I have you. Slow down a bit and I'll pass over and lead you to her. We're going to head south into the desert in approximately five clicks."

"Roger that."

Del smiled. The Nam vets always spoke of clicks, kilometers, not miles. He spotted the plane and turned left off the highway when it banked to the south.

"The car is about eight clicks or so due south. In fact, you may not need me anymore. The vultures were heading in her direction on my last pass."

"Roger that. Not surprised."

"If you've got it covered, I need to make a big decision here."

"What's that?"

"Do I crash or land and see my mother-in-law?"

Del laughed.

"You laugh, but you don't know. By the way, when are you going to settle down? That castle you built must get lonely at times."

"I'm waiting for the next set of Dunes debutantes to be presented. Who knows, maybe this is fate and I'm about to meet my fairy princess?"

"Roger that. You let me know how things turn out. Wait'll you see her—whoooeee!"

"I've got visual on the vultures. One last question before you go—who won today, you or the Red Baron?"

Mike laughed.

"We both lived to fight another day. Now it's back to the Officer's Mess for a root beer! Oh, Del, now that I have you, have you by any chance confiscated any more of that primo Mexican weed that you need to dispose of?"

Del laughed. "I'm sure we can find a pound or so that we need to incinerate. Think you could burn it for us?"

"Down to the last ash."

"I'll have Robin get in touch with you."

"Roger that. Over and out."

"Over and out."

Del could now see the glare off the car windshield and slowed his approach. Mike had been right—there was no cover and no sign of any dust clouds on the horizon, but Del had come to be very respectful of the desert and its many secrets. It paid to be cautious. There were no do-overs in the desert.

As he neared the car, the woman looked startled, and rather than welcome her rescuer, she grabbed the sport bag and started running away to the west. Del realized he had turned on the bubble lights for Mike and forgot to turn them off. The woman wanted nothing to do with the law.

Del pulled alongside the car and took his time taking in the situation before he exited his vehicle. The woman stumbled twice, trying to run in cowboy boots, and was now on her knees barely fifty yards away. One thing was certain—Del could take his time. There was nowhere for her to go and, certainly nowhere to hide.

Del had a veritable arsenal in the back of his Range Rover and selected his .45 ACP for its stopping power, in the event that anyone unexpected dropped by. That was doubtful, as even rogue smugglers wouldn't attempt a move in broad daylight. It was well known and understood that justice in the desert was swift and fatal. Judge Roy Bean would have been right at home.

With the gun at his side he circled around the late model Toyota, which appeared to be a rental car, still erring on the side of caution. The woman hadn't moved and was now standing and watching him. Confident that no one else was around, he opened the driver's side door, noting there was a dent in it, and sat down in the driver's seat. It was an oven outside and even more so inside. He hit the ignition to check the gauges and saw that there was barely a quarter of a tank of gas. Noted. He got out and popped the trunk. It was empty save for the spare tire. No suitcase, clothes, water—nada. Noted, again.

Del was soaking wet from just that exercise, so he knew what state the woman must be in. She hadn't moved, but the vultures had landed and were surveying their prey.

Del got back in the Rover and reached for two bottles of water and a straw cowboy hat in the back. He took his time cooling off a bit in the A/C and rehydrating. Then he turned toward the woman and proceeded very slowly. He put the lights back on for dramatic effect. He parked approximately ten yards away and exited with the .45 at his side. She was standing, holding the bag.

Del glanced at the ground and quickly raised the gun to a two-handed position, appearing to point directly at her.

"Don't move a fucking muscle."

She then heard the explosion of four shots in rapid succession and felt the wind from the bullets. She jumped to the side and, turning around, saw the headless remains of an almost three-foot sidewinder rattlesnake. It had been barely five feet away. She was shaking and dropped the bag.

"See those lines in the sand? It's called a sidewinder because it moves sideways and leaves its distinctive trail. One more step and even I wouldn't have been able to save you."

Del went back to his truck and retrieved the water and the hat. Mike was right, the dress was a sheer fabric that covered little when dry and nothing when soaking wet, like now. He handed her the water, which she dropped at first, her hands still shaking, and reached over to put the hat on her head.

"Sip that water. Don't gulp it. I've got plenty in the truck—you don't have to worry about water."

He kicked the bag out of the way, as much to get a sense of what might be in it. He didn't hear or feel any metal. Still holding the gun at his side he bent down, unzipped the bag, and looked inside.

The woman spoke for the first time. "I want to speak with my lawyer."

"What's your name, miss?"

"Kelsey."

"Kelsey, I'm Del and I understand why you might think there are lots of lawyers in the desert—what with the scorpions, lizards, rattlesnakes, and vultures all part of the same evolutionary chain—but I don't believe you are going to find a lawyer out here—at least not in the daylight. Now, in case you haven't noticed, it is 111 degrees out here and I for one am getting into my air-conditioned truck. Oh, and I suggest if you join me that you take that dress off and spread it out on the hood. It'll be dry in a few minutes, but if you get in the A/C with the dress soaking wet, you may catch cold."

"How convenient."

"Look Kelsey, I could give a rat's ass what you do, but in case you haven't noticed, the dress, particularly soaking wet, leaves nothing to the imagination. So suit yourself and, by the way, you can thank me for saving your life when you get around to it."

"I'm entitled to one call."

"Kelsey, you can make as many calls as you want."

Del got in the Range Rover and locked the doors. He pretended to be occupied with something. Kelsey tried to open the passenger side door and realized it was locked. She freaked and began pounding on the window. Del cracked it a bit.

"You locked the door!"

"You said you had calls to make. I think I'm going to head in. I'll send a tow truck."

"You know there's no cell service out here. You can't leave me here."

"Watch me."

Del put the truck in gear and started to inch away.

Kelsey was pounding furiously on the passenger door.

"OK, OK, you win. Let me in."

Del cracked the window again and took a long drink of water, for dramatic effect.

"I'm sorry, did you say, please let me in?"

"Please let me in. Please don't leave me out here."

Del put the truck in park.

Kelsey had some difficulty getting her dress off as it was literally stuck to her.

She put it on the hood of the Rover, opened the passenger side door, and got in.

Del had never seen such a beautiful woman in his life—even the retouched models in Playboy. He had also never seen a thong in real life. The effect was only magnified by a twenty-four carat gold chain hanging loosely around her waist. She was absolutely stunning and she knew it. There are certain reactions that even the strongest of men have no control over.

Kelsey quickly noticed.

"Is that another gun you're hiding in your jeans?"

"Kelsey, number one, that is a terrible impression of Mae West. Number two, my dick has been harder than Chinese arithmetic since the moment I laid eyes on you, but my primal instinct is for self-preservation and there are way too many things wrong with this picture."

"It just seems like you can do whatever you want with me and there's nothing I can do about it."

"Let's see—you're stranded in the desert with no food, water or even a hat, in deadly heat. I have everything you need to survive. I have a gun and I'm the ranking federal agent in this area. You're very perceptive."

"What happened to justice? Doesn't it apply in these parts?"

"Kelsey, in these parts, as you say, justice is pronounced—just us."

"You said there are things wrong with this picture."

"I said there are way too many things wrong with this picture. For one, no one smuggles drugs in the daylight in the desert. There's no cover and justice is swift and fatal around here. Two, the mules are almost always undocumented Mexicans. The worst that happens to them is they are deported, unless it's an election year. Then they can stay if they vote Democrat at least once. And three, there are a lot of beautiful women and actresses, even, who don't have an ounce of class—despite the efforts of the media to create an image for them. You exude not just class, but also breeding and privilege. Kelsey—you aren't a smuggler. I don't know how you got caught up in this, but I aim to find out. Until then, I'll control my emotions."

Kelsey shifted seductively in her seat and was now turned completely toward him.

"I admire your restraint."

"In the desert, restraint can make the difference between life and death. Many men died of thirst convinced they saw a shimmering lake in the distance. The lake turned out to be a mirage. Maybe you're real or maybe you're a mirage. I'm going to find out, but I'm not going to risk my life doing so."

Kelsey's stomach growled.

"When was the last time you had anything to eat?"

"Yesterday afternoon."

"Do you like Big Macs?"

"Don't tell me—McDonalds delivers out here."

"Kelsey, if you get stranded in the desert without food and water, you die, as you were about to find out. Cars can break down for reasons other than driving them at full speed in triple-digit temps. So I stock up at Mickey D's every chance I get and always have a cooler full of food, beer, and water.

"Now, if you reach behind you in the red cooler you'll find the Big Macs. Take two out to start. You don't need a microwave in the desert. Put them on the hood of the truck in their boxes and they'll be perfect in ten minutes."

Kelsey turned around in her seat and opened the red cooler. She hesitated for a moment, looked at Del, and then pulled out a bottle of Perrier Jouet champagne.

"Perrier Jouet champagne? Are you kidding me?"

"I forgot I put that in with the food. It's for a special occasion."

"Pray tell me your definition of a special occasion?"

"Kelsey, some people can feel in their bones when a storm is coming, or it's about to rain. I can't, but what I can do is sense when danger is imminent and my senses tell me that someone is going to die before this day is done. If it isn't either you or me, that will qualify as a very special occasion. So keep the bubbly on ice"

"Can I—I mean, may I have another bottle of water?"

"I'm about ready to have a cold can of Coors. I suggest you switch to a Coors Light for the nutrients—besides, you aren't going to be driving anymore today. Put the Big Macs on the hood and I'll open the beer."

Kelsey exited with the Big Macs.

Del's mind was throbbing almost as hard as his dick, as he tried to get a grip on the situation. To make matters worse, his dick was virtually undefeated in debates with his brain. The internal debate went like this:

"You're a fucking idiot if you let her get away!!"

"Del, how many times did your mom read the poem 'The Spider and the Fly' to you? Hundreds, and guess what? Kelsey's the spider and you're the fly! Don't walk away —run away while you can!"

"Time out—time fucking out. So she's not innocent, but that may be a good thing. If Snow White did happen to fall out of the sky in this Godforsaken place, how do you explain to her the cash you have stashed offshore and the bags of cash that come every month like clockwork? How do you explain how you built an estate in the desert worthy of the Hamptons on a government salary?"

"Yeah, well, I didn't ask for this. I was forced into it. I didn't make the rules."

"He who hath not sinned. Maybe you should hear her story. You might have more in common than you think."

"That's the problem, you may be too much alike. Opposites attract and likes repel. That's a law."

He was startled out of his inner turmoil when Kelsey knocked on the window.

"Are you OK?"

"Yeah, I just had a little headache."

"You looked like you were a million miles away."

Kelsey held up the dress, which was now dry, for Del to see.

"It's dry. You sure you want me to put in on?"

"Put it on and, by the way, I'm not sure you aren't even sexier with it on."

Kelsey pulled the dress over her head and checked the Big Macs. In the few minutes she was outside she was sweating again and the dress once again was clinging to her. She gave Del the thumbs up and took both sandwiches back to the cab. Del reached over and opened the door.

When Kelsey sat down again she made certain the dress, which was short to begin with, left nothing to the imagination. She turned to face Del and looked at his crotch.

"Seems like your problem hasn't gone away."

"Here's your beer. Eat your sandwich and keep your observations to yourself, while I do the same. When we're through, I have some questions that you're going to answer."

"Fair enough, but please understand that you're a mystery to me, as well."

"I go first. Now eat."

Kelsey had finished her sandwich and most of her beer. Del still seemed deep in thought. He said there were things wrong with this picture and he was spot on, but the so-called picture that was emerging about this federal agent, who wore a gold Rolex, drove a Range Rover, and had a bottle of Perrier Jouet on ice, would resemble a work by Salvador Dali. She tried to suppress a laugh just thinking about it.

"What did I miss that was so funny?"

"I just had a funny thought?"

"You want to share it with me?"

"Not really, but if you want me to really talk—I mean really talk—how about letting me do a couple of lines of coke?"

Del just stared at her for a moment and then shrugged his shoulders. She opened her door and started to get out and get the sport bag.

Del grabbed her arm and pulled her back in.

"Hey, I thought that meant it was OK?"

Del reached in the console and pulled out a baggie full of cocaine and a gold coke spoon. Kelsey's eyes almost bulged out.

"Now even Dali couldn't paint the picture."

"What the fuck is that supposed to mean? Be careful with that—it's almost pure."

Kelsey did two hits and blinked her eyes.

"Holy shit!"

She offered the bag back to Del. He shook his head and reached for another beer.

"One of us has to have our wits about us. Now, three critical questions: What time is your rendezvous at the Oasis? Who are you meeting? And, have you spoken to them since Mexico?"

Kelsey looked truly startled.

"How in the world do you know about the meeting at the Oasis?"

"One of the first things I did was check your gas gauge. You had barely a quarter tank and the only gas station within fifty miles of here is the Oasis."

"I'm impressed."

"Again?"

"Again."

"Good, now start talking or I take the candy away."

"I'm supposed to meet two guys at five o'clock. They extorted money from me and then blackmailed me into making the run. And no, I haven't spoken with them since I left Tucson."

Del took a drink of beer, gazed at Kelsey for a moment, and motioned for her to have another hit of coke.

"This is where it's going to get interesting," she said. To Del's utter amazement, Kelsey appeared to blush and turned her head away.

"I can't wait to hear what could make you blush. I would've bet the ranch that was impossible."

"You want to know how they could blackmail me and I'd rather not have to go there."

"Avoiding the subject isn't an option."

"You're going to think I'm a total slut—which I am."

"Kelsey, the great Muhammad Ali once said, 'A wise man can act like a fool, but a fool can't act like a wise man.' We've already established that you're not a smuggler, even though you were caught red-handed with five keys of cocaine, and, if you're a slut, it's by choice, not fate. Damned good impression of one though."

He raised his beer to her in a mock toast.

"Now it's story time and I can't wait for this one."

"Don't gloat. You aren't exactly Dudley Do Right, although I imagine he'd look just like you. By the way, who'd you piss off to get posted out here?"

"Cute—and for your information, it was a promotion."

"A promotion? Where was your last posting, the North Pole?"

Del liked the spunky attitude.

"In case you've forgotten—I'm in charge here and I'll ask the questions, or your little white ass is going to be left in the desert and Daddy will take your candy away. *Comprende*?"

"Sorry—it's just—it's just fucked up. The truth is, I have a love/hate relationship with men. It goes back to my father and I finally meet someone, by total happenstance, whom I happen to be attracted to, and you're not going to want to have anything to do with me after you find out how fucked up I am."

Del was totally turned on to hear Kelsey admit that she was attracted to him. He couldn't imagine what she could do that would cause him to lose interest in her, but he was about to find out. Knowing her, it would be a doozy. The inner debate was now officially over by TKO. His dick was still undefeated.

"Kelsey, most of us have some skeletons rattling around in our closets. Some are just bigger than others. I have to know what's going on with you and the blackmailers because your life—and maybe mine—might depend on it. If we survive this day, we can share that champagne in my hot tub and I'll let you ask the questions. Deal?"

"Deal—it's just—it's just really screwed up. I've done some terrible things on purpose. My analyst said I was trying to get back at my dad and now I'm ashamed of what I've done. You're not going to like it."

"What did your dad do that was so awful?"

"That's what's so screwed up. He's handsome, smart, a war hero, star athlete, and successful businessman who married the homecoming queen. He gave me everything that money could buy, but there are things that money can't buy and, certainly, can't protect you from. He sent me away to a boarding school, a very expensive and prestigious boarding school, and something happened there that changed my life and I blamed him and my mother for that. I've been acting out ever since and I'm a very bad actor."

"We'll save that story for another time and place. Now, I have to pee and then we have to sort things out."

When Del finished, he again scanned the horizon in all directions and returned to the truck.

"What do you keep looking for? I told you the rendezvous is at the Oasis."

"And I told you I was transferred here, but I don't plan on dying here. Forgive me, but until proven otherwise—I'm going to take everything you say with a grain of salt."

"Ouch."

"You'll get over it. Now it's story time. I need some blanks filled in, like how and why they're extorting you, if they are?"

"How about I give you the Cliff Notes version?"

"Suits me, as long as nothing material is left out. I've had enough drama for one day."

"The alpha dog, so to speak, is a black guy named Franklin. He's one of the two I'm supposed to meet at the Oasis. He's from LA and supposedly associated with one of the big gangs out there."

"What colors does he wear?"

"Blue, primarily."

"The Crips."

"That's it—the Crips."

"And what does Franklin have on you?"

Kelsey laughed.

"What doesn't he have? Let's start with videotape of me with Franklin and a few of his closest friends."

"What's on the tape?"

"Use your imagination. I passed out at some point, but nobody forced me to be there. We were being avant-garde, or so we thought."

"Did you know you were being videotaped?"

"Of course not."

"Whoa—don't expect me to follow any logic here. Logic disappeared at Jump Street with you."

"I told you I was screwed up. There were two of us, me and a local. She was from the opposite side of the tracks, but has looks and a body that could kill."

"And what's your relationship to her?"

"I definitely don't want to go there."

"You don't have that option if she is in any way connected with the cocaine."

"She had absolutely nothing to do with it."

"Fair enough. When did the extortion start?"

"Franklin tried to get money from both of us, but realized that she didn't have any. He demanded twenty-five grand from me and I was too quick to give it to him—so he demanded another twenty-five. If I didn't pay he was going to send the tapes to my parents. I'd been so sure that I wanted to hurt my parents, but now I'd do anything to keep them from seeing the videos."

"Could you get the other twenty-five?"

"It turns out I had fifty thousand in an account my aunt, who was my godmother, had opened for me. I showed him that the account was now empty and convinced him that's all my family had."

"Your godmother gave you fifty grand?"

"I was born with a silver spoon in my mouth."

"Make that gold. Did he give you the tape?"

"He beat me when I asked for it. My eye was swollen shut for several days. Then I'd hear him talking to his friends in LA, telling them he was bringing me out there."

"So you had to continue to act like a slut, for fear he would find out who you really were and up the ante?"

"Exactly."

"Why didn't you go to the police?"

"He threatened to kill me if I did—and I believed him. I was also afraid my parents would find out if the police got involved. I was trying to figure a way out."

"So how did you get mixed up with this coke deal?"

"A few days ago he made contact with some guys across the border who offered him five keys of uncut coke for fifty grand. He knew he could turn that in LA and make a fortune. So he came to me all nicey-nice and apologizing, and said if I did one last favor for him, he'd give me the tape and I would be free—if that's what I wanted. All I had to do was drive across the border and swap the money for the coke."

"Did you believe him?"

"Hell no, but I needed time to get away and think."

"So what happened in Mexico?"

"As much as I feared Franklin, the four guys in Mexico scared the shit out of me. I knew something was wrong. So, I tried to think and parked the car so it wasn't boxed in and was facing out. When they came out they asked if I had the money. I said the money was in the trunk and asked, did they have the coke?"

"One of them brought out the duffel bag and showed me the coke. I popped the trunk and gave him the money. I then had an idea that probably saved my life. My suitcase with all of my clothes was in the trunk. I smiled and said, "Will one of you take my clothes up to the bedroom for me?" They were all smiles now. As we started walking to the casa, I stopped and said, "I need something from my car." I got in on the driver's side and leaned over like I was reaching for the glove compartment and I prayed—I mean I prayed the car would start immediately—and it did.

"I didn't even close the driver's side door, which is where the dent came from. I floored the accelerator and headed due north. I could see them jump in their trucks to follow, but after that, I couldn't see anything for the dust cloud I was creating. I didn't stop until the car overheated and quit. I was sure they were right behind me."

"They would have quit at the border in midday. These guys had to be rogue players and they'd fear the cartels as much as the law. Plus Snoopy was up there today—which is how I found you."

"Snoopy?"

"That's his nickname. He was a decorated pilot in Nam who wanted no more of war or so-called civilization. He moved to the desert and lives in this dream that he's dueling with the Red Baron, hence the WWI plane. He's generally stoned out of his gourd up there, but he alerts us about any unusual activity, like today."

"I've got to say, things are different around here."

"You don't know the half of it, but you've got a major decision to make. Do you have any clue about your situation?"

"I thought I wasn't under arrest."

"You aren't, but Kelsey—let me lay it out to you. Are you paying attention?"

Kelsey nodded.

"First of all, if we pick the two guys up, I've got nothing to charge them with. It's going to be your word against theirs and you got caught red-handed. Secondly, if Franklin is a Crip money-maker, even if we tried to hold him, some mouthpiece would come in and bail him out. Last, and most important, your testimony would be their only risk of prison and you're an idiot if you think they'd take that risk. Black eyes and cut lips are one thing, but do you want to live the rest of your life looking over your shoulder?"

Kelsey started to cry. "It's all my fault. I'm a total fuck up."

Del slid over and caressed her for the first time.

"No argument there, but you have to make a decision."

"What decision do I have?"

"Kelsey, the more I hear you talk, the more alike I think we are. I'm all that stands between you and a fate I don't want to think of—and one that you don't deserve. I told you that if we survived the day I'd tell you how I came to be here. I learned how to make lemonade out of lemons—and I mean a lot of fucking lemonade. I've built a place that would sell for ten or fifteen million in LA, if you could duplicate it. I've got a pool, hot tub, and spa, stables, and an observatory. What I don't have is someone to share it with, as long as I'm here."

"Did you say observatory?"

"I've got a telescope that's the envy of a lot of universities. The sky out here is incredible."

"I minored in astronomy."

"Oh yeah? Tell me about the Pleiades—if you know something about astronomy."

"They're known as the Seven Sisters and are visible from every place on the globe."

"Now I'm impressed. Kelsey, with no promises from either one of us, if we can solve your problem, would you stay for a while and see what happens?"

"You would want me after what I told you I've done?"

"You said you were crazy. Maybe I am too."

"Sounds like a great recipe for success, but how do we get rid of the problem?"

"You were right when you said things are different here. We don't need a jury of one's peers when we know right from wrong. But you have to understand that you'll never be free, as long as he's alive. Do you get that?"

Kelsey bowed her head and nodded.

"So you're going to kill them?"

Del grabbed her face and stared at her.

"You and I are gonna be long gone, but you will never have to worry about them again."

Del picked up his cell phone and dialed a number.

"I thought you said there was no cell service out here."

"I said you didn't have cell service. There's only one provider and he's local."

"Robin, this is Del. What's your twenty?"

"I'm just pulling into the Diner parking lot. I heard Snoopy's call, but it sounded like you got it."

"I did and that's what I'm calling about. We've got a code red here. I repeat—we have a code red. Do you know where the Indians are?"

"You won't believe this. I'm pulling in beside their pickup as we talk?"

"I need you to get the Indians and go to the Oasis. Make sure you go heavy—understand? There should be two black guys hanging around. Take them to the desert. I'll guide you. It's about ten miles west and then five or six miles due south into the desert.

"I'll have my cell. These are bad dudes, but won't be expecting anything. Tell José to turn the security tapes off before you confront them."

"What're we gonna find in the desert?"

"There'll be an abandoned rental car that overheated and a duffel bag with three packages."

Kelsey blurted out, "There are five packages." Del reached over and put his hand over her mouth.

"Del, who was that? I didn't get that?"

"That was the lady we're rescuing. I didn't get it either. I was saying, there are three packages, one for each of you."

"And the bad guys?"

"I repeat—this is a code red. Do I have to say it again??"

"What about the car?"

"Remember the Mexican smugglers who raped the preacher's little girl?"

"How could I forget?"

"That will take care of the rental car and the bad guys. The Indians can have the car they came in, but they have to clean it up—*comprende*?"

"Consider it done."

Kelsey turned to Del. "What happened to the smugglers?"

"Let's just say they were never seen again."

"So you're like the final judge and jury."

"Far from it. The final judge and jury is God. Everybody has to meet their maker at the end of the day. My job is just to expedite the meeting."

Kelsey hesitated as she digested that message and then hopped out of the truck to fetch the sport bag.

She got back in the truck and looked at Del. "You said there were only three kilos. There are five—look."

Del took two keys out of the bag. "These should help get your fifty grand back and the other three are for the dispensers of justice."

Kelsey couldn't speak at first. "Are you for fucking real or am I hallucinating? How about I keep some for myself?"

"You see all the sand around? Cocaine is only slightly less abundant around here. Let's go home and pop that champagne."

"I feel like I fell through the looking glass, but I've never felt more secure in my life. Is this place for real?"

"I promised that I'd tell you my story, and I will, but reality in the desert is what we make it. The Golden Rule out here is, 'He who has the gold makes the rules.'"

"And you have the gold?"

"I have my share, and I make the rules."

"Can I tell you something?"

"Shoot."

"You excite me and scare the shit out of me at the same time. I haven't told you all of my secrets."

"Nor I you, and I think it's best we keep it that way. Just one more thing—what about your family?"

"They disowned me a long time ago. I have two trust funds that are both blocked. My sister is the perfect one. She married a banker, a deacon in his church and the president of the local chamber of commerce, but he salivates every time he looks at me."

"That makes two of us. Pop the Champagne for the ride."

"I thought it was for a special occasion?"

"What could be more special? Oh, I forgot to mention—I also have a climate-controlled wine cellar. There's plenty more where that came from."

"Sounds like you have it all."

"As of this moment I do. Let's get the fuck out of here and you can take the dress off now."

Later that Night in the Hot Tub at Del's Estate

"So, whadda you think?"

"What would anybody think—this is fucking incredible. That is, if it was any other place on the globe but here—no offense."

"None taken. I learned from the best and the lesson is to make the best of your situation, whatever it is and wherever it is."

"Well, you've certainly done that. Now it's time to hear your story. You promised and I can't wait, although I have a pretty good guess where the money comes from."

"Pass me the coke. Now it's my turn to talk."

Kelsey made two large lines and handed him the mirror and a golden straw.

"Here goes, and like with your story, this one is the abbreviated version. I grew up in small town America with red, white, and blue in my veins. My dream was to join the Marines after college and eventually go into some type of government service."

"Bully for you. Sounds like you succeeded."

Del laughed. "Oh, I succeeded, but the path was anything but straight and narrow. After the Marines I went to work for the DEA as an undercover agent in Miami in the thick of the Cocaine Wars.

"Sort of like Miami Vice?"

"Very, very much like Miami Vice."

"What happened?"

"Long story short—I loved the work and the adrenaline. I had a kick ass condo in South Beach and drove a Maserati. After two years we had built an ironclad case against the leading money launderer for the Colombian cartels. I flew to Washington to help prepare the indictments."

Del paused to do another line and take a swig of Champagne.

"And?"

"And a funny thing happened on the way to the forum. When I arrived I was told the operation was being aborted and that all materials were to be destroyed. I was reminded of my oath in re departmental secrecy."

"What the fuck happened?"

"What the fuck happened is that the following day the chief money launderer was named the president's campaign finance chairman for Florida."

"Is that when you got—promoted—isn't that what you called it?"

"Cute. They couldn't fire me, but they wanted me as far off the radar screen as possible."

"Score one for the DEA. How'd they even find this place?"

"The promotion was to senior law enforcement officer in the region. This place is where you're sent if you either fuck up, or succeed too well. It could have been Alaska."

"I'd have to see Alaska before I could comment."

"Cute, again. I wasn't sure what my next move was going to be so I came here to have some time to think."

"And that's when you saw all those lemons laying around and decided to make lemonade?"

"Something like that. Kelsey, it's in a Marine's DNA to obey the rules and not question authority. I didn't make the rules around here—not sure who did, but I understood them."

"Live and let live?"

"More like, live and let die."

"Looks like you've done pretty well for yourself. My dad used to always talk about exit strategies for his businesses. Do you have an exit strategy?"

"It's a work in progress. Now that's the end of story time."

"Whoa. That's not fair. You've hardly told me anything."

"OK—one more story. Once upon a time there was a flock of Geese up in Canada. It was late summer and time for them to head south, but this summer had been unusually warm, with no sign yet of an autumn breeze.

"The head goose rounded everyone up and told them they would be departing in the morning, as was annual custom. One of the younger, and more carefree, of the geese objected. 'I don't want to leave yet. Let's stay a bit longer and enjoy this great weather.' The head goose replied, 'We can't take that risk. This is the time we historically leave, and leave, we will.'

While the rest of the flock said their goodbyes to the young goose and departed, he decided to hang around for a while longer. Overnight a winter storm front arrived, bringing freezing temperatures, sleet, and ice. The young goose freaked out and took to the stormy sky immediately. As the ice built up on his wings, he was gradually losing altitude and certain he was going to die. Just then, he spotted a barnyard down below and in the barnyard was a steaming hot pile of fresh cow shit. He headed directly for it hoping that it might cushion the fall and help melt the ice on his wings.

"He landed in it perfectly and was so happy that he had been saved he began to sing. A cat nearby heard the commotion, and finding the weakened Goose, killed and ate him."

"Wow—what a story."

"Do you know what the moral is?"

Kelsey shook her head.

"The moral is, when you're safe and warm and sitting in a pile of shit, keep your mouth shut."

Kelsey turned to do another line of coke, but clearly got the message.

Del took the mirror away from Kelsey and took her face in his hands.

"Kelsey, I'm responsible for other people's lives and I intend to protect them, like I protected you today. Do you understand me?"

Neither of them spoke for a minute as Del opened another bottle of champagne, even though they were both wasted.

Kelsey looked at Del.

"Doesn't the government know or want to know what goes on down here?"

"You can't stop the flow of drugs if you don't stop the flow of illegal immigrants and the government has no interest in doing so. Plus they're still infected with the Nam syndrome of success."

"I don't follow."

"In Vietnam success was defined by how many VC you killed. If the number was forty, for instance, that was OK, but they'd rather you add at least one zero on the end and get decorated for doing so. In the War on Drugs, success is defined by how few busts you make—implying that you're winning the war."

"So, the cartel tips you off to the little guys and you turn a blind eye to their bigger operations. You make busts, but the busts are relatively small—which means you're successful."

"You said it, I didn't, and that's the last time we will discuss my business—or our business. If there's anything you want that money can buy, you'll have it. But, and I hate to have to say it, my first instinct is self-survival. You know that if you've been paying attention."

"I already told you that you scare the shit out of me. Tell me, when I'm not off shopping on Rodeo Drive or Fifth Avenue, what the fuck do I do around here?"

"That's a little bit of a problem. My deputy is married to a gal who was a pole dancer at a topless club in Tucson. She's a coke whore and white trash, and doesn't pretend to be otherwise. I'll give her credit for that."

"Pole dancers generally have good bodies."

"Trust me, when she cleans up she is a knockout. I could do without some of the tattoos and piercings and she's also a masochist—she likes pain. Go figure. I doubt that you'd get along."

"You never know, but it appears that I don't have a lot of choices. Does she have a name?

"Angie. Don't tell me you know her?"

"Doesn't ring a bell, although Tucson isn't that big."

If Del had been either alert and/or sober he might have noticed Kelsey squirm at the mention of Angie's name.

"So let me ask you this—will I be part of your exit strategy?"

"Like I said, it's a work in progress and it looks like both of our lives changed big time today. Only time will tell, if for the better or worse."

Kelsey raised her glass. "I guess I'm going to find out."

They clinked glasses as Del replied, "Welcome to Apache Dunes".

Chapter One

Mister Chicago

Chicago, August 2011

Howard "Howie" Bloom was a schmo—a schmo with Walter Mitty dreams. *Groundhog Day* was an apt metaphor for his life. He was pushing fifty and so far his whole life had been arranged for him—even his marriage to Ruthie Himmelstein aka "the Hoover." He was never sure what "the Hoover" meant, but knew that Ruthie was the most popular girl in the neighborhood—particularly late at night and weekends. She was the epitome of every young man's dream—a nymphomaniac whose father owned a liquor store. Howie, on the other hand, didn't drink and was resigned to the fact that he might be a virgin for life.

As much as the cool guys, like Jeff Gold, loved enjoying Ruthie's carnal talents, they all wanted to marry a girl like Mom. Thus, Howie was elated when his parents and the Himmelsteins decided that Howie would be good for Ruthie and would make her a good Jewish husband. Howie would have signed in blood just for the thought of getting laid. His notable sexual adventure to date had happened on his senior class trip, when he was pranked into whacking off in the men's room at Denver's airport, believing it would qualify him for membership in the Mile High Club.

So it was with no little angst and chagrin when, during the wedding ritual, Ruthie leaned over and whispered in his ear, as he was getting ready to crush the champagne glass, "Howie, I am so lucky to be marrying a virgin that I have decided to swear off sex too."

It actually brought tears to the eyes of some of the older and more orthodox guests to see Howie have to be restrained from not just crushing the glass, but seeming to stomp on it out of control. "If only all of the young people could be so passionate about tradition!"

The Himmelsteins sold the store and retired to Florida immediately after unloading "The Hoover" on Howie. All that remained was a bottle of their private label single-malt scotch.

But life changed, and dramatically, the day when Jeff Gold, himself, wandered into the office one day and asked Howie to do his taxes. At that time all Howie knew about Jeff was that his last name was fitting, as everything he touched seemed to turn into gold. He had it all—looks, money, a Mercedes convertible, and women by the score.

The first question Howie asked any prospective client was their occupation. His core group of clients over the years had been a group of Greek restaurateurs, who were prone to periodic bouts of fire and/or water damage. Jeff's occupation was a new one for Howie: card counter.

"How much can you make counting cards?"

"If I don't get greedy, I can easily make two fifty a year like falling off a log. And, get this—almost everything else is comped by the Casinos, because they don't know I'm a counter. The travel, the rooms—and I mean suites—and the broads, Vegas broads, not like the Hoover—no offense, Howie."

"None taken. Don't you ever lose?"

"A few shekels every blue moon or so, but when I win, I win big."

Jeff looked around the office and said, "Howie, you ought to try it. You should be doing better than this—again, no offense."

Howie sighed. "Again, none taken. So let's say I wanted to learn. How hard is it and what do I need?"

"Are you kidding me? You were the smartest kid in class—all the way through. If I can do it, you can probably do it better. You still have a good memory?"

"I have a great memory."

"Not surprised. Then all you need is a grubstake. I can teach you the rest."

Howie could remember the conversation as if it was yesterday. Truth is, it wasn't that long ago. What happened next was kismet, in Jeff's words, and just really freaky, in Howie's. His inner Walter Mitty was taking over, but he didn't have anything resembling a grubstake, as Jeff called it. That is, without Ruthie cutting off his balls, but that may be an option—as he had no use for them.

The silence was broken by his secretary Naomi's shrill voice. "Client for Howie on line one, says it's important."

"Who is it? And it's Howard not Howie!"

"Whatever."

"He says it has to do with Mr. Brown—he died."

Howie excused himself for a minute and answered the phone. "This is Howard, how can I help you?"

"Mr. Bloom, I'm Bruce Bender, attorney for the estate of David Brown. Mr. Brown left instructions for you to be his executor."

"Listen Bruce, I hardly knew the man, just did his taxes—some dividends, interest, a small pension, and some social security. Doesn't he have any heirs or relatives?"

"I didn't know him any better, but he never mentioned any heirs or relatives. I've inventoried some stocks he kept in his safe deposit box, and the estate is worth over three million dollars."

"Are you there?"

Howie almost choked and coughed as he replied. "Excuse me—something went down the wrong pipe. So as … so as executor, I would basically oversee the estate until we can determine if there are any heirs?"

"That's right and, again, I asked him several times if he had any heirs and he would only grumble—never replied. My suggestion is that we liquidate the estate and you open a bank account in the name of the estate for the proceeds. I'll help you with the letters and documents you'll need."

"What if—er well, what if he doesn't have any heirs?"

"Well, I guess that you and I would have to decide what to do with the money, unless a will turns up and I never prepared one for him—very strange."

"Yeah, that—that does seem like the thing to do."

"Great, then I will proceed and call you when the funds have cleared."

"I'll stand by. You know, I didn't know him well, but really liked the guy."

"Me too. I'll be in touch."

Howie wasn't sure, but he thought he felt something stirring down below—and it felt good. He smiled.

"So, Howie, what was that all about?"

Howie's demeanor had changed dramatically. After appearing to drift off for a moment, he turned to Jeff, "What could we do with a million dollars?"

Jeff literally jumped up out of his chair and was suddenly animated.

"Are you shitting me? We could break the bank at Monte Carlo! It would be perfect. We split up, five hundred thousand each, and play at separate tables. If, God forbid, you lose a bit—because you're new at the game—I will more than make up for it. Tell me, what happened?"

Howie's Walter Mitty wasn't just waking up—it was taking control. "Let's just say, I have a few million stashed that I've been wanting to do something with."

"Howie, I knew it. I knew it. You were always a mysterious guy. And weren't you the guy who wound up with the Hoov—with Ruthie in the end?"

Howie was soaking up the compliments until the mention of winding up with Ruthie gave him pause. The next two weeks were a blur. While Howie waited for the sale of the stocks to clear and the proceeds to be deposited in the estate account, Jeff was teaching Howie how to count cards and Howie was eager to learn. Even if they lost a million—God forbid—there were at least two more where that came from. And, didn't the attorney confirm there weren't any heirs? More importantly, Jeff said it was a slam dunk, didn't he? What could go wrong?

Las Vegas Strip

What could go wrong? Let's start with Las Vegas, or Vegas as Jeff called it, and the fact that Jeff said that Howie had to look the part, and act the part, if he was going to be at a high roller's table. No problem. Jeff dipped into the stake and replaced Howie's Timex with a gold Rolex—and got himself one too. Why not?

Next came the wardrobe, or wardrobes, as Jeff ordered one also. Howie's inner voice was screaming "Stop!" but Jeff was in control. Next stop was the spa. Howie got a total makeover and was now kind of digging it.

Now that the image issue was resolved, Jeff gave Howie some advice that proved problematical. He told Howie that the casino would be plying them with drinks, as an apparent perk. He knew that Howie had never touched the stuff, but said Howie had to appear to at least sip at a drink, lest he appear too focused on the cards.

That night it was show time. They split up after a "Mazel Tov" and sought out separate tables. That would prove to be the high point of the evening. Jeff forgot to mention the "ladies" who flocked to a stack of chips like moths to a flame.

Howie's moth was a knockout. She was barely legal age, whatever that was in Nevada, and barely dressed. He lost the battle before a shot was fired. It got worse. Speaking about shots—she ordered two single-malt Scotches, neat.

Jeff said to pretend to sip only, but how could he refuse her toast—at least her first few toasts. After the second "sip," Howie's laser focus was more like an old flashlight and a dim one at that. Plus, was it just him, or did her purse seem to be getting bigger as the night wore on?

A crowd had now gathered and were fixated on this really high roller who was betting thousands on a single hand and seemed unfazed when he lost, which was often.

Howie ate up, however, that the dealer referred to him as "Mr. Chicago." That had a very pleasant ring to it and, well, wasn't an unfair description. Just then something happened that promised to change his life—an understatement if there was one. A swarthy looking, self-assured Mexican sat down beside him, a handsome man whose appearance was marred by a scar running from his left ear to his mouth.

"So, Mr. Chicago, you must be very successful, ey? Tell me, what is it you do in Chicago?"

"Oh, a little bit of this and a little bit of that, I guess you could say. I'm a CPA by trade."

"An accountant, very good, very good. I happen to need someone to handle some money for me in Chicago. Do you have a card?"

Howie fumbled looking for one in his jacket, but realized his clothes were new.

"I'm sorry. I have a new jacket on. I'll write down my number on this napkin," which he proceeded to do. "I didn't get your name."

"Garcia. Señor Garcia. Now if you'll excuse me, I prefer the dice to the cards. I'll be in touch."

As he departed, Howie took another swig. Sip time was in the rear-view mirror. He mused to himself, "Success begets success. I just need to get out more."

As the night wore on, it was obvious that Howie's venture was a total failure. Well, maybe not total—he might have had a few thousand bucks left. It was a good bet that his lady friend had more in her purse than he had in his rack. In fact, she wasn't going to hang around for the coup de grace. She told Howie, er, Mr. Chicago, what a great guy he was, but she had just developed a migraine headache and must say good night as she struggled with both hands to carry her purse.

He hoped that Jeff had fared better as promised, but that ship had also sailed as Jeff was led away in cuffs by two burly security guards. A third followed with what remained of his chips.

Howie asked the dealer what that was all about. The dealer replied, "Probably got caught counting cards. They all get caught sooner or later."

Howie just smiled and said to himself, "Not all of them, pal. I'll bet you never even suspected I was counting cards."

Chicago

There were few words exchanged on the flight back to Chicago. Jeff had parked at the airport and offered to drop Howie off at his office. The conversation in the car was strained.

"Look, Howie—I don't know what went wrong, but you didn't follow my instructions either. How many drinks did you have, for God's sake?"

Howie started to reply, but decided not to.

"And, Howie—didn't you say you had a few million stashed away? So you lost a million, it's not the end of the world. You'll get over it. The worst is behind you."

Maybe Jeff's right, he thought, as they turned off of Devon Avenue into the parking lot. He was surprised to see the parking lot full with even the reserved spots taken. Maybe Madame Roux was having a Tarot card sale.

When he entered the office it was total mayhem and he was about to find out that Jeff was wrong again. The worst wasn't behind him—it was staring him in the face. You see, Mr. Brown didn't have an heir—he had eight of them. They seemed to be divided up evenly into two factions, each with a lawyer in tow.

Fearing a battle to the death was about to break out any minute in his lobby, he summoned both attorneys upstairs to his office. They each had copies of the Merrill Lynch statements of the purchases and knew to a penny how much the estate was worth. Howie started to ask how they got the statements, but realized it didn't matter—they had them.

That Howie had any guile was a sentiment open to doubt. After trying to collect his wits, he told the attorneys that the funds had to clear and all the paperwork be completed before he could disburse the funds as the executor—which technically was true and received as such. The attorneys and the feuding siblings departed.

Howie's biggest concern was how to tell Ruthie what had happened. It's not like Howie and Ruthie were a close couple. They had separate bedrooms and Ruthie was a tennis freak. She took lessons late at night five times a week and generally had headaches on the weekends. Twice a year she would spend a month or so at a tennis camp in Acapulco.

Ruthie was out when he got home. He surprised even himself by pouring himself a double scotch from a bottle that had never been opened—a gift from a forgotten occasion.

He was betwixt and between. He dreaded telling her about the loss and the fuck up with the heirs, but something inside of him was yearning to tell her that, for once in his life, he had thrown caution to the wind and the consequences be damned. Not to mention that a very attractive young lady had come onto him – at least for a while – and, get this, he was known in Las Vegas—in Vegas—as Mr. Chicago. What do you think of them apples?

He was confident that she would be shocked to learn that Howie had it in him. Maybe she had misjudged him all of these years. Hell, maybe everybody had. True enough she was shocked, but at his stupidity, not his bravado.

"So let me get this straight—you took investment advice from Jeff Gold? Are you a fucking idiot? Don't answer that—of course you are. Talk about the blind leading the blind. Better yet, the clueless leading the stupid. Listen, I don't have time to deal with this, I am going to tennis camp in two days. Just make sure the life insurance is paid up."

She started to walk away but stopped. "By the way, since when do you drink alcohol? And what's the deal with the new look and the Rolex?"

He smiled. Ruthie was finally seeing the real Howie. He took a sip of the scotch and savored it. He wouldn't be surprised if she changed her mind and hung around. "There's a lot about me you don't know."

"Let's keep it that way. What a putz!"

Chapter Two

The First Rule of Holes

A Hacienda in Northern Mexico by the Arizona Border the Following Day

José Garcia's nickname was "El Diablo," the Devil, and well deserved. His brother Roberto had been the brains behind what was now one of Mexico's largest drug cartels. It was one of the most feared because of El Diablo.

While Roberto, "El Ambajador," the ambassador, was blessed with a combination of effortless grace and charm, Diablo knew only brute and savage force. Truth is, their skills were often complementary, but recently Roberto had perished in a private plane crash of suspicious circumstances. It was well known that the brothers had been feuding, particularly over Diablo's increasing addiction to cocaine. He had violated rule number one of the drug trade: don't put your nose in your own stash. No one had the cojones to suggest Diablo's involvement in his brother's death, so there was an uneasy cloud hanging over the cartel.

Diablo was seated behind the massive oak desk that had been with the hacienda for hundreds of years. The study contained museum quality art, canvasses, ornate wood paneling, oriental carpets, chandeliers and a massive stone fireplace. Roberto had painstakingly returned the estate to its once proud glory, but it was all lost on Diablo. He had a huge line of cocaine in front of him and a bottle of Courvoisier, now a half bottle, at his side as he reached for the telephone.

He had a problem most people would dream of having. He had thirty-two million dollars that he didn't know what to do with. He had been jealous of his brother's intellect and offended by the way the old accountant seemed to dismiss him, but they were the only two people who knew how the money was laundered and now they were gone. He dared not let anyone else know—or show weakness to them. Weakness was a fatal affliction in the drug world. He needed to buy some time and, in the meantime, he needed to get the money out of the safe house, as too many people knew about it for it to be safe anymore. If that wasn't enough to worry about, the Gulf and Sinaloa cartels each claimed part ownership of the money.

He dialed Bertin's cell phone. Bertin was the brother of Diablo's most trusted advisor, Esteban. He was in Chicago doing some "housecleaning," as his brother's death was contemporaneous with the death of the previous accountant/bag man, who had succumbed to prostate cancer.

Bertin recognized the number and answered the call, always with a bit of trepidation these days. "*Hola.*"

"Bertin, it's me. *Que pasa, amigo?*"

"Nada. It's all good, *Jefe.* Have you decided what to do with the money?"

"Maybe. That's why I'm calling. I just got home from Las Vegas and I met someone there who might be a solution—at least for now. I want you to call him and check him out for me. We need a safe—a big one. I'll give you his number. Tell him you are calling for Señor Garcia."

"*Sí, Jefe.* I'll call him first thing *mañana.*"

"*Bueno,* I wait for your call."

Chicago the Following Day

Howie arrived at the office early, but with no clue as to how to repay the million bucks. Naomi was already there, which was no surprise, as she had no other life.

"Naomi, hold all of my calls, I'll be tied up all day."

Naomi held her tongue, which surprised her. The over/under on incoming calls was three for a normal day, save for wrong numbers. She couldn't hold it any longer.

"It may be difficult, but I'll do my best, Howie."

"It's Howard, goddammit. How many times do I have to tell you?"

"Whatever."

Howie had been in the office for half an hour when Ruthie burst in.

"Naomi, what a surprise—you're still alive, I think. Here, let me have a look." She appeared to check Naomi out. "I don't know—the jury's out."

Naomi just grimaced.

"Is Gordon Gecko in?"

"Let me check his schedule."

"Cute. You must tell me where you get your cosmetics someday. That deathly pallor looks good on you."

Ruthie hurried up the stairs and into Howie's office.

Howie was surprised—to say the least—to see her.

"Ruthie, what are you doing here?"

"This isn't a social visit, I've got a car downstairs waiting for me. I forgot to take the Amex card. Give me yours; mine is at home."

Howie looked out the window and saw a limo parked outside.

"Is that your tennis instructor in the back seat?"

"He happens to be going at the same time so we're sharing a ride. Oh, here."

Ruthie put a jar of pills on the desk. "Here's fifty valiums. If you chug them all, you'll go peacefully—no pain. Gotta go."

Howie was transfixed on the jar of pills when Naomi buzzed him. "I thought I said to hold my calls."

"The caller was very persistent. He said he is calling for a Señor Garcia."

Howie woke from his stupor as if dashed with cold water. "Put him through."

"Hello, this is Howie—I mean Howard Bloom."

"Mr. Bloom, Señor Garcia asked me to call you. He say he met you in Las Vegas."

"Yes, yes, I remember. Nice man."

Bertin had to hesitate for a minute to make sure they were talking about the same guy.

"*Sí*, ah—a very nice man. Señor Garcia was wondering if you could help him with a money problem."

"I'm sorry, I didn't get your name."

"Bertin."

"Bertin, I'm sorry, I'm not in the business of loaning money."

Bertin broke out laughing and had to collect himself.

"I'm sorry—I don't mean no disrespect. Señor Garcia's problem isn't that he needs money. It's that he doesn't know what to do with the money he has."

Howie wasn't sure he heard him right. He stood up and almost dropped the phone. "No problem. Please tell me how I can help Señor Garcia."

"Well, our immediate problem is that we need a place to keep some money safe for a while."

"How much, may I ask, are we talking about?"

"Say, maybe thirty-two million dollars."

This time Howie did drop the phone and had to brace himself on his desk. Was this really happening or had he gone completely fucking bonkers?

"*Hola*, *hola*, are you there?"

"Sorry, it's these damn phones. Yes, yes I think I can help you."

"First question—do you have a safe large enough for the money?"

"Oh, I gotta safe, but what are you gonna do with the money?"

"I think we talk too much already. I'll come see you."

"Let me tell you where I am."

"I already know; I'll be there is five minutes."

Howie had trouble containing himself. Talk about snatching victory from the jaws of defeat. Fuck Ruthie's pills. He would try to get her on her cell.

Ruthie saw the number and picked up. "Are you still alive?"

"Very funny. I just wanted to tell you that I have the matter in hand."

"I'm glad you found another use for your hand." He could hear the tennis pro laughing and glasses clink.

"Pray tell me where you found a million dollars?"

"I'm going to borrow it from a new client."

"Does he know you're going to borrow it?"

"Well, not exactly, but I can handle that."

"And what type of business would someone with that kind of money—and someone who would come to you for advice—be in?"

More laughter.

Howie didn't answer as he pondered the question.

"Wait a minute—it's obvious what type of business. So let me—" there was more laughter, "get this straight. You're gonna steal a million dollars from a drug dealer?"

"More like borrow it."

Now there was uncontrolled laughter.

"Stop it. My makeup is running. Can I give you some advice?"

"I was hoping you could as you seem to think this is all a big joke."

She laughed again. "My advice is to forget the pills and use the gun in your desk. It's quicker." She hung up.

Naomi buzzed him. "A Mister Bertin is here to see you."

"Please show him up."

"Mister Bertin—do you see the stairs?"

Bertin entered the office and looked around. There wasn't a lot to see. Devon Avenue is a great area to operate under the radar from, as everything on Devon Avenue is under the radar.

Howie approached. "Mr. Bertin, I'm Howie—Howard Bloom."

"Which do you prefer, Howie or Howard?"

"Either is OK with a friend of Señor Garcia. Now, how can I help you?"

"First, I need to see your safe."

Howie took him around the corner of his office and there sat a massive old bank safe—too big for the room actually.

Bertin whistled and looked around.

"How'd you get it in here?"

"An antique dealer owed my uncle money. It was when they were putting a roof on the building, so my uncle took the safe. It was quite a feat, even with no roof."

"*Comprende.*"

What Howie didn't say was that his uncle was a bag man for the mob and rumor had it that the safe was at various times the storage space for the mob's arsenal of weapons and/or its loot—hence the size.

"May I ask, how long do you propose to keep the money here?"

"Who knows? Maybe a short time, maybe a long time until we can move it offshore."

Howie's wheels were now spinning. "And may I ask, what's in it for me—no offense?"

"Of course—Señor Garcia, he pay you one percent fee on the money he keep with you."

One thing Howie could do was calculate, and he liked the sound of $320,000. If he could cash in some stocks and take out a home equity loan, he could pay back the million with his fee. Could work. Praise Jesus. Wait a minute—he was Jewish. Well, so was Jesus, he laughed to himself.

"Yeah, I think that works. When do you want to get started?"

"I just have to go outside and call Señor Garcia to get his OK. I'll be right back."

Howie paced as Bertin went outside to make the call.

Bertin called El Diablo.

"*Hola.*"

"*Jefe*, this is Bertin. I'm outside the *gringo*'s office."

"You saw him? You saw the office?"

"*Sí, sí.*"

"And, talk to me. Does he have a safe?"

"*Sí, Jefe*. He has a safe—a safe bigger than most banks."

"*Bueno. Muy bueno*. How much can he take?"

"*Jefe*, the safe is huge. I don't know, but he can take most, if not all of it, but—"

"But—you say but—but what?"

"*Jefe*, this guy don't seem like a player to me."

"That's because you don't know him. These guys have two different lives. I saw him in Vegas. The man tossed five hundred dollar chips around like they were pesos. They get back home and they put on an act so nobody knows they got money."

"If you say so. Whatta you want me to do?"

"We got to move that money now. Can you get it over to him?"

"*Sí*, I can get it done today."

"*Bueno.*"

"What do I tell the *gringo*?"

"Tell him anything. When we don't need him, we take care of the problem."

Bertin crossed himself.

"*Sí, Jefe*. I'm on it."

Bertin reentered the office, nodded at Naomi, and climbed the stairs to Howie's office.

"*Amigo*, I have good news. Señor Garcia—he want to proceed."

Howie was struggling to not act too excited.

"Good. Yes, that is good news. What do you need me to do?"

"We will bring the money over in about an hour—maybe take a little longer. No one else is to know about this, *comprende*?"

"Yes, I mean *sí*. I—I *comprende*."

"So that means you should tell your secretary to take the rest of the day off. Tell her you're busy."

"I have a couple of quick items to take care of first."

Howie headed down the stairs with Bertin.

"Naomi, give me the files on my life insurance and the American Express account."

Bertin left and Howie told Naomi that she could take the rest of the day off.

He took the files upstairs and called the insurance company first. He told the agent that he was changing the beneficiary on his policy from his wife to his synagogue. For a fleeting moment, he thought of making Naomi the beneficiary, but the key word was fleeting. The agent said he would e-mail an authorization to Howie. He could print it out, sign it, scan it, and e-mail it back, with hard copy by mail. Howie said he would wait by the computer.

The second call was to American Express to inform them that his card had been stolen by a Mexican tennis instructor and he feared the instructor was headed for Mexico. They replied that they would cancel the card immediately and notify the Mexican authorities.

He leaned back in his desk chair and had to smile. He liked the new Howie—er, Howard. In fact, this called for a toast. He opened the bottom drawer and opened the bottle of Himmelstein scotch that had been captive there forever. He poured himself one, no—fuck it—two fingers and savored it.

Later That Day

Bertin returned with the van and two helpers, each of whom would frighten the bejeezus out of a normal person. Neither spoke, except to Bertin who was clearly in control. They backed the van up to the front door, which was flush with the sidewalk. Bertin and one of the helpers unloaded the van as the other stood guard vigilantly with a MAC-10 just inside the door.

Howie had no conception what $32,000,000 in hundred dollar bills would look like, or how much space would be needed. He learned that each million dollars weighed just over twenty pounds and could fit in a large duffel bag. The van was loaded with thirty-two identical duffel bags from Sports Authority.

It required eight trips, of four bags each, to get the money up the flight of stairs and took less than thirty minutes. It was a bit more problematical getting all thirty-two bags in the safe. They eventually removed a couple of dividers and scrunched up the bags to make it work.

Bertin asked Howie for the combination and tested it to make sure it worked. It did. Then, Bertin gave Howie a slip of paper that said only: "$32,000,000" then said, "Sign it."

Howie was actually shaking when he did so and that didn't go unnoticed by Bertin, who said, "*Amigo*, when Señor Garcia ask for the money to be returned, he mean every dollar, comprende?"

"Yes, I mean *sí*. Except for my fee, of course. Right—I mean *comprende*?"

"Of course, Señor. Except for your one percent fee."

"And—you don't know how long it will be kept here?"

"That's not my business and not your business. It may be just days or it may be a long time."

Howie stuck out his hand to shake, but Bertin just waved the signed piece of paper. "Remember—nobody else is to know about this, *comprende*?"

"*Sí, sí*. Oh, *adios*."

Bertin smiled. "*Adios, amigo*."

As soon as they departed, Howie collapsed in his chair and went for the bottle of Himmelstein scotch again.

The next thing he did was open the safe and withdraw one of the bags—one million dollars.

He called the two attorneys for the Brown heirs and asked if they would prefer one million, of the three million total, by cashier's check or cash in hundred dollar bills. They had the same momentarily stunned reaction and then replied that cash would be … ah, well, fine. One thing Howie did know a little about was taxation and he smiled to himself at the replies.

They agreed to stop by his office in the morning at eleven and appreciated Howie's great work as executor.

He left the office with one major problem solved, but by creating another, with even more serious and potentially fatal consequences. The adrenaline was kicking in. All Howie needed was time to figure out how to get the other $680,000 to make the Mexican's account whole again. He needed to think.

That Night at Home

The combination of scotch, fear, and adrenaline created a potent cocktail that prevented Howie from getting any sleep that night. He was replaying all of the conversations with Bertin in his mind. Something that was said was gnawing at him, but, try as he may, he couldn't recall what it was. Think. Think. Think, dammit.

It was now 4:00 a.m. and time to give up and turn the lights off again, when it came to him—offshore. Bertin said the money would be there until he could move it offshore, or something to that effect. What if Howie could figure out how to get it offshore and into a bank account only he knew about? Garcia should be willing to reward him handsomely for doing so—well more than the $680,000 shortfall.

Regardless, there is no way they would kill Howie if only Howie knew where the money was. He turned the lights off and laid back down with a smile on his face, until he recalled the scene with the chainsaw in *Scarface*. Sleep wasn't going to happen that night.

In the morning Howie called Naomi to tell her he would be out of the office until his eleven o'clock meeting and hung up before she could bust his balls. He had stored his uncle's papers in a trunk in his garage. He knew exactly what he was looking for and finally found it—his uncle's book of contacts.

As a bagman for the mob for over thirty years, his uncle had developed relationships with bankers and players who knew how to get things done. Howie had never had occasion or need to call on any of them and wondered how many would be still alive and/or have their wits about them. He didn't give up when he encountered several disconnected numbers and a few deaths, which were to be expected. His patience finally paid off when he got Fred Harnish on the phone. Howie actually remembered going to a Cubs game with his uncle and Fred. Fred was the quintessential fixer. He knew everybody and had always kept his nose clean and his own counsel. Fred answered on the third ring.

"Yeah, who is it?"

"Is this Fred Harnish?"

"Who the fuck did you call?"

"Mr. Harnish, you may not remember me but I am David Bloom's nephew Howard."

There was a slight pause. "David Bloom was one of my best friends. He was a *mensch*. I miss him to this day. I remember you. You were the son he never had. Tell me, what can I do for you?"

"Mr. Harnish—"

"Call me Fred."

"Thanks, Fred. You see, I need some advice and I don't know where to turn."

"What type of advice?"

"Truth is, I'm in a bit of a jam. I need to get some money offshore and do it in a hurry."

"I'm guessing it isn't your money, right?"

"I'm just the custodian, so to speak."

"I gotta ask you, Howard—does the money belong to the outfit?"

"No."

"That's good. Who does it belong to?"

"A Mexican drug cartel."

"I hope you didn't say a Mexican drug cartel. Do you have a death wish? It would be better if it were the outfit. Maybe then I could make a call or two."

"It's complicated."

"No shit. Howard, I'm an old man and I want to either die of natural causes or be shot by a jealous husband. My name can't ever be connected to this. You understand?"

"Totally understood. I just need to know how best to get the money offshore."

"Let's start with how much money we're talking about?"

"About thirty-one million."

Fred yelled into the phone, "Are you fucking *meshugge*? Do you fucking hate me?"

"If I can just get the money into a bank offshore, everything will be OK and I can pay a fee of one per cent."

"You can pay a fee of two per cent, cash up front. Where's the money now?"

"It's in a safe place in Chicago."

"Here's what you need to do. Are you listening to me?"

"*Sí, comprende.*" The minute Howie said it, he slapped himself on the head.

"What? What the fuck did you say?"

"I'm listening."

"Good. Number one, get yourself a phone with a prepaid card. Throw this phone away and don't carry my number on you or write it down where someone can find it. You understand me?"

"I got it." His mind was racing. Only his wife and Naomi used his cell number.

"Good. It just so happens that my grandson just got accepted to Brown and I can use the money, but I don't want to die for it. Call me in three hours from the throw away phone." He hung up.

Howie was wringing wet from sweating. He took a deep breath. Fred Harnish was going to help him. With the two per cent fee of $620,000, he'd now be down $1,300,000 with the credit of his fee, which didn't seem unreasonable to get the money offshore. The more he thought about it, the more it sounded like a bargain. What Howie forgot was the first rule of holes: when you're in one—stop digging!

He went to the office and wrapped up the business with the Brown heir's attorneys, then told Naomi he would be out for the rest of the day. Maybe she was paying attention, but doubtful.

Chapter Three

Man Plans and God Laughs

The Garcia Hacienda

El Diablo was well into his cups of both cocaine and cognac when he called Bertin in Chicago.

Bertin answered, "*Hola.*"

"Bertin, *mi amigo. Que pasa, amigo*?"

Bertin knew Diablo was blotto and had to tread carefully. "It's all good, *Jefe.*"

"*Bueno, bueno*—hold on a minute."

Bertin heard the sound of Diablo snorting a big line of coke.

"Listen, *amigo*—where was I? Oh, yeah—listen, *amigo*, I have some good news. The Italians decided not to break things off. They're going to launder the money for us."

"That is good news, *Jefe*. What do you want me to do?"

"I'm going to send Flaco up to help you. You and Flaco get the money and take it to the Italians. I'll tell you where."

Bertin grimaced. Flaco was a loose cannon and a coke freak like Diablo. That and the fact that Diablo was fucking Flaco's sister were the only reasons he was still alive.

"*Jefe*, you don't need to send Flaco. I can handle it, plus I still have two men with me."

"I'm sending Flaco. I'll get you his fight—I mean his flight information."

"*Sí, Jefe*. What do we do with the *gringo*?"

"If he has the money, he lives. If he doesn't he dies, *comprende*?"

"*Sí*."

That Afternoon

Howie had tossed his cell phone in the lake and bought two phones with prepaid cards. He dialed Fred's number.

"Who the fuck is this?"

"It's me, Howard."

"OK, Howard. Now listen to me and listen carefully. The easiest and cheapest way to do it is to drive it across the Canadian border at Windsor. It's about a five-hour drive from Chicago. You need to cross at night between midnight and four a.m.—you got that?"

"Yeah. Midnight to four a.m. Then what do I do?"

"You need to give me your car or truck color, make, model, and license plate number. They'll pass you through. You have to give an envelope, with fifty grand in it, to the customs agent who will see you through."

Howie swallowed hard. "Is that part of the two percent fee?"

"That's got nothing to do with the two percent fucking fee. You pay me before you leave. If you have a problem with that, tell me now."

What could Howie say? "No—no problem."

"Good. The customs agent's name is David. After he clears you, you drive to Toronto and call Michael Bendorff at the bank in Toronto. I'll give you his cell number tonight. He'll arrange to meet you and exchange the money for a deposit slip in their Cayman Islands branch—a numbered account."

"Great."

"Hold on. Michael will get a one percent fee in cash, up front."

Howie was now almost crying. "That's almost a million dollars in fees!"

"You don't want to do this tell me now and throw my number away."

"No, no—what choice do I have?"

"None that I know of. Do you have anyone to ride shotgun with you?"

"Yeah, I think I do."

"Good. Then if I were you, I would rent an SUV and hit the road tonight."

Howie looked at his watch. It was not quite 3:30 p.m. He knew where a rental place was. If he could get help, he could get a van or SUV, load the money, meet Fred, and be on the road by around seven and that would put him in Windsor between midnight and four in the morning.

First the help. He took out his phone and dialed Jeff Gold.

Jeff answered, "Hello."

"Jeff, it's Howie."

"Howie, I didn't recognize the number. What's up? Listen I feel terrible about what happened."

"Don't worry about it. How would you like a chance to make it up to me and then maybe some?"

"Are you kidding? Count me in. What do I have to do?"

"I have to drive to Toronto tonight. I have to make a delivery tomorrow. I just want someone to ride shotgun—maybe help drive if I get tired."

"Howie, hold on. This doesn't involve drugs or guns does it?"

"Jeff, when did you know me to be involved with either? It's a debt I have to repay—caused, by the way, by the fuck up in Vegas."

"If it isn't drugs or guns, I'm in. What do you want me to do?"

"Meet me at my office at five. If I'm late wait for me."

Howie rented a Ford E-series Van and was at his office before Jeff arrived. He prepared the envelope for the customs agent—a big fucking envelope. He would put Fred's and Michael's monies in duffel bags. He had an empty one and their combined fees would largely empty another.

They backed the van up to the front door and reversed the process of the previous day. Jeff's eyes bulged out when he saw the thirty-one remaining duffel bags and wanted to know how much money they contained. Howie lied and told him it was approximately a million in small bills—the money they'd lost.

They met Fred in the parking lot of the Field Museum on the way to the Skyway. How he handled it is he let Jeff out approximately fifty yards from Fred's car. Howie told him it was for his safety as he didn't know what would go down. If things went south, Jeff was to run and not look back. Howie loved to see the fear on Jeff's face and the knowledge that he was in control—another shot of adrenaline.

The meet with Fred was short and sweet. He had a goon with him who looked only half human and twice as big. They went to the back of the van and transferred $620,000 in the duffel bag. Wham bam, thank you ma'am. Fred gave him Michael's cell number in Toronto and Howie circled back to get Jeff.

"Did you see how big that guy was?" Jeff was shaking.

"Nothing to worry about. Just a precaution."

"Howie, I don't know if I can do this."

"Nothing to do now. Just sit back and close your eyes if you want. I'll wake you when we get close to Windsor."

All credit to Fred—the rest of the trip went like clockwork, with the exception of Howie being sleep deprived and running on adrenaline for a second consecutive day. No problem at customs and Michael was a real gentleman.

While Howie and Jeff had a late breakfast at Tim Horton's the money was deposited and Michael returned with a deposit slip and account information for the Cayman branch. Howie got the impression this wasn't that unusual a transaction, but he was way too tired to even think now.

Jeff's antennas were way up. Something didn't add up. Who was this Michael guy? This was way too big and mysterious a transaction for just a million dollars. Listen to me, he thought. Just a million dollars!

Howie had deposited thirty million even. They had lost one million in Vegas. Fred got $620,000. The customs agent got fifty g's and Michael a cool $300,000. That left thirty grand, which Howie split with Jeff. Jeff's animal instincts told him he was getting the short end of the stick, but fifteen grand for riding shotgun to Toronto and back could have been worse.

Howie told Jeff he could have the other fifteen g's if he drove all the way home. Jeff was well rested and Howie was exhausted from the ordeal and the rush. When he woke it was 10:00 p.m. and they were running north on LSD, heading into town.

It was after midnight when Howie finally got home. He had several missed calls from Naomi and one frantic message, "Your Mexican friends have tried to reach you at the office and called your cell, like I did—to no avail. They said they're coming by tomorrow afternoon at five to get whatever it is they left with you. They didn't sound happy."

Howie poured himself a double scotch and looked at the deposit slip. He took a pair of scissors and cut off the bank's name, smiled to himself and got up to look for Bertin's number.

Bertin had been frustrated all day trying to reach Howie. He was in a bad humor already thinking about Flaco's arrival tomorrow. He was too restless to sleep and decided to swing by Howie's office and make sure his two shooters were there, sober and awake. He didn't want to even think about the odds for both.

After the transfer of the money he had given them instructions to watch the building and let him know immediately of any suspicious activity. He didn't have a good feeling, as reliability is not one of the inherent traits available with thugs.

He called them on his way, but like with Howie—no answer. His fears were validated when he arrived at the building with no sign of them. The lights were on in the Pakistani's shop and the Tarot card reader, but they were both nocturnal businesses.

He checked the door and it was locked. He went back to his car and fetched his set of keys that could open most of the locks in the world. It didn't take long to find a match. The downstairs office appeared just as he remembered. He turned off the lights and started toward the door and hesitated. I'm here, he thought, I might as well make sure the money is still here as well.

He turned the lights back on and climbed the stairs to Howie's office. Same, same—just as he remembered. He took the combination from his wallet and proceeded to open the safe.

Bertin had never had a heart attack, only heard about them, but his heart definitely skipped a couple of beats as he looked at the empty safe. He had to sit down before he fell down. He got up and opened the window to get some fresh air as he was still hyperventilating. He needed to think.

His first instinct was to call Diablo, but he quickly realized the danger in doing so. Diablo was a psychopath and a schizophrenic and neither received bad news well. He would blame Bertin for the security lapse. More important at the moment was to find the money. For a brief moment he wondered if the shooters could be involved, but realized that only he and Howie had the combination to the safe. His head was throbbing when his cell phone rang. He didn't recognize the number, but answered.

"*Hola*. Who's this?"

"Bertin, it's me Howie."

Bertin literally collapsed back into his seat. What the fuck was going on?

"Señor Howard, I try calling you all day."

"Yeah, I just got the message. Sorry about that. I had an emergency and misplaced my phone somewhere. I had to get a new one."

"I hope this emergency isn't going to be a problem for tomorrow."

"No—no problem, as you say. I will see you at five."

"Señor, let me make sure I understand you. You will be at your office at five tomorrow?"

"Yes, I mean *sí*. Just as planned."

"And you know we are coming for the money, *sí*?"

"*Sí, sí.*"

"And the money—it is in the safe? All the money?"

"I think you will be pleasantly surprised."

"*Amigo*, Señor Garcia, he don't like no surprises—even pleasant ones, as you say."

"I'll explain everything tomorrow."

They hung up and Bertin was even more confused. Why did the *gringo* call him? Was he playing with him? No fucking way he could put the money back in the safe, and where was the money? There was only one thing he could do—forget he was here tonight and knew the money was missing. He would call the office tomorrow morning and if the *gringo* was in, there must be some excuse, but he couldn't imagine what it would be. In the meantime, he had some business to take care of.

Bertin called the shooter's phone again and finally he picked up.

"Who's this?"

"Who's this? This is Bertin. Where are you guys?"

The shooter hesitated. "We—uh, we are by the office like we supposed to be."

"You been there all day—like you were supposed to be?"

"*Sí, sí.* We only left to get some food."

"Listen, I got something for you. I want to pay you tonight as I may be leaving later today. You know where the restaurant Myron & Phil's is?"

"*Sí*, on Devon west of the office."

"That's it. Listen—I will meet you there in about thirty minutes. Park on the far side of the parking lot. I'll pay you and we say *adios.*"

"*Bueno.* Five hundred dollars a day is one thousand dollars, *sí*?"

"*Sí*, one thousand dollars each."

Bertin went into his trunk again and this time found a silencer for his Glock and counted out two thousand dollars in hundred-dollar bills. He put a rubber band around each grand. He then emptied a duffel bag, put the pistol and money in the bag, and closed the trunk.

His next stop was at an Amoco station where he bought a two-gallon can and filled it with gas. It was now approaching two in the morning as Bertin drove into Myron and Phil's and saw the shooters' car in the far corner of the deserted parking lot. He flashed his lights twice as he approached and they did likewise.

He parked beside them and exited with the duffel bag. He motioned for them to open the back seat door and hopped in. He opened the duffel bag and tossed them each one thousand dollars. As they reached for the money he pulled out the silenced Glock and put two slugs in the back of each skull.

He thought for a moment about retrieving the money and decided, fuck it. The insane irony about the drug business was that there was more money than anyone knew what to do with and yet—most of the problems and killings were over money. Truth is, even the loyal soldiers, like Bertin, had more money than they could spend, but no one had the cojones to try to retire, particularly with El Diablo now at the helm.

He fetched the gasoline from his car and doused both bodies, then tossed in a match and heard the fateful whoosh. He crossed himself, not realizing the hypocrisy of doing so—it was just something you did. He pulled out of the lot as if nothing had happened. He pulled over down the street and waited for the car to blow—as it was destined to do. He had to smile as the stress of the day seemed to melt away when he heard the explosion and saw the flames. His smile quickly faded as he realized that the day was just beginning, not ending. He needed to get some shut eye if possible. Flaco's flight was due to arrive at Midway at 2:30 p.m. He would head that way and get a room at one of the no-tell motels on Cicero Avenue near the airport.

Later That Day

Howie slept in that morning—something he very rarely did, but the day was all about the 5:00 p.m. meeting and he needed to be well rested. Around noon Bertin had called to confirm that Howie was at the office and was perplexed by Howie's seemingly chipper mood. Go figure.

Bertin's rest was less peaceful as the room next to his must have been re-let at least three times during the night. He was too tired to protest.

He rented a van and picked up Flaco, who was right on time, but wired to the gills on coke—no surprise.

"Listen Flaco. You do what I say—you hear. Only what I say."

Flaco was paying more attention to the hit of coke he was taking.

"Yeah, yeah. Just you worry about you. I know what I'm doing."

"You know what you're doing? You know what you're doing? You are poisoning your fucking brain—what's left of it."

"Yeah, yeah. You know what I am? I'm a stone-cold killer. You ever kill anyone, old man?"

Bertin just shook his head.

"Flaco—Señor, stone-cold killer—if there is any killing done today, I will do it, *comprende*?"

"Yeah, yeah. *Jefe*, he say, he have the money he live. He no have the money he die. How hard is that? Me, I hope he don't have the money. Then I blow his *gringo* brains out."

Bertin now had a migraine headache and cut over to Little Village to get a late lunch, as they had some time to kill.

The Parking Lot, 4:30 P.M.

Howie saw the rental van pull into the parking lot and park in one of the three spaces reserved for Howard Bloom, CPA. Bertin was driving and had someone riding shotgun. They were early.

He had put the deposit slip in the safe and rehearsed his lines what seemed like a hundred times. "You said you wanted to eventually get the money offshore and I happened to have an opportunity to do so. The deposit slip is there for thirty million. The transfer fee was only two million. I saved Señor Garcia a lot of money."

If that went well, he would give them the bank name and account information. If it didn't go well, that information was his insurance policy—or so he hoped.

As the clock ticked toward five, he helped himself to another bit of false courage and had to smile. The bottle of Himmelstein scotch had been untouched for over twenty-five years and in a few short days had a severe dent in it.

Well, Howie, he said to himself, "You have a plan."

Just then he saw his mother's embroidered sign on the wall that said, "Man plans and God laughs."

Naomi called out that she was leaving and he watched her walk to her car. As soon as she pulled away, the Mexicans got out of their van and walked toward the building. It was showtime.

Bertin came up the stairs first, followed by his coked-up sidekick. Bertin approached, while the one he called Flaco paced by the door.

Howie rose from his desk and went to greet Bertin, who seemed troubled. "Bertin, I was expecting you."

"Señor Howard, I hope you have the money—all the money."

He pulled the signed receipt for $32,000,000 from his pocket and showed it to Howie.

"Yes, well—the money is all—is all accounted for, as you will see. I just have to explain something to you."

Flaco came rushing across the room with his pistol drawn.

"Just open the fucking safe, *gringo*."

Bertin had to restrain him.

"Flaco, go stand over there and shut the fuck up!"

Howie was now visibly shaken.

"Bertin, I just have to explain something."

Bertin was trying to keep one eye on Flaco and one on Howie. He knew it was a mistake to have Flaco there. Howie, he could control.

"Señor, just open the safe and then you can explain."

Howie was shaking so bad that he fumbled the combination twice before the door swung open, revealing only a single slip of paper.

Bertin didn't notice that Flaco had crept up behind them and seeing the empty safe had shot Howie three times before he could react. He grabbed Flaco forcefully.

"What the fuck did you do?"

"I did what *Jefe* told us to do. I kill the motherfucker. He stole the money."

Bertin reached in the safe and withdrew the deposit slip for thirty million. It didn't make sense.

"He didn't steal the money, you moron—at least thirty million. He deposited it. He told us he wanted to explain something."

"So he deposited the money. We go get it, *sí*?"

"Flaco, that's a great idea. Here, you look at the deposit slip and tell me where the money is—so that we can go get it?"

Flaco looked at the deposit slip and then it hit him.

"I was jus doing what *Jefe* said to do."

"Knowing him, I'm sure he'll understand that you just killed the only person who knew where his money was—right before he was getting ready to tell us."

The thought frightened Flaco. "What do we do?"

"What do we do? What do we do? This is all on you. I told him not to send you and I told you that if there was any killing done, I would do it."

"Maybe Esteban can help. *Jefe*, he listen to Esteban."

"That's the first intelligent thing I've ever heard you say. Go sit over there and don't say a fucking word."

Bertin called his brother's cell phone. Esteban answered right away.

"*Hola*, is that you my brother? How are things in Chicago?"

"That's why I'm calling. I have a problem."

"Don't tell me—let me guess. It has something to do with Flaco. I couldn't stop *Jefe* from sending him. He is a cockaroach."

"My brother, you nailed it, but the problem is *muy, muy mal*."

"Tell me what happened."

Bertin proceeded to tell him what had transpired. At the end Esteban was furious.

"Brother, this couldn't be worse. Get this—the Sinaloa and Gulf cartels both claim part ownership of that money. Doesn't the deposit slip give any clue as to where the money is?"

"It look like he cut off any of the identification."

"Where is that fucking cockaroach now?"

"He's sitting down in the corner. What do I do?"

"I hope I don't have to tell you what you do with Flaco. I just wish you could make it slow and painful. As to you—you know you can't come back to Mexico, at least not for a while. Do you have money?"

"I can get all I need."

"Then go somewhere and don't even tell me where. You know, in a way I envy you. If I knew how to get away I would. You find a place for both of us—then let me know."

"What about the deposit slip? Maybe someone can figure it out."

"I tell you what you do. The Latin Devils are sending a truck down tomorrow. They will have a bag full of cash to exchange for the drugs. Put the slip in an envelope and have them put it in with the cash. And Bertin—*vaya con Dios*!"

"*Vaya con Dios,* my brother."

Bertin walked over to the desk and found an envelope. He put the deposit slip in the envelope and put it in his pocket. He then made sure a round was chambered and walked over to where Flaco was sitting.

"What did Esteban say?"

Bertin replied with two shots to Flaco's head and two to his chest.

He went downstairs and looked through Naomi's desk. He found a letter addressed to her home address, which was close by. He then decided he had done enough killing in the past twenty-four hours. At worst, Naomi would describe a Mexican named Bertin as the possible gunman, but Bertin no longer existed. He had another set of papers, including passport, in the name of Manuel Estrada.

He would deliver the envelope to the Latin Devils and then head for the airport. Manuel, the erstwhile Bertin, had always dreamed about living in Spain. The thirty million dollars was now someone else's problem.

Chapter Four

Dodger Blue

Apache Dunes, Arizona, the Following Morning

By any objective assessment, Dylan (aka Geronimo) Reid had the world on a string. At eighteen, he stood six-five with a 220 pound chiseled physique and movie star good looks. If that wasn't enough, earlier that morning the football coach from Yale had come to Apache Dunes to personally offer a financial aid package that would allow him to attend the Ivy League school.

Yet, if you looked at him sitting on the porch steps of his home for the past eleven years, you might have thought he had lost his dog and/or his best friend. Neither was true. Chief, actually Chief II, was right there beside him and he was waiting for his best friend Jake who was—well, who ever knew where Jake was?

This was a major passage for him. If he accepted Yale's offer, which he was likely to do, tonight might be his last night in the only world he had ever known. That was tough enough, as he owed his adoptive parents, Tom and Sue, more than he could ever repay. They had been best friends with his birth parents, who died in a tragic automobile crash, and adopted Dylan when he was only seven years old.

The adoption turned out to be a blessing for all as Tom and Sue were unable to have children of their own. They never adopted Jake formally, but after his junkie mother disappeared, they took him in and he became the brother Dylan never had. Tom was the sheriff and became Jake's guardian. Without Tom, Sue, and particularly Dylan, it is doubtful that Jake could have survived.

By a quirk of fate, a sportswriter for Sport's Illustrated had decided to take a detour through the desert, on his way to an assignment for the Cardinals in Phoenix, and had car trouble outside of Apache Dunes late on a Friday afternoon.

Like much of the South and West, in the Dunes Friday nights meant high school football. That night Apache Dunes was playing one of the Tucson schools—a perennial football power with an enrollment twenty times that of the Dunes.

Both teams were undefeated. The game was made possible by the unexpected run in the playoffs the previous year, when a quarterback nicknamed Geronimo and a running back/wide receiver nicknamed Cochise dominated their foes. They were now seniors and were generating interest from state and regional schools.

What the writer saw he could hardly believe and was up typing about the rest of the night. It was a high-scoring game as the Dunes couldn't stop Central's running game, powered by a massive offensive line, but neither could Central stop Geronimo, who could throw a rope sixty yards in the air, or Cochise who ran over, rather than through, tacklers at will. In the open field he was impossible to catch. The Dunes prevailed, scoring on every possession.

With Geronimo and Cochise on the cover of Sports Illustrated, the recruiting wars were on. When they found out that Geronimo was a straight A student who crushed both the ACT and SAT, all doors were open and the Ivies came calling.

It was stretching it a bit to refer to Jake as a C student, but when you have speed and athleticism, like Jake possessed, and you instinctively run north and south—the football factories are open for business and business is good.

The first recruiting trip they took together was to LA to visit both USC and UCLA.

They split up so that Dylan could visit the USC library and see the campus, while Jake visited with a couple of boosters. A couple of hours later, and before they had even seen UCLA, Jake had signed a letter of intent and had the keys to a new, yellow Corvette.

The coaches obviously wanted them both and it weighed heavily on Dylan as this would be the first time they would be apart, for as long as he could remember.

He was deeply concerned how Jake would survive in La La Land, even if he was present. So there was that.

The other burden weighing on him was even more problematical, if that was possible—Dusty. Dusty, her brother Scooter, Dylan, and Jake had been virtually inseparable for the past eight years. Six of those years were carefree and without complications, but in the summer of Dusty's sixteenth year she had been transformed from a tomboy into a stunningly beautiful young lady and Dylan was still having trouble coping with it. While he had never disclosed his true feelings to her, it was the worst-kept secret in the Dunes and now he was going away.

He was deep in thought when Chief's tail started wagging and they heard the unmistakable sound of the Triumph approaching. Tom and Sue had given the boys matching Triumphs for their sixteenth birthdays. It was a reach for them, but it was either bikes or cars and the bikes were more economical in the desert.

Jake pulled up, dismounted, and stretched a bit. Jake was a couple of inches shorter than Dylan and wirier, but ripped. They wore the same uniform: t-shirt, blue jeans, cowboy boots, and bandanas.

Jake had a big smile on his face as he approached Dylan.

Dylan inquired, "What's so funny? Did I miss something?"

"What's funny is that you're sitting here worrying about things you can't control."

"How do you know what I'm thinking about?"

"Geronimo, everybody in the Dunes knows what you're worrying about—me and Dusty."

Dylan stood up. "Jake, you don't make it easy on me. You know Tom wants me to take the offer from Yale."

Jake laughed. "Dylan, you'd be an idiot not to take that offer and you're no idiot."

Dylan look surprised. "Then—then what happens to you?"

"One of these days I have to learn to stand on my own two feet."

"Jake, you will never survive four years in LA. They will eat you alive."

Jake was now bent over laughing.

"What the heck is so funny?"

"What's funny is you thinking I won't survive in LA for four years. I'll be lucky to last one."

Now Dylan was really puzzled. "What's that supposed to mean?"

"Dylan, God bless you. I love you brother, but you're the only person in the world who would think that I could make it in college. Hell, I was lucky to graduate from high school."

"Jake, they don't expect you to go to class. They want you for one thing—football."

"And I want them for football. Dylan, this is the only thing I've done on my own. I'm juiced man. I did it. You know why I took the 'Vette? Because I earned it. Plus, I'll be lucky if my knees hold out for a full season."

"What's that supposed to mean?"

"You seriously didn't notice? I played with pain the entire last season."

"But, you blew the scouts away when they came to check you out."

"And I was fighting it every minute."

"You know you could try to run away from, instead of over, people."

Jake laughed. "Remember the story of the Scorpion and the Frog? It's my nature, Dude. It's what I do. That's what they love. They don't give a shit about me."

"I'll give you credit for understanding that, but what happens when the knees go?"

"What happens? I'll tell you what happens—I come home to the only home I've ever had and go to work for Tom. I'll drive home in my new 'Vette, by the way."

"Have you talked to Tom about that?"

"I don't have to. He knows us better than we know ourselves. Listen, brother, this was it for me. I made it to the big time. I did it. I sacrificed and I played with pain. I had to prove to myself that I could do it and I did. I won. My Mom, God bless her wherever she is, wasn't strong enough to handle her pain. I had to do this for both of us.

"You, on the other hand, have no doors closed to you. Man, the sky is the limit and you have to go for it. Can you imagine a kid from the Dunes going to Yale and starring on the football team? I'll be OK. I'll miss you every minute of every day, but I'll be OK. Without you, I don't know what would have happened to me. Nine years old—fucking nine years old and you brought me home with you. You knew I was in a bad place. Man, you are some kind of special and everyone knows it."

They hugged. "Thanks, Bro. I just want you to be OK."

Jake looked at Dylan and was still smiling.

"What? What now?"

"You know what now and I can't help you with that one."

Dylan sat back down and rubbed his temples.

"Is it that obvious?"

"Only for the past two years and to everyone but you."

Dylan smiled. "Any advice?"

Jake laughed. "Man, I ain't going near that one."

Dylan looked at his watch. It was almost noon. "I'm going to pick Dusty up and stop by the diner to say goodbye to the coach. He and Tom went there for lunch.

"Then Dusty and I are going to stop by the reservation and say goodbye to Michael. We'll hook back up at the cave. Scooter is going to bring the food and beer in his truck. Can you believe this will be our last cookout at the cave for a while? Maybe ever. Let's try to make it a night to remember."

Jake walked Dylan over to his bike and watched as he pulled out of the driveway and left to pick up Dusty.

The Garcia Hacienda

Ever since Roberto's untimely and suspicious death, there had been a cloud of uncertainty hanging over the Garcia estate. Roberto had started selling grass to college kids from Arizona primarily to subsidize the centuries old estate and the families who depended on it for their existence. At that time they were all impoverished and living off the land. His original entourage were all dependents of the estate, who had a vested interest in its survival.

His younger brother José, by contrast, had long ago left the estate to lead a life of petty crime and preying on *turistas* in Acapulco. The gang he assembled had only one vested interest—greed.

The problems began when José learned of Roberto's success and decided to come home to share in the bounty—and brought his band of misfits with him. It was an uneasy truce as the cultures couldn't have been more different.

The problems escalated and eventually spiraled out of control when José introduced cocaine into the mix. From a monetary standpoint it was a brilliant move, as their distribution channels were already in place, thanks to Roberto, but from any other vantage point it was a disaster waiting to happen. The money was ridiculous and if money isn't the root of all evil—it was for the Garcias.

More by happenstance than design, José and his thugs became a vital cog in the enterprise as the money begat violence and few people, even in the drug trade, were more violent and ruthless than "El Diablo" (the devil). He worked hard to earn and justify his sobriquet.

Truth is, Roberto was content with their grass business and viewed grass as no more harmful than alcohol, tobacco and prescription "downers"—maybe less so. Cocaine—forget about it. It had no redeeming value save taking money from those who had too much to begin with.

But Roberto perished in an airplane crash of mysterious circumstances and the cartel was fairly, evenly split between those who had been loyal to Roberto and those who owed their allegiance to El Diablo. You could feel it in the air.

So, it was with trepidation that Esteban approached the hacienda after being summoned by El Diablo—particularly after Bertin's news from Chicago. He knocked once and entered.

"*Jefe*, you wanted to see me?"

Diablo was seated behind the massive desk with his ever present cocaine and cognac in front of him—never a good sign. He did a line, stood up, wiped his nose, and walked over to the window.

"Esteban—I want to ask you a question."

Esteban was now nervous, but was certain the news from Chicago couldn't have traveled this fast.

"How can I help you, *Jefe*?"

Diablo motioned for Esteban to join him at the window.

"Esteban, is it me, or do I see blue everywhere I look?"

"The hats. Those are the hats of Carlos' gang."

"Carlos' gang? Did you say Carlos' gang?"

All of a sudden another of Diablo's trusted aides, Juan, knocked and entered quickly. "*Jefe*, I have some bad news."

Esteban held his breath. Could it be about Bertin?

"So speak, don't just stand there."

"It's the reservation. They say two more people die because of the bad meth."

Diablo looked stunned. "That can't be. I said to destroy that meth last week."

Juan looked very nervous.

"You have something to say—you better say it."

"*Jefe*, it is your nephew. His men, they take the meth and say they will destroy it, but they sold it to the Indians instead."

Diablo was enraged. He looked for something to throw and went to the desk and hurled the bottle of cognac against the stone fireplace. Esteban winced as he knew the tapestries and carpets were priceless – a fact lost on Diablo.

He waved Juan away and Juan was anxious to leave.

He turned to Esteban, almost pleading.

"Why is Carlos here? I thought he went to LA with his mother after the funeral."

"He did, but he say he come back to take his father's place."

Diablo was pensive as he paced back and forth before speaking.

"Don't we have a shipment for the Latin Devils tonight?"

"*Sí*, it is ready to go."

Diablo sat down and did another line of coke. He instinctively reached for the cognac, then remembered what he'd done with it. He stood up and started pacing again.

"Esteban, I tell you what you do. You tell my nephew I want to see him. You tell him, OK?"

"*Sí, Jefe*. I go find him."

Esteban was always anxious to leave Diablo when he was into the coke. One time he was waving his gun and it accidentally went off, killing one of his men and then he shot another, also by accident, when he was trying to show him what happened to the first one.

He was further relieved that the subject of Chicago didn't come up, but that time would come and soon. If things went well tonight maybe the mood would lighten a bit, as the Latin Devils had threatened to change suppliers when Roberto died.

At least they would have the deposit slip, and how many banks could there be? It might take time, but they would find the bank—wouldn't they? The news of the meth was not good, though. It wasn't hard to read Diablo's mind. There was a bad moon on the rise.

Carlos was in the courtyard with his homeboys, all sporting Dodger caps with the LA logo on the blue background. Esteban thought they were cool hats actually.

He told Carlos that his uncle wanted to see him and escorted him to the study.

Diablo stood as they entered. "Nephew, I heard you were here. How long do you plan to visit?"

Carlos appeared to completely miss the mixed message.

"Uncle, I decided that I would come back and take my father's place. I think he would have wanted that."

Diablo shook his head.

"No, no. Your father—he wanted you to get an education and be a doctor or lawyer. He told me this many, many times."

"I thought about that, but I decided to get involved in the family business. I got some good news for you. I made my first score and I will give you your half."

Diablo was mercurial, but he could control his emotions when it suited his purpose. It was an animal instinct and Diablo was an animal. He gritted his teeth.

"My half, you say?"

"*Sí*, fifty-fifty, straight up."

"The—family business, eh?"

"Yeah, Uncle. I know I have a lot to learn, but I've already put together my own gang. These are our colors, like the Dodgers." He showed Diablo his hat.

"Your own gang, eh? And, what may I ask was this score, as you say?"

Carlos was now animated. "It was fucking brilliant. Some of your men were going to throw some meth away. Just fucking throw it away. I say, we take care of it. I know some Indians I met when growing up in Apache Dunes who love that shit. So we sold it to them. No problem. And I have another deal running tonight."

Diablo had to sit down to control himself. He was rubbing his temples as Esteban went to the cabinet for a new bottle of cognac. He poured a generous helping in a crystal snifter. The timing was perfect as it forced Diablo to catch his breath. Diablo took a generous swig and savored it.

"Nephew, did it occur to you to tell me what you were going to do with the meth?"

"Why would I bother you with such a small deal? What could go wrong?"

Diablo just stared at him. If he had shot him then and there, Esteban wouldn't have been surprised.

"Did you say you have another deal tonight? You want to tell me what that is about?"

"Sure—I have a truckload of illegals to take across the border. It's good money"

"And how, may I ask, are you taking them across the border?"

"In one of the trucks, Uncle."

Diablo now stood and walked to the window again. Esteban could tell his wheels were turning.

He turned to Carlos.

"Nephew, since we are partners—fifty-fifty you say—I'm going to help you out tonight. I have a shipment of marijuana to go to a meet in the hills near Apache Dunes. I will give you a bigger truck, one of the refrigerated ones. You can drop your illegals off in the desert and deliver the grass. I trust you to do that."

At first Carlos seemed surprised, but then smiled at the thought of the added responsibility. This was the big leagues.

"No problem. My men and I will handle it."

Diablo waved his finger.

"No, no, I have a better idea. I will have Juan and his men go with you as they know the drill. In the meantime, I would like to meet your men tonight. Welcome them into the—ah—the family business, as you say. How many are there?"

"Just four not counting me, but we plan on getting bigger."

"Four is fine for tonight. Have them meet me here at seven, say."

"No problem, Uncle."

Carlos then approached to embrace, but Diablo turned away as if he hadn't noticed. After an awkward moment, Carlos shrugged at Esteban and departed.

Esteban approached Diablo who was now deep in thought, staring out the window.

"*Jefe*, the refrigerated truck can't be used for the illegals. It has no ventilation."

Diablo just stared at him and he now understood. Esteban felt a cold chill run through his body.

"And Esteban, send Flaco with Juan's men. Tell him I want to see him before they leave."

Esteban swallowed hard. "Flaco is in Chicago, *Jefe*."

Diablo furrowed his brow. "Chicago? Aren't they back yet?"

"Not yet."

"Well, where are they? Don't you know where your brother is?"

"*Jefe*, I had eleven brothers and sisters. We weren't as close as you and your brother."

Diablo hesitated before replying. Was that supposed to mean something? Did they suspect he was involved in his brother's death? Best to let it slide.

"Well, let me know when they return. Tell Juan I need three of his best men, two to go with Carlos and the truck and one to be waiting in the rocks above the meet. *Comprende*?" His stare left no uncertainty as to the third man's purpose.

"*Jefe*, I don't know if that is a good idea—sending Carlos to the meet. The Devils don't like new faces. We had that problem before, if you remember."

Diablo screamed, "Fuck the Devils! They will do as I say. Just like you do, eh?"

"*Sí, Jefe*. I'll take care of it."

"Oh, Esteban—tell Carlito, you know, the one who knows about the explosives—to come see me right away."

"*Sí, Jefe*."

Chapter Five

Geronimo and Cochise

Apache Dunes, the Diner

Dalian and Dusty pulled into the parking lot, but kept the motor running. Dusty had on her version of Dylan's uniform—a T-shirt that didn't quite cover her midriff and cowboy boots, but with cut offs, rather than blue jeans. Tom and the coach from Yale had just finished lunch and came outside to see them.

Tom spoke first. "Dylan, Dusty. Where are you off to?

"We're going to stop by the reservation and say goodbye to Michael and the kids, then wind up at the cave for a cookout—our last one for a while."

The coach stuck out his hand and Dylan shook it. "Dylan, or should I say Geronimo, it was a pleasure to meet you. I'm glad I came for a lot of reasons. I'm going to keep my fingers crossed that you'll accept our offer. I think—no, I know that you will flourish at Yale, but don't wait too long. I need an answer ASAP."

Dylan looked at Tom first, then the coach, and smiled. "I just need to sleep on it. I think it's looking good."

"That's great news. Be careful on this thing."

They all laughed as Dylan pulled out on the highway. That is, everyone was laughing but Dusty.

The coach turned to Tom. "You know, I have a couple of hours to kill before I have to head to the airport. I'm very intrigued with everything about that young man and this area, too. You don't by any chance have a little more time to spend with me, do you?"

"Dylan and the desert are my two favorite topics and nothing happens around here in the heat of the day. All of the villains around here are nocturnal. There's a little breeze—let's get a pitcher of lemonade and grab those two rocking chairs on the porch."

They sat down and put the pitcher between them. Tom took off his hat and wiped his brow.

"You ask the questions and I'll try to answer them."

"Fair enough. First of all, tell me about the Indian connection—the Geronimo and Cochise part."

Tom pointed off to the low hills. "You see those hills there. Legend has it that Geronimo and thirty or so of his braves held off a combined US and Mexican force of ten thousand soldiers and bounty hunters for over a year. They did it by using a network of secret caves, most that have yet to be discovered. The kids around here play cowboys and Indians, but they all want to be the Indians and Dylan was convinced he has the spirit of Geronimo. I'm not sure he doesn't. Jake chose Cochise."

"The cave Dylan said they were going to—is that one of the caves?"

"He discovered it shortly after his parents were killed. That's why he believes in the spiritual business."

"So, you've been to the cave?"

"Nope. I thought it was important for him to have his own special place, a sanctuary, and the only people who know about it are Dylan, Jake, Dusty, and her brother."

"I definitely want to circle back to Dusty, but can you talk about his parents? I understand that you were close."

Tom took a drink of lemonade and gazed off in the distance before answering.

"Close doesn't do it justice. Dylan's daddy, big Dylan, and I were as inseparable as Dylan and Jake and that's not the only parallel. He and I were the stars of the previous championship team here and we both got scholarships from ASU. Dylan inherited his brains from his daddy and his daddy loved the academics as much, if not more, than the football. He made the dean's list and was starting QB as a freshman.

"I got a lot of playing time, but never found my way to the classroom. I'd lie to his daddy about it, or he would have dragged me to class. Anyway, I don't know what I was thinking about, because I lost my deferment and wound up getting drafted. It was 1969 and they needed warm bodies for Vietnam.

"Well, his daddy was pissed off and then some when I told him. He asked what the fuck I was going to do now. I told him that I was going to meet with the Marine recruiter near the campus that evening and he stomped off.

When I got to the recruiting office, Dylan was sitting there with the recruiter. He had enlisted with the understanding that we were together, under what they called the buddy plan, and that we went to OCS and would be officers, not grunts—lot of difference it meant in country at times."

"Whoa, wait a minute. You're telling me he dropped out of school and enlisted because you got drafted?"

Tom had to look away and rub his eyes a bit.

"That's the kind of man and friend he was."

"That is an incredible story. Sweet Jesus. Then what happened?"

"Then what happened was called Nam and that's all I want to say about that. When we went away to college we both swore we would never return to the desert, but after out tour was up it was the only place we wanted to be. We couldn't get home fast enough."

"What about college?"

Tom laughed. "My college experiment was a distant memory, but Dylan's daddy went back. He lost his scholarship, but had the GI Bill. We were both carrying around some shrapnel, not to mention the emotional scars, so his playing days were over, but he got a job coaching the QBs while he was going to school. After he graduated he came back to the Dunes and got a job as an English literature teacher and football coach."

"That's not your normal combo."

"Yeah, no kidding, but that was big Dylan. Anyway, we ended up marrying our high school sweethearts and had a double wedding. Little Dylan came along late in life for his parents. Sue and I had realized we weren't destined to have children. The docs thought what they now call PTSD had something to do with it. I wouldn't be surprised—nobody survived that war totally intact."

"I know this is painful and if you don't want to go there, I understand, but how did his parents die?"

Tom clearly had to compose himself. He got up and walked to the end of the porch and stood for a while before he came back, sat down, and took a deep breath.

"It was a normal Saturday night. Little Dylan was riding shotgun with me as I made my rounds. He was seven at the time. I cherished the time we spent together. Well, his parents had driven over to Four Corners to have dinner with their new football coach and his wife. On the way home they went to pass a slow-moving car and ran head on into a semi with its light off. It was smuggling Mexicans across the border and they'd keep the lights off to try to avoid detection. Both vehicles went up in flames before help could get there. The truck was padlocked. The coroner estimated that there could have been as many as forty people in the truck."

"I'm sorry. Wow."

"Anyway, we adopted Dylan and he has been the light of our lives ever since."

"And when did Jake enter the picture?"

"Dylan was nine when he came home from school one day with Jake in tow. I can't begin to tell you what a pitiful sight he was. He was filthy—and I mean filthy. His clothes were in tatters and his shoes had holes in them. If that wasn't bad enough, he had lice in his hair, which was why the school refused him entrance. When school was out, Dylan found Jake crying under a tree and brought him home."

"That's pretty exceptional behavior for a nine year old—for anyone, for that matter!"

"That's Dylan. He became a man after his parents died and he's the most compassionate person I know. He got that from his daddy, too. Anyway, Sue made him wash—I should say scrub—in the tub outside and she put his clothes in the trash barrel and burned them. Dylan's a couple of sizes bigger and he always took good care of his clothes, so his hand-me-downs were the finest clothes Jake had ever seen."

"What did she do about the lice?"

"The only thing she could do. She shaved his head—and get this, Dylan then shaved his, so Jake wouldn't feel funny.

"At dinner that night, he ate like a horse and had no table manners whatsoever. Sue and I exchanged glances during the meal. There was something really wrong with this picture. After dinner Dylan asked if Jake could sleepover. I said I would have to check with his mom. When he told me where they lived it all became clear. We used to have a trailer park outside of town that, over the years, was taken over by the worst trash imaginable. Most people avoided even going near."

"You said used to have."

"After a young girl was kidnapped, beaten, and raped by one of the residents, a group of vigilantes burned it to the ground—and I mean to the ground. The residents got the message and scattered to God knows where."

"Were you around when it happened?"

Tom just smiled. "My deputy and I happened to be out of town at the time. Back to Jake—I drove out there and had my deputy stand guard with a shotgun as I found their trailer. His mama was entertaining. I quickly got rid of her guest and couldn't believe the squalor Jake had been forced to live in. His mom was a junkie and she was as infested with lice as he was. I took her into the jail so we could get her cleaned up. One of the visiting nurses came over and attended to her. I noticed that she never once mentioned having a son or asked about him."

"Poor kid. What happened to her?"

"She had bad withdrawals for a few days, but the medication the nurse prescribed seemed to be helping, so I made her a deal. I took her up to a detox center in Tucson where they practice tough love. I told her I would pay for two weeks, but she would have to show progress for me to continue to support her."

"Tom, if more people in the world were like you, what a great world it would be!"

"Thanks, but I was doing it for Jake and Dylan."

"And? I'm almost afraid to ask."

"A person can survive almost anything if they have the will to survive. She was too far gone and had given up long ago. After a little over a week, she disappeared and hasn't been heard from since."

"But you didn't adopt him, right?"

"I would have in a New York second, but she was still his mama and I didn't want him to abandon the hope that she might return someday. I became his guardian, but came to love him like a son and he and Dylan were good for each other."

"Man, I wish he had the grades. I would love to have him. They can both play on Sunday someday if they want."

Tom laughed. "Believe it or not, I'm not sure either one are that crazy about football. There is no way Jake lasts four years at SC running north and south."

"I don't disagree, but doesn't he understand that? He has the speed and athleticism to avoid most tacklers."

Tom laughed again. "That's the point—he doesn't want to avoid them. He wants to punish them. Football was the perfect release for his aggression—that chip on his shoulder. I remember one game where Jake had literally run over and knocked three defensive backs out of the game. The other team was at the bottom of the depth chart and put an undersized freshmen in the game. First play Jake burst through the line and headed straight for him. Tom laughed. "The poor kid tried to run away when he saw Jake coming."

They both laughed.

"You see, football was all about proving something to himself. It was something he had to do and football was the perfect vehicle."

"What happens to him after football?"

"I imagine he'll come back to the desert and maybe work for me. One of his great qualities, and he has many, is that he counts his blessings. He doesn't think the world owes him anything. Even the Corvette was more symbolic than meaningful. By the way, what kind of car are you giving Dylan?"

The coach almost spilled his lemonade and looked at Tom in shock.

Tom eventually smiled and poked him on the shoulder. "I was just messin' with you."

"You got me good. I almost had a heart attack."

"Don't do that. The nearest hospital is more than an hour away."

He smiled. "That doesn't make me feel any better."

He looked at his watch. "Last question. What's the story with the girl—Dusty is it? She's a beautiful young lady."

"Dusty is that, but if you had met her three years ago, you might have thought she was one of the boys."

"I find that hard to believe."

"Imagine how Dylan feels. You see, Dusty is the same age as Dylan and Jake. Moved in down the way when they were ten. She has a younger brother, Scooter, who has a heart bigger than Texas, but two left feet. Dusty was a tomboy and could do almost anything the boys could do, but Scooter was hopeless.

"Their first day of school some of the boys were picking on Scooter when Dylan and Jake came along. From that day forward, Scooter was off limits and the four of them were inseparable."

"I think I'm getting the picture and I can't give any advice in that regard."

"Nor can I. Sue and he have had some long chats, but I'm not included in that dialogue."

"So, Dylan goes away for four years, I hope. Kind of selfish of me. What happens to Dusty?"

"Dusty is a talented young artist. She's won some prizes and she wants to either go to an art school or get a job with a gallery somewhere."

"Well, Tom, this has been a real experience for me. I don't know what it is, but there is something spiritual about the desert and it sure is a change of pace from New England. I feel better for just having met Dylan, Jake—and you. I read the story in Sports Illustrated, but you have to experience the desert to understand the story. I do hope Dylan accepts the offer. I think Yale will be good for him and I know he will be good for Yale."

Tom smiled. "If he can get through his last night at the cave for a while, I think he'll accept. Just say a prayer for Sue and me. It's going to be tough on us, but we knew this day was going to come."

Chapter Six

The Full Moon

The Apache Reservation

Dylan and Dusty spent much of their free time in high school tutoring and mentoring the youth of the nearby Apache reservation. There was actually some dispute as to whether it was an officially recognized reservation, but, as they say, "Possession is nine-tenths of the law," and there was no dispute among the locals that the land, as Godforsaken as it was, was the property of the Apaches—specifically the Chiricahua tribe. Truth is, all of the land had once been their property until it was confiscated under the dubious claim of "Manifest Destiny."

The Apaches were warriors and they lived a rather simple, almost nomadic existence. There was some cultivation of crops, corn mainly, and the women were noted for their basket-weaving ability, but that was more or less the extent of their labors outside of hunting and exploiting the fruit of the agave plant.

In 1872 Cochise entered into an agreement with the government that created the Chiricahua Reservation. After his death, his son Taza assumed the role of Chief, but the reservation was abolished after a deadly conflict with settlers, some of whom had been selling alcohol to the Apaches.

Thus began a painful diaspora for the Chiricahua, with descendants of Geronimo eventually winding up at Ft. Sill, Oklahoma, and others being forcefully relocated to the infamous San Carlos Reservation, where their enemies the Yavapai resided.

Over time, some of the Chiricahua residents of San Carlos slipped away and returned to their ancestral area. The community eventually grew to its current population of a few hundred, who now existed primarily by virtue of government entitlement programs and a few charitable endeavors. In all other respects, save for the ubiquitous satellite dishes and trailers, time had stood still. Having said that, Apache children were like any other children and native culture and traditions were no match for MTV and video games.

The elders just had to sigh and resign themselves to the fact that there was no escape from the white man's culture. It was really just human nature that the young would rebel against their elders—ask the wind not to blow!

Dylan parked near the small school building and what passed for a playground, with broken swings and nets missing from the basketball court. Graffiti was ever present.

As Dylan and Dusty approached the school it was obvious it was closed. The chief's son Michael approached with a long face.

"Michael, why's the school closed? We wanted to say goodbye to the kids."

"Another OD last night. That's two in the last ten days."

"Bad drugs?"

"What else?"

"The Mexicans?"

"Who else?"

Dylan picked up a rock and hurled it at an imaginary target. "I—I don't know what to say."

"Nothin' to say. Nothin' good happens around here—no matter how hard we try. So, my brother, is this goodbye?"

"For a while, I'm afraid."

Dusty tried to break the gloom a bit. "You've known each other a long time."

Dylan smiled, "As far back as I can remember. My dad used to take me out to the desert and I met Michael and his father when I was looking for the cave."

Now Michael smiled, "You mean your secret cave?"

"If I told you where it was, I'd have to kill you."

Now they all laughed.

"Of course, if you tell me where the others are, we might make a deal."

Michael smiled. "I'll think about it."

Dusty looked at them. "I always thought it was ironic that Dylan was called Geronimo and you, the chief's son, were Michael."

"Tell me about it. We would play cowboys and Indians and wrestle for who got to be Geronimo. The loser was the *gringo* and I always lost. How embarrassing!"

They all laughed again.

"At least we can still laugh. There's not much to laugh at around here these days. Take care of yourself, brother."

Dylan and Michael embraced.

"You too, brother."

Dylan and Dusty got back on the bike. He turned to Dusty, "It's pretty hot. We could stop by the wells and skinny dip."

"You never give up do you?"

"I'm running out of time."

"You know it is very hot."

Dylan jerked around as he started the engine. Dusty had a coy smile on her face.

"Is that—do you mean—is that a yes?"

"Careful Geronimo, I don't want you to have a heart attack before we get there."

Dylan let out a war whoop as he pulled away.

The Apache Wells weren't wells at all but rather a group of geothermal pools in the desert. Dylan got off the bike and ripped his clothes off—T-shirt first, then boots. When Dusty took her halter top off, Dylan almost tripped over one of his boots. They laughed and then embraced. Dusty then pulled away.

"Slow down, cowboy—I mean Chief. I've been waiting for this too long to rush it."

She took off her boots and shorts.

Dylan looked shocked. "What do you mean? You mean—you mean you wanted to?"

"I was only waiting for the right time and we're running out of time. First one in!"

Dusty took off her panties ran to the pool and dived in. Dylan followed and they quickly found each other. They embraced again.

"Dylan, slow. I want to do it. I need to do it, but this is my first time."

"You know it's my first time, too."

"Dylan, I love you. I always have."

"I love you, too."

After a few awkward moments, they figured it out and hearts that had once beat independently of each other now beat as one as the sun began to set.

Evening in the Desert in Northern Mexico

Carlos Garcia collected the money from his illegal cargo of twenty-one men, women and children. Juan's men opened the back of the truck and herded them inside. When they were all loaded, the back door was padlocked. Carlos smiled as he counted his money. He and Juan's men, Eloy and Rene, hopped in the cab and headed due north. They were barely into their journey when they heard the banging on the truck's walls.

Carlos shook his head. "What did they expect—first class seating?"

Eloy asked, "We're going to the desert near Apache Dunes. Where do we take them?"

"Easy. I said I would let them off in the desert in Arizona. We'll drop them off before we go to the meet."

The banging started to wane. Carlos smiled. "See, it just takes a little getting used to."

The Highway Outside of Apache Dunes

Del Kennedy, the senior DEA agent and law enforcement official in the area, pulled over to the side of the road to answer his cell phone. He recognized the caller, the senior border patrol agent.

"Del here."

"Del, this is Hank with border patrol. How you doin' this fine evening?"

"I'm fine, Hank. What's up?"

"Well, you asked us to notify you if any vehicles were spotted coming across the border near Apache Dunes. We just spotted a large truck heading north."

"Yeah, we already know about it and will take it from here."

"Roger that. Just making sure you knew. Oh, and by the way, we've been ordered by the DOJ not to interfere with a shipment of guns and ammo to one of the Mexican cartels. Makes you kind of wonder, doesn't it?

"It does indeed. Thanks again."

Del disconnected and then dialed the number of his younger DEA partner, Carl. Carl is also ex-military, but more of a "cowboy" and less discreet than Del.

Carl answered on the second ring. "Hey Del, what's up."

"We have a truck coming through tonight."

"Hot damn. I can use it."

Del paused as he rolled his eyes. "Carl—be cool, be real fucking cool."

"Sorry."

"Just be cool. Now, what I need is for you to take over with the truck. Kelsey's been acting funny lately. I haven't been home much, so I want to surprise her and be home tonight."

"No problem. Can I at least ask, is it a big truck?"

"I was told it's a large one."

"Fucking A!"

"Carl! Oh fuck it. Just take care of the truck." Del rubbed his temples and headed home.

The Garcia Hacienda

Diablo and Esteban greeted Carlos' four main lieutenants. They each had Dodgers hats on and similar tats of an Angel with a cross. Diablo was standing behind his desk and summonsed them closer.

"*Amigos*, thanks for coming. I have a job for you."

Carlos' guys looked at each other and smiled. They were ready.

"By the way, I like the hats. LA—ey?"

They replied in unison, "LA."

Diablo nodded to Esteban, who took his leave.

"Loyalty is very important. Loyalty is everything. So let me ask you—are you loyal to my nephew?"

They nodded in unison as the leader said, "True blue, man. True blue."

Esteban reentered the room and made eye contact with Diablo.

"*Bueno—muy bueno.* My nephew needs you to meet him in Apache Dunes tonight. He'll be at the Diner, which is just west of town. You should leave now so you won't be late."

Diego turned and walked to the window. Carlos' men looked confused at first, but Esteban motioned for them to leave.

Esteban joined Diablo on the veranda as the car left the estate. After it traveled approximately half a mile, it exploded in a spectacular fireball. Diablo was expressionless as he turned to Esteban to see his reaction. Esteban knew what was coming and was careful not to show any emotion. Truth is his senses were dulled long ago.

Del's Mansion Near Apache Dunes

Kelsey felt like she was getting acclimated to life in the desert—life in a mansion in the desert with all of the amenities. It's not like she had a viable choice, or any choice, the fateful day she met Del. Truth is, the solitude that she feared most had actually become an asset, as it afforded her time for introspection that she dearly needed. She particularly treasured the nights, like tonight, when Del was on patrol and she had the place to herself—well, herself, her alter ego, and personal demons. She had warned Del that she had secrets, but he apparently had secrets of his own.

She had just exited the pool and dried off. She put on one of Del's deep V-neck cashmere sweaters that hung loosely on her shoulders and covered the bare minimum. She loved how it felt on her skin and could, and did, literally fall off at any given moment. Her plans for the evening consisted simply of getting stoned out of her mind and listening to Pink Floyd's *Dark Side of the Moon* while enjoying the full moon—and she was well on her way. All other guilty pleasures she was capable of administering herself.

The upside of solitude was that it kept her out of trouble, which is something she had proven incapable of doing without constraints. The problem is—even when you've secluded yourself behind closed doors, trouble can come calling—and it did.

Kelsey was surprised to hear the front doorbell ring as she wasn't expecting any company. In fact, they rarely had any. She was a bit tipsy when she looked through the peep hole and saw Angie standing there. Since she had been in the Dunes, their paths had crossed only in the presence of their husbands. Truth is, she had experienced many sleepless nights fearing what would happen if they were ever alone and that moment had now arrived.

Kelsey opened the door. "Angie, I didn't expect to see you."

Angie brushed past her as she entered and in so doing purposefully caused the sweater to fall off Kelsey's left shoulder and expose her perfect breast. Kelsey recovered as quickly as possible, but knew it was no accident.

Angie always unnerved her. She was a knockout even with the white trash tats and piercings. Her greatest and most disarming trait was a peculiar variation of self-confidence, which she exuded. She wasn't self-confident because she was undaunted by life's whips and scorns; rather, she readily accepted them without a hint of defiance. She didn't just expect to be used and abused—she welcomed it.

As her eyes devoured Kelsey, she broke the ice. "Kelsey, you look fantastic, but you always did."

Angie was wearing a loose and very short sundress that left little to the imagination. She did a pirouette that proved there was nothing underneath. "So, Kelsey, how do I look after all this time?"

"Like a slut, but you always did."

Angie laughed and moved closer, noting that Kelsey didn't retreat. "Same old Kelsey. I wondered if you had changed."

Kelsey had to adjust the sweater again. "Angie, I'm not the same old Kelsey and I have changed. I'm married and trying to make it work, if you haven't noticed."

Angie advanced again and they were almost touching. She reached up and brushed Kelsey's hair back and put her mouth next to her ear. Kelsey showed no sign of resisting. Angie's tongue went in Kelsey's ear as she whispered, "Oh, I noticed, but old habits don't die easily."

Kelsey shivered and her chest was heaving with desire as their mouths found each other. Kelsey pulled Angie's sundress over her head as her sweater dropped to the floor. As they tumbled to the sofa as one, Kelsey caught the glimpse of headlights coming up the driveway. She quickly jumped up and ran to the window. By the lighting arrangement, Kelsey knew it was Del's Range Rover and went into full panic mode.

"Angie, quick—into the bathroom and get dressed. You have to leave as soon as Del gets here." Kelsey had trouble getting the sweater back on—at least, getting it to stay on. Her heart was still beating out of control as she tried to straighten her hair.

She was standing by the door when Del came in. He had seen Angie's car and looked perplexed. Kelsey spoke first, "What are you doing home? I thought you were on patrol tonight?"

Del was taking in the scene and particularly the askew sweater. "I got Carl to take over and thought I would surprise you. Apparently I have. Isn't that Angie's car?"

Kelsey replied as Angie exited the hall bathroom and walked right by Del as if he weren't even there. "Yeah, she just stopped by to borrow something."

Del watched Angie get in her car and leave. "I thought you said she was a slut."

"I did and she is."

"What did she want to borrow?"

Kelsey let the sweater drop to the floor. "Do you want to talk about her or us? Why don't you get some coke and I'll get some bubbly and meet you at the hot tub?"

Del quickly rose to the occasion. "Sounds like a plan."

As Kelsey passed a mirror on the way to the wine cellar, she paused and looked at herself. She realized two things: all of the champagne and cocaine in the world wouldn't help Del pass through the portal that Angie entered and exited with ease, and old habits don't just die hard. Some don't die at all.

The Sheriff's House in Apache Dunes

Sheriff Tom Ward and his wife Sue were having dinner, but Tom seemed distracted.

"Tom, you've hardly eaten anything and this is your favorite meal. I know what's on your mind, but we both knew the day would come when Dylan and Jake would have to go away to college."

Tom moved his plate aside and laughed. "I'm not worried about Jake and the only way he was going to college was on a football scholarship. Truth is—I've worried about Dylan every day he's been with us."

"You're going to make yourself sick. Just relax. He'll be fine."

Tom got up from the table and walked over to the window, where a full moon was in view.

"It's just that nothing good ever seems to happen around here and he has so much potential. As much as I hate to see him go, I know he has to get out of here."

"Where is he tonight?"

"Where else? With Jake, Dusty, and Scooter cooking out at the cave."

"Well—you knew he'd want to be with them if he's leaving. Poor Dusty."

"Poor Dylan."

Carl's SUV

Carl pulled into the Diner parking lot and got his cell phone out. He dialed his bookie.

"Yeah."

"This is the Cowboy. Whatta you have on the D-backs and Rockies tonight?"

"D-backs are minus 160, but it starts in a couple of minutes."

"OK—put a nickel on the D-backs minus 160. In fact, I feel lucky tonight. Let's double that."

"I have you for a dime on the D-backs minus 160. You want your number?"

"I know where I am."

"I hope for your sake you do."

Just as Carl hung up, his phone rang—it was his wife Angie.

"Hey, what's up? I thought you were out with a girlfriend tonight?"

"I was, but plans changed. Speaking about being out—I am out of something."

Carl pounded his fist on the dashboard. "Angie, how the fuck can you be out?"

"I don't need a lecture. Shit happens. You know what I need and if you bring it to me we can party like you like."

"Angie, I can't. Not tonight. I promised Del I would look after business tonight and it's big business."

"Yeah, well—Del's home fucking Kelsey while you do all the work."

"Wait, how do you know what Del's doing?"

"I'm just saying. If you don't want to come home, I'm sure I can find somebody to keep me company—maybe somebodies."

Carl hit the steering wheel with his fist. "OK—I'm coming home, but Del can't know about me coming home, or about the evidence."

"Why would I say anything? Hurry Baby."

Carl looked up at the full moon and turned on the radio as he exited the parking lot.

"Back-to-back homers by Helton and Tulowitzki and the Rockies lead now four zip in the top of the first and still no outs! That's four hits on just five pitches. It looks like a long night for the D-backs!"

"FUCK!!!!!!!!!!!!!!!!!!!!!!!!!"

The Cave

Dylan and Dusty arrived first and started the fire. After an awkward silence, Dusty turned to Dylan. "If you go out East, you won't be coming back."

Dylan shook his head. "You don't know that. I don't know that."

"I don't want you to stay just for me—well I do, but do you think you will—you know—fit in out there?"

"Dusty, I'll be playing football and studying. I won't have time for anything else."

Jake and Scooter entered. Jake had hot dogs, buns, Fritos, and ice in a cooler. Scooter had a couple of six packs of beer.

Jake set the cooler down and motioned to Scooter. "Scooter, ice down the beer."

Jake tossed a beer to Dylan and one to Dusty and took one himself. Dusty looked at Jake. "So Jake, are you leaving tomorrow?"

"Hollywood here I come. I can't wait and there is a sweet little yellow Corvette waiting for me. Is this a great country or what?"

Dylan clinked cans with Jake, but raised his eyebrows. "Jake, you better be careful about that. Tom warned you."

"You were there, Dude. The parking lot at practice looked like a luxury car show. Everybody had a nice ride."

Dylan just shook his head. "Whatever."

"I wanted to ride my bike out, but the coach put the kybosh on that. He asked if I had a lot of stuff to bring with me. I told him, I don't have a lot of stuff."

They all laughed. Scooter finished with the cooler and stood up. "Dylan, can I borrow your rifle?"

"Sure, in fact you can have it when I leave."

"Cool, but I mean right now."

"What do you want it for now?"

Jake handed him Dylan's rifle. "He thinks he saw something big up above. Might be a big cat."

"I did see something and it was big."

Dylan patted him on the shoulder. "Just be careful. OK?"

Scooter took the rifle and left.

Jake sensed the tension between Dylan and Dusty. He grabbed another beer. "I'm going to watch the full moon for a while. Call me when you want to eat."

Jake exited the front of the cave to the rocks above the desert floor.

The Refrigerated Truck in the Desert on the Way to the Meet

Carlos motioned for the driver to stop the truck. "This is good. Let 'em out and point 'em toward the highway. It's a full moon so they have plenty of light."

The two gunmen exited the cab and unlocked the back door. Carlos stayed in the cab and did another line of cocaine.

The first gunman yelled, "*Ondolay, ondalay.*"

When no one moved, the gunmen looked closer and realized that everyone was dead. They both crossed themselves and one stumbled and fell as he moved backward. They went to the cab to tell Carlos, wide-eyed with shock.

Carlos was puzzled. "Where are they? What's wrong?"

The gunmen just motioned for him to follow. Carlos stepped down and walked to the back of the truck where he saw the bodies and jumped back himself. He grabbed his head with both hands.

"The fucking truck has no vents! Why didn't I see that? Shit! Listen—get the bodies out. You can have whatever they have on them, but this doesn't get back to my uncle. *Rapido*! We have to get to the meet."

The gunmen looked at each other and then pulled the bodies out.

The Cave

Jake entered in a rush. "We've got company—closing fast from opposite directions. Put the fire out."

In all of the years they had been coming to the cave, they had never seen anyone in the desert and nothing good happened in the desert at night. They doused the fire and Jake grabbed his rifle. Dylan realized that Scooter had his.

"Jake, where's Scooter?"

"He went out the back way. He's on the back side of the hills."

"Dusty, you wait here for Scooter and tell him to be quiet. Jake and I will check things out."

Dylan grabbed his bow and some arrows. He and Jake went out among the rocks where they were hidden from view from the desert floor. They each had binoculars.

A large tractor trailer was coming from the south and a medium-sized van was approaching from the north. It was obviously not a coincidence. They parked approximately twenty-five yards from each other and left their lights on. Three men exited the trailer and four got out of the van. All appeared to be armed. One man from each party approached the middle. The one from the van was dragging a large duffel bag.

Jake whispered to Dylan. "Where's the DEA when you need them?"

"According to Tom they're probably in on it."

Jake did a double take. "Holy shit! If it isn't our classmate Carlos Garcia? The fucking punk."

Carlos and his counterpart appeared to be arguing in Spanish, but Dylan and Jake couldn't hear the conversation. All of a sudden, a series of rifle shots rang out from the rocks above. After a stunned moment, both sides started shooting at each other. They were all exposed and it was pandemonium.

When the smoke cleared, all four from the van were down and likely dead. One of Carlos' gunmen was down and Carlos was wounded and bleeding badly as he tried to drag himself back to the trailer.

Jake and Dylan were both stunned. Dylan motioned, "Cover me. I'm going down for a closer look."

As Dylan made his way through the rocks he saw Carlos' remaining gunman walking toward Carlos with his gun drawn.

Carlos turned and saw the gunman. "*Amigo*—it's me Carlos."

The gunman stood over Carlos and aimed his pistol. "Your uncle wants you dead and now you die, motherfucker."

Before he could pull the trigger, he stopped and looked at his chest where an arrow had just come through his back. He dropped the gun and collapsed.

Dylan moved down through the rocks. He turned to Jake. "Check the others."

Dusty and Scooter came down. Scooter was shaking and Dusty was trying to calm him down. Dylan looked over, "What's wrong with him?"

Scooter replied, "I … I sh … sh … shot some … somebody."

Jake checked the other bodies. He looked at Scooter. "They're all dead. What's with you?"

"I sh … I shot a guy. He was in the rocks up above. I didn't know it was a man until I was about ten yards away. I thought it was a c … cat and I was scared … so I had my rifle aimed at it. He heard me and turned with his rifle. I just shot and kept shooting. I'm c … c … cold."

“Dusty, take him back to the cave and get him a blanket. Jake, let’s go check on Carlos.”

As they approached they saw that Carlos was bleeding from his side. He looked up and saw Dylan. “Geronimo! Where’d you come from? You saved me man. I didn’t know you cared.”

“I don’t, so shut the fuck up while I look at you.”

Jake turned to Dylan. “He’s a dead man. Let’s get out of here. He’s a piece of shit anyhow.”

“Listen to me, Jake. There’s been enough killing for one night. I don’t know if he’ll make it or not. Get me a bottle of water and a blanket while I try to stop the bleeding.”

“OK, but I don’t know why you give a shit.”

Dylan took off the old checkered shirt he had put on in the cave. He tore some strips from it and tried to stanch the bleeding. Jake returned with the water and a blanket.

Dylan gave Carlos a drink and covered him with the blanket. Carlos tried to speak.

“You better save your breath. Jake, see if there’s a flare in the cab.”

Jake found a flare and tossed it to Dylan. Dylan lit it and put it near Carlos.

“Let’s get out of here.”

They headed back to the cave where Dusty and Scooter were having an animated discussion. Dylan took charge and commanded everyone’s attention.

“This is some fucked up shit. Go straight home. Don’t stop for anyone and don’t talk to anybody. We heard nothing—we saw nothing. We’ll talk tomorrow. Dusty—you go with Scooter.”

The Oasis Gas Station

Dylan pulled up to the phone booth near the road. He was wearing the torn shirt. The phone booth was full of moths and other bugs attracted to its light. He squeezed in and put a quarter in the phone and dialed 911.

"This is 911."

"There's been a killing—there's been a lot of killing, in the desert about five miles north of Apache Dunes. One person may be alive, if you hurry. I left a flare at the site."

"Who am I speaking with?"

Dylan hung up, got on his bike, and headed home.

Chapter Seven

A Buzzard's Banquet

The Desert the Following Morning

The crime scene was an absolute zoo. The site of the gun battle was taped off and numerous federal agencies were present, as were the sheriff, the coroner and several media outlets.

Del parked his Range Rover off to one side and was waiting for Carl, who drove up in his Lexus. Del immediately charged the car.

"Carl, I swear I would kill you if these people weren't here."

Carl looked sheepish as he exited his car. "Del, I saw the truck pass into the desert. No one was around—what more could I do? We can't get involved in their deals."

Del backed off a bit. "This was a major league pay day. The money has disappeared and our dicks are hanging out."

A five-year-old Buick pulled up beside their cars. It was Hank, the border patrol agent.

Del shook his head. "Fuck! What else can go wrong? Carl, get lost for a few minutes, but don't say a word to anybody. You understand?"

Carl walked away as Hank leisurely strolled up. He took his sunglasses off and wiped them as he seemed to be inspecting the Range Rover and the Lexus.

"Whooey. I must be workin for the wrong agency. Will you look at these luxury automobiles? No siree Bob, I could never afford a car like them on my salary."

Del stared for a moment. "Hank, if you've got something to say—spit it out."

Hank took a step back. "My, my—did somebody get up on the wrong side of the bed this morning?"

"Hank, in case you haven't noticed, we have a fucked-up situation here—a seriously fucked up situation."

"Oh, I noticed. I noticed, indeed. In fact, that was why I was gonna seek your advice. It seems like that truck I let pass because of your—your federal investigation—it seems like that truck had twenty-one illegals in the back. Men, women, and little boys and girls—and they're all dead. I was just tryin' to do you a favor and make sure I reported our conversation correctly when I fill out them damn forms. You see the position I'm in?"

Del removed his hat to wipe his brow and then took a deep breath. "Hank, let's cut the bullshit. What is it you want?"

Hank was clearly enjoying his perceived advantage and was in no rush to let it go.

"Now, Del—you shouldn't want to offend me at a delicate time like this. Me, I'm a real simple man. I never had much and never needed much, but my wife—my wife is what you call upwardly mobile," he said with a hard *o* and a hard *i*, "and she gets upset when she sees everybody else drivin' new automobiles and we got more than one hundred thousand miles on ours."

Del removed his hat again and rubbed his temples.

"Hank, talk to me. What do you want?"

"Del, I was hopin' this conversation could be more cordial, but if you want to be direct, I'll cut to the chase. How about twenty-five thousand cash, tonight, and how about twenty-five thousand cash every time I have to yield to a—to a federal investigation, like last night? You see—it'll be like a partnership. All nicey nice."

"And you don't file a report about last night?"

Hank smiled. "What report—partner?"

"Come by my house tonight. No—meet me at the Apache Wells at eight."

"I'll see you tonight at eight—partner."

Hank smiled and walked away, stopping to admire the Range Rover and Lexus again. He looked back at Del, then turned and gave a little hand wave as he walked to his car. The proverbial cat that just ate the canary—or so he thought.

When Del looked back at the scene he noticed that the sheriff was watching him.

Carl returned and approached Del. "What did Hank want?"

Del clinched his teeth and needed all the restraint he could muster not to attack Carl. "What did he want? What did he want? I'll tell you what he wanted—twenty-five fucking thousand dollars tonight and twenty-five fucking thousand dollars every time he lets a truck pass."

Carl's mouth was agape as he watched Hank slowly drive away. Hank smiled and waved again.

"Where—where are we getting that money?"

Del stared at Carl, "Where are we getting the money? We aren't. This is all on you. You fucked up—you pay."

"But Del—"

Del lost it and grabbed Carl by the collar. Just then, he saw the sheriff approaching and let go of Carl—appearing to pat him on the shoulder.

"Everything all right boys?"

"Doesn't appear to me like anything is all right this morning. Carl here was just leaving."

Carl hesitated for an awkward moment and then walked to his car.

The sheriff turned to Del. "I'm a little confused about jurisdiction here. With all of the letters on the shirts and jackets I thought this was a Wheel of Fortune convention."

"Yeah, well—it does get confusing at times, but this is a federal case and if we need your help I'll call you."

The sheriff took off his hat and wiped his brow as he took in the killing zone. "Looks to me like you got all the help you need."

"You can say that again."

"Can I ask you a question?"

"Shoot."

"With all of you alphabet guys, with all of the help you got, how the hell does something like this happen?"

Del was at a loss for words as the sheriff smiled and turned to leave.

The Sheriff's House Later that Morning

Tom knocked on Dylan's bedroom door and entered to find him still sprawled in bed with a sheet covering the lower part of his body. Dylan rubbed his eyes and sat up on the edge of his bed. Tom's uniform was drenched with sweat from the desert heat. He took off his hat and wiped his brow with his handkerchief.

"I just put Jake on a bus to LA and told him not to look back. I didn't wake you as you were snoring up a storm. Get your gear together. You're going to Yale and I got you a late afternoon flight. The coach will meet you at the airport."

"I was going to come see you when I got up. I had trouble sleeping."

Tom sat down in a chair. "I don't doubt it. Let me see—so far we've got twenty-eight dead bodies, a trailer with a ton of grass in it, and a van with Illinois plates. I've never seen so many alphabet shirts in my life. Every fed within five hundred miles is here, not to mention the media—and I mean all the media. Geraldo's people are camped out and waiting for him."

Dylan was visibly startled. "Twenty-eight dead bodies?"

"Yup, up the road a bit from where the gunfight was, we found twenty-one men, women, and children—all dead. The coroner says they suffocated. It was one of them refrigerated trucks that doesn't have any ventilation. Go figure. It was like a buzzard's banquet out there."

"I don't know anything about that."

"I know that. I already talked to Jake. Oh, and by the way, one of the dead gunmen was killed by an arrow."

Dylan winced and then changed the subject. "What about Carlos?"

"He's a very lucky young man. Somebody saved his life or he would have bled out. Funny thing is—he had some bandages that look like they came from an old shirt of mine."

Tom got up and walked over by the bed and picked up the torn shirt. He looked at it, dropped it, and sat down again.

"We were at the cave—just the four of us, like always. They all just showed up. All of a sudden the shooting started and it was crazy. When it died down I went down to get a closer look and one of the gunmen was going to shoot Carlos—so I shot him with my bow. I just reacted, I didn't know what to do."

"The guy the, ah, the Indian killed with the arrow was a known executioner for the cartel. No great loss there. In fact, if it were me, I would have shot him after he killed the Garcia kid. Good riddance."

"It just all happened so fast. Too fast—and unexpectedly."

"Dylan, son, I know you as well as you know yourself in some ways. I know you all weren't tied up in that mess, but I don't want you to become collateral damage, so I want you gone today and everyone will swear you left yesterday. Oh—and the feds think that millions of dollars are missing."

Dylan winced as he thought about the duffel bag. "I didn't see any money, but there was a duffel bag. The guys in the van brought it."

"I was the first one on the scene with the EMTs and there was no duffel bag. This is a mess and I don't know if we'll ever know the truth. The Garcia kid will probably survive, but he's lawyered up and his lawyer asked for special protection. He claims his uncle set him up and wants him dead."

"It was one of the men he came with who tried to kill him."

"Well, with all of the drugs confiscated he'll be looking at ten to fifteen minimum, with maybe some time off. If his uncle wants him dead he's going to be hard to protect in prison."

"What about Dusty and Scooter?"

"Dylan, I know this is going to be tough. I know that you and Dusty are more than friends and we love Dusty, but there's nothing here but trouble for either of you right now. You'll have to leave it to me. If it's meant to be with Dusty, it will be some day. Trust me on that."

"When can I come back?"

"I don't know the answer to that. It's more likely that last night was the start of something, rather than the end of it. Now Aunt Sue has made you breakfast and you know she's gonna be fragile today, so be gentle with her."

"I'll have some money and some checks for you before you leave. Your offer is for four years even if you get injured. If the feds, or anybody, tries to contact you about this business—you refer them to me. You don't talk to anybody. Now hop in the shower and get ready."

"Tom, I—"

"Save it, Son. The last time I cried was when your parents died. I don't feel a whole lot better right now. It's just best you go. My deputy will take you to the airport."

They embraced. Both had tears in their eyes.

Chapter Eight

All the News Is Bad

The Garcia Estate in Northern Mexico

Diablo was in his study, wired to the gills on coke and on a rampage. Esteban was trying to explain the situation to him. "I talk to the DEA guy. He say he don't know nothing."

Diablo was just further enraged. "He don't know nothing—nobody knows nothing." He screamed, "Where's my fucking money?"

"*Jefe*, the only survivor is Carlos. He's the only one who knows what happened."

Diablo calmed down a bit, but continued pacing. He turned to Esteban. "But *amigo*—tell me this—who saved Carlos' life and where is the money? No, there had to be someone else involved, but who?"

"They say Eloy was killed by an arrow. Maybe it was an Indian?"

Diablo stopped pacing and stared at Esteban. "*Amigo*, when was the last time you saw an Indian running around with a bow and arrows?"

Esteban shrugged. "What do I tell Chicago?"

Diablo raised his hands and affected a nonchalant tone. "Oh—you jus' say—hey, we're sorry. You lost your money, your drugs, and—oh, by the way, four of your men were killed, but we hope that doesn't have any effect on our relationship."

Diablo then grabbed his snifter of cognac and threw it across the room. Esteban winced as it crashed against the wall. He made a note to order another box of snifters.

Diablo roared, "You set up a meeting with our DEA friend and then you send a shipment by truck to Chicago—pronto. You tell them it is coming and you tell our friend that it has to reach Chicago."

"*Sí, Jefe.*"

"Oh—and Esteban, tell the lawyers to find out what Carlos is being charged with."

The Apache Wells, Late Afternoon

Del was parked and waiting outside his truck when Carl drove up. Del opened the rear hatch on the Range Rover and took out a shovel as Carl walked over.

"Del, what are we doin' out here and what's with the shovel?"

Del handed the shovel to Carl. "The way I see it, you've got two options. Hank is meeting me here tonight at eight to get twenty-five g's—that's twenty-five thousand from you, because you fucked up."

Carl started to speak, but Del held up his hand. "And, he wants another twenty-five grand every time he lets a truck come through. There are two problems with that. Number one, that's the twenty-five g's that presently go to you, so you'll be getting nothing. Number two, that greedy fuck will never be satisfied. This will be just the start of our problems. Or—you bury your mistake."

Carl looked shocked. "Del—are you saying we kill a federal agent?"

"No, I'm saying you kill a federal agent—unless you can talk him into jumping into his grave."

Carl shook his head. "Del … I … I don't know about this."

Del took the shovel from his hands. "Carl, I'm actually impressed with your ethics. I've never seen that side of you. Go get the twenty-five thousand."

Del had walked halfway back to his truck when Carl called out, "Give me the shovel."

Del smiled as he walked back and handed him the shovel. "Everything has a price in the desert. Actually, this could work out perfectly as his disappearance will cast the shadow of doubt on him, and we need a scapegoat or we'll all be fucked."

Carl started digging.

The Garcia Estate

Diablo was having a drink by the pool watching two young señoritas swim in the nude. Esteban approached warily.

"*Jefe*—"

Diablo made a dismissive gesture as he leaned down to do a line of coke. He motioned for the girls to join him and they giggled as they got out of the pool *au naturel.*

"This better be *muy importante*."

"*Jefe*, it is *muy, muy importante*, I'm afraid."

Diablo motioned for Esteban to sit down.

"*Jefe*, I speak to our man in Chicago. I ask where Bertin and Flaco are."

"And?"

"And *Jefe*, this is bad news."

"All the news is bad these days."

"He say the accountant and Flaco are dead and that Bertin has disappeared."

Diablo was enraged. "Are you saying Bertin stole my money?"

"No—he say the accountant put the money in some bank—he say an offshore bank, but he was the only one who knew which bank. He had the bank numbers in the safe, but when Flaco didn't see no money he shoot him before he could tell them the name of the bank."

Diablo jumped up and screamed, "NOOOOOOOOOOOOO!"

The girls ran off to the cabana as Juan and three other soldiers came running with guns drawn. Esteban held up his hand and waved them away.

"Bertin then shot Flaco and he was afraid to come back. He told the couriers to put the bank information in the bag with the cash. It's in the missing bag."

"*Amigo*—you get the word out—I mean to everybody in every prison north of the border. No one touches my nephew. He has to be behind this. He knows where the bag is. *Comprende*?"

"*Sí, comprende.*"

"And you tell the lawyers that I want the best lawyer in the country for Carlos. I don't care what it costs."

Apache Dunes Sheriff's Office, Following Morning

Tom was at his desk when his deputy, Frank, knocked on his open door.

"Come in Frank. Whatta ya got?"

"I just got a call from that Eloise—you know—the one married to the border patrol agent."

"I was beginning to wonder what happened to her. She hasn't complained about anything for almost a week."

They both laughed. "I hear ya, but she didn't call to complain about anything. She's worried because her husband didn't come home last night."

"I'm guessing it was go home to her or commit suicide."

"I'd take suicide."

More laughter. "But get this—guess who she said he was going to meet with?"

"I saw him yesterday morning in the desert talking to Batman—the DEA agent."

"Bingo."

"And it didn't look like a real happy conversation."

"You think this is related to the business in the desert?"

Tom stood up and strapped on his gun. "Probably just a coincidence, but I don't believe in coincidences. What I do know is that a large tractor trailer somehow waltzed over the border, despite the fact that half the people around here seem to work for the DEA, ATF, ICE, FBI, XYZ, ETC. And—and that ain't the first time it's happened. It'd be a more efficient use of the taxpayer's money if we built the smugglers a toll road."

"Whatta ya gonna do?"

"I think I'll pay Batman a little visit."

"You want me to come along?"

"No—you stay and watch the shop."

The Crime Scene in the Desert

It was even more of a mob scene with all of the media outlets. Geraldo was on the air live in front of the trailer. Tom saw Del speaking with some guys from ICE. He approached and Del saw him coming.

"Excuse me guys. Hey, Sheriff—I thought I said I would call you if I needed help."

"You did, indeed, but I need to speak with you about another matter—probably unrelated, but maybe not."

"What would that be?"

Tom took his sunglasses off and cleaned them to make Del wait a bit.

"Well, you see, we got a call from the wife of the border patrol agent you were talking to yesterday."

Del was almost never without the reflecting sunglasses, so it was impossible to see his eyes, but Tom sensed him squirm just a bit.

"Keep talkin'."

"Well, it seems her husband Hank didn't come home last night."

Del laughed. "If you met the missus, you'd be surprised he ever went home."

Tom smiled. "I've met her and I hear ya, but she said he left to meet you."

Del looked around furtively and then motioned Tom away from earshot of the crowd.

"Sheriff."

"You can call me Tom."

"Thanks. Tom, I like you and we've never had any problems, so I'm gonna share something with you that is strictly off the record. Understood?"

"Understood."

"Good. I hate to say this, but the agency has been watching him for some time. We could never figure out how those trucks got across the border so easily. Well, we think we finally figured it out. Yesterday when you saw us talking, he knew the gig was up and he was trying to cut a deal, but he wanted immunity and immunity is above my pay grade. So I told him I would talk with my superiors and meet him last night, but he never showed."

"Any chance your partner has seen him?"

"Carl? No—he had to leave for a couple of days on another mission. Now what I told you is off the record—understand? This is a federal investigation."

Tom was pensive. Everything Del said was plausible, but he didn't trust anything Del said. It seemed too convenient.

"Yeah, well thanks for your time. You take care now."

St. Mary's Hospital in Tuscon, the ICU

There were two armed guards outside Carlos' room as his attorney approached and showed his ID. He entered the room and closed the door. Carlos was heavily bandaged and hooked up to an IV and monitors, but sitting up in bed.

"My mouthpiece. *Hola*."

"Carlos, we've got some things to discuss. Do you feel like talking?"

"Man, I feel fine. I like this shit they give me for pain, but I think I broke the clicker."

"I'll tell the nurse. OK, first off—I called all of the numbers you gave me for your … associates and no answer by anyone."

"Call them again."

"Carlos—listen to me. We've had them on robo dial. They're not answering. Also, your uncle's attorney contacted me. He's a well-known and very high-profile attorney. He wants to help with your case and your uncle is paying him."

"My uncle tried to have me killed. He set me up."

"The attorney says it wasn't the uncle. He says it was a couple of his men who were traitors."

"Bullshit, but let's say I believe it. Why's he being so nice?"

"Your uncle wants the money and what was with the money. He says you will be protected in prison and he'll get you out as soon as possible."

"Wait—you said, and what was with the money. What does that mean?"

"He didn't say. He said you would know. In fact, he said he would split the money with you if you returned the other item—whatever it is."

Carlos closed his eyes for a minute and was lost in thought.

"Whadda they call that secret stuff between a lawyer and his client? I mean is it really secret?"

"It's called attorney–client privilege and I can't disclose anything you tell me in confidence."

Carlos sighed. "OK, I gotta trust somebody. Check this out—I don't know what happened to the money. The bag was there when I passed out. When the ambulance came to get me it was gone and I don't have a fucking clue what the other thing is."

"I don't think that's what he wants to hear."

"Let me ask you this—how long am I going down for?"

"My best guess? Ten years maybe. With time off for good behavior, you could be out in four, maybe five years. Regardless, you'll still be a young man and have your life ahead of you."

"Yeah—well that life won't be worth much if my uncle doesn't get his money back."

"Any ideas?"

"I think I'm alive as long as he thinks I know where the money, and the other thing, whatever it is, are located."

"Agreed. Let me work on a response and we'll talk tomorrow."

"Do me a favor—tell the nurse about the clicker."

The Sheriff's Office

Tom was at his desk when his secretary Rosa buzzed him.

"Sheriff, there's a Detective Sandowski from Chicago on line one for you."

"Put him through."

"This is Sheriff Tom Ward."

"Sheriff, Max Sandowski here, Gang Crimes Detective in Chicago. How ya doin' today?"

"Call me Tom. Well—it's a little hectic around here right now."

"I saw the news and that's why I'm callin'. The van with the Illinois plates belongs to an associate of the Latin Devils street gang up here—a late associate, I should say. The Devils are like my franchise. We have an undercover guy pretty well placed in the gang and we've known for some time about their connection with the Garcias, from your neck of the woods. I was working a homicide a few days ago and am now pretty certain that it may have something to do with what happened down there."

"I'm all ears."

"One of our local accountants got whacked recently and we found out he was a bag man for the Garcias. The safe in his office was cleaned out, but nothing else was touched—except the accountant."

"Could be a robbery?"

"Coulda been, but his secretary said he was expecting to meet with some Mexicans who were coming for something. She said they were waiting in the parking lot when she left. Our CI said that one of Garcia's men added something to the bag with the money that was payment for a load of grass. Looked like an envelope."

"Max, please understand we haven't met, so I have to be a little guarded, but I was the first responder to the scene and there was no bag, no money, nada, but the drugs were still in the trailer. It's a mystery right now, but a little bird told me that one of our alphabet boys might have been involved."

"That's old news, but we could never pin down who it was."

"Stay tuned—we may know soon."

"I'd appreciate if you'd keep me in the loop. By the way—I've had asthma all my life and if we'd had the money my folks would have moved to the desert. The doctor said it would be good for me, but it was hard enough putting food on the table. But, I'm getting ready to retire and I'm thinkin' about where to go. A sleepy little place that has only twenty-eight homicides in one weekend sounds pretty good."

Tom laughed. "It's an acquired taste kind of thing, but you're welcome to be my guest anytime. Oh—and I have a feeling that a border agent may be number twenty-nine. He didn't make it home last night."

"You ex-military by any chance?"

"Marines."

"Semper fucking Fi! I knew I liked you."

Chapter Nine

The Devil You Know

St. Mary's Hospital, the Following Morning

Carlos' attorney followed the usual drill with the guards and entered the room as an attractive young nurse was leaving.

"How's he doing?"

The nurse scowled as she looked back at Carlos. "His biggest problem is with his hormones."

The attorney sat next to his bed. "Good morning, Carlos."

"My mouthpiece. *Buenos días.*"

"Carlos—you watch too much TV. You can call me Mr. Dennison or you can call me Roger, but no more mouthpiece, OK? Or you can get yourself another attorney."

"Whoa—whoa. Check this out—I didn't mean no disrespect."

"If that's an apology, it's accepted. Let's move on. We had an investigator check out the addresses you gave us for your associates. The houses were all empty and it doesn't look like anyone's been there for a while."

"Shit!" Carlos crossed himself.

The attorney just shook his head. He handed Carlos a letter.

"I've drafted a response to your uncle's lawyers. The intent is to say that you have no information to share with the authorities and will be grateful for any and all assistance. When you are released you will be pleased to work with your uncle to help recover any assets that may have been lost or misplaced."

"I told you, Roger. I don't know where the fucking money is and I don't have no fucking clue what the other thing is."

"You also told me that you're a dead man if your uncle knows that. So it appears to me that you need to buy some time. Further, since that time is going to be spent as a guest of the US government, you will benefit from your uncle's protection."

"I knew you was a smart guy. That's good, man."

"That buys you some time, but it doesn't help much if you don't even have a clue where the money is."

"Oh—I got a clue. I got a clue."

"You want to share it with me?"

"No offense, but right now I don't share that with nobody. That's my—whatta you call it? My insurance policy."

"Fair enough. That's probably a smart move. One more thing—and I have to ask this. The feds are willing to discuss a deal if you will work with them against your uncle."

"Man, I gotta choose my devil and my uncle is El Diablo—he is the devil. Tell the feds I got nothin' to say."

"I had to ask. Let me start working on a plea. I'll speak with your uncle's lawyer. You won't skate, but it won't be as bad as it could have been. Plus—it appears you need some time."

The Sheriff's Office

Tom was walking back to his office when Frank approached.

"The *Federales* called. They found a Buick with Arizona plates torched about sixty miles south of the border."

"I'll call his wife."

Tom entered his office and sat down behind his desk. Frank lingered in the doorway. "We always thought that Batman and Robin were the bent guys. Maybe we were wrong."

Tom shrugged his shoulders. "Maybe."

He dialed Hanks' wife. She answered immediately.

"Hello—Hank is that you?"

"Ma'am, this is the sheriff."

"Did you find Hank?"

"Ma'am hang on a minute. We haven't found him, but the Mexican *Federales* found your car—torched—in Mexico."

"Torched? What does that mean? I can't drive it?"

"Ma'am—it means all burned up. I'm sure the insurance will replace it."

"Oh yeah—I'm sure they'll replace a five-year-old Buick with a hundred thousand miles on it. My husband worked for the government for over twenty years and we drive a five-year-old car and live in a small house while the DEA guys drive new cars and have fancy homes. Have you seen the place the head agent lives in? It's a mansion. Tell me how that happens."

"It's a puzzle—I agree."

"Just when Hank said all of our problems were solved—he disappears."

"I'm sorry—did you say he solved your problems?"

"The day he disappeared he said I could get me a new car—any kind I wanted and that we would be moving into a bigger house."

Tom was silent as he digested this news.

"And one more thing, Sheriff. I've been callin' for months about that stoplight near the square that blinks all the time. When are they gonna get off their butts and fix it?"

Tom smiled. "I'll look into it. I'll call you if we get any news about your husband."

"And another thing—"

Tom hung up.

Frank had been standing in the doorway the whole time. "How'd it go?"

Tom laughed. "She's more concerned about the car and the broken stoplight on the square than she is about Hank. Listen, I've got an errand to run and then I'm gonna take the weekend off and visit Jake in LA—make sure he's settled in. I don't expect much to happen here until Carlos' trial. Oh—and Eloise wanted to know how the DEA guys can afford their cars and homes on a government salary."

"I've wondered the same myself."

Dusty's House In Apache Dunes, Early Afternoon

Dusty was loading suitcases and boxes into her Jeep Cherokee as Tom drove up. Dusty didn't appear too happy as Tom parked and approached.

"Hey Dusty. You goin' somewhere?"

Dusty appeared nervous and her eyes were red as she turned to respond. "The lady in Key West, who bought one of my paintings, has offered me a job. There's no reason for me to stay when everyone else has gone."

"Dusty, why don't we sit down for a bit?"

They walked over to the swing on the porch and both sat down, but neither spoke right away. Tom broke the ice. "You said everyone else has gone. Scooter's still here isn't he? I'd like to talk to him."

Dusty remained very nervous. "Scooter left yesterday. He said he was going away for a while."

"Did he say where he was going?"

"You know Scooter. He probably doesn't know himself."

"Dusty, there's no sense in beating around the bush. I made Dylan and Jake leave quickly because I didn't want any of you getting caught up in that mess in the desert."

Dusty started to cry. "Then why didn't you make us leave as well?"

Tom gave Dusty his handkerchief and gently patted her on the back. "Dusty, I shouldn't have to tell you that Sue and I love you and Scooter. You've always been part of our family, too, and we would be very happy if you and Dylan wind up together. Having said that, the feds found motorcycle tracks on the other side of the hills. If they asked anybody in the Dunes who might ride their motorcycles in the desert—you know what they would say."

Dusty was still emotional. "Did you tell Dylan that he couldn't at least come over and say goodbye?"

"Dusty, the feds were all over the place—still are. I wanted him out of here. You think it was easy for me—for us—to see him go so quickly? He asked about you."

Dusty looked up.

"He wanted to know about you and Scooter and I told him that I would look after both of you. I told him that if it is meant for you two to be together that it will happen, but right now there's nothing here for either one of you—so I'm not unhappy to see you go."

Dusty leaned into Tom and he put his arm around her.

"I'm sorry, it's just—it's just that everything seemed like it was working out so perfectly. Even Dylan going away to college I understood, but then it turned into a nightmare."

"Life is never gonna be perfect. You kids were in the wrong place at the wrong time. In Nam we called it collateral damage and I didn't want any of you to become victims. Dusty—I do have to ask you something about that night."

Dusty pulled back and appeared nervous again. "If it's about that night, I was in the cave most of the time—so I really don't know what happened. Dylan made me stay in the cave and wait for Scooter."

Tom picked up on it quickly. "Where was Scooter?"

Dusty realized she made a slip of the tongue. "He was—he was on the other side."

Tom was pensive. "Dusty—they found a shooter dead up on the ridge—on the other side. Did Scooter see or hear anything?"

Dusty laughed nervously. "You know Scooter. He's afraid of his own shadow."

Tom gazed at the Jeep. "One last thing. Did either of you see a duffel bag out there?"

Dusty was clearly nervous and Tom sensed it. "A—a duffel bag? No—no I told you that I was in the cave and Scooter was on the other side."

Tom stood and wiped his brow. "Is your mom home?"

Dusty stood and tried to compose herself. "She's volunteering at the clinic today. Do you need to see her?"

"No, I was just gonna pay my respects. I'll tell you the same thing I told Dylan and Jake. If anybody, and I mean anybody, tries to contact you asking questions—don't say anything. You tell them to talk to me. Now you take care of yourself and drive carefully."

Dusty hugged Tom and teared up again. "If Scooter comes back—look after him please. He's got such a big heart. It's just—it's just that he's … well, he's just Scooter."

"Don't you worry."

Tom walked to his truck. Dusty called out to him. "Is everything going to be OK?"

Tom turned, "Only time will tell."

Chapter Ten

Geronimo's Homecoming

A Boarding House Near Yale's Campus in New Haven, Four Years Later, May 2015

Dylan was walking in when he ran into one of his roommates on the stairway.

"You didn't come home last night."

"I slept on Lola's couch."

"Yeah, right. Anyhow, someone named Jake has called for you several times. He said it's important. I left his number on your desk."

"Thanks, dude."

Dylan entered his apartment and went right to his desk. He picked up the phone and dialed the number.

Sheriff's Office, Apache Dunes

"Apache Dunes sheriff's office, this is Rosa."

"Rosa—is that you? It's Dylan."

"Dylan, thank God. Are you OK?"

"Whoa, I'm fine. I'm returning Jake's call. What's up?"

"I better let him tell you. I'll transfer you."

"Jake, I have Dylan on line one."

Jake grabbed the phone. "Dylan—where are you?"

"The same place I've been for the past four years. Where do you think I am?"

"I don't know man. I called several times and they said you didn't come home last night."

"News flash—I have a girlfriend, Jake. What's up?"

Dylan—I hope you're sitting down. I'm acting sheriff right now."

"Where's Tom?"

"Tom's in the hospital, but he's gonna make it. He was wearing a vest."

"Whoa—Jake, what's going on?"

"Dylan … Scooter was murdered—after he was tortured. Tom saw the Mexican cars coming and going and he and Frank followed them to Scooter's house. There was a gunfight. Tom was wearing a vest, but Frank wasn't so lucky. They killed four *pistoleros* and we've got two of the Mexicans in jail—one bad guy and, get this, Carlos Garcia, who may have been a victim, too. The jury's out on that one."

"Holy shit! Is this related to four years ago?"

"Fraid so, but let me start at the beginning, because there is a lot of shit going down. You know that Carlos was sent away. Well, he was paroled recently. He got a lot of time off for—get this—good behavior. He claims he got religion in the joint."

"What kind of religion?"

"I hear you. Anyway, as soon as he was released, the shit hit the fan. Tom called it. He said there were millions of dollars missing from four years ago and Carlos' uncle apparently thought Carlos knew where it was. That's what kept him alive in prison. In the meantime, Tom has been sharing information with a Gang Crimes Detective in Chicago who has an informant inside the Latin gang that lost four of their soldiers that night in the desert."

"Tom told me that some money was missing. I told him I remembered seeing a duffel bag that the gang brought with them, but don't know what happened to it."

"Ditto for me. I just wanted the fuck out of there. It was there when we left."

Dylan paused before speaking again. "Jake—did you leave before or after Dusty and Scooter?"

"I know where you're going. Scooter said he forgot something and went back to the cave. I took off."

"I can't believe he would have the balls—or the brains—to do something like that."

"Keep in mind he'd just killed a guy—a bad guy. He was never the same after that."

"Did you ever talk to him about it?"

"By the time I came home from LA, after I blew out my knees, Scooter wasn't the Scooter we knew and he seemed to avoid me whenever possible. He was running with a bad crowd and spending a lot of time—and money, they say, in Vegas."

"So what happened to Scooter?"

"One way that Scooter never changed was not knowin' when to keep his mouth shut and apparently he was running his mouth one night and the wrong people heard him brag that he was in the desert that night."

Dylan rolled his eyes. "You say Tom's gonna be OK?"

"Like I said, he was lucky that he had the vest on. I never saw him wear one. He'll be out of commission for a while, but he wanted me to tell you to watch your back."

"Me? What's this got to do with me?"

"I hope you're still sitting. According to Carlos, Scooter sang like a lark and he kept saying the bag was in the cave, but they gouged out his eyes so he couldn't take them there. If Tom hadn't shown up when he did, they would have started in on Carlos, but he swears he doesn't know what happened to the bag. He said he passed out right after we left."

"Again—what's this got to do with me?"

"Carlos said that Scooter told them about you, me, and Dusty being with him, but it could just as easily have been Carlos who told them. Anyway, the money is still missing and we all have targets on our backs."

"Jake, I can't believe that Dusty could have been in on this."

"Let me ask you a question—when did you last speak with her?"

"I don't know what to say."

"There's nothin' to say. It is what it is. I spoke with her yesterday. She's coming in for the funeral day after tomorrow, but I better warn you—there's some serious scar tissue there."

"Where was she?"

"Just like you—the same place she's been since she left—Key West."

"Oh, right—she's working at some art gallery."

"She owns the art gallery and a sailboat."

"Oh man."

"Don't jump to any conclusions. My wife Ashley is an artist and she's familiar with Dusty's work. She says her paintings sell for fancy prices."

"If I get a flight into Tucson can you pick me up?"

"You know I will, but there's a bad moon rising around here and who knows what Scooter told the Garcias."

"Sounds like it's time for Geronimo to come home."

The Garcia Hacienda

Diablo was pacing as Esteban and Juan brought José, another member of the gang, into the massive study. José's hands were tied and he was gagged and wide-eyed with fright. He was trying to speak. Diablo stood face to face with him.

"Take his gag off."

Juan took it off and José started pleading. "*Jefe*, what did I do?"

Diablo was furious. "What did you do? What did you do? You had my nephew and the *gringo*. All you had to do was make one of them talk, but you—but YOU gouge the *gringo*'s eyes out so that he can't show you where the cave is. And you—YOU create such a disturbance that the *policia* come. Four of my men are dead, one is in jail, my nephew was rescued, and one of the *policia* was killed. Oh—and I don't have MY FUCKING MONEY!"

Diablo ripped a gun out of Juan's hands and started shooting José point blank. He fired until the gun was empty. Esteban and Juan had jumped out of the way. Diablo looked at the gun and nonchalantly handed it back to Juan.

"Get him out of here. Esteban—how many men do we have left?"

"We have at least twenty soldiers."

"When is the *gringo*'s funeral?"

"They say in two days."

"It is bad luck to disturb a funeral. Get the men together and in three days we go to Apache Dunes and get my nephew, the sister, Geronimo, and my money."

"*Jefe*, you said we. Are you going?"

"If you want something done right—do it yourself."

"Should I call our friends—the agents?"

"Tell them to take a vacation. Who's guarding the prisoners?"

"The sheriff is in the hospital and one deputy was killed. That leaves the young deputy in charge and guess what, *Jefe*?"

"*Amigo*, I am not in the mood for games."

"Scooter, he say that the young deputy was with him, his sister, and the one called Geronimo in the desert that night. He say the deputy is the one called Cochise."

Diablo smiled at the news. "*Bueno, muy bueno*. Tell our friends we are coming back."

The Sheriff's Office

Jake was at Tom's desk looking at a file when Rosa buzzed him.

"Jake, it's Detective Sandowski from Chicago. He wants to know about Tom."

"Put him through."

"Detective, this is Jake here."

"Jake, call me Max. How's Tom doin'?"

"They say he's gonna be laid up for a while. Some bones were shattered by the bullets and he lost a fair amount of blood, but the vest saved him."

"Saved my sorry ass more than once. Don't leave home without one."

"I hear you."

"Listen, Jake, a little heads up. There's a rumor that the Garcias are making another visit to your neighborhood and they're coming heavy. They want the nephew and the money and they're bringing an army with them."

"What's an army?"

"Twenty bad *hombres*—well armed, I hear—and El Diablo himself."

"Uh huh."

"If you need some help, I've got some vacation time coming."

"Thanks, but we'll figure something out."

"The more I talk with you people, the more I like the place. You'll figure something out. Sounds like my kind of people."

Chapter Eleven

Hotel California

Del's Estate

The desert was an apt metaphor for Kelsey and Del's relationship. During the day, the desert can easily reach triple digit temps, as the sand reflects, rather than absorbs, the rays of the sun. However, when the sun sets there is no warmth stored to protect from the dramatic change of temperature and the desert assumes a totally different and darker nature.

Anyone on the outside looking in would see a perfect "atomic" family, relaxing together on the patio in the late afternoon, but—and like the desert—nightfall often found Del lost in his dark thoughts about how to find a way out of this maze and Kelsey drawn like a moth, to Angie's flame.

Del felt that in time he could somehow finesse or deal with the loose ends in the Dunes, principally Carl and Angie. His biggest concern, bordering on paranoia, was how to deal with the schizophrenic and mercurial El Diablo. To that end, he had just completed a project cloaked in total secrecy. He had imported a team of eight private contractors to construct a completely concealed, soundproof, fireproof and bombproof safe room in his house. It was equipped with state-of-the-art electronics that provided audiovisual access to every room in the house plus its own air, water, sewage, and power supply. They accomplished it by moving a wall in the spacious library upstairs. Entry was virtually invisible and accessible only by an electronic device that moved a section of the wall. The dimensions were tight, but they could remain concealed and safe for a minimum of thirty days at a time.

To maintain total secrecy on the project, Del had the contractors fly into Tucson, where he picked them up and drove them to his estate. They each had to sign a nondisclosure agreement and relinquish all electronic devices while they worked on the project. They were housed in four RVs that he had rented in Tucson and stationed by the stables. In exchange for the extraordinary conditions they received extraordinary compensation. The six contractors each received fifty thousand dollars for the two week period and the two supervisors were paid double that.

Last night Del hosted a cookout for the team to celebrate their successful completion of the project. He paid and thanked them and advised that he had arranged for a private jet to arrive at, what served as, the Dune's airport at noon the following day to fly them to Tucson, where they could make their final connections.

Kelsey had gone for a late-morning ride in the desert when she saw the jet pass over head just past midday. She reined in and watched it arc toward the north when it exploded into a massive fireball and disintegrated in midair over the desert. She wasn't sure, later, how long she sat there paralyzed with a mixture of shock and fear, but eventually returned home—which was all that she could do. She was still shaking when she got up the nerve to call Del.

"Hey, what's up?"

"What's up? What's up? You don—you don't know? Del, I just watched the plane blow up over the desert!"

"Calm down. I know. Carl and I are out there right now."

"I ... I don't understand."

"Kelsey, I got a call from the air traffic control. They detected an unidentified object on their screen. It showed up and then vanished. That generally means smugglers."

"Smugglers? Del, this was your contractors. The plane had just turned toward Tucson."

"Kelsey, get a grip. That wasn't the contractors. I dropped them off at eleven thirty and they decided to change their destination to Santa Fe."

"Then … then, who was in that plane?"

"How should I know? Probably smugglers. It's happened before."

"Don't they send inspectors to a crash site?"

"They do if there's been a crash. Look, Kelsey, the last thing we need are Feds snooping around. I told them that we didn't find anything. The vultures had already arrived and by the time they'd get a team down here there'd be nothing left. The desert will reclaim the rest."

"What about Snoopy? Isn't he at the airstrip? What will he say?"

"He generally is, but he had an errand to run today, so no one was there. Now, you need to relax. Take a chill pill if needed. When I get home I'll grill some nice steaks, make a salad, and open one of our Caymus cabs. Just chill out 'til then. I've got some other news, but it can wait."

Kelsey wanted so badly to believe him, but all the alarms were sounding.

"Del."

"Yeah hon?"

"Can I ask you a couple of questions?"

"Of course—shoot."

"The errand Snoopy ran today—was it for you, by any chance?"

"By the way it was. What else?"

"The contractors—did you pay them in cash?"

"That would have been too much cash for them to carry. I gave them certified checks from the Cayman account."

"What happens if they don't cash them?"

"What kind of question is that? They have sixty days to cash them."

"And then what?"

"You mean if they don't? Why wouldn't they? But—if they don't, the checks are cancelled and the money credited back to the account. Why do you ask?"

"No—no reason."

"OK, I'll see you later."

Although it was in the high nineties, Kelsey shivered as she put down the phone. They knew too much—she should have known. There was no way Del was going to let them live. Which means this is my Hotel California—I can check out any time I like, but I can never leave.

Later That Evening

They retired to the patio after dinner. Kelsey hardly touched her meal and few words had been spoken since Del came home. Del was enjoying one of the Cohiba Edicion Limitadas, a gift from Roberto Garcia during less stressful times, and a forty-year old vintage Tawny Port. Kelsey had taken a Quaalude and was complementing it with champagne.

Del admired one of his smoke rings and then broke the ice. "Kelsey, do you know it was almost five years ago when we first met?"

Kelsey didn't respond.

"During that time, I've done everything in my power to protect you—including the safe room, which you'll understand better when I share some news with you. I've given you space. I don't question where you go, or who you see. I spend almost every waking hour trying to find a way to let go of this tiger's tail without both of us—without all of us—getting eaten."

He paused for a pull on his cigar followed by a sip of port. "Yet, I see you like this. You can believe me, or not, about the plane, but … at least I told you what you wanted to hear. Maybe you need a little trip down memory lane."

There was more choreography with the cigar and port. Del was clearly in control and enjoying the moment to the point of smugness. "So let's see—five years ago, if Snoopy hadn't seen you and I hadn't been nearby and followed up—your little white ass would have lasted no more than another hour, if that. If I hadn't reacted swiftly to the sidewinder, you would have likely died. If I had done my job—my government job," he chuckled, "I would have arrested you and you would be doing a minimum of ten years in prison. Now I don't know what you think happens to a young white beauty queen in prison, but death would be a better option. Yet, here you are with all the comforts that money can buy, sipping champagne, and you're unhappy."

Neither spoke for a while as Kelsey digested Del's comments—all of which were true. Kelsey finally responded.

"Del, I know I owe you my life and appreciate all you have done, and continue to do, for me, but I remember telling you in the beginning that I was afraid of you and five years later, I still am. It's one thing to have an acute instinct for survival—in college we called it Social Darwinism—but as long as we are here, meaning this situation, I live in the fear that I'm next, and that's no way to live. And what about our child? He's being raised by the nanny, and thank God we have her."

Del noticed her tears and handed over his handkerchief.

"Kelsey, when I first arrived here—as disillusioned as anyone could possibly be—I met briefly with the guy I was replacing. He was the architect behind all of this; I simply inherited it, although I wasn't aware of it at that time. He asked me one question and gave me one piece of advice."

He paused for more cigar and port.

"The question was, did I know how to make lemonade—which is where the phrase came from. I replied, 'Do me a favor and don't speak in riddles.' He laughed and said, 'Fair enough, what I mean is simply that there are times in life that fate gives us a bunch of lemons. It happens and you have a choice to make: do you accept your fate, or do you make lemonade out of the lemons? You'll figure it out as one thing this place gives you is plenty of time to think. The advice I give you is simply: know when to get out.' Kelsey, look at me. Kelsey, I was more than halfway out the door when I answered the call five years ago. I stayed just because of you. Now—I'll be honest with you …"

"That will be a refreshing change."

Del laughed. "*Touché*. That's the Kelsey I fell in love with. The truth is things keep getting more complicated, particularly after what happened yesterday."

Kelsey turned toward Del. "What happened yesterday?"

"I was wondering if you'd heard. Your friend Kato—"

"You mean Scooter?"

"Kato, Scooter, whatever—anyway, he was murdered and tortured first."

Kelsey dropped her champagne glass and bolted upright. "Who? Why?"

Del reached over and gently guided her back to a sitting position. "Let me get the Dirt Devil. I'll clean up the glass. Be right back."

Kelsey's heart was racing and her mind was totally blown. Her only hope of escape, as faint as it may be, was to get her hands on some money of her own. Her parents had blocked her trust funds, and while she had a handful of credit cards, they could easily be tracked and cancelled on a moment's notice. Scooter was a local personality and, like most everyone else in this godforsaken place, a drug dealer. Kelsey devised a scheme where she would periodically raid Del's evidence stash of cocaine. Scooter would sell it and they would split the profits. Scooter dreamed that he would be leaving with her, but that wasn't in the cards. The problem is that Scooter was holding on to Kelsey's share, which now should be over a hundred grand, as she couldn't risk Del finding it. If Scooter was dead, she had no hope of escape.

Del returned with the vacuum and cleaned up the remains of the champagne glass.

"What happened?"

"All I know is that the cartel thought he had something of great value that belonged to them. It apparently goes all the way back to that massacre in the desert four years ago. And, rumor has it, they are coming back to get whatever it is."

Kelsey was now shaking. "Did he talk?"

Del laughed, "From what I heard they did to him—anybody would have talked. Are you cold? I'll go get you a sweater."

Kelsey stood. "I'll get it, I need to pee anyway."

She hurried up the stairs to the master bedroom and paused to make sure Del hadn't followed her. Something of great value … when Scooter found out that her brother-in-law owned a chain of banks in Tucson, he entrusted her with a partial deposit slip showing a thirty-million-dollar deposit and an account number. He claimed it was cartel money, but they didn't know where it was and—if we could find it—it would be ours. Few people took Scooter seriously and he had a big mouth, which probably led to his demise, but she had kept the receipt. Once more checking the stairway for Del, she went to a stack of books she kept in her nightstand. There it was, *Love Story.* She flipped through it and found the receipt. Just then she was startled by Del's voice from downstairs.

"Hey, Kelsey. Carl just called and wants me to meet him at the Oasis. Are you gonna be OK?"

She put the receipt back in the book and returned it to the nightstand, then headed back downstairs.

"Yeah, I'll be OK."

"I'm sorry about Kato. I thought you were going to get a sweater."

Kelsey was momentarily flustered. "I—I realized it must have been a hot flash. I'm OK now."

"Good. Hey—maybe it's a good thing we have the safe room."

Kelsey just nodded, but if Scooter talked—it was a very good thing.

Kelsey headed back upstairs to take a longer look at the mysterious receipt when her cell phone buzzed. It was Angie. She briefly debated answering, but picked up on the fourth ring.

"Hey."

"Hey, you. Are you OK? I heard about Scooter. What's up with that?"

"Are you surprised? He was an accident looking for a place to happen and it happened."

Angie knew nothing about the receipt. In fact, no one knew unless Scooter told the cartel and just the thought made her shiver.

"Well, I have some other news that I thought you might be interested in—Bobbie is coming to visit for a while."

Angie was a temptation that Kelsey could handle, could take or leave, but her heart skipped a beat just hearing Bobbie's name and Angie picked up on the silence.

"I thought that might get your blood flowing."

"Angie, you know that nothing ever happened between us."

"Oh—I know, but I also know both of you. I never told you, but we all talked about betting on which of you Divas was going to give in first."

"I'm dying of suspense. What did you decide?"

"Nothing. No one would bet on you."

Kelsey was silent as she digested the slight and lacked a retort.

"Carl just left to meet Del. You wanna come over and take your frustrations out on me?"

"Angie, you of all people shouldn't try to be clever. I studied psychology in college, but then I doubt you even know what college is."

"It's where they play football."

"Close enough. I'm going to pass on tonight. I have to make a trip to Tucson tomorrow."

"What're you going to Tucson for?"

"I have a business matter to discuss with my brother-in-law."

"I'll let you know when Bobbie comes in."

"Whatever."

Bobbie was a temptation that she didn't have the bandwidth to deal with right now. "No one would vote for Kelsey." Deep down, she was afraid they might be right.

Chapter Twelve

A Bad Sign—A Very Bad Sign

Tucson Airport, the Following Afternoon

Jake was waiting for Dylan by the carousel. They embraced. Dylan grabbed his bags.

"Welcome home. I wish it was better circumstances."

"I missed the desert. Lots of strange dreams lately."

They walked outside. The sheriff's SUV was parked at the curb. Jake thanked the policeman and they pulled away. When they exited the airport, Jake handed Dylan a small bag. Dylan opened it and found a Glock nine millimeter inside.

"That's a Glock 9. Ever see one?"

Dylan smiled as he inspected it. "One of my teammate's father was big in the NRA. The whole family were gun nuts. We used to go to the range to get rid of stress. The Glock 9 was his gun of choice—maybe mine too."

"Good. I've got Tom's Browning in the back with a vest and plenty of ammo."

Dylan looked at Jake. "Am I coming to a funeral or a war?"

Jake looked over with a serious expression. "If the rumors are correct, it may be both."

"What rumors?"

"The detective from Chicago said El Diablo is coming and bringing twenty of his fraternity brothers with him to finish what they started."

"Uh huh … twenty. I'm afraid to ask—how many do we have?"

Jake smiled. "You and me to start with."

"Well, if Geronimo and thirty Apaches could keep ten thousand soldiers and bounty hunters at bay, I guess we can figure out how to deal with twenty Mexicans."

Jake laughed. "That's what I told the detective. It's good to know that Geronimo is still alive."

"Jake—Geronimo never died."

"Neither did Cochise. Weird isn't it?"

"Did Dusty get in yet?"

"I picked her up last night."

"You say anything?"

"Let's let her get through the funeral. Scooter was a world class fuckup, but he was her brother—and our friend at one time."

"Jake."

"Yeah?"

"How's she look?"

Jake smiled. "Let's just say that time has been very, very good to her. And, if I remember correctly, she could shoot as well as we could."

"Rabbits and snakes don't shoot back."

The Sheriff's House

Jake pulled into the driveway.

"Your room is ready, just like the day you left it—except it's clean."

They laughed.

"And, I charged the battery and gassed up your bike for you. I'll pick you up in an hour and we'll stop by the jail so you can get reacquainted with our buddy Carlos."

Apache Dunes Jail

As Jake and Dylan entered the jail, Carlos jumped up. The other prisoner sat silently and scowled. He was wearing a yellow Mexican soccer jersey.

"Dylan, you remember our old friend Carlos. Gee—this is just like a homeroom reunion."

Carlos was animated. "Geronimo! Man you saved my life, but you gotta get me outa here. I didn't have nothin' to do with Scooter, man. Check this out—check out these bruises. Tell him, Jake—they had me too."

Jake replied with a lack of interest. "I told him."

"Geronimo—you got to save me. After you saved my life, I got religion in the joint—I mean the prison. That's why they released me early, but my uncle tricked me. They killed Scooter after he told them about you guys and Dusty—so we're all in this together."

Dylan approached the cell. "If you got religion in the joint—I mean prison—you better pray that Tom recovers. Scooter may have died a violent death, but you will die an Apache death. *Comprende, amigo*?"

"Check this out, man. I told you—we're on the same side."

The Cemetery

A very small graveside service had just ended. Dylan overslept and missed the visitation at the church beforehand. He sheepishly approached Dusty after the service.

"Dusty—I'm so sorry. I overslept."

"Save your breath, Dylan. I can remember other times you overslept. I appreciate you coming."

"Whoa."

Dylan grabbed her arm to slow her down, but then felt awkward as she stopped and looked at him. He released his grip.

"Hold on a minute. You didn't think I wouldn't come, did you?"

"Dylan—a lot of water has flowed under the bridge, so to speak, and, frankly, I don't know what to think anymore. Now I need a stiff drink and to get out of these fucking clothes. I'm going out to the reservation this afternoon to see the new school. We can talk later, if you're still around."

"They have a new school at the reservation?"

"That's what I heard—some anonymous donor."

"Listen, Dusty—I was planning on riding my bike out there to see Michael. Why don't you ride with me?"

"Just like old times, huh?'

"Dusty, when my parents were killed, Tom told me that God put our eyes in the front of our heads so that we would look forward and not back. Let's just focus on today for now."

"Pick me up at my house in a half hour."

"Dusty"

She turned as she was walking away.

"You look great."

Dusty's House, Early Afternoon

Dylan pulled up on his motorcycle wearing a T-shirt, blue jeans, his old cowboy boots, and one of his old bandanas. He had the Glock 9 velcroed on his thigh.

Dusty came out of the house with a halter top, sans bra, blue jean short shorts, and cowboy boots—just like old times. She had her hair in a ponytail. She hesitated when she saw the gun.

"Afraid I'm going to bolt without paying the fare?"

"Cute. In case you forgot why we're here—there are some real bad guys who think we have something that belongs to them."

Dusty got on behind Dylan.

"And what would that be?"

Dylan craned his neck around and stared at Dusty. "What that would be is a duffel bag that disappeared that night four years ago. You wouldn't know anything about that, would you?"

Dusty got off the bike and started walking toward the house. She turned with tears in her eyes.

"Fuck you, Dylan. If you came by just to give me some bullshit grilling—fuck you. I hardly hear from you for four years and all you are interested in is some duffel bag."

Dylan jumped off the bike and grabbed her.

"Dusty, look at me. I'm sorry, I didn't mean it like that. It's just that I had to ask because Jake said we're all in danger right now—and you know what they did to Scooter. Why do you think I'm wearing a gun?"

Dusty's arms were crossed and she was crying. Dylan embraced her.

"You know I'm emotional right now about Scooter—and about you. I'm still not over you—damn you!"

Dylan held her tight and stroked her hair. "Let's take a ride. It'll do us both some good. It's been four years since I've been on a bike."

They got back on the bike and headed toward the reservation. Dusty clutched Dylan tightly. He put one hand on hers.

The Apache Reservation

As they pulled into the reservation they saw the new school building and playground. It was obvious that no money was spared on either.

Dylan was stunned. "Wow! Some anonymous donor did this?"

"I heard it was either Bill Gates or Warren Buffett—maybe both."

They dismounted and were admiring the building when some teen-aged Apaches approached from behind.

"We ain't givin' no *gringo* tours today."

Dylan and Dusty turned quickly and the teens saw the Glock and stopped in their tracks.

One of the teens recognized them. "Hey, I know you two. You were my tutors."

Dylan frowned, "We didn't teach you to be rude."

"Yeah, you're Geronimo. Sorry, man. It's just that things are way different since you were here."

"I'd think they would be better with the new school and playground. I can't remember when there were nets on the hoops."

"Only the little ones go to school anymore. It ain't cool for the older ones to go."

"So let me get this straight—it's cool now to be stupid?"

"Everybody wants to be hip hop, man—you know, like the rappers."

"What's Michael say about all this?"

"Man, nobody listens to him anymore. The chief has that thing where you don't remember nothin'. He don't even know his own son."

"Do me a favor and tell him we're here."

One of the youngest boys ran to get Michael.

"So tell me, if the chief is ill and nobody listens to Michael, who's in charge?"

The teens exchanged glances. "It's like this, man. Some people, mostly the older ones, listen to Michael, but almost all the young ones follow Black Snake."

"I don't remember any Black Snake. Who would I know him as?"

"He used to be called Kennedy—after the president."

Dylan made a face. "Kennedy? Kennedy was a punk."

"Yeah well—you might call him that, but he's got the Mexicans behind him and they got the money, the drugs, and the guns."

"By Mexicans—you mean the Garcias?"

"Who else, man?"

Michael approached. Across the street a small crowd was gathering. Michael embraced Dylan first and then Dusty.

"Dusty, I heard about Scooter. He didn't deserve that."

"Thanks."

He turned back to Dylan. "Geronimo! Am I glad to see you, but what brings you out here?"

"Number one, I want to talk to you about something. Number two, we heard about the school."

Michael turned and gazed at the school. "It's a beautiful building. If only we could get the kids to use it."

He then glanced at the growing crowd. "This isn't a good place for us to talk. You remember the wells?"

Dylan feigned a look of doubt. Dusty elbowed him in the ribs, smiling. "We know."

"Good, I'll see you there in fifteen minutes."

He noticed Dylan's gun for the first time. "That's a good thing to have these days."

The Apache Wells

Dylan and Dusty arrived first, but didn't say anything as they walked over to the wells, lost in their own thoughts. Dusty sat by the water. Michael arrived shortly after.

"Geronimo, my blood brother. It's good to see you."

"It looks like you can use a friend these days."

Michael laughed. "I could use many friends. It's a bad moon."

"Maybe we can help each other. First—who has control of the reservation, you, or that little punk Kennedy?"

"He calls himself Black Snake now."

"I heard."

"Truth is he has more of the young men, but many are hangers on. Some have told me in private that they would support me if they thought I could win."

"What's preventing him from taking over?"

"The elders still have power and we're all Apaches. This isn't the first time in our sad history that there has been a power struggle. My father's days are numbered. When he dies, Kennedy will challenge me and the elders won't interfere. It is our way."

"What if that happened tomorrow?"

"If we fight, it will be a war and many will die. The Mexicans will back him and they're ruthless."

Dylan motioned and they sat down on the rocks. "Our fates are tied together once more. In the next few days, the Garcias and El Diablo, himself, will come to the Dunes looking for me, Jake, and Dusty."

"But, why?"

"They think we have something of theirs—their money, and a lot of it. It's why they killed Scooter."

"But, I heard you saved Carlos Garcia's life."

"Don't remind me. Regardless, he and his uncle appear to be at odds. Let me ask you this:if we could eliminate the Garcias—"

"Eliminate like kill?"

"Like kill. What would that do to the reservation?"

"Without the Garcias, Kennedy's support would disappear."

"How many men can you raise without others noticing—total secrecy?"

"Five, maybe six for certain, not counting me … possibly ten."

"Ten would be enough, but I would settle for six or seven whose absence won't be noticed. This has to be done without the Garcias' knowledge."

Dusty wandered over. "Am I interrupting anything?"

"Not at all. Michael—we'll need all the caves."

Michael laughed. "Even yours?"

Dylan smiled, "Even mine. How many are there?"

"There are seven we know about, including yours, and that may be all. The elders say the Spanish were referring to the caves when they talked about the seven cities of gold, because the gold was mined nearby and stored in the caves. Each cave has two separate, but connected sections."

"Mine only has one."

Michael smiled and Dusty seemed nervous.

"I promise you, Brother, that yours has two sections too. The second section was created as a safe room. They are identical in all of the other caves, so I'm sure yours is the same. You just haven't stumbled on it yet. There's a secret to it."

Dylan shrugged and glanced at Dusty, who appeared to look the other way.

"Whatever. Get your men together and wait to hear from me. This has to be done the Apache way—silently."

They embraced. "One of the elders, a medicine man, told me that help would be coming—that the great chiefs would be on my side."

After Michael departed, Dusty turned to Dylan. "Are you sure it's a good idea to tell him where the cave is—your cave?"

"Sorry—our cave. We need each other's help and we can only win if we use the caves, all of the caves, like Geronimo did."

"I like Michael, but you haven't seen him for four years. Are you sure you can trust him?"

"Dusty, I saw your look back there. If you've got something on your mind—just tell me."

"I'm just saying is all."

"Then let's get back."

"I'm pretty hot. I thought I'd take a dip first."

Dylan stopped in his tracks. "You think that's a good idea?"

"Funny—you never asked me that before."

"It's just—I don't want to hurt you."

"Dylan—I mean, Big Chief Geronimo, you couldn't hurt me anymore if you tried."

Dusty stripped and dived in. Dylan hesitated only briefly, but then followed. They quickly found each other and made passionate love.

They were dressed and ready to get on the bike when Dylan noticed the front tire was low.

"We need some air in the front tire. What's closest?"

"The only place near here is the Oasis."

The Oasis Gas Station

Dylan and Dusty pulled up to the air hose. As Dylan was getting the hose Dusty decided to get something to drink.

"I'm gonna get a Coke—you want anything?"

"I'm good. I'll have a sip of yours."

Dusty entered the mini-mart as Dylan was putting air in the tire. He looked up to see two matching black Escalades with Mexican plates pull in to get gas. Five bad-looking *hombres* exited each vehicle and stretched. Dylan noted that several were wearing yellow soccer jerseys identical to the one the prisoner wore. It's clear who the boss was as all eyes were on him. He was tall and swarthy and had a scar running from his ear to his mouth. Dylan knew, immediately, that it was El Diablo.

He tried to get Dusty's attention by rapping on the glass, but she didn't notice. She came out as some of the Mexicans were going in. They checked her out and were smiling and laughing. Diablo had stayed by the highway and was gazing in the direction they came from. He turned and headed toward the mini-mart.

Dusty was sipping her Coke and was oblivious to the situation. "What's up? You look like you saw a ghost."

Dylan grabbed her arm and pulled her close. "Don't say a word and don't look around. Get ready to get on and leave quickly."

Diablo was entering the mart when he noticed Dylan and the pistol strapped to his thigh. He stopped to take in the situation.

"Hey *amigo*—is it dangerous around here?"

"I'm just passing through. I heard there were snakes in the desert."

Diablo laughed. "*Amigo*, you always hunt snakes with a nine millimeter?"

"You never know. I heard they run in pairs—sometimes more. Are you a writer or something?"

Diablo laughed again. "Me a writer? No, *amigo*—I'm just a businessman. What is it you do, *amigo*?"

"Me—I'm sort of a fortune teller."

Dylan got on the bike and Dusty got on behind him.

Diablo was still smiling, but no longer laughing. "A fortune teller? Maybe you can tell my fortune, *amigo*?"

"All depends. What sign are you?"

"The crab, *amigo*."

Dylan seemed to ponder for a moment. "A Cancer, huh? That's too bad. These aren't good times for Cancers."

The smile was now gone from Diablo's face. "No? Tell me—what sign were you born under, *amigo*?"

Dylan started the bike and slowly let out the clutch. "A bad one, *amigo*—a very, very bad one."

Dylan pulled out near the road and stopped.

Dusty was shaking. "What was that about? "I've got goose bumps. That guy was scary."

"That was El Diablo. Do you have Jake's cell phone number?"

"It's on my phone."

"Good. Now listen carefully—hang on tight and don't look back."

Dylan drove between both SUVs, shooting out the tires on either side. He then took off. Diablo and his men were inside when they heard the shots. They rushed out, but the bike's taillights were already fading in the distance. They walked over and surveyed the damage.

One of the gunmen shouted, "*Jefe*, the motherfucker shot our tires."

Diablo was standing on the highway staring at the distant taillights with a sinister smile on his face.

"*Jefe*, why'd he do that?"

"*Amigos*, we just met Geronimo, but not for the last time."

As they were standing there, two more black Escalades pulled into the station. The men got out and one of them approached Diablo.

"*Jefe*, sorry—we had to stop for gas earlier."

Diablo grabbed him by the collar and pulled him close. "Next time you are late, I cut your eyeballs out and feed them to the chickens. *Comprende*?"

"*Sí, Jefe. Sí, sí, comprende.*"

The Highway to Apache Dunes

Dylan pulled off the side of the highway. He turned to Dusty. "Get Jake on the phone."

Dusty dialed Jake's number and handed the phone to Dylan. Jake was in his truck when the phone rang. He saw it was Dusty.

"Hey Dusty."

"It's me, Jake, and the shit's begun."

"Slow down a bit. Where are you and what's up?"

"Dusty's with me and we're about five miles west on the highway, but we're heading straight for the cave. We stopped at the Oasis and who pulls in but two carloads of bad guys and—and El Diablo himself. As I left, I shot out a few tires to buy us some time."

"Holy shit! OK, I'll meet you there. What do we need?"

"Do you have any of those spike pads for puncturing tires?"

"We've got two that I know of."

"Perfect. OK, bring those, all the guns and ammo you can lay your hands on, plenty of food and water—and jackets and blankets."

"You say all the guns—we've got a small arsenal."

"Good, we'll need all we can get. We're going to get some help."

"Help? From where?"

"That's what I was working on today. I'll fill you in later."

"What about the prisoners?"

"Bring Carlos, but keep him cuffed. As for the other guy—tell him to tell Diablo we're in the desert and have his money, but make sure he can't pull a trigger. Understand?"

"Got it."

"And Jake—make sure that Rosa and everyone else stays away until we give them the all clear."

"Geronimo—I hope you have a plan."

"Old Apache saying—the way to kill a snake is to cut off its head."

"Roger that. I'll round up the supplies."

"Jake, get Carlos first. I don't see them attacking in the dark. Tell Homer to stay out of harm's way, but to keep an eye on things and stay in touch with us."

CHAPTER THIRTEEN

Groundhog Day

Apache Dunes Sheriff's Office and Jail

The jail, an adobe structure, was over a hundred years old. It was adjacent to, but not connected with, the sheriff's office. Inside there were two cells, a desk, chairs for the jailer and a potbelly stove.

The sun had set by the time Diablo got the tires replaced. The street was deserted and the only light was from the street lights and the single bulb above the entrance to the jail. Diablo and his entourage of four black Escalades cruised slowly past the jail, looking for evidence of an ambush, but there was none. They hesitated at the end of the block and then returned to park near the entrance.

The Deputy Homer was hidden from view in the alley across the street. Diablo waited another several minutes before exiting the truck and entering the jail with two bodyguards. The jail was empty except for the prisoner who was huddled in the corner of his cell in obvious pain.

Diablo called out, just in case. "*Hola*—anyone here?"

When there was no answer, they opened the cell with keys that were left in plain sight. The prisoner struggled to get to his feet.

He cried, "*Jefe*, they broke my arms."

Diablo winced as if sympathetic. "Where did they go?"

The prisoner was sobbing. "The desert. They say to tell you they go to the desert and they have your money and Carlos. I don't say nothing so they broke my arms."

Diablo put his hand gently on the back of the prisoner's head as if to console him. "You don't say nothing? *Bueno,* but what good are you to me now?"

Diablo jerked the prisoner's head back by his hair and in one swift motion slit his throat. He jumped back as the prisoner collapsed, spurting blood from his gaping wound. Diablo leaned down and wiped his blade on the prisoner's jersey. The two gunmen were stone-faced even though they knew the prisoner. They had become accustomed to Diablo's spontaneous acts of violence long ago.

Diablo walked out to where the trucks were parked and addressed his entourage. "Let's find a place to stay the night. I'll fight Geronimo in the daylight—on my terms, not his."

The Shady Rest Motor Court, on the Outskirts of Apache Dunes

The Shady Rest was a ten-unit motel that belonged to another era. The neon sign resembled a Wheel of Fortune puzzle with the vowels missing. Its only amenities were clean sheets, plumbing, and electricity that worked most of the time. But, the price was right, and for the less fortunate traveler, it might as well be a Four Seasons. In El Diablo's case, the Shady Rest was the only option tonight without driving another forty miles.

When they pulled into the parking lot, there was a light on in the office and four older-model vehicles parked in front of the units. Diablo, Juan, and Esteban entered the office. No one was at the desk, but they heard a television and voices in the back. Diablo rang the bell and the manager came quickly. He wiped his hands on his pants and was still chewing some food.

"*Hola,* welcome. Welcome—you need a room for the night?"

Diablo stared at the manager before he spoke. "Why else would we be here?"

The manager saw through the window that there were four trucks parked outside. He answered nervously, "*Sí, sí*—how many rooms do you need, Señor?"

"All of them."

"That would be six rooms, *sí*?"

Diablo moved closer. "How many rooms do you have, *amigo*? I counted ten."

The manager had now broken a sweat. "*Sí* … *sí*, there are ten rooms total, but four are occupied—so I only have six available."

The manager's young daughter entered from the residence. "Daddy, Mommy wants to know if everything is OK."

The manager was now very nervous and tried to gently push his daughter back out of the office when Juan stepped in to block the door. The manager held his daughter close.

"Señor, would you like the six rooms? I'll give you a special rate."

"How much are the rooms?"

"They are twenty-four ninety-nine plus tax, but for you—"

Diablo cut him off. "Esteban, give our friend four hundred dollars for the ten rooms and for the inconvenience we have caused."

The manager held his hands out, pleading, as Esteban counted out four hundred-dollar bills.

"Señor, please. What can I do? The people are in the rooms."

Diablo grabbed the manager's hands and appeared to inspect them. "I will make you a deal, *amigo*. You have ten rooms and you have ten fingers. If you give me ten rooms, I will let you keep all ten fingers. If you give me only six rooms, you will only get to keep six fingers. *Comprende*?"

The daughter was clinging to her father. The manager was now sweating. "Let me get my shoes, I will try to talk to the people."

Juan didn't budge and continued to block the doorway.

"You don't need the shoes, *amigo*. Esteban will send some men to help you. We will look after your daughter. Oh—and have your wife make up the rooms."

"Señor, my wife isn't the maid."

Diablo stared at the manager. "*Amigo*, are you trying to make me angry?"

"No señor. I'm sorry. I will take care of everything."

"*Bueno, muy bueno.*"

Homer had been observing from his truck across and down the road a bit. He dialed a number on his cell phone.

The Cave

Dylan, Dusty, Jake, and Carlos (in cuffs) were sitting near the fire. Several rifles, shotguns, and boxes of ammo were nearby. Jake's phone rang and he got up to go outside and answer it. He returned and sat down.

"That was Homer. He's pretty shaken up. Diablo has four carloads of soldiers.

Carlos was animated. "Check this out—I told you he would come heavy."

Jake replied, "Shut the fuck up. If it wasn't for you we wouldn't be here. Anyway, Diablo and two of his men went in the jail. They left the prisoner. One of them cut his throat."

Dusty gasped.

Jake continued, "They're spending the night at the Shady Rest south of town. Homer says they evicted some people to get their rooms."

Dylan started laughing. Dusty couldn't believe it. "Please tell us what's so funny? I didn't hear anything remotely comical."

"It's not funny, funny. It's funny, ironic. Geronimo fought the Mexican army right here in these hills and it's like Groundhog Day—it's happening all over again."

Dusty shook her head. "Dylan—this isn't a game. We aren't kids anymore. What are we gonna do?"

"Michael is getting us some help. I'm going to ride over and tell him we'll need them in the morning."

Carlos spoke up. "Check this out—I'll tell you what you can do."

Everyone looked at him. Dylan was all ears. "Which is?"

Carlos now looked directly at Dusty.

"Which is—you can give the money back and the bag. Scooter told them that you and him took it and hid it in the cave. He said the bag was still there, but some money had been spent. If Diablo's men hadn't messed with his eyes, he would have shown them where it was."

Everyone was quiet. Dylan and Jake looked at each other. Dusty started sobbing, jumped up, and hurried out of the cave.

Dylan was angry at Carlos. "Maybe Scooter said what they wanted to hear. He was tortured."

"Check this out—the bag was there when the shooting started. I know you guys didn't take it, but after you left I saw Scooter coming down the rocks. I must've passed out. When the sheriff came, the bag was gone."

They heard Dusty returning. She was dragging the bag. Dylan jumped up.

"I can't believe you lied to me."

"Fuck you, Dylan. I never lied to you—I just didn't tell you. You told me you loved me and then disappeared for four years."

"I didn't disappear. I was at school. You knew where I was."

Jake stood up and intervened. "Everybody cool it. It is what it is. We need to stay focused. Dusty, how much money is left?"

"I'm not sure. It looks like more than half is gone."

Jake turned to Carlos. "Do you know how much was there to start with?"

Carlos shrugged. "Three maybe four million, I think. This ain't good news."

Dylan looked at Dusty. "Where'd all the money go?"

"It's just gone, OK? What difference does it make now?"

It suddenly dawned on Dylan, "The school!"

"That was part of it."

Jake looked puzzled, "The school? What school?"

"On the reservation."

"I heard some anonymous millionaire donated the money."

Carlos piped in, "She ain't anonymous any longer."

Dusty had gone outside and was sitting alone in the rocks, still crying. Dylan approached.

"Dusty, I'm sorry. I just don't get it."

She wiped her eyes. "It was great that you and Jake let Scooter hang around and always protected him. You guys were like gods—still are—everybody's heroes.

"But, try as he may, Scooter could never be like you guys. One day he just stumbled on the other passage. I don't know how we all missed it. He was so proud of that and was just waiting for the right time to show you.

"Well, that night when he went back for the bag and found it full of money, we got into a big argument. I said we had to tell you about it. He said you would give it to Tom and we'd never see it again."

Dylan started to respond, but Dusty cut him off. "Scooter said you were going away and would probably never come back. I didn't believe him—I didn't want to believe him. He said Carlos was going to die and no one would know.

"He said he would put it in the secret passage and not touch it for a month. If no one said anything by then, it was finders keepers."

"How about the school?"

"I came home when my Mom was ill and took a ride out there for old time's sake. It was so sad and barren to me that it just came to me and … I guess it made me feel less guilty about the money."

"I gotta admit, that was a nice thing to do. How about your shop and the boat?"

Dusty finally smiled, but it was a sad smile. "The shop is all legit. I worked for the previous owner and she wanted me to have it. The terms she gave me were very generous. The boat, the Garcias paid for. I had this pipe dream that we would reunite someday and sail away together."

Dylan gently took her face in his hands. "Who knows? Maybe we'll do just that."

They embraced.

Dylan left to meet with Michael and Jake did guard duty outside the cave. Upon his return, Dylan was coming up through the rocks and spotted Jake.

"Aren't you supposed to say, 'Who goes there?'"

"I'm glad to see you still have your sense of humor."

Dylan sat down. "Listen, Jake, you don't have to do this. You have Ashley to think about."

"You heard Carlos. Scooter told them about us, me included. Plus, this isn't just about the money, or Dusty, or even us. The Garcias have been a cancer around here for as long as I can remember. It was a Garcia truck that killed your parents. This has to end sometime and if they are foolish enough to try to fight us here, we can end it—we will end it. I can see how Geronimo held off the Mexican and American armies. I don't care how bad his twenty men are. El Diablo will die here, particularly if we get some help from Michael."

"Good news and bad news: Michael's got five men plus himself. The others were afraid."

"You know what is sad? Losing their land is one thing, but it seems like they've lost their heart, as well."

"Not all of them, Jake. I'll take six good men any day."

"That's eight plus Dusty and we have the high ground and the caves. Hard to believe El Diablo would be that stupid."

"It's not stupidity—it's arrogance. Plus, Carlos said Diablo's brain is fried on coke. He said the men aren't so loyal—it's more like they fear him."

"If we can take him out somehow, cut off the snake's head, maybe that would end it."

"I doubt seriously that he will get too exposed. We'll have to finesse it somehow. Jake, you and I always thought that one of Michael's caves was right over there. Remember how he would seem to disappear and reappear when we would play out here?"

"If they could put a sniper over there and we could create a diversion,

Diablo might be exposed."

"I'll take the watch for a while. Try to get some rest—we're gonna need it."

Jake departed and Dylan leaned back to gaze at the trillions of stars in the desert sky. He missed that dearly. The silence was broken by Carlos' appearance—still cuffed. Dylan sat up.

"I thought you were sleeping."

"How can I sleep, man? These cuffs don't help."

"Yeah, well, you'll get used to them."

"That's cold man. Check this out—I'm on your side. My uncle wants me dead. He thinks I'm in on this. See these tats—the crosses and angels—I got religion in the joint, man. It's because of you, man. You saved my life, now twice."

"Carlos, cut the bullshit. You had tats in high school."

"Yeah, the angels, but the crosses are from the big house."

Dylan appeared skeptical as Carlos held his shirt up.

"They look like a prison job—the crosses."

"Word, man. That's what I'm sayin'. There was this chaplain—an old dude, Padre Gomez. He took me under his wing. He turned me onto all kinds of books, man."

"I didn't know you could read."

"Ouch, man. Why you dissin' me? I'm opening my heart here. I know I ain't ever gonna be as smart as you are, but I'm a lot smarter than some people think. You know what my dream is?"

"I have a feeling you're gonna tell me."

"Dude—I'm baring my soul."

"Sorry, go ahead."

"Check this out, man. When I saw what one guy, like Padre Gomez, could do … I'd like to open a place for young gangbangers like I was."

Dylan looked at him. "You don't know how much I would like to believe that."

"Check this out, man. I got my own reasons for wanting Diablo dead.

He ain't gonna sleep until I'm dead, and what they did to Scooter would be like a Disney movie compared to what he'd do to me."

"Carlos, let's say, for the sake of discussion, that Diablo dies tomorrow. What happens to the gang?"

"That snake has three heads, not just one. Nobody's as ruthless as Diablo, but Esteban and Juan ain't no choir boys. The men would follow either of them. If I get back together with some of the men it will be to help them. That's all."

"Best guess—will the others quit if we take out all three of them?"

"Maybe I can talk to them. How about you take these cuffs off?"

"If you get tired enough, you'll sleep. Maybe tomorrow."

"Man, that's cold."

Chapter Fourteen

A Good Day for Killing

The Desert, the Following Morning

Dylan was scanning the nearby rocks with his binoculars and saw mirror flashes off the sun's first rays. He acknowledged with a wave. Jake, Dusty, and Carlos emerged from the cave.

Dylan motioned to Jake. "Take the cuffs off."

Even Carlos looked surprised.

"Dylan, you sure about that?"

"We need all the help we can get and you have my permission to shoot him if he tries to escape."

Jake smiled as he unlocked the cuffs. "Please try to run."

Carlos massaged his wrists. "Man, you got a black heart."

Dylan addressed the group. "Let's take the spike pads down there and get them situated and covered as much as possible. They'll be coming from the west through the desert so they'll be looking into the sun. That should help."

Jake nudged Dylan. "We've got company."

They saw Michael and his men coming up through the rocks.

"They're coming for guns and ammo."

Jake seemed surprised. "You gonna show them the cave?"

Dylan smiled. "It's part of the deal. Take Carlos and Dusty with you to place the spike pads and I'll take care of Michael."

When the Apaches exited the cave, a short time later, each was carrying two rifles and ammo belts. Michael and Dylan surveyed the scene.

Dylan pointed. "All of the action is going to be up here. Leave one man on the other side of the hill so they can't flank us or take us by surprise. Nobody is to fire until we have them in a crossfire. The primary targets are Diablo and his two lieutenants. Anything else?"

Michael grabbed his pouch. "There is one more thing."

He pulled out two small tubes of paint. He put red and yellow lines on Dylan's cheeks and forehead, then did the same to himself. They embraced and Michael yelled an Apache war cry as he returned to his position.

The Shady Rest Motel

Diablo was addressing his men. "We'll go through the Taco Bell in town and get something to eat. Then we have a date with the one who calls himself Geronimo. I want the duffel bag. If all the money is there, maybe we spare the girl, but my nephew has to die."

The Desert

Dylan, Jake, and Dusty were armed and watching the desert. They placed Carlos directly below them where they could keep an eye on him. All of a sudden a mirror flash came from the opposite rocks. They looked to the horizon and saw the dust cloud from the Mexicans' approach.

Dylan gave his final instructions. "It's showtime. Spread out and keep down at all times. They can't hit us unless we expose ourselves. Dusty, anytime you want, you head to the cave and wait there until it's over. Now if we're lucky, at least one car will hit a pad. If it does, aim all your fire at that car and be relentless. We have plenty of ammo. We'll take them out one at a time."

Diablo was in the second car. He put the visor down to block the sun's glare. He uncapped a vial of coke and snorted some off the back of his hand.

"It's a good day for killing, *amigos*."

His men laughed.

Esteban gazed warily at the hills ahead. "How do we get them down from the rocks?"

"*Amigo*, when they see us, they will want to surrender." More laughter.

Suddenly, the lead car hit a pad and swerved violently out of control before stopping. Diablo's car just missed the pad as a hail of gunfire erupted from the surrounding rocks. All of the men in the first car were killed as they tried to exit. A bullet pierced the gas tank and the first car exploded. Diablo was cut with flying glass as he exited his vehicle. The third car swerved, but in doing so hit the other pad and immediately drew the incoming fire.

Diablo jumped back in his car and signaled for the remaining two cars to move back. When the gunfire halted, at least six of Diablo's men were dead, one car was disabled, and the other destroyed.

Diablo and his men were clearly shaken. Esteban broke the silence. "Maybe we should wait until Jesus gets in position behind them."

Diablo looked at him wild-eyed. He exited his car and the others followed, all being careful to keep the cars between them and the rocks.

Diablo called out, "Geronimo—I underestimated you. My mistake. I only want what's mine. Give me the bag and you can keep the girl and my nephew. I forget about the men and the cars. They can be replaced."

The silence is pierced by the sound of rifle shots coming from the other side of the hill.

Dylan yells back, "It sounds like you just lost another man, *amigo*."

Diablo was furious. Esteban tried to reason with him. "*Jefe*, there is no way we get them out of the rocks without losing most of our men—maybe all of them."

Diablo yelled out, "*Amigo*, let's talk."

Dylan replied, "You send one man, unarmed, and I send Carlos. They meet halfway."

Diablo looked at his remaining men, but all tried to avert his gaze.

"José, you go. You know my nephew."

José was anything but thrilled, but put his guns down and tied a white handkerchief to a broken aerial. He started up the hill.

Dylan approached Carlos. "Are you ready for this?"

Carlos shrugged his shoulders and crossed himself. Waving a white rag back and forth, Carlos proceeded to meet José halfway in the rocks. Dylan caught the brief mirror flash of acknowledgement from Michael's position. Carlos and José appeared to have an animated discussion, then returned to their respective positions.

Dylan motioned Carlos over. "What did he say?"

Carlos laughed, "He wanted to come with me. He didn't want to go back. I told him they were surrounded, but we only wanted Diablo, Esteban, and Juan. I told him what you say about getting his men out of the way so that Diablo is exposed. He say he try. I told him I split the money with them if they help us."

"I don't recall saying anything about the money."

"You want me to call him back?"

Dylan just shook his head. "I could give a shit about the money."

José had returned and was huddled with Diablo, Esteban, and Juan. José was then seen walking over to talk to a group of four gunmen behind one of the SUVs.

Dylan and Jake had been watching closely with binoculars. He and Michael again exchanged mirror flashes. One of the gunmen appeared to be getting into the driver's side door of the SUV as José and the four others stood by with their rifles.

Dylan uttered under his breath, "Do it … do it."

All of a sudden the silence was broken as the engine started and the SUV jerked back. José and the gunmen jumped in and took off, while Diablo and the others looked on in confusion.

After a stunned pause, Diablo realized they were now exposed on their flank. Michael and his men seized the moment and gunfire erupted from their side of the rocks. The din was made even more frightening by the Apache war whoops that accompanied the gunfire.

When the barrage ended and the smoke had cleared, Diablo, Esteban, Juan, and at least three others were dead. They had no chance after being exposed, unaware that the Apaches occupied their flank. Three others dropped their guns and held their hands up. José's SUV slowly returned, but kept a safe distance.

Dylan stood and waved to Michael. Both parties headed down through the rocks with weapons aimed at the prisoners. Dylan turned to Jake, "You have any claim on that money?"

Jake looked surprised at the question. "Good riddance."

Dylan called out to Dusty, "Dusty, give the bag to Carlos."

On the desert floor Dylan and Michael embraced again. The Apaches continued with the war whoops until Michael held up his hand. The prisoners looked terrified. José and his men hadn't yet exited their SUV.

Dylan got everyone's attention. "Carlos, split the money with Michael and his men. Without them we might not have survived."

Carlos didn't object, if he could have. He reached into the bag and started throwing out bundles of cash, all hundred-dollar bills. Each time he did so, it appeared he was looking for something. He looked up, "It's going to take a while to count it out."

Dylan eyed the cash on the ground. "If Michael's OK with it, I think that looks like half."

Michael nodded. "I'm cool with that."

Dylan turned back to Carlos. "Well, Carlos, I hope you do what you said you were going to do."

"Geronimo, you saved my life a second time. I owe you."

Dylan appeared skeptical. "Just don't let me down."

Carlos took the bag and motioned for the prisoners to follow him to José's SUV. They ran, not walked, to the car.

"Michael, can you get some help with the bodies and what's left of the trucks?"

"When the news that Diablo is dead reaches the reservation, they will want to help just to see that he's really dead. Plus," he said waving a wad of bills, "I can afford to pay for the help. I know exactly what to do with the trucks. We have a tow truck on the reservation and a pit that needs to be filled. Tomorrow no one will suspect that anything happened here."

Dylan turned to Michael. "Now that you will be the new chief, you'll need an Apache name."

Michael smiled. "I've been thinking about that. Since Geronimo and Cochise are already taken, I've decided on Taza, Cochise's son."

Dylan and Jake smiled and they all embraced a final time.

Jake then did a final survey of the scene. "I don't know about you and Dusty, but a pitcher of margaritas and some burritos would taste mighty good right now."

Dylan quickly replied, "I'm in."

Dusty grinned, "Do you have to ask?"

Chapter Fifteen

The Past Isn't Even Past

The Cantina in Apache Dunes

Dylan, Jake, and Dusty were joined by Jake's wife Ashley. Two empty pitchers were on the table.

Ashley looked at Dusty, "Dusty, I was hoping you would stay a few days. I really admire your work."

"Thanks, but believe it or not, my ticket is for tomorrow morning. How's that for planning? I need to get back. I have a captain hired for a trip I've been planning."

Dylan appeared surprised. "Where are you going?"

"That's the funny thing—I don't have a destination in mind. I've always wanted to do something spontaneous."

Jake looked at Dylan. "What about you, big chief?"

"You don't need to say that. I'm already self-conscious. I feel like people are staring at me."

The others laughed as Dusty handed him her mirror and he saw that he still had the war paint on. They roared when they saw his reaction.

"Thanks a lot. You could have said something."

Then he laughed too as he tried to remove it with a wet napkin.

Dusty raised her glass, "Cost of wet napkin—a few cents. Seeing the great Geronimo embarrassed—priceless!"

They all laughed.

Dylan savored his drink for a bit. "Well, as for me, I have two days left. I want to visit Tom tomorrow. Graduation is next week."

Dusty started to stand. "Well ... I have to pack and get cleaned up. Dylan, how about one more ride?"

"I would love to."

Dusty blushed as everyone laughed. "I meant on the bike."

"Seeing the great Dusty blush—priceless!"

"Touché, but I want to speak with Ashley before we leave."

Tucson Airport, Two Days Later

Dylan approached the counter. "I've got a ticket to New York. How hard is it to transfer to Key West instead?"

The agent replied. "It's possible, we can get you there, but it won't be a direct flight. Let me see if there's any additional cost."

"Do me a favor and just get me there. If it's extra—I'll pay it."

Sheriff's Office

Jake was sitting at Tom's desk looking at some files when Homer poked his head in.

"Did Dylan get away OK?"

"Yeah—Ashley took him to the airport this morning. He told her he was going to try to switch tickets and go see Dusty for a few days in Key West."

"Maybe things will settle down a bit now?"

"That's what I thought, but Tom told me to look at a couple of files he'd tucked away and it's like—whatta they call it? Pandora's box."

"Is this about the Garcias?"

"It's about Carlos Garcia AND Scooter."

"I don't follow."

"It seems like Scooter visited Carlos at least twice in prison."

Homer looked incredulous. "He what?"

"Scooter visited him in prison and those calls are taped. The prison officials told Tom that Scooter was trying to cut some sort of deal to give back something that belonged to Carlos."

"The money?"

"That's the thing—it appears something else was missing besides the money and something that was more valuable."

"What the hell is more valuable than three or four million dollars?"

"That's the question that never got answered—at least on the tapes."

"You said Carlos got the bag back with the money."

"Yeah, but come to think of it, when he was taking money out of the bag, it seemed like he was looking for something."

Homer was pensive for a moment. "Jake."

"Yeah?"

"Now, I'm just sayin' is all, but if Scooter knew about it—did Dusty, too? You said she knew where the bag was."

Jake stood up and was now pacing. "You read my mind."

"You think we ought to let Dylan know—I mean, if he's with her?"

"I know we let seven bad guys and that piece of shit Carlos go with what was left in the bag. I've got a bad feeling about this. Dylan was way too anxious to believe Carlos' bullshit. There's a big piece of this puzzle missing. Where'd I put Dylan's cell number?"

Duval Street in Key West, Late Afternoon

Dylan got out of the cab and paid the driver. He spotted a group of what appeared to be locals and approached them.

"Excuse me, I'm a friend of Dusty Loader. Do any of you know where I might find her?"

It was clear they were checking him out, but figured he was OK.

One of the locals finally replied. "Her shop is right down the street, but I saw her a little while ago on her boat at the marina."

He pointed the way and Dylan walked as quickly as possible, hoping she hadn't left. He was directed to her slip, but when he arrived it was empty. A man was sitting in his cockpit in the adjacent slip—sipping a beer and reading.

"Excuse me, I'm looking for Dusty Loader."

The guy stood up and looked out at the harbor. A forty-foot sailboat was just leaving.

"You may have just missed her. That's her going out on Geronimo."

He saw that Dylan was distressed. "Is this something real important?"

Dylan had a hangdog look. "It is to me."

The guy put his beer down. "I've got an idea—hold on."

He went below and emerged with an air horn. He blasted it twice.

Dylan asked, "You said the Geronimo."

"That's the name of her boat."

The Geronimo

Dusty was standing by the mast when she heard the horn. She turned and squinted—then yelled at the captain. "Turn the boat around."

"Say what?"

"Turn the fucking boat around.

After returning to the dock and picking up Dylan, they cleared the harbor and were getting ready to set sail when a cigarette boat with three men aboard came dangerously close. Dylan seemed fixated on them.

"You gotta relax. You're in the Conch Republic now. They're just jerks—they're not locals."

"Did you see their shirts?"

"What about them? Some type of yellow jersey. What's so unusual about that?"

Dylan shook his head. "I guess it's just me."

"So tell me—what are you going to do about your graduation?"

"Any suggestions?"

"Yeah—why don't you tell them you're too well to attend?"

They laughed as Dylan's phone rang.

"It's Jake."

Dusty grabbed the phone from him. "Here—let me say hello."

She tossed the phone in the ocean.

"What the—?"

"Dylan, you need to relax and forget about things for a while. That's all in the past, now."

Dylan looked pensive as the sails caught the wind. The spinnaker had a portrait of Geronimo on it.

Dusty nudged him. "What's that look?"

"Faulkner said the past isn't dead—it's not even past."

CHAPTER SIXTEEN

Liability

A little more than two weeks had passed since the fateful battle in the desert and Sheriff Tom Ward was finally cleared to go back to work. The local "sawbones," as Tom referred to him, actually suggested it was time for Tom to hang up his spurs—particularly since things were now so calm. However, for Tom, calm had the same connotation in the desert as it had in the jungles of Nam. It simply meant that a storm was soon to follow.

His first order of business after his checkup was to drive out to the reservation and pay his respects to Michael, the new Chief Taza. Michael's father, the old chief, had finally succumbed to a long battle with several health issues.

Michael had succeeded him with virtual unanimous support of the elders after the one they called Black Snake and four of his lieutenants had perished in a house explosion. The cause of death was listed as a natural gas explosion—which was interesting, as they didn't have natural gas, and even further interesting that a case of dynamite had disappeared from a mom-and-pop mining operation in the area. As far as Tom was concerned it was good riddance.

The Reservation

When Tom turned into the reservation he saw Michael and a small group of what appeared to be elders talking with a dapperly dressed man beside his late-model Cadillac. Seeing Tom, Michael excused himself and approached Tom's truck.

Tom exited his vehicle and gave Michael a warm embrace. Michael had spent many nights sleeping over at Tom's with Dylan and Jake while growing up.

"Tom, it's great to see you up and about. We were praying for you."

"Thanks, Michael. I wanted to pay my respects. Your father was a great man in a very difficult time."

"Thanks, that means a lot."

"And I also wanted to congratulate you on becoming the new chief."

"Yeah, well I don't know if congratulations or condolences are more appropriate," Michael said with a smile. "Have you heard anything from Geronimo?"

"Not a word, but he's on a sailboat somewhere in the Caribbean. Probably doesn't have cell service."

"You think he'll return?"

"Oh, I think he'll come back, but not for good. There's nothing here for him—as much as I'd like him to stay."

"I hear you. What about Dusty? You think they'll get back together?"

Tom smiled, "If they don't it won't be for a lack of prayers from Aunt Sue, but ... me ... my gut says that too much water may have flowed under that bridge."

"I've gotta say, Dusty seemed different somehow."

"Remember when you were kids and I used to call you big dummies?"

Michael laughed.

"Well, Michael, the only things that don't change around here are those hills and the desert. We've all changed."

"Too bad we can't stop the hands of time, huh?"

"Oh, how I wish. Are you gonna be OK?"

"Well, it's me against TV and the internet and it's not going to be easy. I'm sure that affected my father—broke his heart. The young kids don't care about the culture. They say it isn't relevant. I'll tell you one thing I won't allow, if I can help it—I won't let Carlos Garcia or anyone else just walk in here and peddle their drugs anymore."

"So you don't buy that Carlos was born again?"

Michael scoffed. "He was a punk, he is a punk, and he'll always be a punk. Geronimo wants to see the best in everybody, but there is no best in Carlos."

"If they do try, do you have any of that er, natural gas left?"

Michael smiled. "There might be a little left over."

Tom returned the smile. "I'll let you get back to your meeting—looks important."

"The jury's out on that. He wants to build a casino, says it will create jobs and money. More money means more TV, internet, and consumerism. Maybe I'm just swimming against the tide."

"If you need me, you know I'll be there for you. Oh, by the way, I've got something for you. Aunt Sue baked you your favorite casserole."

"I smelled it. I was hoping it was for me. Let me know when you hear from Geronimo."

They embraced and Michael suddenly turned around as he was walking away.

"Oh, Tom—there is one more thing I thought you'd like to know. The DEA guys have been out here a couple of times asking questions about the Garcias. Nobody's said anything. You'd think they'd be happy they were out of business."

Tom appeared pensive for a moment. "Like you said, the jury's out on that one, too. Somebody was paying for those homes and cars and it wasn't Uncle Sam."

Tom waved as he drove away, heading back to the Dunes.

Tom called Jake from his truck. "I'm heading in. You want me to get you anything from the diner?"

"Thanks, but I'm all set. When you get in, Detective Sandowski wants you to give him a call. He's a funny guy—I really like him."

"I imagine you have to have a sense of humor in his business—gang crimes in Chicago."

Tom stopped at a four-way intersection just as a red Cadillac Escalade came to a rolling stop and turned right in front of him. The driver was wearing reflective sunglasses and appeared to be in an animated discussion on his cell phone.

"Well, whatta ya know. If it isn't Robin on the bat phone and he just committed no less than three traffic violations."

"I was going to tell you—I heard they've been out at the reservation making inquiries about the Garcias."

"I just left Michael; he told me. I'm going to stop for lunch at the diner and then head in."

"Roger that."

Del's Mansion

Del's house was easily the most spectacular residence in Apache Dunes. No expense had been spared. It was situated on a massive manicured lot with palm trees and had an in-ground pool, observatory, and stables. A new Range Rover and a new Lexus were parked in the cobblestone, circular driveway.

Carl, "Robin," pulled into the driveway way too fast and didn't see the child's bicycle until it was too late. The sound of the screeching brakes and twisted metal brought both Del and Kelsey from the house. As Carl exited his truck it was apparent he was coked to the gills.

Del screamed, "Carl, what the fuck is your problem? Are you blind?"

Kelsey stared at both of them. "What's his problem? What's his problem? Maybe you're blind too. He's totally wired. What an asshole."

Del grabbed Carl by the arm as Kelsey returned to the house in disgust. "Don't ever come here like this again. You hear me? Now what is so important that you had to rush over?"

"Del, we need to talk. I've got a problem."

"No shit, but make that plural. Let's go around to the patio. Try not to wreck anything."

They sat down on the patio out of earshot of the pool and the babysitter.

Del got two Coronas from the wet bar and handed one to Carl. "Now pull yourself together. What's your problem?"

"It's the Garcias. Where the fuck are they? Twenty-five g's a week like clockwork and all of a sudden they disappear."

Del sat up in his chair and stared at Carl. "Don't tell me—do not tell me that you went through all of that money. I built this place and have enough stashed offshore to retire without a care in the world. You had the same chance as I did. Truth is, I sleep better now that they're gone. It makes an exit from this game easier."

"I had a run of bad luck."

"A run of bad luck? How bad?"

"A hundred and fifty large."

Del stood up and paced back and forth before sitting again and scooting his chair closer to Carl. "Carl, you should have had that much under your mattress. What happened to the rest of the money?"

"It went—I don't know."

Carl pulled a wad of hundred dollar bills out of his pocket. "See this. It's about eight grand. It's all I have left. I took it out of the bank or it would have gone up Angie's nose.

Del got up and emptied the Corona and poured himself a shot of Don Julio Real tequila—then another. He sat back down.

"OK, let's start at the top. Who do you owe the money to?"

"The Italians in Vegas and they aren't happy, but they said they would take some AK-47s and ammo in trade."

Del reached over and forcefully grabbed Carl by his collar. "Carl—you listen to me and you listen carefully. There will be no trade of any kind. You got in this jam and you better find a way out. Sell your fucking house."

"I – I can't. I put it in Angie's name."

"You put your house in a fucking pole dancer's name? Are you fucking insane?"

"I don't think—"

"Shut the fuck up. That was a rhetorical question."

"But Del—what happened to the Garcias? How could they just disappear?"

"Carl, we have asked our Apache informant. He swears that Geronimo and Cochise apparently came back to life and wiped out the Garcias in a gun battle in the desert. The Indians believe in that shit. We've been to the supposed site twice and there were no bodies and no burned up trucks. What more can we do?"

"Del, just listen to me please. I've been thinking about this."

Del scoffed at the idea of Carl thinking.

"Just listen to me. If there was a gun battle, they couldn't have picked up all of the spent cartridges. You've got a metal detector. How about we take the metal detector and pick up the breed and go there one more time? If we find nothing—it's over."

Del was silent as he mulled over the situation. When Carl tried to speak, Del raised his hand to stop him. Finally Del spoke, "OK, Carl, here's the deal. We'll do as you say, but if we don't find anything, it is over, period. You understand? You're becoming a liability to me. I'll go get the metal detector. We'll take your truck, but I'm driving. Wait for me in the truck."

Carl stood, but didn't move. Del turned around. "What? What now?"

Carl looked sheepish. "Del, Angie's out of coke."

It took all of Del's will power to restrain himself from attacking Carl. He took a deep breath. "Go wait in the truck."

Del put on a pair of leather gloves and went to his safe where he retrieved a thirty-eight caliber pistol with handle taped and serial numbers filed off. He made sure it was loaded and stuck it in his belt. He then took a quart baggie full of coke and went to fetch the metal detector from the garage.

He put the detector in the back of the truck and hopped in the driver's side. He tossed the coke to Carl. "Put that in the glove compartment and don't ask me to do this again."

Carl opened the glove compartment and then turned to Del. "Is it OK if I take just one hit?"

Del literally banged his head on the steering wheel. Composing himself he looked at Carl and sighed. "Knock yourself out."

Carl took one massive hit and glanced at Del, who was now driving, and took one more before putting the bag away.

It was a breach of longstanding protocol to pick up their informant at the reservation in broad daylight, but Del didn't seem to care and Carl was in la-la land. The informant, however, was visibly uncomfortable as he was seen getting into Carl's vehicle. No words were spoken during the ride to the scene of the supposed battle.

The Desert

When they exited the truck the Apache led them to the spot where he said El Diablo was killed. He gestured around, shading the sun from his eyes. "El Diablo—he was here behind his truck. There were two trucks over there. One was shot up and the other was on fire."

Del and Carl looked around, but could see no evidence that any vehicles had been there. Carl pulled his gun and lunged at the Apache, who stumbled and fell to his knees. "This is the third time you've told us this bullshit story. Maybe you think we're just a couple of stupid *gringos*. Maybe I'll blow your fucking half-breed brains out!"

Del stepped between them. "Carl—chill out. Do you have any water in the truck?"

"In the cooler."

Del shook his head as Carl just stood there."

"Carl, I was asking for a reason. Get me two bottles."

Carl fetched the two bottles and then looked a little miffed as Del took one and gave the Apache the other one.

Del reached down and helped the Apache to his feet. "Take a drink and relax. So you're saying there were three trucks and two were destroyed?"

The Apache shook his head. "No—no. There were four trucks."

Del took off his hat and wiped his brow. "Where was the fourth truck?"

The Apache pointed. "Over there."

Del still couldn't get a handle on it as Carl was pacing like a wild animal.

"OK, *amigo.* Tell me again where you were and what you saw."

"I was up in the rocks over there. No one see me. The Apaches don't trust me and the Mexicans would have killed me. The truck was on fire when I got here. There were dead Mexicans all over the place. Geronimo and Cochise were up there and the Apaches were over there."

Del whistled. "No wonder—they had them in a crossfire. It was suicide to try to attack them in the rocks. Then what happened."

"El Diablo, he send a man with a white flag and Geronimo he send a man with a white flag—a Mexican—and they meet up in the rocks. When El Diablo's man return, they talk for a while, then the man and three others jump in the fourth truck and drive off. El Diablo, he didn't have no cover then and the Apaches killed him and his bodyguards."

"Carl—go get the metal detector and run it over this area."

Del was still trying to process the Apache's story when Carl returned with the detector. It immediately went crazy as he passed it over the battle site. Del kicked at the ground with his boot and found several spent cartridges.

Carl threw the detector down and ran over to Del. "Del—he was telling the truth. Maybe this isn't over."

Del was still pensive. "If he's telling the truth, El Diablo is dead."

"But, but he said that some of the gang got away."

Del motioned the Apache over. "What happened to the bodies and the trucks that were destroyed?"

"I don't know. I don't know. I was scared of both of them—the Mexicans and the Apaches. I left when El Diablo was killed."

"And no one on the reservation said anything about this?"

"I told you. They don't trust me because they say I work for you and the Garcias."

Carl was animated. "Del, Del—Diablo may be dead, but the gang is still alive. Maybe things will be just like before."

Del wiped his brow again and took a swig of water. "I don't know what we're dealing with here—somebody who can make bodies and trucks disappear, just vanish in thin air. Nothing is going to be just like before."

Carl looked at the Apache who had moved away and then back to Del. "What are we going to do with him?"

"What do you think we're going to do with him? He's a liability to us. You know what to do."

Carl walked over to the Apache and calmly shot him twice in the chest. Only then did the word liability register on him. When he turned around Del shot Carl twice in the chest with the throwaway pistol.

Del then placed the pistol in the Apache's hands and fired off one more round to leave a trace of residue. After doing so, he laughed to himself. After a few hours in the desert there would be little left to analyze. That's why there wasn't any desert CSI.

He then extracted the roll of bills from Carl and took all but two hundred dollars, which he put back in Carl's pocket. He hesitated for a moment and then spoke to the corpse, "Sorry, buddy, but you made your own bed and became too much of a liability. I tried to help you, but you wouldn't listen. See you in Hell."

Del took off his gloves and called Kelsey on his cell phone, almost panicking when he had trouble getting a signal. She finally answered. "Kelsey, listen to me carefully. Don't speak—just listen. I'm in the desert near the low hills. I'm going to walk toward the highway. Come pick me up immediately. Keep your phone on and we'll find each other."

Chapter Seventeen

Who's Your Daddy?

Sheriff's Office, Two Days Later

Jake was in his office reviewing some files when Rosa knocked on his door and said that Dylan was on the line. He picked up the phone. "So you didn't get shipwrecked or drown? We were worried about you."

Dylan laughed. "When I handed her the phone, thinking she wanted to say hi, she tossed it into the water. She thought we both needed a break from the events of the past. In some ways, I think she was right."

"In some ways? Was there trouble in Paradise?"

"I wouldn't say trouble, but some things have definitely changed."

"Duh!"

"Yeah … I get it, I think. How's Tom? Anything going on in the Dunes?"

"Tom's back in the saddle, but taking it easy for a bit. No fallout yet and very quiet. The Feds have been sniffing around the reservation asking questions, but I don't think they got anywhere. There is one interesting thing—which is why I was calling you in Key West."

"Which is?"

"When Tom was laid up he had me review some of his private files. One of them was for Carlos Garcia and Scooter."

"You said Carlos AND Scooter? Like together?"

"Like when Scooter visited him twice in prison."

Dylan exhaled. "What did Scooter get himself into?"

"The prison conversations were taped and from what we can make out, I mean—can you imagine Scooter trying to be sly? Scooter was trying to make a deal with Carlos."

"For the money?"

"Here's where it gets interesting. Apparently there was something else in the bag that was more valuable than the money."

"More valuable than three million bucks?"

"Apparently, but get this—Carlos didn't appear to know what it was, just that something was missing."

"So let me see if I've got this straight. One total moron was trying to make a deal with another total moron over something that moron number two knew nothing about?"

"That pretty much sums it up and we know how that worked out for Scooter. Also, we checked with the prison to see if that whole religion things was a hoax, but the old Padre, the one Carlos claimed mentored him, died a couple months ago."

"I can't say I'm surprised, but if he was acting, he deserves an award. Have you heard anything more about him?"

"Nada, which may just be the calm before the storm. Oh, our pal from Chicago, the gang crimes detective, Sandowski, says he has an informant who has infiltrated one of the Latin gangs the Garcias supplied. Apparently, supplies have dried up and there's tension in the hood. He faxed me the sheets on a couple of shooters who are coming down to investigate. And get this—he says they're armed and dangerous."

Dylan laughed. "Well they should feel right at home."

Jake laughed. "Exactly what I said. One more thing—he says the gang has protection down here with one or more of the alphabet boys, but they don't know who."

"Alphabet boys?"

"You know, FBI, DEA, ATF, ICE."

"I always wondered who has the franchise on the blue windbreakers? That's gotta be a moneymaker."

Jake laughed again. "Yeah, no shit. He says all they know is they refer to them as *nada ojos*, no eyes—like the guy with the reflecting sunglasses in *Cool Hand Luke*."

"That doesn't narrow the playing field much."

"Tom has some suspicions. Sandowski's going to give us their flight info and we're going to try to tail them and find out."

"Speaking of flight plans, I'll let you know mine as soon as I book a plane. Over and out, *amigo*."

"You're catching on fast. Over and out."

As Jake was hanging up, Tom knocked on Jake's door and entered.

"Hey, Tom. I didn't know you were in the office. I was just talking with Dylan. He's coming home in a few days. I told him all was quiet so far."

"Well, it ain't quiet any longer. I just got a call from the reservation. A couple of Apache kids stumbled onto a couple of dead bodies in the desert—what's left of them—and a red Cadillac Escalade."

Jake bolted up out of his chair. "There's only one of those around here that I know of."

Tom replied, "Robin."

"Didn't you just see him a couple of days ago?"

"Roger that. Tell Rosa to call the coroner—lot of good it will do now. Oh, and grab some crime scene tape."

As Jake was leaving his office he turned to Tom. "Should we call the Feds—maybe his partner?"

Tom was silent for a moment and then shook his head. "Let's see what we've got first. Remember what Sandowski said. Maybe this wasn't a random act."

The Desert Crime Scene

Tom and Jake were drenched with sweat as they watched the coroner examine the remains. The coroner approached, wiping the sweat from his face. "As near as I can tell, maybe forty-eight hours. It doesn't take long for the varmints. Lucky anything is left."

Tom nodded. "Don't need cremation in the desert—that's for sure. I called for the hearse. We're going to check out the scene now. Thanks for coming out."

A truck pulled up to the scene with two passengers. Tom recognized one of the Apache elders. When they exited the truck, Tom called out, "You guys stay outside the tape. I'll be over in a few minutes."

The Apaches nodded.

Tom and Jake put on plastic gloves and walked over to the bodies—what remained. Tom picked up the Glock, checked the cylinder—two bullets missing—and bagged it. He then stooped and took the pistol from the Indian's hand. He turned to Jake. "That was one tough Indian. He was shot at close range and didn't lose his grip on his gun."

Jake looked at Tom. "You're being sarcastic, right?"

"Totally. Look at this. They call this a throwaway or drop pistol—numbers filed off, handle taped up."

"What are you saying?"

"Maybe I watch too many cop shows, but I'd bet money that the Indian was shot first and the gun planted on him."

He checked the cylinder and three bullets were missing—two bullets missing from the Glock and three from the drop gun. "You know where the other bullet went?"

Jake shook his head. "I've got no idea."

"Whoever planted the gun fired off another round with the Indian's hands on it. That would leave residue, implying the Indian had fired the weapon. That is, if the vultures and coyotes hadn't got here first. The average Joe Six-pack wouldn't even think of that. Somebody had some experience."

"Then who killed Robin? I mean, if that is Robin."

"Excellent question, my dear Watson. Who indeed? Bag this gun, too, and check out his ride."

Jake walked over to the Escalade. Tom took off his hat and wiped his brow as he walked over to where the Apaches were standing. The elder spoke first. "His name is Benjamin. He's been missing for two days."

Tom wiped his brow again. "Well, first of all—I'm sorry. You have any idea what happened?"

Jake approached with the bag of cocaine. "This was in the glove compartment."

"Put it in an evidence bag and check the pockets of both victims."

Jake left and the elder resumed. "He was always in and out of trouble, but not any violence I know of. He was known to sell drugs for the Garcias, so he was an outcast to many. His friends said that the Feds picked him up two days ago and he left with them."

Tom furrowed his brow. "You said Feds—plural. You sure about that?"

"His best friend, Little Dog, they call him Barney, said that two *Federales* picked him up in a red truck. He said Benjamin got in. He wasn't forced."

"Yeah, well the other body—what's left—belonged to a DEA agent name of Carl."

The Apaches looked at each other. "We know of him. He was bad medicine."

Jake approached again with two bags of items. "It was Robin all right—badge, driver's license, wallet, about two hundred bucks, ring, watch, and bracelet. The Apache had an ID, a couple of dollars in change, and a necklace."

Tom nodded. "Give them the Apache's stuff and go get me the drop gun."

When Jake returned with the bagged gun, Tom handed it to the Elder. "Don't take it out of the bag. I just want to know if you recognize the gun."

The Apaches looked at it closely and shook their heads. "We've never seen a gun like this before. New guns are cheap around here—no reason to have something like this and like I said, Benjamin had his share of troubles, but he wasn't into guns and violence. He sold drugs to be popular—or so he thought."

A hearse pulled up and two attendants brought out body bags.

"Sheriff, can we take the bodies?"

"Leave the Apache."

Tom turned to the Apaches. "I'll let you take him. If you hear anymore let me know."

After the Apaches departed, Jake asked Tom, "You think we should have called the Feds?"

Tom appeared to gaze off into the horizon. "Under normal circumstances, whatever that is in the desert, but like you saw—there wasn't much left to see. You take the Escalade to the station. I'll pay a visit to Batman."

Del's Mansion

Del's two cars were parked in the circular driveway when Tom arrived. When he rang the doorbell, Kelsey greeted him.

"Can I help you?"

"Ma'am, is Del home? Tell him the sheriff would like a word with him."

Tom's shirt was still soaked with sweat. Del came to the door in swimming trunks, T-shirt and ever-present reflective sunglasses. He had a bottle of Corona in one hand.

"Sheriff, what a surprise. You look like you could use a dip in the pool. Come in where it's cool."

"Thanks. Actually, we need to talk. How about the patio?"

"Works for me. That's where I was. How about a cold beer?"

"That would be great."

"Glass? Bottle?"

"Bottle's fine, thanks."

They sat down in the shade of the patio. Tom savored the cold beer as he took in the huge pool and manicured grounds.

"So, Sheriff, to what do I owe the honor?"

"You can call me Tom." Tom sat his beer on the table and leaned forward. "Del, I'm afraid I have some bad news."

"Is there any other kind in the desert?"

"I hear ya, but this hits close to home. We got a call this morning. Some Indian kids playing in the desert came across two bodies—one Anglo and one Apache. Appears to be a double killing. The Anglo was your partner, Carl."

Del bolted up—a little too dramatically, thought Tom. He walked to the edge of the pool and gazed off into the horizon for a few moments before returning to his seat.

"Sheriff—er, Tom, when did you get the call?"

"Like I said, this morning. All we knew at the time was there were two dead bodies. By the time we got there, there wasn't much left. Coroner said they'd been dead for two days probably. We bagged his body, personal effects, and the weapons and drove his truck to the station."

Del appeared deep in thought.

"Tom, I'm going to have to take you into my confidence and, obviously, we're taking over from here—including the return of all of the property and evidence. You see—we've been watching Carl for over a year as part of an internal affairs investigation into drug trafficking. This is and must remain confidential. You understand me?"

Tom took a drink and savored it a bit, sensing Del's unease. "I seem to recall that's what you said about the border patrol agent a few years back. Hank, wasn't it?"

Del hesitated, but the sunglasses prevented Tom from reading any eye movement.

"You've got a good memory. The two killings could actually be connected."

Tom seem surprised. "Two killings? I didn't know Hank was killed."

Del was now visibly nervous. "I just, er, I just assumed he was killed. I mean to just—to just disappear like that. Anyway, we had pretty solid evidence that Carl had gone over to the other side. He was still my partner and I didn't want to believe it—still don't. It's like I'm surprised, but I'm not at the same time."

"What in the world would make him do that?"

Del scoffed, "Money—what else. It's always about the money."

Tom took his time looking around. "I guess I don't get it. I mean—look at what you've got here."

Tom was pretty sure Del squirmed at that last comment. "Tom, hold that thought. I've got to hit the head and now I can use something a little stiffer. How about some Scotch or Tequila?"

"If you don't mind, another beer will do fine."

Tom fanned himself with his hat and digested the conversation while Del was gone. Del returned with the drinks.

"You were saying, Tom?"

"Oh, I was just saying this is quite a spread you've got here."

"We got lucky with some investments. Dot com stuff and got out before the crash. What a wild ride. Who knows about this so far?"

"If you mean about the killings—me, my deputy, the coroner and a couple of Apaches. Oh—and the hearse guys. The coroner and the hearse guys don't know the identities. It seems like Carl and you are both pretty well known on the reservation, though."

"Yeah, well we've been there a few times on investigations. They got a real problem with the kids. All they want to do is get high."

"Plenty of town kids and Anglos that could apply to as well."

"I hear you. Let's talk about the killings."

"The Apache's name was Benjamin. Apparently, he's been selling dope for the Garcias."

"Benjamin—I think I know who you're talking about. By the way, what the fuck happened to the Garcias? You guys hear anything?"

"I didn't know anything happened to them."

"No kidding? It seems like they just up and disappeared without a trace. Poof. And you know what the Apaches say? They say that

Geronimo and Cochise took on an army of the Garcias and killed most of them."

Tom offered his bottle in a toast, but Del didn't seem to get it. "That would be great news. Make your life easier, certainly." Tom chuckled "Those Indian legends don't die easily."

"Yeah—great news if it's true. What do you think happened with Carl and the Indian?"

"Can't say for certain. Mind you, after two days in the desert there wasn't much left. Carl had a Glock minus two shells and the Indian had what looked like one of those throwaway guns, numbers filed off and handle taped up. It was missing three shells. The Apaches said that Benjamin's best friend swears that he was picked up by two *Federales*, not just Carl. You know anything about that?"

Del took a long drink before replying. "Number one, those Indian boys are stoned most of the time. Number two, I haven't heard or seen Carl since Tuesday morning, two days ago. I'm pretty sure he knew we were on to him. Maybe it was a drug deal gone bad?"

Tom felt he had gotten what he came for and saw no reason to prolong the meeting.

"You might be right. There was a good deal of white powder in Carl's glove compartment. We bagged that, too."

"Well, like I said, we've got to pull some rank here and I hope we can keep this as quiet as possible. It's a little embarrassing when the good guys are dirty too. How about another beer?"

"No thanks, or I'll never leave. Did Carl have a wife or family?"

"A wife—no kids, thank God. I'll handle that, as well."

Tom finished his beer and stood up to leave. "You can stop by the station and get the effects. I'll check with the state's attorney about the weapons, drugs, and vehicle."

Del stood up. "We'll let the suits sort that out. You come back anytime. I meant to ask, is your body all healed?"

"It takes a little longer to heal, the older you get, but I'll be fine."

Del walked Tom to his truck. "Good to hear. You take care, now."

"Thanks. We'll be in touch."

Sheriff's Office

Jake was sitting on the edge of the desk. Tom was in his chair.

Tom gestured with his hands. "We always called them Batman and Robin. Kinda figured if one was dirty, both were."

"So Del said they knew about Carl?"

"Said they suspected him. The problem is, they're the Feds and they can pull rank on us, which is what they are doing."

"What about the Apaches saying that two Feds picked the Indian kid up?"

"He's tough. Said those kids are stoned most of the time. He's probably right. It would be an Indian kid's word against the word of the senior Fed in the region. Mind you, the kid didn't say it was Del—just that there were two of them."

"Did Carl have a family?"

"Wife, no kids. Del said he would notify her."

"You think she might know something?"

"Maybe—probably, but she'll be off limits. I'll tell you what we'll do. Take the ring out of the evidence bag. Bag it separately. If that bag got misplaced, maybe I can drop it off with the wife—honest mistake."

"Won't he see through that?"

"It'll be too late. I know he was playing me—trying to play me. He was way too cool and those glasses help hide his emotions. I think he knows I have my suspicions, but we've got to be careful not to spook him with the shooters coming down. We need to find out who the contact is."

"It's quite a coincidence isn't it?"

"Is what?"

"As I recall, you had doubts about him years ago and all of a sudden the border patrol agent disappears. Del said he was under investigation.

Now, his partner turns up dead and it turns out he was under investigation too."

Tom smiled. "You're gonna be a fine lawman someday, Son. In fact, you are already."

"Thanks. You believe in coincidences?"

"Never have."

Del's Mansion

Del opened his safe. He donned his gloves and lifted out a package of cocaine even larger than the one he gave Carl. He put the coke in a duffel bag with three thousand dollars of Carl's money and a bottle of champagne.

Carl's House

Del pulled up in his Lexus. A late model Mustang was parked in the driveway. The garage was closed and all of the blinds in the house were drawn. Del got out with his bag and walked to the door. He could hear music inside. He rang the bell and heard voices.

Carl's wife Angie answered the door. She had likely been a knockout in another time and place, but it was obvious, as the locals might say, that she had been ridden hard and put away wet too many times. She was tatted up on her neck and back and both nipples and her belly were pierced. It was obvious to Del that she had been on a coke binge as her hair was mussed and any makeup had long since worn off. Oh—and she had a spiked collar around her neck. She was wearing white bikini panties and had one of Carl's long sleeve shirts on, but unbuttoned. She cracked the door slightly.

"Angie, let me in. We need to talk."

Angie stepped aside and Del entered. The living room was in total disarray. A mirror was on the coffee table with coke residue and a gold razor blade. Empty glasses and full ashtrays completed the scene. The stereo was blaring music that Del couldn't identify. He walked over and turned it off. Then turned back to Angie.

"Angie, sit down so we can talk."

Angie got right in his face, open shirt and all. Del's eyes opened wide and a smile came to his face.

"Fucking A we need to talk, but I can talk while I'm standing," said as she almost stumbled over the coffee table. "Where the hell is Carl and where is his payoff?"

Del winced at the mention of the word payoff. He had hoped that Carl had been more discreet—particularly with a cokehead wife—but knew that would have been too much to ask. That was reinforcement, if he needed any, for why Carl had to go. Carl would have had the right to remain silent—he just wouldn't have had the ability.

She continued. "I know all about you guys, so don't fuck with me!"

Del held up his left hand for her to calm down. Just then a drop-dead brunette appeared from one of the bedrooms holding a leash in her hand and smiling seductively. She was totally naked except for black bikini panties. Del was momentarily stunned.

"Whoa, who do we have here?"

"That's Bobbie, but she's leaving because she's a coke whore and I'm out of coke—so go ahead and leave you fucking whore."

Bobbie turned to leave. "Whatever."

Del took charge. "Everybody hold on a minute. No one's going anywhere. First, I've got some news and Angie, you're going to sit down for it. You too Bobbie."

Del set the duffel bag down, but remained standing. Angie's attention went to the bag.

"What's in the bag?"

Del held up his hand again. "I'll get to that in a minute. Angie, Carl was killed in a shootout."

Angie jumped up. "What happens to me? Carl looted our bank account. I'm broke and out of coke. I'm totally screwed."

Del had to smile at the lack of sorrow or emotion. "That's what I'm here for. You think I wouldn't take care of you?"

Del put the bag on the table and opened it. He pulled out a roll of bills. "Let's see what we have here ... looks like three thousand dollars."

Angie rushed over and grabbed the money. She hugged and kissed Del. She then turned to Bobbie. "Bobbie, call José—now! Tell him we need an eight ball."

Del quickly called out to Bobbie. "Bobbie, honey—sit back down. No one's calling anybody."

He reached back in the bag and pulled out the bag of coke. He held it up for all to see. Angie hugged Del again as he dangled the bag of coke.

"Baby, baby, baby, I was wrong about you."

She lunged for the coke, but Del continued to tease her by holding it out of her reach. "Who's your daddy?"

Angie finally understood the game. Del asked again, "I said, who's your daddy?"

"Baby, you're my daddy!"

Angie rubbed up against him seductively as he tossed the bag to Bobbie, who spoke for the first time. "Oh, great. Now you'll have fucked the whole family."

Del reached into the bag for the champagne, but hesitated at Bobbie's comment. "What is that supposed to mean?"

Angie scowled at Bobbie. "Don't pay attention to her. That's just white trash talk."

Bobbie shot back. "Like you aren't white trash too."

"At least I'm not trailer park trash you fucking slut."

Del smiled at the catfight as he stepped between them. "Ladies, ladies. Hold on a minute. This is a solemn occasion that calls for a toast to the dearly departed. Angie—trade panties with Bobbie and lose the shirt. The grieving widow is supposed to wear black. And, Bobbie—hang on to that leash. We may need to keep Angie under control with her grief and all."

Bobbie and Angie exchanged panties and then Bobbie fastened the leash to Angie's collar without any protest from Angie.

Del popped the cork and took a drink from the bottle, then seemed to be lost in thought for a moment. "I think I know exactly what you two need and I'm going to try to arrange it."

Angie finally noticed the gloves. "Hey, what's with the gloves by the way?"

"I cut my hands on some barbed wire. Now it's time for that toast."

As Del raised the bottle, Bobbie chimed in. "He doesn't want his prints around here, you idiot."

Del raised his eyebrows and looked at Bobbie in a new light, as Angie slid down his front and was now on her knees. He raised the bottle again. "Here's to Carl. I hope he's in a better place now. I know I am."

CHAPTER EIGHTEEN

Capiche?

Sheriff's Office

The sheriff's office was abuzz with activity. The shooters from Chicago were due to arrive; they were waiting for Dylan's flight information and, to top it all, Del had called the sheriff to advise him that, owing to the condition of the body and the widow's wishes, a burial service had been hastily arranged for that afternoon.

Jake was having his morning Joe at his desk when Tom entered. "Here's the flight info for the shooters. Their flight gets in at thirteen hundred hours, so if you leave here by eleven, you'll have plenty of time to park and get to the gate."

Jake nodded.

"You can lay back a bit on the highway. We know what direction they're going. Call me when you get near the Oasis and I may meet you and take over the tail. It depends on how I make out on my end."

"No luck yesterday dropping by her house?"

"I went by a couple of times and both times Del's car was parked in the driveway. I'm going to Plan B, which is to approach her at the cemetery service and pass along my condolences. I'll invite her to drop by and get Carl's ring."

"You think she's in any danger?"

"Hard to read it any other way with Carl out of the picture. It all depends on how much she knows. I'll have my cell with me. Call me when you get to the gate."

"Roger that. Oh, any word from Dylan?"

"All I know is he's trying to get in this afternoon. That's a lot of excitement for one day in Mayberry, as Sandowski calls it." They both laughed. "He's in for a real surprise."

Tucson Airport

Jake waited at the gate for the shooters, but they didn't get off the plane. He walked back to the main counter of US Airways and approached an airline rep.

"Ma'am, I need some help, please. I was supposed to meet a couple of associates on Flight 90 that just arrived from Chicago, but they weren't on the plane."

He consulted his paper. "Their names are Edwin Santana and Felix Herrera."

The rep checked her computer. "Sir, it seems like Mr. Santana cancelled his flight earlier today and changed destinations. I don't see anything for Mr. Herrera."

"Huh. I must have missed the message. Do you happen to know the new destination?

"It looks like Acapulco and that's on United."

As Jake walked away from the counter, deep in thought, he almost ran smack into Carl's wife Angie and her girlfriend Bobbie. They were walking hurriedly through the airport, oblivious of everyone else. The opposite was true for everyone else, as Angie and Bobbie both wore revealing outfits and were turning heads. The sky cap with their luggage was struggling to keep up. Jake barely avoided a collision and dodged them at the last moment.

He followed them to the United counter, where they got in line. He stepped in behind their baggage. When they were motioned up to the counter, he edged as close as possible.

The United rep greeted them. "Good afternoon ladies. May I help you?"

Bobbie handed the tickets to the rep. "We, ladies," Angie chuckled, "are going to Acapulco and we need adjoining seats. We're very close."

Angie added, "Very, very close."

They both laughed.

Apache Dunes Cemetery

It was approaching 2:00 p.m. in the sunbaked cemetery when the very small graveside service concluded. An American Legion detachment fired a salute to the Army vet, which was followed by Taps played by a high school band member. The so-called mourners consisted of Tom, his Deputy Homer, Del, and a couple of the local old ladies who never missed an opportunity to grieve.

The widow was MIA. After the service, Tom was trying to get a handle on things when he noticed a black Lincoln Town Car parked by the hillside. He turned to find Homer and saw Del approaching.

"Thanks for coming, Sheriff. He was a good man."

"It's apparent he touched a lot of lives. Was the widow too consumed with grief to attend?"

Del smiled. "Something like that."

Tom's cell phone rang. It was Jake.

"Excuse me for a minute. I've gotta take a personal call."

Tom walked out of hearing range and answered the phone. "Jake, what's up? I've been waiting for your call."

"Change of plans apparently. I was at the gate, but our friends weren't on the plane. I waited a while, then went to the airline counter and was told that one of them changed his destination to Acapulco at the last minute."

"What about the other one?"

"Nada. He just cancelled his flight. It gets more interesting. I'll bet you didn't see the widow at the cemetery."

"How'd you know that?"

"As I was leaving the counter, who do I almost bump into but Carl's wife and a girlfriend who could stop traffic—in fact, she did in the airport. Neither one was in what you would call mourning clothes. Quite to the contrary."

"You have any idea where they were heading?"

"You don't pay me minimum wage just because I'm handsome. They don't know me, so I got in line behind them at the United counter, and guess where they're going?"

"Don't tell me—Acapulco?"

"That's why you're the sheriff. You want me to head back?"

"Might as well as we still haven't heard from Dylan. Call me when you get back."

"Roger that. What do you make of all this?"

"I don't know. The Apaches would say there's a bad moon on the rise."

When Tom hung up from Jake he walked back to where Del was waiting—still with a smile on his face. Homer was sitting on a bench nearby playing a game on his phone. It was clear that Tom was agitated.

"Well, the widow has apparently decided to do her grieving in Acapulco."

"I was just getting ready to tell you that when your phone rang. The doctor thought it might be too much for her."

It was all Tom could do to keep his composure. He shook his head. "It's like Yogi Berra said, 'It ain't over till it's over.'" He paused. "Now tell me what you know about that car over there."

Del appeared to squint at the car. "If I was to guess, I'd say those are Carl's EYEtalian bookies tryin' to figure out how to collect from a corpse. Rumor has it, he was into them big time. Maybe they'd like a word with the missus."

Tom called over to Homer. "Get me a ticket book out of my truck and meet me down by that Town Car. Del, you take care now and let's hope the widow does the same."

Del now had a big grin. "Sheriff, she's a big girl. I've got my own family to worry about. Mexico's a dangerous place for tourists these days—or so I've heard."

Tom just stared at him. "By the way, speaking about Mexico. How do they say no eyes in Spanish?"

"*Nada ojos*. Why do you ask?"

Now it was Tom's turn to smile. "Just curious is all. *Hasta luego*."

"*Hasta luego*."

Tom walked down the hill toward the car and Homer met him with the ticket book. Tom approached the driver's side and motioned for Homer to go to the rear. Inside the car were two Italians with shades, silk shirts, and enough jewelry to make Mr. T jealous. The car was running with the air conditioner on. Tom took out his night stick and tapped on the driver's window. The driver lowered the window and glared at Tom.

"Whatta you want?"

"What do I want? I want a blow job from Jennifer Lopez, but what I need is your driver's license and registration."

"What the fuck for? We're just sitting here minding our own business. We didn't do nothing wrong."

"No kidding. What about the busted taillights."

"What busted taillights?"

Tom motioned to Homer, who shattered both taillights. The driver and the passenger both started to exit, but stopped as Tom drew his pistol.

The driver looked at the gun and then back to Tom. "What—you're gonna shoot us? I don't think so."

Tom replied very calmly. "There's only one way to find out. Homer, tell those diggers to hang around. We might need two more holes."

The Italians looked at each other and got back in the car.

"You boys apparently don't understand the customs or the law around here. Some things are still sacred around here—like funerals. Now, you already have a five-hundred-dollar fine for the busted taillights. How bad do you want to make this?"

The driver turned to his companion. "You believe this fucking guy?"

He handed Tom his license and registration.

Tom looked at them for a moment before handing them back. "Now, what are a couple of guys from Las Vegas doing at a cemetery in Apache Dunes?"

"The stiff—er, the departed guy was a former client. We wanted to pay our respects to his widow, but she ain't here, apparently. You happen to know where she is?"

"She was too consumed with grief."

"No kidding? I never saw that sensitive side of her."

"She had to hide it well, with all of her civic responsibilities."

"Don't tell me. She was chairman of the local pole-dancing society?"

Tom had to smile. "They're talking about making it an Olympic sport."

Now the companion was animated. "Ooh, ooh, Sonny, you know who would win a medal—"

The driver, Sonny, cut him off. "Vince—it was a fucking joke."

Sonny turned to Tom and shook his head. "Busted taillights ain't my only problem."

Tom took his time wiping his sunglasses before putting them on again. "I'll tell you what I'll do. I'm going to forget about the ticket."

"What about the lights?"

"Don't push your luck. If I see you around here later, those lights will be the least of your problems. *Capiche*?"

Sonny turned to Vince. "You believe this fucking guy? *Capiche*, he says?"

Sonny flipped off his chin and drove away. Homer was smiling, but Tom was still agitated. They walked to Tom's truck. When they got in, the phone rang. Tom didn't look to see who the caller was he just answered—and gruffly.

"This better be good."

It was Detective Sandowski. "Whoa, what happened? Did Aunt Bea burn your bacon this morning?"

"Sorry. I'm having a shitty day."

"Poor baby. Why don't you come up to Chicago and have some fun? Let's see—so far today, we ended a standoff with a guy who killed his common law wife, her mother, and six kids with six different last names. You know why? Because the kids ate all of the Captain Crunch. We asked him, Why'd you kill everybody? Know what he said? They was there."

"*Touché*! I need to talk to you more often. So far today every one of our plans has blown up on us—that includes the shooters, who changed destinations."

"Acapulco. That's what I'm calling about. I just got the news."

Tom banged the steering wheel. "Fuck! I knew it."

"Knew what?"

"It's the wife. She was a no-show at the funeral and Jake literally almost ran into her at the airport in Tucson—buying a ticket for Acapulco."

"You got any friends in the insurance business who will make us beneficiaries of a life insurance policy?"

"Don't even joke about that."

"Who said I was joking?"

"You have any ideas?"

"None that don't include a private jet."

"Dylan is supposed to be flying in this afternoon, but not on a private jet."

"Sheriff, this isn't the type of situation you want an Ivy Leaguer to handle."

Tom started laughing.

"What'd I say was so funny?"

"Nothing. He was still laughing. "It's hard to explain. Let's just say he has an alter ego."

"Listen to me. He may have a fucking alter ego, but the odds are still two to one and these guys are dangerous—especially Santana."

"It's a long story. Let's just say he might call those manageable odds."

"Maybe you ain't listening to me. These guys are professional shooters. Your boy ever pull a trigger?"

"Max, everybody around here knows how to shoot. Someday over a bottle of good tequila, I'll tell you a story—the real story, and even then you may not believe it."

"I'm starting to feel like this could be the start of a good friendship."

"Just like *Casablanca*."

"*Casablanca, Cool Hand Luke*—you guys must be movie buffs?"

"Jake certainly is. He said Classic Cinema was the only class he attended at SC."

"I remember him playing there. A white running back in the program is almost unheard of. Didn't he have a nickname?"

"Cochise."

"Wait a minute. Didn't the Indians claim that it was Geronimo and Cochise who wiped the Garcias out?"

Tom chuckled. "Something like that."

"I know the other one, Dylan, played college ball, but I never followed the Ivy League."

"I'm stunned. I always pictured you with a boater, raccoon coat, and a Yale pennant singing 'Boola Boola.'"

"Yeah, fuck you too. Now let me take a wild guess. Was his nickname Geronimo?"

"Pay the man, Shirley!"

"Are you shitting me? Those guys were fucking insane to take on the Garcias."

Tom just laughed again. "They think they're still playing cowboys and Indians. It's a game to them."

"Some game."

"Back to the matter at hand. Even if I could get Dylan to divert to Acapulco, how do we locate them in time?"

"That's the easy part. I've got a geek here who can find out where they're staying in less than an hour."

"I'll try to reach him and get back to you."

"Fucking unbelievable! I think I'm dealing with Gomer and Otis and it turns out to be Geronimo and Cochise! You'll have to get me one of those Indian names."

"I'm thinking Pocahontas."

"Everybody's a fucking wise ass!"

After Tom hung up with Sandowski he sent an email to Dylan asking him to call him immediately. Dylan called within minutes.

"Hey, Tom, what's up?"

"Where are you?"

"At the airport in Key West, waiting for my plane. Why?"

"You feel like switching your destination to Acapulco?"

"Who wouldn't want to go to Acapulco? What's going on?"

"Long story, short, I need to get a message to someone whose life is in danger, but I don't want you to take any unnecessary risks. We'll cover the cost of the trip."

"I've got nothing better to do. Tell me more."

CHAPTER NINETEEN

Two Dead Bodies and an Invitation to Lunch

Dylan's jet approached for landing in Acapulco. The city and surrounding hills were sparkling with lights. He'd had to switch planes in Atlanta, but the flight to Acapulco had been enjoyable as he sat next to a great guy, Marvin, who flew choppers in Iraq and Afghanistan. He had some great stories to tell, but seemed to change the subject anytime Dylan inquired about his current occupation. Marvin was also staying at the Princess and after they retrieved their bags they decided to share a taxi to the hotel.

Back in Apache Dunes, Tom had fallen asleep in his office chair when his cell phone rang.

He fumbled with it while trying to answer. "Yeah?"

It was Sandowski. "Did I wake you?"

"I—I just nodded off apparently. I stayed at the office tonight."

"Have you heard from Geronimo?"

"Not yet, but he should have landed. He said he would call from the hotel—the Princess. What's up?"

"What's up is that one of the shooters was supposed to be a punk named Felix Herrera. My guys were on the street yesterday looking for my CI, who dropped off the radar screen, and guess who they run into—Felix Herrera. They asked Felix if he'd seen my boy and Felix said he took a trip to Acapulco—a last minute change of plans."

"You got a name for me?"

"Normally, I wouldn't say it – even over the phone, but this ain't normal. His name is Davey Lopes—L-O-P-E-S. Just like the baseball player—used to play for the Dodgers."

"Keep your phone on. I'll pass it on to Dylan when he calls. Should be anytime now."

"Tom, I gotta bare my soul a bit. This kid is like a son to me—like you said Dylan is to you. If anything happens to him it's gonna get real personal. I don't have a lot to show for my life—two failed marriages, a daughter who hates me, with good reason, I guess, and more bad relationships than I can count. Saving this kid might be the only good thing I ever did, but then he wanted to be a cop like me and wouldn't take no for an answer. He's been undercover for three years now and due for a promotion, because most guys don't last on the street that long."

Tom was silent as he processed the information. "Keep your phone on."

Acapulco Princess, Three in the Morning

Dylan was in his room trying to call Tom, but having trouble getting a line. Maybe it was the time, he thought. He hadn't been to bed yet and was nursing a Dos Equis when he finally got a connection. Tom answered on the fourth ring.

"Yeah?"

"I've been trying to call, but couldn't get through."

Tom reached for the light switch. "What time is it?"

"It's just past three here."

"Did you find the girls?"

Dylan hesitated a bit. "Tom, this is pretty messed up. I got here as fast as I could—got a taxi right away, but it was still too late. By the time I arrived, the place was crawling with *Federales*. I knew then it wasn't good. I had to wait outside with the other arrivals for at least an hour before they let us check in. That was a little after midnight. After I got my room, I went down to the bar and hung out for a while. A large tip later, here's what I found out. They're calling it a murder–suicide, a lover's quarrel between the blonde named Angie and a Mexican, but not either Santana or Herrera."

"Did you get the dead guy's name?"

"Lopes with an S—Davey Lopes."

"Holy shit!"

"You know the guy?"

"I heard his name for the first time a few hours ago. It turns out he is like an adopted son to Sandowski, the detective from Chicago."

"Oh man, that's messed up. What happened to the two other guys?"

"Sandowski said they switched Herrera and Lopes at the last minute. Lopes had been an undercover informant for three years. They must've found out. Santana is the main triggerman. He must have done the hits, but where's the other girl?"

"I checked. The room was in just Angie's name. One of the guys in the bar said he saw her with another gal earlier, a knockout brunette, but she seems to have vanished—like Santana."

"Are the police still there? I mean, is there an investigation?"

"That's what I asked in the bar and they looked at me like I'm a dumb *gringo*. The bartender said this must be my first time in Mexico. He said there are so many dead bodies these days that they can't keep track of them all. He said Acapulco used to be off limits, but no place is off limits these days."

"OK, listen to me. Come home. It's over. Get some rest and get the first flight out. I'll have Jake pick you up."

"I can't just yet."

"What do you mean—you can't?"

"I've been invited to lunch today."

"You what? By who? You aren't making sense."

"I was in the bar and a little paranoid to start with. A guy appeared to be staring at me, but then he left. As I was getting ready to leave, he returned and came up to me. He had some nice tats of angels and crosses on his arms."

"Dylan—listen to me …"

"Wait—he asked me if I was Geronimo. When I asked who wanted to know, he said that Carlos wanted to take me to lunch and that he would pick me up at noon."

"Dylan—listen to me. Get on the first plane out. Come home. Do you hear me?"

"Tom, if they were going to kill me, I would be dead already. You said you had some questions about Carlos. Well, he's the only person who can answer them—and I saved his life at least twice, if not three times, so I think I'm safe today. Anyway, I told him that I'd meet Carlos here by the pool, on neutral ground."

"Can you hire some backup?"

"Believe it, or not, I think I have just the guy."

"Man, I would pay money to have somebody else tell Sandowski, although he already had bad vibes. He said if anything happened to his kid, things were going to get real personal. I don't think I'd want to be his enemy."

"It was bad enough with El Diablo, but now we've got a Latin gang from Chicago, a dangerous hit man, a mysterious female, and a bent Federal agent. Oh—and our old friend Carlos, whoever he really is. We need all the help we can get. I'll be back tomorrow night."

"Get me your flight info and I'll have Jake pick you up. And, Dylan—be careful, please."

A Modest Condo on Chicago's North Side

Sandowski was passed out on his sofa. There was an empty bottle of Jim Beam and several empty cans of Old Style beer on the end table to complement the overflowing ashtrays. He fell asleep holding a picture of Davey in his police uniform the day he graduated from the academy.

The phone rang and he struggled to get rid of the cobwebs, but, even then, dreaded to answer. He finally picked up, knowing it would be Tom, who dreaded just as much making the call.

"Don't say it. Don't fucking say it."

"I'm sorry. I'm really sorry."

Sandowski could be heard knocking the bottles over and making a guttural cry. Tom could only let it be. Sandowski tried to compose himself as much as possible and picked the phone up again.

"What happened? Do you know?"

"Dylan got there as fast as he could, but was too late. The story they're peddling is it was a murder–suicide, a lover's quarrel between Davey and the agent's wife. Just another day in Mexico, these days."

"What about Santana and the other broad?"

"Poof. Like they didn't exist."

"Where's Geronimo now?"

"Get this. He was in the bar trying to get information and one of Carlos Garcia's guys approaches him and says Carlos wants to have lunch with him."

"The Garcias are involved with this?"

"I don't see Carlos' connection to the wife, but he was there, so who knows?"

"Tell me that Geronimo's not going to meet him."

"Like I said earlier, you don't know him very well, but I have a feeling you're going to meet real soon."

"Tom, I told you, I got nothing more to lose and I won't—let this go."

"Max, if you could, that friendship we talked about wouldn't last very long."

"You don't know what that means to me. Is there a motel down there?"

"You think we put our friends up in motels? We'll have a place for you."

"I really appreciate that, but you know I'm coming heavy don't you?"

"I told you before—if you aren't armed around here, they'll think you're a tourist."

The Pool Café at the Acapulco Princess

Dylan was having coffee with Marvin, his seatmate from the plane.

"Dylan, what a hassle last night. When I finally got to my room I was dead."

Dylan replied, "That makes three apparently."

Marvin laughed. "Yeah—right."

"Listen, Marvin, I know we hardly know each other, but I need a favor. When I tell you what it is, if you're the least bit uncomfortable, just say no—no harm, no foul."

Marvin leaned forward, intrigued by the comment. "Talk to me."

"In about half an hour, a guy will be meeting me for lunch—someone I have some history with. I'm sure neither of us expected to run into the other in Acapulco, but one of his— let's say associates—ran into me last night and asked for the meet. I don't expect any trouble, but he will almost certainly have some, ah, friends with him."

Marvin smiled, "So you want me to be like the guy at the hospital in *The Godfather*?"

Now Dylan smiled. "That's exactly what I had in mind, but there won't be any shooting—not here. If there is anything you see that makes you uncomfortable, you just take off."

"You're a mysterious young man, Dylan. I have some secrets of my own and I could use an adrenaline rush."

"I'm not surprised, which is why I asked you. I really appreciate your help—and, again, I don't expect any trouble. In fact, I've saved this guy's life at least twice."

"I'm in. What do you want me to do?"

Dylan looked around. "Take that table over there and keep the shades on. Have a newspaper in front of you so that you could be hiding something."

Marvin lifted one end of his guayabera shirt, exposing what appeared to be a .38-caliber pistol in his waistband. "You mean something like this?"

Dylan seemed surprised at first, but then laughed. "I'm glad we're friends. Regardless, if anything goes wrong—this isn't your fight. Worry only about yourself."

"What's so hard about that? Self-preservation is the first rule of survival. Without it, the other rules don't matter."

"The hard part is looking serious, but I'm not sure you have another look."

They both laughed.

"Oh—and I'm buying lunch."

Marvin smiled. "If you don't, I know how to find you."

They both laughed again as they did a man hug and Marvin left for his new table.

Dylan ordered a mimosa and it had just arrived when Carlos showed up. He had two men with him. Carlos spoke to them briefly and directed them to a table on the opposite side of the café from where Marvin was sitting. Carlos then approached Dylan. They waived the waiter away.

"Geronimo, *mi amigo*. I didn't expect to see you again so soon."

Dylan didn't get up, rather motioned for Carlos to sit across from him.

"Me either, but it seems like wherever trouble is, you just happen to be nearby."

"Check this out, man. I was gonna say the same thing about you."

"Then I guess we're even."

"That's not the only way we're even, which is why I wanted to meet."

Dylan looked puzzled. "You lost me, as you tend to do."

"I'm gonna ignore the dis—like you tend to do. You saved my life and I don't forget that."

"I seem to recall saving it twice."

"Word, man—twice—but now I've saved your life twice so we're all even."

"I realize math wasn't one of your strong subjects—in fact, I don't think you had any strong subjects."

"There you go again."

"But, how do you figure you saved my life—and twice?"

Carlos lowered his shades and stared at Dylan. "Man, you can't be that naïve, and whatchu doin' coming to Mexico all alone?"

Dylan smiled. "Who said I was alone?"

That startled Carlos and he quickly scanned the café. Marvin lowered his paper just a bit, smiled, and gave a small wave. Carlos' guys saw the exchange and looked toward Carlos for direction. Carlos smiled as he shook his head and signaled for them to stand down. He turned back to Dylan.

"Fucking Geronimo, man. My mistake to ever underestimate you. It won't happen again, but, like I said, we're even—so there won't be no trouble today."

"You still haven't answered me. How did you save my life twice?"

Carlos pointed at his men.

"You see *mi amigo* on the left? The one with the scar on his cheek."

Dylan nodded.

"His name is Manuel Garcia. He's a cousin and he lost all three of his brothers that day in the desert. They all belonged to a cult called Santa Muerte, the saint of death. They believe the saint protects them from death, but the saint must have taken that day off and they blame you for that. Last night we were watching the crowd outside the hotel and who do I see? Fucking Geronimo! I remembered his vendetta and stopped him from bustin' a cap in your ass right then and there."

Dylan glanced over at Manuel, who was staring at him and then turned back to Carlos.

"That's one."

Carlos shakes his head and stares at Dylan. "That was numero dos. Like I said, you have a habit of showing up in the wrong place at the wrong time—like last night. Numero uno was on the boat, the Geronimo, in Key West."

Dylan was visibly caught off guard.

"What the hell are you talking about? How'd you know about the boat?"

Carlos studied Dylan for a moment and took a sip of water before replying.

"You don't have any idea, do you?"

"Not a clue and I don't like this game."

"This game?" Carlos laughed "*Amigo*, this ain't no fucking game. School's out. You're up to your ass in something you know nothing about and we're even."

Dylan was scrambling to try to figure things out. "Why don't you educate me? Let's start with last night. Were you involved in that? Or, do you just happen to appear wherever trouble is and you're never involved in it?"

Carlos was enjoying the moment. He laughed, again. "Check this out—you can believe me or not. It don't matter to me. I had nothing to do with last night and didn't know what was going down. We just heard that a couple of bad *hombres* were coming down from Chicago. There aren't many secrets down here."

"How about the boat?"

"That's a little more of a problem and I am involved in that. You see, there was something else in that duffel bag. Something a lot more valuable than the money—the three million."

"I'm all ears."

"The bag man in Chicago had his hands in the cookie jar and the cookie jar had over thirty million bucks in it. My uncle sent a couple of bozos to get the money and take care of the bag man, but one of them pops the guy before they got the money and wound up with only some deposit numbers, but no bank name. The guy had transferred the money offshore and only he knew where. Afraid of what my uncle would do to them, they put the bank information in the duffel bag. Then one of the shooters offed the other one and disappeared."

"If all that's true, why didn't you say anything that night in the cave? Or the next day?"

"Check this out, man, I didn't even know about it. My uncle's lawyers told my mouthpiece that something was missing and that that something was more valuable than the three million cash. We didn't say nothing, 'cause we didn't know nothing, and my uncle thinking I did was what kept me alive in prison. Then—get this—Scooter came to see me in prison and he was, like, trying to bargain with me, but he was trying to be like a spy or something and was talking in riddles. I got the impression he knew what was missing, but I still don't know what his game was. He was a strange dude."

"So how did you find out what was missing?"

"How did I find out? I found out when I was released from prison and my uncle's goons were ready to take a blow torch to me. They thought I knew. I had to tell him about you guys being out there. That's how he found out about Scooter and Scooter spilled the beans. If they hadn't gouged his eyes out, he would have led them to the cave."

"So you thought if Scooter knew, Dusty knew?"

"Check this out, man—you're having a hard time trying to figure out who I am and you need to do the same thing with some other people as well."

"Meaning Dusty?"

"You're a smart guy. You were the smartest guy in our class, by far, so you can't be dumb; you're just blind. That girl has some scars from you that might never heal. Bones heal, skin heals, but the heart's another thing. Four years is a long time to be away. When I found out what was missing, I naturally had to consider that she might have it and—guess what man? You believe in coincidences? The day after her brother's funeral the money was transferred from the Cayman account. Thirty million dollars—poof!!"

"You're telling me that Scooter figured out where the money was all by himself?"

"We both know that dog won't hunt. He had help and all signs point to Dusty. Maybe there were others."

"So you had her followed?"

"Followed? Followed? There were four pounds of plastic explosives and a timer on her boat when we found out she was leaving! Guess what? My guy was waiting to detonate the explosives when the boat cleared the harbor, but the boat turned around and came back to the docks. Why?" Carlos' voice was rising. "Because my guy calls me and tells me that Geronimo just got on the boat! That was the longest and toughest fifteen minutes of my life. I prayed, man. I couldn't forget that you saved my life—twice—so I tell my man the hit was off. So, Geronimo, we're even. *Comprende*?"

Dylan was pensive for a moment. "So you don't know for sure it was her?"

"Check this out, *amigo*—you don't know it wasn't. Now, I don't know about you, but I've sort of lost my appetite. I know you and Jake too well to know you will just walk away, but this doesn't concern you guys. That bag was there when you two left. That story about Geronimo we were taught as kids—the one where he held off the armies and bounty hunters for several months with a small band of warriors? In the end, they got him. You know that, right?"

"You forgot one thing: that was then and now's now."

"Go home, Geronimo."

Carlos stood up, but Dylan remained seated. They looked at each other for a moment and then Carlos walked away and motioned for his men to follow. Dylan called out to him.

"How do I get in touch with you if I need to?"

Carlos returned to the table and wrote his number on a napkin, then left without another word spoken.

Tucson Airport Later That Day

Jake was waiting by his SUV when Dylan approached with his bags. They did a man hug and then departed for Apache Dunes.

"I wasn't in favor of you going to Acapulco, by the way. It was a lost cause."

"Jake, I'm a big boy and it was good that I went. I heard some things I didn't want to hear, but needed to. I'm pretty confused right now, but it is what it is."

Jake looked over at him. "You feel like talking it out?"

Dylan leaned over his seat and got a pad and pen out of his bag.

"My edge was that I always tried to think in a linear fashion, rather than try to outsmart everybody. So let's see what we've got."

"OK, let's start with the double murder in the desert. All signs point to the DEA agent—right?"

Dylan made a chart. "Almost a no-brainer, but proving it is another thing—especially with a Fed."

"Don't forget—you're back in the desert. The jury may be us and Sandowski and I don't get the impression that he's a bleeding heart."

"What's his status?"

"Tom's been talking to him. Apparently he went through channels and got clearance for his boy's body to be shipped home. He's going to see that he gets a proper funeral with honors and then he's coming our way. My guess is a week or so."

"What about the dead gal?"

"As of this afternoon, no one has claimed the body."

"Any word on the other two—the shooter and the mystery gal?"

"Nada."

"OK, back to work. We've got the DEA agent for the double in the desert. Hey, that's kind of catchy. It's easy, then, to connect the dots to the hit on his partner's wife—tying up loose ends. Why take a chance, huh?"

"That's the way I see it. Can't see it any other way, but how did he orchestrate the hit?"

"Sandowski said the Chicago gang had protection on the border. If it was the DEA agents, that line goes straight to the gang and Santana. They found out about Sandowski's informant and decided to do a Groupon."

"A what?"

"A deal—kill two birds with one stone."

Jake pondered that for a moment. "I'm good with that. Hard to see it any other way. If we're right, Sandowski is gonna want dibs on the agent. Del's his name, and I wouldn't trade places with him for all the tea in China."

Dylan took a deep breath and closed his eyes. "Now it gets a little harder and a lot closer to home."

"I was wondering when we were going to get to that. You believe that Dusty's involved?"

"Jake, and this is just between us—I don't want to believe it, but it doesn't look good. I told you what Carlos said about the timing of the money transfer. Could that be just a coincidence? And, whether I believe it or not, Dusty came within a few minutes of getting blown up, and her Captain with her? That's our buddy Carlos."

Jake looked at Dylan and shook his head. "Don't say I didn't tell you."

"You told me I should have let him die. I know. Trust me, I won't make that mistake again."

"You think Carlos will try again?"

"He said the only reason he called it off was that I showed up unexpectedly and he owed me one. He says we're even now—so, yeah, he's not going to stop until he gets the money."

"I just thought of something: what if someone is trying to frame Dusty?"

"I've plowed that ground over and over and as much as I would like to believe it, I can't connect the dots on the timing. How do you explain the four-year window? I can't explain it and Dusty has changed."

The SUV swerved as Jake did a double take at Dylan. "Did you play without a helmet at Yale? Of course she's changed! We all have—even you, by the way."

"*Touché*!"

Jake smiled. "I've missed hearing you say that."

"What I mean, is that it's deeper than that. When we first got involved, she was fragile almost, but now it's way different. Not only is she no longer fragile—she's in control and she knows it. I hate to say this—and would only say it to you—but I can see Dusty doing this. Her eyes—you know what they say, the eyes are the windows to the soul? Her eyes are different. It's like I'm looking into a vacuum."

"So there was trouble in paradise?"

"Jake, it would be hard enough for any two people to reconnect after four years of different experiences. I know I broke her heart, but mine was broken too—we were kids. That's a rite of passage. But with Dusty—it's not like a scar. It's like a festering wound that never healed."

"Maybe we all need to breathe out a bit. You've had a ton of shit to process recently. All I can tell you is that Ashley loves her. They communicate frequently. Let's get back to our puzzle. Where are we?"

"Final chart. Can we connect Carlos to Del in any way?"

"This is just speculation, but if Carlos has taken his uncle's place—it isn't hard to imagine they would've met—particularly if the system remains the same. Ditto for Carlos and the guys up north."

"I don't know about you, but I didn't risk my life just to help Carlos take over the cartel."

"Your Glock is in the glove compartment, by the way."

"One more missing link—Santana and the other gal?"

"He's a contractor so she may not even be alive. If she is, we need to figure out why."

Jake's cell phone rang.

"Jake here. He paused. "Roger that, we're almost home. I'll see you in the morning."

He turned to Dylan. "You have a message from Dusty. Said she tried to reach you, but couldn't. Said she had to make an unexpected trip to Switzerland to see an art collector. She'll be in touch."

Chapter Twenty

Survival Instincts

Three days had passed since the murders in Acapulco. Del was in his living room watching TV with Kelsey when his cell phone rang. He saw the number and told Kelsey it was business, so he'd take it on the patio. It was Santana.

Del answered. "Where are you?"

"Is that any way to greet your *amigo*? I'm at the dead woman's casa."

"Are you fucking crazy?"

"*Amigo*, she don need it no more." He laughed. "I parked in the garage and all the blinds are closed. You got to chill. We finish our business and I'm gone, *amigo*."

Del was trying to process how Santana knew where Angie had lived. "I'll chill when you're gone. I'll be there in about ten minutes."

"*Bueno*—and don forget the money—twenty thousand."

"Twenty? The deal was for ten."

"I said ten for the woman. The other ten is for the snitch. You do the math."

Del was silent while he tried to absorb the change. "How is the snitch my problem?"

"*Amigo*, the snitch was your problem—trust me. You seriously want to fuck with me?"

"I'll bring the twenty. Open the garage door so I can drive in."

Del went to his safe and took out twenty thousand dollars. He started to close it and hesitated. He reached back in and grabbed another throw-away gun. He checked to make sure it was loaded and then velcroed it to his ankle.

Carl's House

The blinds were all drawn and there was no sign of life as Del pulled into the garage. As soon as he exited his Lexus, he heard the garage door close. He saw Santana in the doorway to the kitchen with a bottle of tequila in his hand.

Santana motioned him in. "*Hola, amigo. Mi casa, su casa.*"

"Very funny."

Del walked past him into the living room.

"You have the money, *amigo*?"

Del handed him the brown paper bag. Santana tossed it on the kitchen table.

"Aren't you gonna count it?"

Santana spread his hands. "*Amigo*, I trust you. You got to chill."

Del looked around and it looked much the same as it did when he was there last. There were lines of coke on a mirror on the coffee table, razor blade, rolled up hundred-dollar bill, and two glasses.

"Have a line, *amigo.* I'll put some music on."

Santana set the tequila bottle down and went over to the stereo. Del took a glass from the cupboard and poured himself some tequila. He took a sip and paused to look around again.

"How come there are two glasses?"

No sooner were the words out of his mouth when Bobbie appeared in the bedroom doorway, almost exactly as she had done before—nude save for black panties and with leash in hand.

"How soon you forget."

Del was visibly caught off guard, but now understood how Santana knew about the house. Bobbie walked over to the coffee table and did a line, as if basking in the limelight.

Santana noted Del's surprise and grinned. "You look surprised, *amigo.* You didn't think I could kill somebody who looks this good, did you?"

Del threw his hands up. "Hey—hold on. She was never part of the deal. Tell her."

Santana reached behind his back and drew his gun. He motioned to Bobbie. "Baby, see what our *amigo* is carrying."

Bobbie walked over and patted Del down. She maintained eye contact with him the entire time. She took the Glock from behind his back, but when she clearly felt the throwaway, she acted as if nothing was there. Del was now really confused. Bobbie handed the Glock to Santana, who put it in his waistband.

Santana shrugged his shoulders. "Sorry, *amigo.* You can't be too careful these days."

"No problem. We're all friends."

Santana put some music on and turned back to Del. "Man, you too tightly wound. Maybe Bobbie can take you in the bedroom and give you a massage?"

Bobbie did another line and then wrapped the leash lightly around Del's neck and led him to the bedroom. When they were inside, she closed the door and then pushed Del onto the bed. She reached down to his ankle, took his gun with little resistance, and then got on top of him. Brandishing the pistol, she leaned close and whispered in Del's ear, "I have a feeling only one of you is leaving here alive and I'm going to belong to the survivor. You and I have some issues to work out, but I would prefer it be you."

Del was still trying to process the situation. "Wh—what do I have to do?"

Bobbie sat up, still astride him, and handed him the pistol. "Take your clothes off. I'll lay on the bed and you tell Pancho Villa that Bobbie wants him. When he walks past you, kill him and don't hesitate for a second. He's a psychopath—don't underestimate him. Can you do that?"

Del nodded yes. He was frightened and turned on at the same time. He disrobed as Bobbie shed her panties and then lay on the bed very seductively.

"You said we have some issues."

Bobbie propped herself up on her elbows. "You had Angie killed. I understand why, but Angie and I were close—or didn't you notice?"

"Bobbie, listen to me. You were there—you heard her threaten me. What else could I do? Can't she be replaced?"

Bobbie hesitated, then smiled. "Well, I do have someone in mind. Do you like surprises?"

Del shrugged. "Surprises are good sometimes."

Bobbie then seemed more serious. "There is one other thing."

"What's that?"

"The thing is—we, ah, we like to play a little rough. A little b and d. Do you think you can handle that?"

Bobbie looked down and Del's dick wasn't just rock hard—it was throbbing. "Never mind—you just answered. Now do what you have to do."

Del checked the gun and tried to will his dick down, but to little avail. He took a deep breath, held the gun down his leg, and cracked the bedroom door. Santana was dancing by himself in the living room. Del called out. "*Amigo*, Bobbie wants you, not me."

Santana laughed and stooped to do another line before heading to the bedroom. "She need a real man, ey?"

As Santana passed by, Del deftly put the gun to the base of his neck and pulled the trigger. Santana collapsed on the floor. Del grabbed a pillow to suppress the noise and fired three more times into Santana's head.

Bobbie stepped around Santana, as if a pile of clothes, to nuzzle up to Del. She grabbed the dog collar off the dresser and handed it to him. She then took the pistol from him and placed it on the dresser. She rubbed up against him and fastened the dog collar around his neck with no protest. She then attached the leash to the collar and led him to the bed—both seemingly oblivious to the dead body in the room.

Bobbie sat on the side of the bed. "We need to talk."

"What do you want to know?"

"The night we met, Angie was right. I was her coke whore. I came from less than nothing and have nothing other than my looks and instinct for survival. I wind up where I wind up. Santana inherited me when he killed Angie and now you've killed him. I want to know what happens to me?"

Del sat down beside her. "Baby, I will take care of you—very good care—and I can afford it. I wanted you the moment I laid eyes on you."

Bobbie motioned for Del to lie down and then straddled him.

She seemed to think for a moment. "I seem to recall Angie saying you are married, and if I recall right, she said your wife is a knockout. How would that work out with her?"

"You leave that to me. I'll take care of her."

Bobbie arched her eyebrows. "Like you took care of Angie?"

"You said you had an instinct for survival. We have that in common. I'll do whatever I have to do. There are things you wouldn't understand."

"Try me."

"It's like this—my wife is every man's dream, but so are you, by the way. Our marriage was doomed from the start. We're too much alike. We thought, maybe even believed, we could be something different—be like Ozzie and Harriet—but you can't change the spots on a leopard. We are what we are."

"Who are Ozzie and Harriet?"

"Nobody—a couple of made up TV characters. Anyway, we gave it a shot, hoping to save each other from our dark secrets, which we chose not to share, all the time having 'sympathy for the devil,' as we liked to say. I actually think that I pulled it off, the public persona, but I'm not sure she even tried. She was never gonna be a soccer mom. I've stayed out of her private life, whatever that might be. Temptations are limited in the desert."

"You might be surprised, but just assure me that she isn't going to be a problem. I, on the other hand, have only one side and it's dark, very dark, but very transparent. Even if I could change my spots, so to speak, I'm not sure I would. I've always been someone's property. I don't know anything else, and—in case you haven't noticed, I'm bisexual—with an emphasis on the bi. I'm the dominant partner with all of my girlfriends. Angie may have owned me, but I was the boss."

"I'll take care of Kelsey—that's my wife. I know she's been seeing someone else anyway."

Bobbie raised her eyebrows again. "And you don't know who—with all of your resources?"

"She was very careful. She always had a girlfriend as a cover and I've been up to my ass in alligators with some problems that affect everything."

"Sort of like damage control—like Angie?"

"Look, I didn't make the rules. In fact, I hate them, but I learned that you have to play the hand you're dealt. Angie gave me no choice."

"How much more damage control do you have to do?"

"Just one more and you will live in luxury you never dreamed of. Now tell me about the surprise."

"Then it wouldn't be a surprise, would it?"

Bobbie got up and walked over to the dresser, where she got a pair of handcuffs from one of the drawers. Del was excited, but sat up at the sight of the cuffs. "What's up with the cuffs?"

Bobbie didn't answer immediately. She got back in bed and straddled Del again. She took one wrist in her hand with only modest resistance. "Your problem doesn't seem to want to go away without some help. I need you to trust me and, don't forget, I just saved your life. You see, I was raped brutally and repeatedly when I was a child and I have a fear of having sex with a man for the first time. After that, I'm fine. So, if you want me to fuck your brains out and get you ready for your big surprise, you're going to have to put these on."

Del surrendered both wrists willingly and Bobbie slapped on the cuffs. "One other thing. I just need to secure the leash—same reason."

Del was now in turmoil. His dick was saying "Go, go, go!" and his brain was saying "Stop!" This wasn't the first time he'd experienced this dilemma, but it would have been the first time he listened to his brain. He was desperately trying to focus now, but to no avail. Bobbie wrapped the leash around the cuffs and secured it to one of the faux brass bed posts. Back astride of him, Del started to cry out in joy when Bobbie reached over and stuffed a wash cloth in his mouth. Del was now wide-eyed with a mixture of joy and fear, while Bobbie was wide-eyed with joy and domination—and soon to be revenge. As much as one side of her wanted to stop, she didn't, she couldn't, and she literally jumped up and down on Del's dick until he exploded. To her surprise, and ironic regret, she exploded too! Go figure, she thought, as she tried to sort out her mixed emotions. She had just had the best sex of her life with a man and he was about to die.

Bobbie rolled over as both tried to catch their breath. She got up and left the room. She made no attempt to release Del or even remove the gag. A new and frightening picture was emerging in Del's mind.

Bobbie went to the kitchen and poured first one and then another shot of Tequila. She sat down on the sofa and struggled to sort things out. She had survived a life and experiences that few could imagine, let alone overcome, but she was angry with herself and, frankly, scared that she had missed so many warning signs recently. She was lucky to be alive.

What the fuck was she thinking about? When Del showed up with the news that Carl was dead, with three grand, an ounce of cocaine, and a bottle of champagne—and the following day brought more money and two first class tickets to Acapulco, all the while wearing gloves? She'd picked up on the gloves, but allowed herself to forget about "Greeks" bearing gifts. She was alive only because she convinced a psychopathic

Mexican assassin that she was attracted to him!

The Mexican was now dead on the bedroom floor. The so-called mastermind of the scheme was cuffed, tied up, and gagged on the bed where she had just had sex with him—and enjoyed it! Had she totally lost the survival instincts that had kept her alive and out of harm's way? If so, she was truly screwed. She had to think and quick.

Truth is, the arrangement with Angie was never destined to last—rather just one more temporary oasis on her improbable journey, but the suddenness and violence could not have been foreseen. Or could they? She needed to take stock of the situation. Del had brought Santana twenty thousand dollars, which solved a crucial problem, but wouldn't last forever. There were two cars in the garage, but one was stolen and one belonged to the leading federal agent in the area who would not, could not, survive the night.

Her thoughts kept returning to Kelsey, but how much of that was the obvious synergy and how much was the desire that had burned in her since the moment they met? It was obvious from her conversation with Del that Kelsey's life was in danger and Bobbie had no illusions about her own future with him. It was a given that Del had a fortune stashed away somewhere. The sixty-four-thousand-dollar question was, did Kelsey know where?

What was even more problematical was how were two such dominant personalities going to coexist? Bobbie had to be brutally honest with herself. This was a matter of life and death and she needed Kelsey more than Kelsey needed her. Her head ached, however, from the darker voice that told her that she had always been in control, still was, and this was nothing more than an excuse to finally submit to Kelsey.

In any event, Bobbie had to make the call. She had nowhere else to turn. Things would be what they would be. She had never been truly free. It just wasn't in the cards she'd been dealt. The fact that someone like Kelsey desired, but couldn't have her, was maybe her only claim to self-esteem. It was a luxury she could no longer afford.

Bobbie went to the kitchen and dialed Kelsey's number. Kelsey answered on the second ring. "Hello."

"Do you know who this is?"

"The caller ID says it's Angie, but it can't be Angie, because she was murdered in Acapulco. Which begs the question—why are you still alive?"

"Look, I know we have our issues, but this is a serious call—a deadly serious call. Angie's murder was a contract hit paid for by your husband. The reason I'm still alive is that I wasn't part of the contract and the shooter told me he was very, very attracted to me."

"Attraction can sometimes be fatal."

"Funny you should say so. In his case it was."

Kelsey hesitated a moment. "And you know for certain that Del was behind it?"

"Kelsey—I was here at Angie's house when she tried to extort him. Del came over to tell Angie that Carl was dead. We'd been up for two days. Angie told Del that she knew about the payoffs and would burn him if he didn't take care of her."

"That fucking idiot. How did Del react?"

"He didn't, which should've been the tip-off. He gave her three thousand bucks and at least an ounce of blow. Oh, and all the time he was wearing gloves. Then Angie blew him and all seemed cool. He showed up the next morning with more money and two tickets to Acapulco and even arranged for a ride to the airport. He said we needed to get away for a few days. Even I didn't see it coming. I missed all the signs."

"I'm beginning to get the picture. Now you're broke and homeless and you think I give a shit. You have a very short memory. You had numerous chances with me, but blew them all."

"First of all—I'm soon to be homeless, but I'm not broke. The shooter was kind enough to bequeath me over twenty thousand in cash."

"The shooter had a will?"

"A very strong will, but a very weak mind. And, Kelsey, the problem between us was that we were too much alike. We were both dominant—very dominant."

"I noticed you said the problem was, as in past tense, and you have no idea how much you piss me off by saying we're alike. I was born dominant. My parents were old money. I was born with a golden spoon in my mouth. You were born in a fucking trailer park to a white trash whore who had no clue who your father was. I can only imagine what was in your mouth when you were born."

"I thought what mattered most was where you wound up, not where you began."

"How quaint. We were Anglicans and we believed you accepted your station in life, or station wagon, as was the case with you."

"News flash—there was a revolution two hundred years ago that said people were free to be what they could be."

"OK, let's test that theory. You were born a bastard child to a white trash whore and years later you worked your way up to be the coke whore of a burned out ex-pole dancer. What an inspirational story. You should think about going on Oprah—or, better yet, becoming a motivational speaker."

There was silence and muffled sobs on the other end of the line. Kelsey waited and then spoke, "Are you still there? Reality sucks doesn't it? By the way—I wanted you, I never needed you. There's a big difference."

Bobbie tried to regain her composure. "If your aim was to hurt me, you succeeded. Everything you say is true. I didn't want to believe it, but this is no time to play games as both of our lives are in danger."

"Tell me something I don't know. I was packing when you called. I almost didn't answer."

"That's a lot to walk away from – the house, the money, and don't you have a child?"

"Apache Dunes has always been like Hotel California to me and none of that means anything if I'm dead. I'm a liability now to Del and I've seen that movie before. My parents were all too happy to come get my son. They wanted to take him when he was born and should have. He's better off with them. They never liked Del. As for the money—they've cut me off and I had the benefit of Del's money, but never access to it. It was his way of controlling me."

"Where will you go and what will you do for money?"

"Let's just say I won the lottery."

"Knowing you, it would have to be a pretty big jackpot."

"How's thirty million sound?"

"Like a pretty big fucking jackpot."

"The problem is—the money's in a bank in Switzerland and I need money to get there. If I use an ATM I leave a trail, so, you might come in handy with your, um, inheritance."

"Whatever it takes. I think I can also help with Del."

Kelsey laughed. "Trust me, he's way out of your weight class, but there's comfort in having an ally—a submissive ally, that is."

"I told you I'm finished pretending. You win. I'll do whatever it takes, as I said."

"You've been honest with me—maybe—so I'll reciprocate. I never stopped wanting you, but it may be just the thrill of the hunt and I may lose interest real fast. Now, why do you think you can help with Del?"

"If you come pick me up at Angie's, I think I can explain."

"I'll be there is fifteen minutes and expect to see the new you—the real you."

"You won't be disappointed. What are you wearing?"

"Diamond earrings, a gold Rolex, a two-carat flawless diamond ring, a twenty-four carat gold chain around my waist, a twenty-four carat gold ankle bracelet, and Jimmy Choo high heels. And a light jacket, of course. What do you have on?"

"Lipstick."

Bobbie heard Kelsey's car arrive. In anticipation she had put on a dog collar with a leash attached and did her makeup as much as possible. She had to admit to being a little turned on by the change of roles. She had dominated more women—and men—than she could count, but ultimately it was all role-playing. Being submissive, however, didn't require any mental energy. You just ... submitted. She didn't even fear pain as she had dished out more than her share and didn't Sartre say, "Pain is a condition of existence." Today was all about existence.

Kelsey rang the doorbell and Bobbie answered it immediately. Kelsey was wearing a Burberry raincoat. She handed it to Bobbie and Bobbie handed her the end of the leash. Kelsey gently tugged on the leash as she was transfixed with Bobbie's perfect body. She then let go of the leash, "Hang my coat up and fix me a glass of Tequila and a line of cocaine."

As Bobbie seductively walked away, Kelsey took in the scene. When Bobbie returned with the coke and Tequila, Kelsey had moved over to the sofa. Bobbie started to sit down beside her, but Kelsey jerked hard on the leash and pointed to the carpet. Bobbie obediently knelt down in front of her.

In the bedroom Del had managed to loosen the bed post a bit, but was afraid to make too much noise. He stopped when he heard voices. He could swear that he heard Kelsey's voice, but that made no sense at all. On his next tug the bed post banged against the wall. Kelsey looked toward the bedroom and noted the door was closed. "What was that? Is someone in the bedroom?"

Bobbie looked up, "That's part of the surprise I have for you, but let me please you first."

Kelsey sniffed, "Why does it smell like you just had sex?"

Bobbie stood up. "I think it's time for the surprise. Follow me."

When Bobbie opened the door, Kelsey saw Santana's body on the floor and Del bound and gagged on the bed. It was difficult to say who was more surprised—Kelsey or Del.

Bobbie broke the ice. "That's Angie's killer and I think you know the man who paid for the hit."

Del was now totally freaked out and thrashing around as much as possible—to no avail. Kelsey turned to Bobbie. "You fucked Del?"

"It was the only way to get him to wear the cuffs and tie him up. He thought it was a game. I didn't do it until he told me he was going to kill you."

Del was struggling to protest.

"Still doesn't explain why you fucked him, but nothing surprises me anymore. Tell me—you ever kill anyone?"

"No—I had Del kill Santana. How about you?"

"Whatta you think? However, I have an idea. I dated a Greek guy in college. His family owned some restaurants. When they needed renovation, they just happened to burn down. He told me how they did it. Close all the windows and get our coats. Leave everything except your leash. I'm going to turn the gas on and light a candle and then let's get the fuck out of here."

"So we don't kill him directly? While you're turning on the gas and lighting the candle, do you mind if I have some private time with him?"

"I don't mind at all."

Del was consumed with fear, but doubtful he could escape. He had to survive somehow. Bobbie returned from the living room with a fireplace poker. Her first two swings were aimed at Del's left arm and leg. The sounds of the bones breaking were unmistakable. Del had gone into shock by the time Bobbie connected with his skull, leaving a deep gash that spewed blood. Kelsey reentered the room after hearing the noise. She grabbed Bobbie's arm as she was about to swing again. She took the poker from her hand and tossed it aside. Bobbie collapsed into Kelsey's arms and Kelsey gently consoled her."It's time for us to go."

Bobbie brushed back the tears from her eyes and neither looked back as Kelsey led her from the room.

Del wasn't sure how long he'd been blacked out, but knew he was seriously wounded and in shock. His left arm and leg were definitely broken, yet he felt no pain. Blood was still coming from the gash on his head, but it had clotted a bit. He had the bedpost almost disconnected before the attack, but didn't want them to know for fear they'd shoot him. He summoned his strength and dislodged the post, which slipped through the leash and allowed him to use his hands to remove the gag, collar, and leash. He smelled the gas and realized what they had done. The bedroom had a door leading to the patio and the garage must have a side or back door. The gun was still on the dresser. If he could make it to the garage, he could use the gun to shoot out the lock, if needed.

He tried to remember his Marine survival training and understood that the next few minutes were the difference between life and death. As the fog cleared, a thought came to him—the cuffs, where'd they come from? Think. He remembered seeing Bobbie getting out of bed and going to the dresser. He gently edged off the bed. He knew that people in shock could do some amazing things—even run on broken legs—but he also knew that the shock would wear off soon. He had to move as fast as possible. He lurched toward and grabbed hold of the dresser. He opened the top drawer and found nothing.

He tried the second drawer and bingo! It looked like a porn shop with all of the toys. He found the key with another set of cuffs and a second key. He couldn't use his left hand, but was able to use his right and he was right handed. He unlocked the left hand cuff and didn't bother with the right one—he would worry about that later. He exited the patio door and used a chair as a crutch to take the pressure off of his leg. Surprisingly, the back door to the garage wasn't locked, but the garage was totally dark. He steadied himself on the cars as he worked himself toward the kitchen door and garage door opener. The opener was just out of his reach. Gripping the barrel of the pistol, he could barely reach the opener and the door started to rise. As important, the garage lights went on and he could see more clearly. He reached his car and fought through unbearable pain to get behind the wheel. He was able to back out of the driveway and did the best he could to exit the subdivision and pull over to the side of the road. He had left his cell phone in the car and used it to speed dial another DEA agent, who groggily answered. "Who's this?"

"Ray, it's Del. This is a code red. I repeat—a code fucking red. Meet me at the safe house and bring a doctor—fast!"

Just then, in the background, Carl's house blew up.

"Del—what the hell was that noise?"

"Get me a doctor—quick!"

Chapter Twenty-One

Payback

Sheriff's House

Tom was awakened by his cell phone. It was not quite 6:00 a.m. He turned on the light and saw it was Jake. "Jake, what's up?"

"Sorry to wake you, but I just got a call that the dead DEA agent's house blew up this morning. I didn't call earlier because the fire department initially thought it was an accidental gas explosion, but then they found a body inside—a male. The body was burned pretty badly, but it looks like he might have been shot in the back of the neck. There was a car in the garage with Mexican plates. I ran the plates and the car was stolen two days ago in Acapulco."

"Were you able to get any ID on the body or a print?"

"No papers, but we were able to get a pretty good print and we're running it now."

Tom thought for a moment. "What about the alphabet boys—particularly Del?"

"That's what's funny—nobody has been around or called."

"OK, I'll get some breakfast and head into the office. I'll wait for the wire on the print. If Del hasn't surfaced by then, I'll pay him a visit. Get some rest and check in with me later."

The DEA Safe House Near Apache Dunes

Del had been sedated and his head was immobilized. There was an IV hooked up and casts had been put on his left arm and leg. The doctor was speaking with the agent Ray.

"I've sedated him and he should be out for several hours, but I still think his head needs to be examined. At minimum he has a severe concussion, but he could have a skull fracture. Keep him strapped down and his head immobilized. He was worked over pretty bad. It's amazing he could drive, but that's what shock does. I'll come back periodically and change the IV, but you need to call me immediately if his condition worsens. If it does, he needs to get to a hospital."

"Doc, I know that this is hard maybe to understand, but we need to avoid a hospital at all costs, if possible. This was a very sensitive mission he was on and it's better if the bad guys think he's dead at the moment. Here's ten grand to start with."

The doctor took the money, almost reluctantly, then looked back at Del. "Listen Ray, I appreciate the money and helping the government even more, but I don't understand any of this. If he has brain damage he can die. I don't think he would have made it this far if he did, but we can't be sure. Have somebody watch him at all times and call me if you need me. If he takes a turn for the worse—call the ambulance first and then call me."

Del's Mansion

Kelsey and Bobbie were in bed. They were startled by the doorbell. Kelsey sat up. "Who can it be at this hour?"

Kelsey got out of bed and peered through the blinds. The sheriff's SUV was parked in the driveway. "It's the sheriff. He's probably come to give me the bad news about Del. I don't want to speak with him. Answer the door and get rid of him."

Bobbie stretched and smiled. "Only if you promise to pick up where we left off."

"Baby, you don't have to worry about that. We've now got all the time in the world."

Bobbie ran her hands through her hair and stooped to do another line of cocaine before putting on a robe and heading downstairs. Tom was starting to walk away as she cracked the door open. "Can I help you?"

Tom pivoted, expecting to see Kelsey, and was a bit startled. "Ma'am, I'm looking for Del. Is he around?"

"No—he didn't come home last night."

"Is his missus in?"

"She is, but she isn't feeling well. I'm looking after her."

Tom removed his hat and scratched his head. "Well, when he comes home or calls, tell him to watch the morning news."

"I'll tell him."

Tom started to walk away again, then turned back toward the door. "Oh, I didn't get your name."

"I know, have a good day."

Bobbie closed and locked the door. Tom stared at the door for a moment, perplexed by her response, but just shook his head, got in his SUV, and left.

Bobbie went back upstairs, tossed the robe on the floor, and climbed back into bed. "It was the sheriff. Said he was looking for Del and if he came home or called we're to tell him to watch the morning news."

Kelsey sat up with a start. "Why would he tell him to watch the news if they found his body in the house and his car in the garage? Hand me the TV control."

Kelsey channel surfed until she found the local news station and waited for the commercial to end. With the remains of the house as a backdrop a local reporter was on the scene.

"When the Apache Dunes Fire Department responded to an apparent gas leak explosion at a home in the exclusive Buena Vista subdivision, early this morning, they discovered the body of an unidentified male in one of the bedrooms with multiple gunshot wounds to his head area. A police spokesperson said they were able to retrieve a fingerprint, which they are running through the FBI's data base. A car in the garage with

Mexican plates had been reported stolen in Acapulco. Stay tuned as we follow this breaking story."

Kelsey was visibly shaken. She clicked off the TV and turned to Bobbie. "Let's get our stuff together. We're out of here—now!"

Bobbie appeared confused. "Where are we going?"

"I have no fucking idea, but we can't stay here."

Sheriff's Office

Jake was back at the office and called Dylan's cell phone. Dylan saw Jake's number and answered. "Hey, Jake. What's up?"

"Just your normal night in the Dunes. Remember Carl, the dead DEA agent? His house blew up last night and there was a body inside, a male with a few bullet holes in him. We got a print and are running it."

Dylan exhaled, "Whew!"

"Oh, and there was a stolen car in the garage with Mexican plates. Guess where it was lifted from?"

"Just a wild guess—Acapulco?"

"You're getting good at this. How about Final Jeopardy—the identity of the guy who bought the bullets?"

"I'm going to risk it all, Alex. Who is Santana?"

"That's my guess, too."

"Jake, while I have you—I need to run something by you. I've been thinking. You said that Tom has a file on Carlos and Scooter. Did you read it?"

"More like glanced through it."

"Where's the file now?"

"Last I saw it, it was in the file cabinet. Why? What's up?"

"I was thinking. Everything points to Dusty for the thirty million transfer, because we think that only three people knew about the money: Carlos, Scooter, and Dusty, and neither Carlos nor Scooter transferred it. So it all points to Dusty, right?"

"And?"

"Jake, you knew Scooter. He couldn't keep a secret if he tried and he had four years to try. What if he involved someone else and they found out he was dead? They might think they were free. I was with Dusty and nobody could pull off a score like that without betraying some emotion."

"It makes some sense, but how do we ever prove it?"

"I've got an idea. I'll get back to you."

"I'll be here."

Dylan was still at Tom's house. He looked for the napkin with Carlos' cell number. He sat down and dialed the number. Carlos answered, "*Hola*, who the fuck is calling?"

"Carlos—it's me Dylan."

"Geronimo! You got my money!"

"Carlos, cut the shit. I may have an idea what happened to it, but I need you to back off and give me a few days."

"A few days so you can hide Dusty?"

"Carlos, at first it even looked bad for Dusty to me, but I have another idea and, I think, a better one."

"Check this out, man. I need a little more than that. Give me something."

"Fair enough. You're thinking Dusty because you think it had to be either Scooter or her and you know it wasn't Scooter, right?"

"Keep talking."

"Carlos, you know Scooter was a loose cannon. That's how your uncle found him. You telling me he kept that information secret for four years? He couldn't keep a secret for ten minutes! You also know that if it had anything to do with codes or numbers, there's no way he could figure it out by himself."

"Geronimo, you so smart, everything you say makes sense, but check this out—Scooter ain't able to tell us who he might have told."

"Listen to me. The sheriff kept a secret file on Scooter. I haven't seen it yet, but I will later today. By the way, it includes transcripts of the conversations that he had with you at the prison."

"How the fuck? I told you man. We're even—I don't owe you nothing. And Geronimo?"

"Yeah?"

"I didn't understand a thing he was saying. I told you—he was playing spy."

"Understood. Now I owe you a favor and the way you live it may come in handy. By the way, the longer you're away from the joint, the worse your grammar gets."

"Fuck you, *amigo.* You've got a week."

"Oh, Carlos—there is one more thing. Have you heard from your *amigo* Santana?"

"Uno, he's not *mi amigo*. Dos, he's *muy peligroso. Comprende*?"

"He WAS very dangerous. My guess is that he's the guy they found in the Dunes with a few bullets in his neck. You forget how dangerous the desert is."

Carlos was silent for a moment. "You find out for sure, you call me."

"Certainly, now we're even, again."

Dylan hung up and reached for his wallet and the piece of paper with Dusty's number in Geneva. He dialed the number and a man answered.

"*Bonjour.*"

"Hello—I mean *bonjour. Parlez vous Anglais*?"

"Yes, I speak English. May I help you?"

"Please. My name is Dylan and I'm a friend of Dusty. I was told I could reach her at this number."

"Ah yes. One moment, please."

Dylan heard a muffled conversation and then Dusty answered. "Dylan, I'm glad you called. Did you get my message?"

"I did and it's just as well you didn't come back now. There's a bit of a problem."

"Problem? What problem?"

"Look Dusty, I don't want to upset you and I know you aren't responsible, but, apparently, there was something else in the duffel bag."

"The bank codes."

"Dusty! You knew! Tell me you didn't do it."

"Do what, for God's sake?"

"Dusty, someone transferred thirty million dollars the day after Scooter's funeral from an account in the Cayman Islands to God knows where. Carlos was convinced it was you, but I've held him off—at least for a while. That's why you shouldn't come back right now."

Dusty paused a moment. "I don't know how to say this, so I'll just say it. I don't know where you got the idea that I was coming back to Apache Dunes anytime soon. I'm not—in fact, I may never return."

Dylan started to speak, but Dusty continued. "You know how Tom and Sue said if it was meant to be, it would be? Well, for four years now I've been keeping that hope, that dream alive, and when we were brought together again, I just assumed it was fate, but what is clear now—at least to me—is that it's going to take more than a few days on a sailboat to make up for those four years apart."

"You didn't answer my question about the money."

"And I don't intend to. I can't believe you keep asking me. Dylan, have you forgotten I lost my brother and all you seem to care about is some drug cartel's money?"

"Dusty, that's not fair."

"What's fair got to do with it? Was it fair what happened to Scooter? And when did you become Sherlock Holmes?"

"I'm just trying to protect you."

Dusty scoffed. "Dylan, you don't protect someone by leaving them for four years. It was foolish of me to think that things could be the same as they were. Nothing stays the same. You take care of yourself and I'll look after me. What I need most is some time."

"If you need me, you know how to reach me."

Dusty said, "Likewise." And hung up.

Chicago

Max Sandowski pulled up to the Starbucks on the north side of Chicago in his unmarked police car and parked in a no-parking zone. He got out of the car and tossed what was left of his cigar before entering the coffee shop. He hadn't shaved for two days and his clothes looked like he had slept in them, because he had. Inside, he immediately made eye contact with Marta, a very attractive twenty-something Latina barista. Marta was showing a baby bump. When she saw Max, she started to tear up and asked the manager for a few minutes off. He understood and she came around the counter and rushed into Sandowski's arms with tears now flowing down her cheeks.

"Let's go sit in my car."

"I—I'm sorry. I can't help it."

He tried to brush away the tears. "Shh … don't worry. I don't have any tears left, or I'd be crying too."

He opened the passenger side door for her, then went around to the driver's side and got in. "I'll go get some napkins."

Marta touched his arm. "Hold on, I have plenty of Kleenex. All I do is cry."

"Marta, listen to me. I know all about you and Davey and the baby and I'm going to get things straight with the department. Trust me on that."

She leaned over into his arms and started crying again.

"Shh, we're gonna work through this thing together." He reached in his coat pocket and handed her a small envelope. "Here is the key to my condo. It's a fucking mess—sorry. It's a mess, like me, but I'm going away in a few days and might not return. Inside is also the card of a lawyer friend of mine. I told him that you would be moving in and that if I don't return to transfer the title to you. All you gotta pay are the electric and phone bills, the condo assessments and the real estate taxes. The mortgage has been paid off and, like I said, I know the department will do the right thing. Everybody loved Davey."

"I—I don't know what to say."

"Don't say nothing. Just take care of that baby and let him know what kind of man his father was. Name him Davey, Jr. That's all I ask."

"Davey wanted to name him Max—after you."

Sandowski choked up and looked away from Marta. He took a deep breath and exhaled. "Trust me—we want the boy to be like him, not me."

The DEA Safe House

Del was still immobilized and hooked up to the IV, but he was awake and coherent and Ray was at his side. Ray had just turned the pain drip up a notch at Del's request. "Ray, go by my house and see if anybody's home. Call first. If anyone answers, hang up. If nobody's there, put out an APB on my Range Rover. The license plate number is on my insurance card in my wallet."

"What do I tell the police?"

"Give 'em some bullshit—undercover case and we need the occupants of the car, two women, held for us until we can pick them up for questioning."

Del's voice was trailing off at the end. He was fading out.

"Del, where do I take them? Del—Del?"

Belmont District Police Station, Chicago

Sandowski was sitting outside the chief's office. A few fellow officers had walked over to shake Max's hand and offer their condolences. The chief's door opened and a detective motioned for Max. "Sorry to make you wait. The chief will see you now."

Sandowski entered the chief's office and took a seat in front of the desk. The chief was directly opposite him and had his head in his hands. When Max sat down, the chief looked up and clasped his hands in front of him. "Max, we all know what Davey meant to you. He meant a lot to all of us. Jesus—we watched him grow up right before our eyes, from gangbanger to the best undercover cop we've ever had and none of that would have happened without you."

The chief hesitated for a moment and looked more closely at Max. "Max—you look like shit. Are you OK? What can I do for you—anything?"

"Listen, Chief."

The chief cut him off. "Fuck the chief shit, Max. You and I started out together—both Marines. It's Pete in this office."

"Thanks, Pete. That means a lot right now. Here's a letter—excuse my handwriting, it was never good. It's got all the details on Davey's fiancée Marta who's five months pregnant."

The chief grimaced. "Shit—that's what I heard. Is she OK?"

"She's pretty far fucking from OK. I just left her. She's a tough gal, but it ain't gonna be easy for her. All I want is for the department to do right by her."

"Max, you have my word on that. We'll write her up as his wife with full benefits. I'll personally take care of it. We did it once before. What else?"

"Pete, I'm tired. I think this is it for me. I'm thinking about tying up some loose ends and retiring down to Arizona. I got some friends there."

The chief sat back in his chair and shook his head. "Max—don't bullshit a bullshitter. How the fuck do you have any friends in Arizona when you hardly have any here? And isn't somewhere in Arizona connected to the Devils? What are you up to? I've gotta know?"

Sandowski stood and laid his badge and service revolver on the desk. "Pete, I gotta do what I gotta do."

The chief put his face back in his hands for a minute, then looked up. "Max, you know Sandoval—the young cop Davey used to hang with?"

"I seen him around."

"He's young, but he knows his way around the neighborhood, so to speak. Why don't you have a beer with him?"

The chief came around the desk and gave Max a man hug. "Semper Fi, Max."

"Semper Fi."

The Highway Outside of Apache Dunes

Kelsey pulled the Range Rover over to the side of the road. It was obvious they left the Dunes in a rush. Kelsey turned to Bobbie. "You have any bright ideas?"

"Mexico is an option, but that little issue of killing Santana doesn't help us. I've been thinking—I don't know if it's a good idea or not, but some guys from Las Vegas stopped by Angie's house one day looking for Carl and they were right out of *Goodfellas*. They said they had a business matter to discuss with Carl and one of them left his card."

"Del told me Carl owed some bookies a lot of money."

"How's this sound? Maybe if we offered to pay off Carl's debt, they could help us get new IDs and a new ride. I don't see we have a lot of options. If Del is alive he'll have every cop and fed in the country looking for us. Vegas is the best option as far as I can see."

"What's the guy's name?"

Bobbie fished through her purse. "Here it is—Sonny Del Giorno."

Kelsey did a U-turn on the highway. "Las Vegas here we come!"

Higgins Tavern on the North Side of Chicago

Sandowski was waiting at the bar with a boilermaker in front of him when Manuel "Manny" Sandoval entered. Sandoval was late twenties to early thirties, pushing six feet, with a shaved head and physique that looked as if it had been carved out of marble . He was wearing his signature shades, sweatshirt with the sleeves cut off, tight blue jeans, and cowboy boots with steel toes. Sandowski rose to greet him.

"Hey Manny, thanks for comin'."

"No problem. The chief called me. Said we should meet."

Sandowski motioned to a back table. "Let's move over where we can talk. You want something?"

"Water's fine for now."

They sat down at the table. "Manny, we never got a chance to know each other, but Davey talked about you a lot and I know you two were tight."

"Tight doesn't do it justice. Davey was like a brother to me—particularly after my two real brothers were decapitated and left in the middle of a road in Mexico. That was their retirement plan from the cartel. My mom brought me to Chicago—illegal aliens. I met Davey running the streets and gangbanging. I know the story about how you saved him. He told it many times and always if we'd been drinking. He was the one who referred me to the immigration attorney you had handle Davey's case. I never had a father figure, so I invented one—you." Sandowski looked surprised. "When Davey joined the force I followed in his footsteps. My mom eventually died of a broken heart over my brothers and Davey was my only family. So whatever you're gonna do—count me in."

Sandowski nodded. "Good. You got any ideas?"

"Man, I ain't been thinking about anything else. I got an idea maybe."

Sandowski got the bartender's attention. "Can I get another one over here? Manny, you want anything?"

"A double shot of your best tequila."

"Let's hear your idea."

"Hang on."

The drinks were served and Sandoval raised his glass. "To Davey."

Sandowski clinked glasses. "To Davey."

"And to payback."

"To serious fucking payback!"

Sandoval took a sip. "OK—here's my idea. You may have read where the mayor convened all the gang leaders for a sit down."

Sandowski nodded.

"Well, I read where the mayor is meeting with local business leaders in Bucktown tomorrow night. It's no secret that Flaco Escobar runs the Latin Devils—so he had to order the hit. So what happens if I contact him and tell him the mayor wants to meet with him privately after the meeting—hush, hush?"

"You think he'd buy it?"

Sandoval smiled. "That fucking chumbalone has an ego the size of Texas. I'll tell him the mayor was impressed with him—regards him the big cheese."

"So then what happens?"

"There's a Mexican restaurant near where the mayor is meeting. It's got a backroom for parties with a back door on the alley. The owner owes me big and I give a shit if he catches any hell. You cover the alley. We let Flaco bring a bodyguard, but Flaco has to be clean to see the Mayor, so his man has to stay in front where we'll have a couple of tables full of plainclothes guys—friends of Davey. As soon as we enter the back room, they'll neutralize the bodyguard and I'll take care of Flaco. We take him out the back and I got a destination in mind that would make a Nazi doctor blush."

Sandowski stared at him, finished his beer, and was silent for a moment.

"What's wrong? You got a better idea?"

"The only thing that's wrong is I hate to have to wait until tomorrow night." He signaled for the barkeep's attention. "Another round over here."

CHAPTER TWENTY-TWO

The Wire Transfer

Las Vegas

For most of its storied history, Las Vegas had been the personal ATM of the mob bosses in Chicago and their associates in Milwaukee and Kansas City. With just a wee bit of discretion, it would remain so today, but discretion wasn't one of the lessons learned on Grand Avenue in Chicago and the mob couldn't have chosen a worse person to oversee their operations there. Joe Pesci's depiction in *Casino* was, if anything, understated. The resulting skimming scandal led to a slew of prosecutions for the mob bosses. The net-net was that the Golden Goose flew the coop and corporations replaced the mob. Shangri-La would never be the same.

Even though Vegas was now a family destination controlled by suits, it was still a union town and the Mecca of gambling in the US. As such, there remained plenty of opportunity for the mob, just on a much smaller scale than before. A lot more forethought went into their new overseer. Sonny Del Giorno, aka Sonny Day, was a safe choice. First of all, at six-four, 260 pounds, and a meticulous dresser, he fit the role perfectly. More importantly, he was respected by the bosses and the so called "young Turks" alike. It was for that reason, ironically, that Sonny agreed to the move. It's just a fact of life in the mob that when the boss dies, there is generally a war for the vacant throne, and the current boss, Little Tony Mondelli, had seemingly been on his last legs for several years. When the war comes, neutrality isn't an option and Sonny didn't want to be caught in the middle at his age.

Sonny liked Vegas and what wasn't to like? His heart, however, would always remain in Chicago. There just wasn't another place like it on the face of the earth. Like a lot of Italians, food was important to him and Chicago had real Italian restaurants like Carlucci, Gene & Georgetti, Italian Village, and La Scarola, to name just a few. Toss in a couple of Italian beefs at Mr. Beef, an afternoon with Steve at Sluggers, prior to a Cubs game, and fuggedabout it! Regardless, a man's gotta do what a man's gotta do and it was time to make a move.

Sonny was the type of guy who could fit in anywhere and Vegas worked out well for him. Truth is, there wasn't that much to oversee anymore. A more apt job description would have been mediator and judge for the wise guys and wannabes who were still attracted to the glitz, but didn't get the memo that times had changed. The lieutenant he inherited from the old regime, Vince "Vinny" Alliota, was the source of most of his angst. If Sonny was the Hollywood stereotype for a mob captain, Vinny, at five-eight on his tip toes and matching Sonny pound for pound, was a clone of Clemenza in *The Godfather*. Vinny was a dinosaur. Vegas and the mob life were the only life he knew. Sonny never referred to him as his lieutenant because there was no way Vinny could ever spell it. He had a good heart and was a good companion for Sonny, but he had some serious baggage in the person of his nephew Petey, who was a few bricks shy of a load—make that several bricks shy of a load. Sonny admired Vinny's efforts to look after his family, but Petey didn't have to look for trouble, it found him, and Vinny usually got caught up in it. On no fewer than three occasions Sonny had to call in markers to keep Chicago from whacking Vinny and Petey.

Sonny and Vinny were relaxing in Sonny's penthouse suite in the Pompeii, the strip's newest hotel. Sonny was going over the latest racing form and Vinny was reading the comics section when the phone rang. Sonny answered.

"Sonny here."

"Is this Mr. Del Giorno?"

"Isn't that what I said? Who's this?"

"You came to Apache Dunes looking for the DEA agent's wife. I'm Bobbie—I answered the door and you gave me your card."

"I hope you ain't callin' to tell me the broad got whacked in Mexico. That's old news."

"Mr. Del Giorno, I was thinking I might be able to do you a favor."

"First of all, they call me Sonny Day. Now, what kind of favor can you do for me?"

"How about if I pay off the husband's gambling debt?"

Sonny clicked his fingers and motioned for Vinny to pay attention. He put the phone on speaker.

"Excuse me—I don't hear so well. That's better. Now tell me. Mother Teresa, I mean Bobbie, why the fuck would you do that?"

"Well, it just so happens that I may need a favor from you."

"Bobbie, honey, you have any idea what he owed me? This isn't chump change."

"Carl was a world-class fuck up, so I know it wasn't incidental."

Sonny laughed, "That's a good one. No, it ain't incidental."

Vinny looked at Sonny and squinted his eyes trying to figure out what incidental meant. Sonny waved him off.

"So, you gonna tell me how much he owed?"

Sonny covered the phone with his hand and motioned for Vinny to whisper. "How much was the bent fed into us for?" He then motioned for Vinny to write it down. Vinny wrote $150,000.

"Bobbie, I hope you're sitting down. The number is three hundred large. You know what that means?"

Vinny looked at Sonny, wide-eyed.

"I can handle that, but not until the morning when the banks open."

Now both Sonny and Vinny were wide-eyed. "Listen, Bobbie—you ain't plannin on knocking off a bank are you?"

"It's called a wire transfer. Now let me tell you what I need from you."

"Whoa, stop right there. No more talking on the phone. Where are you?"

"We're on the Strip in our car. I've got a girlfriend with me. We haven't checked in anywhere yet. You have any suggestions?"

"I can do better than that. I'll get you a suite comped at the Pompeii—that's the new place. Go to the front desk and mention my name, Sonny Day, and they'll take care of you. When you get settled in, call me and I'll stop by."

"That's great. Hey, why does your card say Sonny Del Giorno if you go by Sonny Day?"

"This is your lucky day. I'm gonna start you on the road to being bilingual. Del Giorno means day in Italian."

"Sonny, I got news for you—if bilingual means mouth, I already am."

"You know, I was afraid you might be one of them brainy broads. I'm likin' you more every minute."

"Is that supposed to be some kind of compliment?"

"Some kind. Get checked in and call me. Room service is comped too."

After they hung up, Sonny turned to Vinny, who was still amazed. "Vinny, whatta they call that suite where we got the hidden cameras and microphones?"

"I think they call it the Congressional Suite."

"Call down and tell them I need it indefinitely."

Vinny made the call, then holding the phone turned to Sonny. "They say they got the senator coming in for two nights."

"Like we need more shit on that douchebag. Tell them to put him someplace else—anywhere. I need that suite and tell Harry that no one sees or hears those tapes but me. Period. You tell him that."

"The senator?"

"No moron, not the senator—Harry, the manager."

Comped Suite at Pompeii

Kelsey tipped the bellboy and locked the door after he left. Kelsey and Bobbie took in the suite and its incredible view of the Strip. They hugged each other, happy and relieved with their good fortune. Bobbie then walked over to the bags and turned to Kelsey. "Unpack our bags and put our clothes away while I shower."

Kelsey couldn't have been more stunned. At first she thought it must be a joke, but Bobbie wasn't laughing. "Excuse me? Are you forgetting who's in charge here, you little slut? Not to mention I drove all the way and in MY car!"

Bobbie approached Kelsey, who backed up a bit, completely off guard. "Kelsey, play school is over. You keep pointing out that I'm a slut, but I've never claimed to be anything else—I can't. I never had the chance to be anything else. You, on the other hand, are a slut by choice."

Kelsey raised her hand to slap Bobbie, but Bobbie caught it and pushed Kelsey down on the bed and straddled her. Kelsey made no apparent move to escape.

"In fact, Kelsey, I may know you better than you know yourself. You may have a college degree, but I've forgotten more about psychology than you'll ever know."

"Bullshit. How could that be? You weren't even enrolled in college."

"I didn't have to be enrolled. I went to the classes."

"Liar! You would have been caught and kicked out."

"I was caught and I was sent to the Dean's office. We had a closed-door session and afterward I had a front row seat in any class I wished to attend. Of course, I had to meet with him periodically to keep him apprised—he liked to say—of my progress. What a sick fuck he was."

"What's that got to do with me?"

Bobbie got up and walked over to her suitcase and took out her dog collar and leash. She then proceeded slowly back to the bed, where Kelsey hadn't moved or made an effort to escape. Bobbie remounted her and fastened the collar around her neck, meeting no resistance. She then connected the leash to the collar and leaned down to give Kelsey a passionate kiss. Kelsey squirmed with desire.

Bobbie sat back up and gave a little tug on the leash. "What that's got to do with you is this—all of your life you've had it all handed to you, but you were bored, never satisfied, and the wild side of life attracted you like a moth to a flame. It's not that you couldn't stay on the safe side of the street—you didn't want to." Bobbie leaned down and kissed her again. "This, here and now, is the last frontier for you. People have kissed your ass and groveled for you all of your life, but you repaid them with contempt. You could never reconcile the fact that they got what they wanted, what they needed, yet you were never satisfied. You are dying to know what it feels like to be on the other side of the leash," Bobbie gave it a stronger yank, "and I'm going to show you. Starting today, I'm in charge and you're my bitch. Whatever you have, including the money, is now mine—and want to know why? Because you want me to have it. You're dying to be treated like the piece of shit that you've secretly always wanted to be and class is now in session."

Kelsey now tried to throw Bobbie off of her, yelling, "Wait just a fucking minute."

Bobbie hit her right on the nose and blood erupted. Kelsey appeared to be in shock. Bobbie stood up. "Go get a towel. I don't want your fucking blood all over the carpet."

Kelsey ran to the bathroom, holding her nose. Bobbie looked around the suite and smiled.

Sonny's Suite

"The broads are in, Vinny. I'll give them a chance to get settled in then have a little chat with them, find out what's going on. Bobbie is supposed to call me. In the meantime, go down to the safe room and watch 'em. If there's anything interesting, call me right away. Before you go, give me our guy's number at the bank."

"You mean the president?"

"No, moron. I want to talk to the janitor. Of course the president—John something."

"John Carlson, but he's current with us. I picked up a payment two days ago."

"What's he into us for now?"

Vinny took out his book. "A little less than fifteen g's."

Sonny thought for a moment. "Good, now give me his number."

Vinny gave Sonny the number for Carlson and left for the safe room as Sonny made the call. Carlson's secretary answered the phone. "Mr. Carlson's office, this is Sarah speaking."

"Sarah, this is Sonny Day calling. Tell John I need to speak with him."

Sonny listened to a couple of minutes of elevator music before Carlson picked up the phone, sounding nervous. "Sonny, I gave Vinny a payment two days ago. I've done what I promised."

"John, relax. We're friends, right? This is a social call. I need a favor from you and, if you can help me, maybe we can wipe the slate clean."

That obviously didn't calm Carlson's nerves. "Friends, sure, but, but what kind of favor?"

"John, chill out. I just need the use of your office for an hour tomorrow afternoon and you can pick the time."

"I—I don't understand. What do you mean—use my office?"

"Just what I said. I need to meet with someone and I want to use your office."

"How about a conference room?"

"John—I thought we was friends. You trying to piss me off?"

"No Sonny, sorry. I just don't understand. You say if I do this for you, we're square?"

"John, not only will we be square, but I'll have five grand in chips for you at the cage tonight. How's that?"

"Wow … that would be … great. And all I need to do is let you use my office for an hour?"

"One hour and you pick the time."

"How about four p.m.? I'll leave early."

"Perfect. Oh, there is one more thing."

"Oh no—I knew it."

"I told you to chill. It's just a banking question. What information do you need to make a wire transfer from someone's account to mine?"

"That's easy. You just need to give them your bank name, location, routing number, and your account number, and they do the rest."

"Thanks. See, that was painless. We'll be there at four tomorrow. Tell your secretary to take off early too."

Comped Suite at Pompeii

Kelsey returned from the bathroom with a washcloth to stop her nose bleed. Bobbie sat down beside her and stroked her hair. "Baby, I don't like to hurt you, but you have to behave. I don't know what happened to you to make you like this, but you've got some serious issues and this is not the time to deal with them. We're in some deep shit here. You have to listen to me if we're going to get out of this alive. You understand?"

Kelsey was sobbing, but nodded her head yes.

"Now tell me—how in the world did you get thirty million dollars?"

Kelsey wiped away her tears. "It's a long story."

"It's also a necessary story. Give me the short version."

Kelsey took a deep breath to compose herself. "There was this guy named Scooter, a local who was cute, but harmless. We called him Kato. Anyway, we had an arrangement. I'd rip off some of Del's confiscated dope and Scooter would sell it. We'd split the profits. I was trying to get some money of my own, in the event I had to get out of Dodge someday. Well, one day I was talking about my sister, the good daughter, who was married to a banker. His ears perked up and he said he needed some help from a banker. He said he had some numbers and codes that he thought had something to do with banks, but he didn't trust anyone enough to ask. He said, knowing the source, it could be a lot of money. I copied the information and dropped it off for my brother-in-law. He said they were for a numbered offshore account in the Cayman Islands.

He told me I should stop by the bank in Tucson and explain how I got them. Now, he is the upstanding president of the bank and a deacon at his church—the perfect family man—but I could read his sick mind every time he looked at me and I would play him by leaving a button loose or brush up against him. So I said that I was staying at the Marriott, maybe it would be better if he came over there and we could discuss it in private. He said, 'Well, yeah … yeah, yes … that might be, ah … ah be best.'" They both laughed.

"Long story short—he explained everything to me and would have left my sister and kissed my ass for the rest of my life if I had let him. He told me how to transfer the money, thinking we were running away together. I taped our conversation and mailed him a copy at this office."

Bobbie and Kelsey were both laughing as they embraced. Kelsey had now officially submitted. "Take me now. You can do what you want with me."

Bobbie got up and removed the sash from her robe. She tied Kelsey's hands without resistance. Then Bobbie made a gag out of the sash from Kelsey's robe. Kelsey appeared to resist, but half-heartedly.

"Since our roles have now flipped, we have a few more changes to make. If you're going to be my bitch, you have to look butch—not like a movie star."

Kelsey totally freaked when Bobbie returned from the bathroom with a pair of scissors and started cutting off Kelsey's long blonde tresses. She did try to resist, but resistance was futile. When Bobbie finished, Kelsey looked like a Marine recruit. She sobbed as she saw the damage in the mirror on the wall. Bobbie removed her robe and started to make love to her. "Can I take the gag off? Are you gonna behave?"

Kelsey was breathing heavily as she nodded yes. When Bobbie removed the gag, Kelsey said, "I love you."

Bobbie held Kelsey's chin up. "Shh—I know you do."

Sonny's Suite

The phone rang. It was Vinny, out of breath.

"Boss, boss—you gotta see this to believe it. I'm gonna whack off.

Sonny jumped up. "I'll be right down. Nobody else gets in the room."

Comped Suite At Pompeii

Almost two hours had passed since they checked in. Kelsey was naked on the bed—still tied up, but no longer gagged. Bobbie walked into the bedroom.

"I just called our friendly mobster. He'll be here shortly; he must live here. I'm going to close this door and tell him you're out if he asks. Don't make any noise. I'll set things up for tomorrow and then we can get out of here. I don't know what it is, but something doesn't feel right."

The doorbell rang. Bobbie closed the bedroom door, ran her hands through her hair, and checked her makeup before she opened the door. Bobbie was wearing only the robe with the sash reattached. Sonny appeared surprised. "Hey, now I remember you. You didn't have to get all dressed up just for me."

Bobbie led him into the living room. "Cute. This is a business meeting, remember?"

Sonny pretended to be checking out the suite. "So where's your friend? Did she get tied up or something?"

Bobbie was caught visibly off guard by the remark and the smile on Sonny's face. "What did you say?"

"What did I say, what?"

"About my friend—you said—"

"I asked if she was tied up. You know, detained or somethin', since she ain't here?"

Sonny seemed way too relaxed and confident and Bobbie had to struggle to regain her composure. "She had a beauty appointment. She wanted to get her hair done."

Sonny laughed—too easily, "Yeah, well that's women ain't it. I mean—you know what I mean."

"Look Sonny, Sonny Day, why don't we talk business?"

Sonny held his hands out. "That's why I'm here. So you're gonna wire transfer three hundred large to my account tomorrow?"

"That's the plan. We just need a bank."

"I'll make it as easy as possible. We'll do it at my bank; the president's a friend. He's agreed to see us at four tomorrow. Does that work for you?"

"That works. Will you pick me up?"

"I'll pick you up in front at three forty-five. Oh, where's your bank, by the way?"

Bobbie hesitated a bit, which Sonny caught, but she had to reply. "It's what they call offshore."

Sonny just nodded, his wheels turning even faster.

"Hey, Sonny—I need to get some cash too. If I make the wire out for, three fifty, say, can you give me fifty?"

"No problem. In fact, I can give you the cash without adding it to the wire. Let me ask you a question. You ever done a wire transfer before?"

Bobbie looked a little nervous, but didn't want to get caught in a lie. "This will be my first. It's good the president will be there to help."

Sonny smiled and nodded. "You need anything else?"

"We do. My friend is married to the dead agent's boss and she wants to get as far away as possible. We have a new Range Rover in the garage that we'll trade for anything that's reliable, but you have to ditch the plates. Plus, we need new IDs."

Sonny raise his eyebrows. "Anything else?"

"That should do it."

"I'll need your driver's licenses for the new IDs."

"Hang on a minute, they're in the bedroom."

Bobbie went to the bedroom, opening and closing the door quickly. She returned with the driver's licenses. She handed them to Sonny, who looked like the cat who just ate the canary. He looked at the licenses and then back at Bobbie. "I should be able to get the IDs by the time we meet. When are you leaving?"

"As soon as we get our business done. We've got friends in LA."

He nodded and looked around one more time, then headed for the door. "I'll pick you up at a quarter to four tomorrow."

After Sonny left, Bobbie locked the door and almost collapsed. Remembering the conversation, she went to the bedroom and sat down next to Kelsey. "You ever do a wire transfer before?"

Kelsey shook her head. "Of course not. You're the one who mentioned it. Don't you know how to do it?"

"I heard about it in some movie. Not to worry, the bank president is going to help."

Kelsey was nervous. "What if it doesn't work? Do we have a plan B?"

"Sonny's a man and the way to a man's heart isn't through his stomach. Leave him to me."

The Casino at the Pompeii

After leaving Bobbie, Sonny went directly to the casino where he approached Angelo, one of the floor bosses. "Hey, Angelo."

"Mr. Day, how are you tonight? It always sounds funny when I say that. What can I do for you?"

"I'm looking for Wall Street."

Angelo looked around. "He's working table seven tonight, but it looks like he's on break." Angelo spotted him coming back to the table. "There he is now."

"Listen, Angelo, I need a few minutes with Wall Street before he goes back to work."

"Sure thing, Mr. Day. Is everything OK?"

Sonny smiled. "They couldn't be better."

Sonny walked over and greeted the dealer nicknamed Wall Street. The moniker was appropriate, as Wall Street looked like a clean-cut banker, which he was for twenty years. "Wall Street, my man. How ya doin'?"

"Hey, Mr. Day. I'm great—how are you?"

"Never better. Listen, you remember that little issue I helped you out with a couple of years ago?"

Wall Street nodded. "How could I forget? And it wasn't so little at the time. It's like they say about minor surgery – that's when it happens to someone else."

"Well, we take care of our friends and now I need a favor from you. It'll take only an hour or so—say three thirty to five tomorrow afternoon, not far from the Strip."

"No problem. What do you need?"

"I need you to play a banker. Can you do that?"

Wall Street laughed. "I played one for twenty years until Barney Frank and the Fannie Mae melt down."

"Good. So let me ask you a question. You familiar with wire transfers?"

"Did 'em every day."

"Give me the short version of how they work."

"There is no long version; it's simple. The person wiring the money just needs the banking coordinates of the person receiving the funds. Which one are you?"

"I'm the receiver. A lady owes me some money, a lot of money, and she's not familiar with the process."

"I'm glad to help, but you really don't need me. She just needs to contact her bank and give them the instructions."

Sonny appeared pensive. "What about her bank account information?"

"What about it? You don't need it."

"It's a little more complicated than that. What if I want it?"

Wall Street shifted a bit as he got the drift. "Oh … oh, well … you said she was unfamiliar with the process?"

"Totally."

"This is just off the top of my head, but it might work."

"I'm all ears."

"Where are you meeting?"

"At my bank. I've got the use of the president's office. He's a friend, John Carlson. You may have seen him around."

Wall Street nodded. "I know who you're talking about. He hasn't figured out that the house has the edge."

Sonny laughed. "He and millions of others. Let's hope they never do. What's the idea?"

"Well, no money can be wired tomorrow as the banks will be closed—at least yours here in town. Where's her bank?"

"She said off-shore."

Wall Street raised his eyebrows. "No problem, they all have US correspondent banks and that might be even better, particularly if it's a numbered account. OK, here's what I would do. I'd have John, as the bank president, tell her to fill out a form with her account information also and he'll facilitate the transfer in the morning."

"That's a good idea, but John isn't gonna be there. He's leaving early. You're gonna be the president."

Wall Street took a deep breath and exhaled as Sonny watched him closely. "I—I see. So then we'll be even, right?"

"Not just even, but there will be something in it for you. I'll get to that in a minute. I got one more question. What if I wanted to increase the amount of the wire?"

"You mean, with her—with her approval?"

Sonny just shrugged.

"Whew. Well, assuming that she would approve, here's what I suggest: you, I mean I, ask her to fill out two separate applications—one with the amount of the transfer and one blank. I can tell her that it's routine in case the first wire gets botched up in transmission—which does happen. It's rare, but it has happened. That way she doesn't have to come back to the bank."

"That's good, that's real good, because she's leaving town right after the meeting. So, we can send in either of the forms?"

"Well, you'd have to fill out the blank one and it couldn't be for more than she has in the account—which there is no way to know, right?"

"You let me worry about that. Any chance that her bank doesn't play ball?"

"Oh, there's always a chance, and particularly the offshore banks, but, on the other hand, if it's a numbered account and she has the information, it shouldn't be a problem. Sonny, I hope this can't come back and bite me on the ass. Is she—is she gonna know my name?"

"Of course, John Carlson. Oh, and there's ten g's in it for you—maybe twenty if things go well."

"That'll help with the tuition. I'll get my Brooks Brothers and Alan Edmonds out."

"Whatever that means. You ever miss that life?"

"Sonny, I work nights, which keeps me out of trouble, and when I leave here the only thoughts I take with me are of a particularly nice set of tits at my table. I make good dough, I sleep like a baby, play golf during the day, and repeat the process. I have one more college tuition to pay and then I'm done, and the alimony is the best money I've spent in my life. With no small thanks to you—every morning I wake up, I feel like I won the lottery."

"I'll have Vinny pick you up at three thirty."

Gene and Georgetti Restaurant, Chicago

Two bodyguards escorted mob boss, Little Tony Mondelli, past the bar and into the backroom of the restaurant. Mondelli was using a walker and had an oxygen hose attached to his nose. As soon as he sat down, he ripped the hose out. One of his lieutenants picked it up. "Boss, maybe you oughta keep this thing in—in case there's Feds around."

Mondelli was irritated, his usual demeanor. "Fuck the hose and fuck the Feds. Now what's so important that Johnny needs to see me tonight?"

"I dunno. I think it's somethin' about Vegas. The union guy is bitchin about somethin'. Here comes Johnny now."

Johnny Bellini walked in, as always, immaculately groomed and dressed. Bellini was Mondelli's personal emissary. It was understood that when Bellini spoke, he was speaking for Mondelli. He either nodded or shook hands with the other members of the entourage. "How ya doin'? How ya doin'?"

Mondelli motioned for him to sit. "Sit down. It's not like I don't have enough problems. What the fuck is the problem in Vegas? If it's got to do with that moron Vinny and his idiot nephew, this time I want them whacked and I don't care what Sonny says. You got that?"

Bellini held his hands up. "I got a call from the union guy. He was yelling and screaming about Sonny."

Mondelli looked surprised. "Sonny? What did Sonny do?"

Bellini gave the gangster shrug. "I ain't taking sides here. I haven't heard Sonny's side and we all know Sonny. The union guy said he had the senator set up with a couple of hookers in the suite with the cameras and Harry, the manager, tells him that Sonny took over the suite indefinitely, for a couple of broads."

"Whatta ya mean a couple of broads? We spent a lot of money on that suite. Johnny—you fly out there. You tell Harry that I want copies of the tapes of the broads. That comes from me. Tell Harry not to say nothin' and if you see Sonny or his idiot sidekick, you don't say nothin' either. Oh, one more thing—you tell the union guy not to call every time he has his period. You tell him I said that."

Chapter Twenty-Three

The Best Laid Plans …

The DEA Safe House, Apache Dunes, the Following Day

The doctor arranged for them to use an ambulance to take Del home. The doctor spoke with Del before they left. Ray was by his side.

"Del, you're lucky to be alive. You definitely have a concussion so you have to take it easy—and I mean easy, for a while. Get plenty of rest and drink plenty of liquids. If you feel faint or have severe headaches, call me immediately."

"Thanks, Doc. I'll feel better when I'm home. Ray will be with me."

The doctor departed and Del told the EMTs to hold on a minute. He motioned for Ray to come close. "Any word on Kelsey and her bitch?"

Ray shook his head. "I put out an APB as soon as you told me. It's like they vanished."

"That probably means Mexico. Ray, you ready to step up and take Carl's place?"

"I been waitin' for you to ask. Carl was a fuckup."

"You got that right. Get me home. If we're right and Carlos is taking over, he'll have to make contact soon. We'll let him make the first move."

The Office of the Pompeii, Las Vegas

Johnny Bellini walked in unannounced. Harry, the manager, was behind his desk. When he saw Johnny, he jumped up. "Mr. Bellini—this is a surprise. Nobody told me you were coming."

"Relax, Harry. This is a little business trip—spur of the moment thing."

"Is there anything I can do? Anything?"

"Our suite, of course, and Harry, the old man wants the tapes of the broads that Sonny put in the Congressional Suite."

Harry was visibly nervous. "I—I don't have them. Sonny had Vinny pick them up."

Johnny thought for a moment. "Are the broads still there?"

"As far as I know. Sonny told me that only he and Vinny go near the safe room until further notice. Nobody told me differently."

"You didn't do nothin' wrong. Here's the deal—don't say anything to Sonny or Vinny about me askin' for the tapes, or that I know anything about 'em. You have any idea where Sonny is now?"

"No idea. Vinny got the new tape about an hour ago."

Comped Suite, the Pompeii

Bobbie laid down next to Kelsey and pretended to nibble on her ear, but was whispering to her. "Baby, I'm convinced this place is bugged and probably has cameras, too. Don't say anything—just act like you're turned on."

"I don't have to act. Are we in trouble?"

"I don't know. Probably not as long as we've got the money, but I don't trust Sonny and it's funny they want to do the transfer after banking hours. Something's wrong."

Bobbie got out of the bed and called Sonny.

"Sonny here."

"Sonny, it's Bobbie. How you doing on the car and IDs?"

"I told you everything will be ready this afternoon."

"That's great. Oh, there is one little problem. If we meet after hours, we may not be able to get the money until tomorrow morning and we were hoping to leave right after the meeting. We want to drive to LA while it's still light out."

"You mean the extra fifty?"

"Yeah—the extra fifty thousand."

"How come I can't say no to you? I'll give you the fifty after you fill out the forms and then you can be on your merry way. You got to promise to keep in touch."

"Sonny, I know you'll be thinking about me when I'm gone."

The Casino at the Pompeii

Sonny sent Vinny down to the cashier's cage to get the fifty k for Bobbie—all Benjamins. When he walked away from the cage with the money, he almost ran smack into Johnny Bellini. Johnny spoke first. "Hey, go figure—just the man I was lookin for. Vinny, how ya doin'?"

Vinny was definitely caught by surprise. "Johnny—I didn't know you was in town. How ya doin'?"

"Just a quick business trip. Listen, Vinny, I need to talk to Sonny. You know where he is?"

"Sonny? Gee, I'm not sure. If I see him you want me to tell him you're lookin' for him?"

"Yeah, do that. I'm here for a couple of days. I'm gonna get a massage and have lunch in our suite. Hey, is the Oriental gal still around?"

Vinny smiled. "You mean Suzy Wrong? Yeah—she's still here and in great demand."

"Do me a favor. Find her for me and tell her to cancel all her other appointments. You got that?"

"Sure thing, Johnny. No problem."

Sonny's Suite

Vinny returned to the suite with the money. Sonny sensed something was amiss.

"You get the money?"

"Yeah, I got the money, but guess who I ran into in the lobby? Johnny Bellini."

"Johnny Bellini? I didn't know he was comin' to town."

"He just got in and he told me to tell you he's lookin' for you."

Sonny was pensive, trying to digest this new development. "Listen, we got to avoid him until we get this bank thing done."

Vinny smiled.

"What's so funny?"

"You said we got to avoid him until after the bank thing. Well, that ain't gonna be hard to do. He asked me to set him up with Suzy Wrong."

"That's perfect. You get her for him and I don't care if she's with the Pope."

"No shit—is the Pope in town too?"

Sonny could only stare at Vinny.

"What?"

"Listen, moron. Go get the broad and tell her she is to keep Johnny occupied until after five. Can you handle that?"

"I'll take care of it and how about I tell Johnny you'll meet him for dinner?"

"It's amazing that you can come up with a good idea, but that's perfect. Tell Johnny I'll meet him at Carlucci at six thirty—he loves the food. Call Genti and tell him I'm comin' in. Oh, and one more thing. I want two guys to tail the broads when they leave here. They said they're goin' to LA. I want somebody following that car wherever it goes."

"I'll call Petey."

Sonny closed his eyes, took a deep breath, and exhaled before looking at Vinny. "Vinny—I know he's your nephew, but he's a total fucking moron. It must run in the family. You guys grow up in Appalachia by any chance?"

"We ain't even been to Europe."

Sonny stared again. "OK, but you better listen to me. If he fucks this up, I'll whack him myself."

"Sonny, with Petey you just gotta be … whatta ya call it … explis something?"

Sonny raised his voice. "You mean explicit? I'll be very … whatta ya call it—explicit. Tell him he is to stay with the fucking car wherever it goes. If it goes to the moon, he fucking follows it. Is that whatta ya call it explicit enough? Can he understand that?"

Vinny held his hands up. "I'll tell him to stay with the car. Stay with the fucking car."

Mexican Grocery Store, Northwest Side of Chicago

Sandoval parked his unmarked car in front of the grocery store that was the hangout of the Latin Devils street gang. Several gang members were loitering in front. Sandoval and Davey had grown up and run with several of them when they were younger, but it was common knowledge that Sandoval had crossed over and joined the police force. How they found out about Davey remained a mystery. Sandoval exited his car and walked toward the store hoping to find Flaco, the leader of the gang. One of the bangers called out to him. "Man, why donchu come home and get some devil love? You won't have to drive no piece of shit like that."

The homeys all laughed.

Sandoval walked over to the jokester. "How you know I ain't home? When did I ever bust any of your sorry asses?"

"You ain't here for groceries. Whatchu up to Homes?"

"I'm lookin for Flaco. I've got an invitation for him."

"I hope you don't mean warrant. You can't be that stupid."

Sandoval got in his face. "I hope to God you weren't callin' me stupid. You got to take the shit out of your ears. I said invitation—an invitation from the mayor no less. He happens to like Flaco. Good thing he doesn't know the trash he hangs around with."

Flaco emerged from the doorway just in time to cool things down. He looked at Sandoval. "Whassup? Look at chu? Let *mi amigo* through. It's been a long time, Homes. You don't come around much anymore. I thought you forgot where you came from like our old friend Davey."

Sandoval struggled to show no emotion at the mention of Davey's name.

"In fact, Homes, I ain't seen Davey around lately."

"Neither have I, but I ain't here about Davey."

"No? Then whatchu here for Homes?"

"I have a message from the mayor—an invitation to meet with him one-on-one tonight at La Cantina after his big speech in Bucktown. It seems he was impressed by you at the gang summit. He must impress easy."

Flaco held up his hands to prevent a reaction to the slight. "Why you come here and insult me? You got some big *cojones*, but you always did. That's why you're just a punk ass cop and the mayor is the mayor. He can recognize talent when he sees it."

The gang all hooted.

"Let's all chill out. Now tell me about the meet."

"It's top secret. The mayor isn't even telling his closest aides. He told me he had a favor to ask, but he doesn't want his opponents or the newspapers to know about it."

"What kind of favor?"

"Didn't I just say it was secret? You think he would tell me? I'm just the messenger."

"So, how's this go down?"

"After his speech, he'll appear to head back downtown, but he'll stop at La Cantina and meet you in the backroom—just the two of you, and you'll be patted down first."

"Man, you crazy you think I'm gonna go anywhere unarmed."

"I explained that and he agreed that you'll each have a bodyguard, but they stay in front while you meet in the back."

"I dunno—it don't sound right."

"Flaco, this is the mayor. He likes you. Why you think he singled you out of all the gang leaders he met with? He thinks you're the man."

Flaco ate up the flattery with a spoon.

"Yeah—you right. He must have something big in store for me. I got some ideas to run by him."

"Fucking A man. You can't read it any other way."

"What time?"

"I'll pick you and your man up around seven—right here."

"You better be straight up man."

"When was the last time I hassled any of you? Flaco?"

"Yeah?"

"Devil love, man." Sandoval flashed the gang sign. The gang erupted and Flaco beamed.

"Devil love, my man. Hey—you and I got to get together after I see the mayor."

"I'm counting on it."

Bellini's Suite at the Pompeii

Johnny answered the door to find Vinny standing with a stunning Oriental dressed in black leather, with a studded necklace and large purse.

"Hey Johnny. You remember Suzy?"

Johnny stepped aside as they entered. "How could I forget? Come in."

"I'll leave you two alone. I got some errands to run."

"You find Sonny?"

"Oh yeah, he's playin' golf. He said he'd meet you for dinner at Carlucci at six thirty."

Johnny looked surprised. "When did Sonny take up golf?"

"He's one of them whattaya callits—one of them dumpsters?"

"One of them whats?"

"You know—a guy who doesn't play very often."

"A duffer."

"Yeah that's it. Sonny's a duffer."

Johnny stared at Vinny in amazement.

"Well, I gotta go."

Johnny and Suzy were standing in the middle of the room when Vinny left. Suzy reached in her purse and took out a short black whip. She gently wrapped it around Johnny's neck and then whispered in his ear. "We have some work to do. Now tell me—you been a good boy or a naughty boy?"

"I've been very, very naughty."

The Bank, Las Vegas 4:00 Pm

Sonny walked in with Bobbie and Kelsey. Bobbie was wearing a sundress. Kelsey was dressed in blue jeans, a T-shirt, a baseball cap, and sunglasses. Vinny greeted them and escorted them to the president's office, where Wall Street was seated behind the desk. Bobbie noticed the curious glances from the employees who remained, and that the president's secretary wasn't one of them. When they entered the office Wall Street rose to greet them. "Hello, Mr. Day."

"Hello John. John, this is Kelsey and her friend Bobbie. Ladies, this is John Carlson, the bank president. I'll leave you with Kelsey—she's the one doin' the wire for three hundred fifty thousand dollars."

"The forms are already prepared except for the sender's account information. It should only take a few minutes. Of course, you all know this won't go through until tomorrow morning."

Sonny nodded. "No problem. We just want it done right—like we discussed."

Bobbie sensed a little nervousness on the banker's part after Sonny's comment.

"Of course. Very routine matter. Kelsey, why don't you sit down right there and I'll get the forms."

"Bobbie and I will excuse ourselves now as we have other business to discuss."

Sonny took Bobbie by the arm and gently guided her out of the office to the seating area where Vince was waiting.

Kelsey was seated when Wall Street handed her the forms. She looked up at Wall Street. "Why are there two forms when I'm only doing one wire transfer?"

Wall Street sat across from her and gave her a paternal smile. "Kelsey, have you ever done a wire transfer before?"

Kelsey shook her head no.

Wall Street was relieved by her answer. "No problem. You see, Kelsey, we always fill out a second form in the case there's a problem with the first one. Standard operating procedure."

"But, the second one doesn't have an amount."

"Again, standard operating procedure. If we had the amount on both, someone might get confused and think there were two separate but identical wires. It's rare there's a problem."

Kelsey couldn't put her finger on it, but something didn't seem right. One thing she had learned from Del was to be suspicious of everyone and that had generally proven to be good advice.

"Now, Kelsey, if you're ready to proceed, all I need is your account information."

"I could use a glass of water, if that's OK."

Wall Street jumped up. "I'll be right back."

When he returned with the water, Kelsey appeared to be transcribing the account number from a slip of paper in her purse. She looked at the number one more time and then put the pen down—her hand still shaking.

Wall Street stood up. "See, that was painless, wasn't it?"

Kelsey could only manage a weak smile.

"Let's go find Mr. Day and your friend. We're all finished here."

The Bank Seating Area

Sonny turned to Vinny. "Vinny, you got the money and the IDs?"

Vinny handed Bobbie a briefcase. She opened it.

"There's fifty large—I mean thousand, two very good California driver's licenses, and the keys to a like-new Buick. We figured you didn't want anything that would stick out. And you got car insurance cards and a vehicle registration card in there too."

Bobbie was impressed and smiled. "You guys have been great."

Wall Street approached with Kelsey. Sonny looked up. "That was quick."

"All she had to do was fill out the two forms—pretty routine."

Bobbie thought there was a slight emphasis on the number two, but couldn't be sure. It was obvious, though, that Sonny and Vinny received the news well—as they should. They were getting a net of three hundred grand. She clapped her hands. "You've all been great, thanks. When can we get the car?"

Vinny stood. "It's waiting at the hotel with a full tank of gas."

"Great. If you take us back there, we can hit the road right away."

Bobbie looked over at Kelsey, who seemed a million miles away.

Sonny noticed it too. "Doesn't your friend speak?"

"Only when I tell her to."

Pompeii

Bobbie and Kelsey were putting their things in the Buick. Sonny and Vinny were standing nearby. "Vinny, where's Petey? I swear to God I'll put his head in a vice if he fucks this up!"

"Relax, Sonny, he's right over there."

Sonny looked where Vinny was pointing and saw a vintage Dodge Charger, fire engine red with yellow flames on the hood. Sonny was too stunned to speak.

"That's his Starsky and Hutch car."

Sonny grabbed Vinny forcefully. "You fucking moron—you fucking moron! I don't know how you're gonna do it, but you got fifteen minutes to get him in a car that doesn't stand out like a sore thumb. I don't care if you have to carjack someone on the Strip!"

Vinny was shaken. He ran over to the valet stand. Bobbie noticed the commotion and walked over to Sonny. "Everything OK?"

Sonny had to take a deep breath. "Oh yeah, no problem. Hey, I almost forgot—I got a little going away present for you girls. Give me fifteen minutes while I go get it."

Sonny went inside. Vince gave a wad of cash to one of the parking valets who then drove a gray, late model Toyota across the street and swapped cars with Petey. Bobbie noticed everything and just smiled.

Sonny reemerged with a couple of fashion tees with Pompeii in glitter. He handed them to Bobbie. "It's just a little something to remember me by."

Bobbie acted surprised. "You shouldn't have."

It was hard to tell who was the most smug—Sonny or Bobbie.

"Well, you gals want to get on your way. I'm sure your friend has a lot to talk about."

"Sonny, there are things you can do with your mouth besides talk."

Sonny laughed. "I won't forget you two."

"Sonny, I can guarantee that."

Sonny watched as they got in the Buick and pulled onto the Strip, only to be nearly rear-ended by Petey. Sonny could only gaze in amazement.

Bobbie was way too exhilarated by the dramatic turn of fate to be concerned about Kelsey's somber mood, ascribing it to her having difficulty in adapting to the change of roles. Let's see, in just the past few days Bobbie had averted certain death in Mexico at the hands of a psychotic assassin, whose death she had subsequently finessed, while picking up a cool twenty g's. All indications were that Del somehow survived the explosion, but, even if he did, that wasn't all bad in that she then wasn't responsible for his death. If that wasn't enough, she had outwitted two Vegas mobsters—check that, outwitted one, as the other one was witless—and pocketed another fifty g's, plus they had new IDs and a new ride. Not to mention that it appeared the thirty million was legit. Was this a great country or what? She glanced again at Kelsey, who remained lost in a funk. A few days in Acapulco would be just the tonic she needed.

Chapter Twenty-Four

What's Twenty-Nine Divided by Two?

Sheriff's House, Apache Dunes

Dylan was on the patio reading the file and reached for the phone to call Jake, who answered immediately.

"Jake, I've been reading the file, but nothing jumps out at me. There are a couple of names that are unfamiliar to me and one is underlined. It seems like Scooter turned into quite the ladies man, but this is the only name underlined—Kelsey."

"I must have missed that."

"It appears that she might have been involved with his venture into the drug business."

"I wanna see that file again. The only Kelsey I know of around here is married to the head DEA agent—the one who appears to have disappeared. That Kelsey, however, is a stunning—and I mean stunning—blonde. She's way out of Scooter's league. Having said that, I don't know anyone who knows anything about her or her husband, for that matter. If he's still alive, he's our prime suspect in his partner's murder."

"Any ideas?"

"Let's follow up with Tom and see if he knows more than is in the report."

"What happened to sleepy old Apache Dunes?"

"You mean Mayberry, as Sandowski calls it?"

"Any news on him?"

"I spoke with him an hour or so ago. He said he had an errand to run tonight and he would be on a flight tomorrow that would get into Tucson around five p.m."

Carlucci Restaurant at the Pompeii

Sonny was sitting in booth number one nursing his drink when Johnny arrived.

"Johnny, how ya doin'? Welcome to Vegas. What brings you to town?"

Johnny sat down and ordered a drink. "This is a business trip, Sonny. The old man sent me."

"What's up?"

Johnny looked at Sonny. "That's what the old man wants to know and he sent me to find out. First, the union guy called up bitchin' and moanin' about getting that special suite taken away from him. Said he had something important set up."

Sonny jumped in. "Johnny, the guys a cunt—you know that. You know who they had booked in there? The fucking Senator! If they don't know he's a pervert now, they never will."

Johnny held up his hand while his drink was served. "Let me finish, OK? And Sonny, understand one thing, cause I ain't gonna say it again—Harry works for us. He's our manager. No harm better come to him. You hear me?"

Sonny looked stunned. "Why would anybody harm Harry? What the fuck did I do?"

"You're no dummy, unlike that fucking moron you hang around with. Harry told me the facts."

"Facts? What facts?"

"What facts? How about the fact that you took over the suite for a couple of broads and then you tell Harry that only you and Vinny can see the tapes?"

Sonny took a drink and savored it, hoping to defuse the situation a bit. "Yesterday, I got a call out of the blue from a broad I ran into in Arizona, when I went to collect on a marker from a bent fed down there—at your request."

"It wasn't a request."

Sonny shrugged. "Sorry—at your demand. You happy now? In the meantime, as you know, the fed got whacked in the desert and his wife got whacked down in Mexico—leaving us stiffed for one hundred fifty large."

Johnny waved his hand for Sonny to speed it up. "Tell me somethin' I don't know."

"That's what I'm tryin' to do. This broad tells me she needs a favor and is willing to pay off the dead guy's marker in exchange."

Johnny now leans forward. "She said she was gonna pay off one hundred fifty large?"

Sonny now took his time and had another sip. "No—I told her it was three hundred large and she said, no sweat, she'd do a wire transfer tomorrow morning."

Johnny was now fully engaged. Sonny smiled. "It's getting good, isn't it?"

Johnny motioned again. "Keep goin'."

Sonny milked the situation by motioning to the waiter for another round before continuing.

"So I'm thinking. Put them in the suite with the cameras and bugs and maybe find out how these broads got three hundred large."

"I gotta say—that was good thinking, Sonny."

"Excuse me, was that a thank you?"

"I'll wait for the rest of the story."

They both paused as the waiter replaced their drinks.

"Johnny, that's why I didn't want anybody else to see those tapes."

"But, you were eventually gonna tell the old man everything?"

Sonny threw up his hands. "Why do you insult me like this? I told you—this all happened in the past twenty-four hours and just ended, a very happy ending indeed, about an hour ago."

Johnny nodded, but still appeared skeptical—as was his nature.

"So I comped them the suite and told them I'd see 'em later about what they wanted in return."

"Which was?"

"I'll get to that. So they check in and I send Vinny down to check the tape."

"How'd he find his way down there by himself?"

"I hear ya, but he has his moments. Anyway, Vinny calls me and says I gotta get down there immediately and see the tape. Turns out these chicks—and Johnny, they're both fifteens on a scale of one to ten. I ain't lyin. They'd make a fortune in this town. Turns out these chicks are lesbos and into B&D—serious B&D!"

"So you guys got to watch some real live porn."

Sonny closed his eyes. "That's the second time you busted my balls."

"You'll get over it. Finish the story."

"So, the one chick asks the other how she got the money in the first place."

"The three hundred grand."

Sonny is now animated. "The thirty fucking million!"

Johnny choked on and spilled part of his drink. He wiped his chin and dabbed at his silk suit. "Say that again."

"The thirty fucking million."

It was clear that Johnny's wheels were turning. He savored his drink and sucked on a piece of ice before speaking. "Sonny, who all—and I mean, all, knows about this?"

Sonny smiled. "Only three people. Me, you, and Vinny."

"Sonny, Vinny's a fucking moron."

"I tell him that at least twice a day, but whatta ya gonna do? He saw the tape."

"I dunno. We'll have to think about that."

"About what?"

"About Vinny."

Sonny was quiet for a moment. "Whatever. Let me tell you what I did."

"Hold on. First, what'd they want from you?"

"Simple. The one broad wants away from her husband—the dead fed's boss. They needed new IDs, to swap their car, a new Range Rover, and fifty g's."

"Time out. I thought you said she was giving you three hundred. Why did she need fifty from you?"

"Let me finish. She said she would do the wire transfer to me for three hundred, but would make it out for three fifty so she could get some walkin' around money. Now, I'm thinkin' about the thirty million, not the three hundred grand—and certainly not the fifty. They wanted to leave right after the wire. If I waited until tomorrow morning, I could only make the wire for three fifty. If I gave her fifty today, which I did, they would take off tonight, which they did. Tomorrow morning the wire will go through for twenty-nine million!"

"Sonny, I hope to fuck you know what you're doin, cause I'm getting a headache tryin' to figure this out. First of all, how you gonna make the wire for twenty-nine million? Secondly, why twenty-nine million and not thirty? I hope you ain't tryin to get cute and fuck this up."

"Johnny, I never did a wire transfer before, so I didn't know anything about how they were done."

"Me either."

"Neither did the broad. Then I remembered that we got a dealer here who ran a bank for twenty years, before it collapsed in the crisis. He went through a messy divorce and some other stuff. When he wound up here lookin' for a job, he was a mess. In fact, I helped him out of a jam and had never called in the marker. His nickname is Wall Street. So I pay him a visit and he explains the ins and outs of a wire transfer. It's pretty simple except generally it's the sender's bank that initiates it and there is only one form to fill out with the amount and the receiver's banking information."

"So now you're an expert on wire transfers. How's that help?"

"You keep interruptin' me. The president of my bank, just off the Strip, is into us for fifteen. Was more, but he's got it down to fifteen. He'll die before he makes money at the blackjack table. Anyway, I kill two birds with one stone, so to speak. I tell the bank president that I'll wipe out his debt if I can use his office. I told Wall Street that we're even if he plays bank president today and tells the broad it's routine to fill out two forms, not just one, and one of them is blank. They both agreed and it worked like a charm. The broad got her fifty and couldn't wait to get out of town. The wire goes in tomorrow morning."

"You still ain't explained why the wire is for twenty-nine and not thirty."

"Wall Street told me that if you made the wire for more than was in the account, it would get kicked back. I'd get nothin'. I had no way of knowin' if they had spent any of that money, but knew they didn't spend a million, or they wouldn't need me."

"That was good thinking Sonny. No reason to get greedy. You know what they say back home? The pigs get fat and the hogs get slaughtered. You said they left. You have any idea where they were goin'?"

"They said LA, but I wasn't takin' any chances. I got two guys tailin' the car and they checked in just before you showed up. My guys are with the car."

"So tomorrow morning, twenty-nine million bucks shows up in your account?"

"Tomorrow morning."

"Sonny, I'm sorry. I underestimated you. It's the fucking idiots we have to deal with today. They're not much smarter than the politicians—just more honest."

They laughed. The waiter approached, but Johnny waved him away.

"No problem, Johnny. I always looked up to you."

Johnny's demeanor turned very serious. He even glanced around to be sure no one was within ear shot. "Sonny, listen to me. We gotta sleep on this and talk in the morning. *Capiche*?"

"*Capiche*."

"Now, I ain't sayin anything and I ain't implying anything. You hear me?"

"Loud and clear."

"It's just—all I'm saying is, the old man is, well—an old man, and he's got the feds up his asshole. When he goes out he wears an air hose to look like he's sick, but, the truth is, he is sick. He's pissing blood. He tries to hide it, but one of the guys has to take him to the john. Some of the guys ain't happy. It's not a good situation. I'd stay out here if I could."

"I've heard some rumblings. Twenty-nine million is a lot of money—even split three ways."

"It's even more split just two. *Capiche*?"

"*Capiche*."

"Listen, Sonny—I think I'll eat in my room tonight. I got some thinkin' to do and I wanna be up when the banks open."

"No problem. I might do the same. Tell me what you want and I'll have them send it up to your room."

They both got up and embraced. Johnny winced as Sonny patted him on the back. "Sorry, I forgot about the massage."

"No problem. How was the golf game?"

"What golf game?"

"Never mind. What's twenty-nine divided by two?"

"Fourteen and a half."

Sonny's Suite

Vinny was surprised that Sonny was back so quick and jumped up when he heard him enter. "That was quick. I thought you was having dinner? What'd Johnny want?"

"You know—da beep, da bop, nothin' really. Have you heard from Petey?"

"Just got off the phone. They're still with the car."

"He say where they are?"

"You want me to ask?"

"Not necessary. They're at least three hours away. Just make sure he stays with the car. I'm hitting the hay. It's gonna be a big day tomorrow and, Vinny—you stay with me tomorrow at all times. You hear me?"

"Where am I gonna go?"

Chicago

Sandoval was on his way to pick up Flaco and his bodyguard. He called Sandowski who was on his way to La Cantina.

"Max, I'm about five minutes away from picking up Flaco. You all set?"

"Almost there. I'll be in the alley. A couple of unmarks are gonna cover both ends."

"Good. A pal of mine drives one of the Channel Seven trucks. He's gonna circle the restaurant a few times—make it look like they suspect something."

"Great idea. Listen—you watch yourself. I don't trust that rat fuck."

Sandoval laughs. "When the ego goes up against the brain, take the ego and give the points."

"I used to tell Davey that."

"Where you think I heard it?"

They both laughed.

The Mexican Grocery Store

Sandoval pulled up in front of the Devil's hangout. "The Eagle has landed."

"Roger that."

The usual suspects were hanging out on the street corner. One of them ran inside the store when Sandoval pulled up. He parked his car and got out.

One of the Devil's approached. "Whatchu about, Homes?"

Sandoval flashed the Devil's sign. The bangers liked it. Flaco appeared dressed like he was going to a pimp's convention. "Hey Homes, how do I look?"

"You look great. I think I saw that outfit at Brooks Brothers."

"Who the fuck are the Brooks Brothers?"

"Never mind. Where's your man? We gotta get goin'."

The bodyguard walked over and flicked open a switch blade, pretending to clean his nails. He stared at Sandoval. "I'm his man tonight."

"Whatever. Get in—you're in the back."

"Donchu forget it. I'm always right behind you."

Del's Mansion

The sheriff pulled up in Del's driveway. An unfamiliar car was parked there and there were lights on in the house. He rang the doorbell and a new face in a DEA polo shirt answered the door. "Can I help you?"

"I'm the sheriff. My name is Tom—I don't believe we've met."

"Ray with the DEA. What can I do for you?"

"I'm actually looking for the missus if she's around."

Del's voice can be heard from inside. "Who is it, Ray?"

Ray turns to answer. "It's the sheriff. Says he's looking for your wife."

Del scooted up in his wheelchair. One arm and one leg were in casts and his head was still bandaged. "Aren't we all? Come on in Tom. Take a load off."

Tom entered, visibly surprised by Del's condition. "What in the world happened to you?"

"Car wreck. Lucky to be alive."

"I didn't hear anything about a car wreck around here."

"Wasn't around here. Down south, if you get my drift."

"All I knew is that I heard you were away."

"Just as well. So you're looking for Kelsey?"

"A few questions is all. Is she here?"

"She was gone when I got home. Ran away with a girlfriend. Let her parents take the kid and flew the coop. No warning—no nothing."

"I don't know what to say."

"Nothin' to say. That's life and life is way different these days. I saved her life and this is the thanks I get. Can I help you with the questions?"

"I doubt it. They were about a local kid named Scooter that she may have been friends with."

"I remember him. Wasn't he the one the Garcias tortured and killed before they just poof—disappeared?"

"I believe we had that discussion before."

"Kelsey used to call him Kato after OJ's boyfriend. Worthless as tits on a bull, but the ladies thought he was cute."

"That pretty much describes him. You ever hear of him dealing?"

Del laughed, then winced. "It hurts when I laugh. We just assume everybody around here, present company excepted, is involved in the trade. There's no industry to speak of—yet people seem to get by pretty well. We have to focus on the big dogs."

Tom nodded and started to walk away. He pivoted. "Del, there is one more thing. Do you know if Kelsey had any friends who were bankers?"

"Banker friends? I don't know of any friends who were bankers, but her brother-in-law runs a chain of banks in Tucson. I don't think they got along too well, though."

"You happen to recall his name?"

"I told you, he was her brother-in-law, J.R. Blake."

"Thanks, Del. You take care—hear?"

La Cantina Restaurant, Bucktown, Chicago

Sandoval pulled up to La Cantina just as a Channel Seven News truck passed by—slowing, but not stopping.

Flaco was excited. "Hey, man, we gonna be on TV."

Sandoval turned to him. "Not if we can help it. The mayor insists this is strictly one-on-one tonight. He said he has something big to propose."

Sandoval parked the car. After he got out, he scanned the area for any sign of Devils lurking around, but saw none. They walked inside.

The restaurant was quiet. There was only a couple at the bar and two tables occupied in the bar area. They walked to the rear, where the cop pretending to be the mayor's bodyguard blocked the door to the backroom. Sandoval motioned to Flaco, who stepped forward, smirking at the bodyguard. "I hope your hands are clean."

The cop patted him down and then turned to look at Flaco's bodyguard.

"Donchu even think about touching me, Homes."

The cop looked at Sandoval, who shrugged, and then escorted Flaco into the empty backroom.

Flaco looked around. "When's the mayor comin'?"

Sandoval made sure the alley door was unlocked and then walked toward Flaco. "You and I have some business to discuss first."

Sandoval put on brass knuckles. Flaco freaked and tried to run for the door, but Sandoval caught him squarely in the jaw and sent him sprawling. Flaco's bodyguard heard the commotion and moved toward the door with his switchblade open. The couple at the bar and the two tables of patrons were all cops. They pulled their guns in unison as one of them put the closed sign in the window and motioned for the bartender to vamoose—which he was only too happy to do.

The cop blocking the door pointed his pistol at the bodyguard's head. "What're you doin' asshole? Don't you know better than to bring a knife to a gun fight? This is for Davey."

Eleven guns fired in unison and kept firing in the event that the first eleven at point blank range hadn't done the job. Flaco was on the floor and dazed when he heard the deafening sound of the execution. Sandoval slipped cuffs on him and gagged him. Sandowski also heard the gunfire and came rushing through the alley door. Sandoval had to restrain him from stomping Flaco to death.

"Let's get him out of here. Your trunk open?"

Sandowski was still hyperventilating. "I want this to be slow."

Sandoval smiled. "It'll be better than that. I got a cousin who manages a hog farm in Indiana, about an hour from here. He knew Davey. He told me that hungry hogs will devour a human body—even the bones."

Flaco's eyes were wide with fright.

"I hope they're hungry."

"He's got forty big hogs that ain't even sniffed food since we came up with the idea. Let's take the bodyguard too. Come to think of it—it won't be slow, but it sure will be fun."

Sandowski's mouth was open. "Remind me never to piss you off."

Aeromexico Flight from Las Vegas to Acapulco

The pilot announced that they would be touching down in fifteen minutes. Kelsey still appeared nervous while Bobbie was enjoying the first-class perks.

"Bobbie, are you sure Acapulco is a good idea? Las Vegas didn't work out so well."

Bobbie looked shocked. "We've got fifty thousand dollars to go with my twenty and new IDs. What am I missing?"

"You think that Sonny is going to just forget about us?"

"Why does Sonny care? He got his money. He's probably like a pig in shit. We have driver's licenses, not passports. It kinda limits our options."

"What about the Mexicans?"

"I would think that Acapulco would be the last place they'd think we'd be. Only an idiot would think we'd come here."

Kelsey frowned.

"What?"

"Del's an idiot."

Sonny's Suite, the Following Morning

Sonny stretched and answered the door to let Vinny in. "You hear anything from Petey?"

"Not since last night. You want me to call?"

"Yeah, you call and I'll put the coffee on."

Vinny went to the phone to call Petey, who yawned when he answered, as if still asleep.

"Petey—it's Vinny. You still with the car?"

"We been with it all night. It hasn't moved."

Vinny called out to Sonny. "Petey says they been with the car all night—it hasn't moved."

Sonny hesitated for a moment and then darted over and grabbed the phone. "This is Sonny. Whatta you mean it hasn't moved?"

"It hasn't moved. It's been here all night."

"It's been where all night?"

"The airport here in Las Vegas."

Sonny screamed. "You fucking idiot! You mean they went straight to the airport and you never said anything?"

"Vinny said to stay with the car. That's what I did."

Sonny threw the phone across the room and grabbed Vinny by his collar, still screaming. "I told you—I told you—I told you. I said I was gonna put his head in a vice and I'm gonna fucking do it!"

Vinny was pleading. "Sonny you was expli-whatever. You said for him to stay with the car—stay with the car. That's what he did."

Sonny plopped down in his chair and rubbed his temples. The phone rang. Vinny handed it to Sonny. "This better be fucking good."

Johnny Bellini was the caller. "What kind of hello is that? I was gonna invite you for breakfast, this bein' our big day. I hope nothing has gone wrong?"

Sonny tried to compose himself. "Sorry, Johnny—no, nothing wrong—just a little personal issue I have to deal with."

"Do me a favor and keep your fucking personal issues to yourself. I've got enough of my own. What time does the bank open?"

"It should have just opened. I'm waiting for the call."

"I'll wander down to the café and read the paper. Meet me there as soon as you hear."

Sonny hung up and started to dial a number, but changed his mind.

He walked over to the window overlooking the strip and was lost in thought. Vinny tried to speak. "Listen, Sonny."

Sonny walked toward Vinny pointing his finger. "Vinny don't say a word, not a fucking word. In fact, go take a walk. I need to think."

Vinny departed quickly. No sooner had Sonny sat back down than the phone rang again. Sonny grabbed it. "Sonny here."

"Sonny, this is John—John Carlson."

"I know who it is. Just tell me the wire went through."

"Sonny, er, I'm afraid we have a problem."

Sonny was now enraged and almost out of control. "You listen to me John. We don't have a problem. I want my money!"

"Sonny, I wasn't even there. I didn't have anything to do with it. You asked for my office and I gave it to you. You wanted me gone."

Sonny exhaled. "Sorry, John—but, how can there be a problem?"

"It's the account number. Their account number was wrong."

"So somebody misread a number. Try another one."

"It's more than that. All of the numbers were wrong. They don't match the bank or the account. Sonny, Sonny are you there?"

Sonny had dropped the phone and collapsed in his chair.

Chapter Twenty-Five

St. Christopher

Sandowski's Condo in Chicago

Sandowski was awakened by the banging on the door. He had fallen asleep on the couch again. He tried to clear the cobwebs, reached for his gun, and went to the door. "Who the fuck is it?"

"It's me, Pete, the chief. Open up"

Sandowski opened the door. The chief entered in a huff, but motioned for his entourage of cops to wait outside.

"Chief, what's up?"

"What's up? What's up? I knew you had some cleaning up to do with the Devils and we looked the other way because of Davey, but what the fuck was the massacre all about? Are you fucking nuts? Don't answer that."

Sandowski appeared at a loss. "Massacre? What massacre?"

The chief got eyeball to eyeball with him. "Do not fucking play me! You swear you don't know?"

"Pete, I've never lied to you. I have no idea what you're talking about."

The chief backed off a bit. "Where's Sandoval?"

"How would I know? What happened?"

"What happened is—the night—the very night the mayor gave his speech about how he had a plan to stop the violence and the killing, somebody drove by the Groceria the Devils call home and opened fire with an automatic and didn't stop until nine people were dead!

Fortunately, none were bystanders. There are no witnesses—at least none that aren't scared shitless."

Sandowski sat down on his couch and motioned the chief to a chair. "We had some business over in Indiana and got back around shortly after eleven. He dropped me off. What time was the shooting?"

"Around midnight."

"I'm glad he's on our side."

The Chief just stared at him. "When are you leaving?"

"As soon as I get cleaned up. My flight is at one."

"You're taking Rambo with you and cancel the flight—you're driving. I'm afraid he'll blow up the plane if the peanuts aren't fresh."

"What about the mayor?"

"The mayor's a fucking asshole. Fuck him and his tutu. Where are you headed again?"

"A place called Apache Dunes, Arizona."

"Drive slow. I want time to call my broker and short their municipal bonds."

Jake's SUV Traveling to Tucson

Dylan and Jake were headed to Tucson for an appointment with Kelsey's brother-in-law, the bank president.

"Jake, he's expecting us, right?"

"Sounded like he'd rather get a root canal."

"How'd you spook him?"

"That's what's odd. I hardly said anything. I simply introduced myself and said we'd like to ask him a couple of questions about his sister-in-law, Kelsey."

Valley of the Sun National Bank & Trust, Tucson

Dylan and Jake arrived and approached the receptionist inside the bank. "May I help you?"

"Yes ma'am, please. We have an appointment with Mr. Blake."

"Are you Mr. Devlin and Mr. Reid?"

"Yes ma'am."

"They're waiting for you in the boardroom. Follow me."

Dylan looked at Jake. "They?"

Jake shrugged.

Inside the boardroom J.R. Blake was seated at one side of the long conference table flanked by his attorney on one side and a court reporter further down the table. A tape recorder was positioned in the middle of the table. Jake and Dylan were visibly surprised by the scene. They were seated on the opposite side.

Blake's attorney opened the meeting. "Gentlemen, my name is Oscar West. I'm Mr. Blake's attorney. This discussion will be recorded and everyone will be provided with a transcript upon request. My assistant will also be creating a transcript of this meeting. Please identify yourselves for the record."

Dylan and Jake looked at each other, still a bit confused. Dylan motioned for Jake to go first. "Nice to meet you all. I'm Jake Devlin, the deputy sheriff of Apache Dunes. To my right here is Dylan Reid. Neither of us expected all this. I told Mr. Blake that I just wanted to ask him a couple of questions about his sister-in-law."

Blake started to speak, but his attorney cut him off. "I'll be speaking for Mr. Blake today. Now, please explain what this is all about."

"Mr. West, I'm Dylan Reid. We're simply trying to clear someone who is suspected of making a fraudulent wire transfer and we believe that Mr. Blake's sister-in-law may have some information that could be helpful in that regard."

"You say fraudulent wire transfer. Two questions: How much was the wire transfer for and in which jurisdiction have any charges been filed?"

Jake fielded the questions. "The transfer was for around thirty million dollars."

Blake, sipping water from a bottle, choked when he heard the amount. It took him a couple of minutes to regain his composure.

West intoned. "For the record, we had a brief recess and are now back on the record. Please proceed."

Jake continued. "I'm not aware of any charges being filed."

West looked at Blake and then back at Jake. "Please repeat that and a little louder, please."

"I said, I'm not aware of any charges being filed."

"Have you interviewed Mr. Blake's sister-in-law?"

"We don't know where she is."

West leaned over to Blake and whispered in his ear. Blake shook his head no.

"My client has no knowledge of her whereabouts either. Therefore, I see no reason to continue this meeting. If you have any questions for Mr. Blake, please submit them directly to me—my card is in front of you. Please refrain from any further contact with my client. Good day, gentlemen. This meeting has ended."

Jake and Dylan glanced at each other in total surprise while the attorney, his assistant, and Blake quickly departed the room.

In the parking lot afterward, Dylan smiled. "You see his reaction when you said thirty million?"

Jake laughed. "Not to mention that I thought we were in a federal hearing or something."

"No kidding—he's definitely hiding something. Problem is, we're not going to find out from him."

"It gets curiouser and curiouser."

Master Suite at Las Brisas, Acapulco

Bobbie tipped the bellboy and closed the door. Kelsey still appeared miserable. "Don't you think a regular room would do? Isn't this a bit extravagant?"

"I don't know what you're problem is, but it shouldn't be money. We left Vegas with over seventy thousand cash and you've got access to thirty million."

"Bobbie—there's something I gotta tell you."

"Something's been eating you since we left Vegas. We should be celebrating. If you're having second thoughts about Del or your family, it's a bit late."

"It's not that. I've finally admitted how fucked up I am. It's about the money."

"What about the money?"

"You're not going to be happy. When I went to fill in the bank account information for the transfer, I realized I didn't have it."

Bobbie was stunned. "What do you mean, you didn't have it?"

"I mean that we were so fucked up and in such a hurry to leave, I forgot to get the information. I hid it where Del couldn't find it, but I forgot to take it."

"How did you do the wire?"

"The only thing I could do, I made up some numbers."

"Are you telling me that we have to go back to Apache Dunes?"

"If we want the information, we do?"

"What about Sonny's wire?"

"He's probably not a happy camper right now."

Café at Pompeii

Johnny Bellini was having a cup of coffee and reading the sports section when Sonny showed up.

"Sonny, why the long face? This is our big day."

Sonny sat down. "Johnny, we got a problem."

"Stop right there. WE don't have any problems. If there is a problem, and I hope for your sake there isn't, YOU got a problem. Not we, not us, not them—you!"

The waiter approached with menus. Johnny scowled at him. "Get the fuck outta here and leave us alone. I'll let you know when we want something."

"It's the broad. She gave us a bogus account number."

"Maybe somebody made a mistake?"

"It was all bogus."

Johnny knocked over a glass of water when he reached across the table and grabbed Sonny's shirt. When he realized the commotion he made, he let go and took a deep breath. "Let me get this straight. You pissed off the union guy and some broad took you—and notice I didn't say us—I said you, for fifty g's?"

Sonny could only shrug.

"Where are the broads now? You said you had 'em tailed."

"That's another problem. Vinny had his nephew tail her and he lost her."

Johnny lost his grip and threw a roll at Sonny. "Didn't I tell you the guy's a moron? Didn't I?"

"I told Vinny I'd kill Petey."

Johnny leaned over and grabbed Sonny's shirt again, but spoke softly this time. "Sonny, you're gonna kill Petey AND Vinny—TODAY. You hear me?"

Sonny hung his head.

"And Sonny—you better find that broad. If you don't, don't come back here. In fact, disappear, because I can't protect you."

"Johnny, I might need Vinny for backup."

Johnny rubbed his temples. "Sonny, the nephew has to go. Period. No debate. I gotta send a message. You got two weeks to find the broad."

Sonny's Suite

Sonny called Vinny. "Vinny—listen to me. You and I have to find those broads. Get packed and I'll pick you up in two hours. In the meantime, I got an errand I need Petey to help me with. Tell him to meet me in front in half an hour."

Vinny hesitated for a bit. "Sonny—is Petey OK?"

"Would I trust him to help with an errand if he wasn't?"

"Where are we goin'?"

"How do I know? I guess we go back to where this all started and see if we can pick up the trail."

"What about that sheriff?"

"That sheriff is the least of our problems right now."

Sonny picked Petey up outside of the Pompeii.

"Sorry, I'm runnin' a little late."

Petey was fidgeting with his necklace. "No problem, Sonny. Where we goin'?"

"We got to meet someone out in the desert, won't take long. What's with the necklace? I don't recall you wearing one."

"It's a St. Christopher medal. Uncle Vince gave it to me this morning. He said it was my father's."

"What happened to your dad?"

"He was killed in Sicily before I was born. Uncle Vince said that St. Christopher is supposed to protect you. Didn't work for my dad, I guess."

"How'd you get over here?"

"I had two older sisters and my mom had her hands full. She said nobody wanted to adopt us all. Uncle Vince saved up some money and brought us here—all of us. He's tried to be a father figure for me, but I think it's been tough on him. He said he thinks I fell on my head as a child, maybe—I don't know."

Sonny was silent for a while, then beat his hands on the steering wheel.

"Sonny, is everything OK?"

"Yeah—it's just that sometimes a man's gotta do what a man's gotta do, even if he don't like it."

Sonny pulled off the highway and drove a couple of miles into the desert.

Petey looked around. "We meetin' them here?"

"Yeah, they should be here shortly. Let's get out and stretch our legs. I gotta get something out of the trunk."

They exited and Sonny opened the trunk. A pair of gloves and a taped-up revolver were in a small bag. Sonny put the gloves on, but then ripped them off, slammed the trunk door and screamed, "FUCK!" at the top of his lungs.

Petey was startled. "Sonny, you OK?"

"Nothin' is fucking OK. Get in the fucking car and don't say a fucking word. I mean not a fucking word!"

They got back in the car and Sonny banged his fists and then his head against the steering wheel. He grabbed a necklace from under his shirt and turned to Petey. "You see this? And don't forget, not a fuckin' word. This is a St. Christopher's medal that my grandmother gave me for my First Communion. She said it would protect me and I'm still here. Maybe your dad wasn't wearing it—you don't fucking know, cause you weren't there. We're gonna find out if it protects us very soon, because we're all in deep shit now."

Sonny accelerated and the car spun around, kicking up a cloud of sand.

Sandowski's Car, Northern Arizona

Sandowski was driving while Sandoval seemed lost in his thoughts. Sandowski nudged him. "Can I ask you something?"

"Shoot."

"I get you wanting to go back and take out a few Devils, but I don't get how you went about it. You're lucky to be alive."

"I didn't expect to be."

"You tellin' me that was a suicide mission?"

"It's a bit more complicated than that. I just kinda felt like my life was pretty much over. I did what I came to do. Now, it's kinda funny. It's like somebody was lookin' after me last night—protectin me. It's like, maybe I've got a purpose. I just don't know what it is."

"Stop right there. I'm the last guy to give anybody any psychological advice."

They both laughed.

"You don't know this, but I envied Davey that he had you. Neither of us knew our fathers and life can be tough even with a dad, but it sucks bad if you don't have one. It's like bein' alone in one of them mazes with all those roads to go down and all but one bein' a dead end. I don't know where we're goin' now, but I'm glad we're together."

Sandowski reached over and patted Sandoval on the back.

"We, my friend, are going on an adventure, but we ain't getting there if we don't stop for gas soon—like the next exit."

They took the exit ramp to a gas station and mini-mart in the middle of nowhere. Sandowski pulled up to one of the pumps.

He got out and headed directly to the mini-mart. "I gotta piss like a race horse. You pump and I'll pay inside."

Sandoval was pumping the gas when two young Latinos pulled up to the adjacent pump in a lowrider with rap music blaring. Sandoval looked over at the car.

The driver got out and stared back. "What the fuck you lookin' at?"

Sandoval replied, "I hope you weren't talking to me."

"Who you think I'm talkin to, Melvin?"

Sandowski emerged from the restroom and approached the cashier when he glanced outside. "Oh shit —I'll be right back."

The cashier grabbed Sandowski's arm and whispered. "*Amigo*, those are bad dudes, very bad dudes."

The cashier then motioned to the second Latino, who approached the cashier with a bag of Doritos and a coke.

Outside, Sandoval approached the punk, who made a move as if he was reaching for a gun or knife. In a flash, Sandoval grabbed his pistol from his waistband and proceeded to pistol whip the shit out of him. The punk was bleeding and trying to crawl away.

His friend dropped the snacks and started toward the door, but was tripped up by Sandowski's extended baton. Sandowski took out his anger and frustration on the guy until he was unconscious.

Sandoval sprayed gas into the lowrider and then drove it off to the side. He lit a match and flicked it inside. The car erupted in flames. The cashier was in absolute shock. "*Madre de Dios*!"

Sandowski turned to him. "Rap music isn't his genre."

He reached for his wallet. "Here's money for the gas, but I'm gonna need your video tapes."

The cashier was shaking. "The video doesn't work."

"Good—those boys are lucky there isn't a hog farm nearby."

"Wha—what?"

"It's a private joke. Sorry for all the blood."

Sandowski and Sandoval drove away as the lowrider exploded. Sandoval noticed Sandowski gazing at him. "What?"

"Nothin'– I'm just impressed."

"About what?"

"Your anger management progress. We're halfway to our destination and you haven't killed anybody yet."

They fist bumped and laughed.

Sonny's Car

Sonny called Vinny as he was driving back to Vegas. Vinny had been expecting a call and had been pacing in his room. He answered his phone.

"Yeah."

"Vinny, listen to me and listen carefully. Meet me at the hotel's loading dock. Get one of them laundry carts and plenty of sheets. I'm goin' up to Johnny's room. You and Petey are gonna bring the cart up and wait for me in the hallway. I already talked to the Oriental gal. She knows what to do."

"Wait—Sonny, is Petey still alive?"

"I regret it already, so don't remind me. If we don't find those broads we're all dead.

"Sonny, I owe you big time."

"Tell me something I don't know."

Las Brisas, Acapulco

When Bobbie returned to the room, Kelsey was sobbing.

"Chill out. We'll get the information if it's in the house."

"It's not just the bank information. It's not just the money."

Bobbie sat down next to her and gently patted her back. "OK, I give up. What's the problem?"

"What's the problem? Everything is the problem. I'm the problem."

Bobbie took her in her arms and tried to console her. "Let's start again. What's the problem?"

"I'm the problem. This is all my fault."

"Baby, slow down. Have a drink of water."

Kelsey got up and got a bottle of water. She drank some water and took several deep breaths before she sat down in a chair.

"You were right. I had it all—looks, money, and popularity, but I wasn't happy. In fact, I hated myself. I had—I still have a huge guilt trip, and I can't shake it. I tried to self-destruct and did a pretty good job of it. You know what I miss? I miss my son and I miss my parents, but I'll probably never see them again. I'm totally fucked up."

"Kelsey, the fact that you miss your son and parents doesn't mean you're fucked up. It means you're sane."

"I don't get it. I thought you would be pissed, and please—no more beatings."

Bobbie walked over and knelt before Kelsey's chair. She took Kelsey's head in her hands. "Baby, baby—I only ever did what I thought you wanted. You had it all. I, on the other hand, had only my looks, body, and wits—none of which last forever. Sex was never my objective. It was more like my passport to survival. As much as I resented you for your arrogance, these past few days I have loved you for your humility—even if it was forced upon you."

"What about us? What about the sex? Was that all just a game?"

Bobbie laughed. "Sex is just a game in the scheme of things, and a short one at that. Shakespeare said the world is a stage and we're all actors. You and I happen to be damn good actors—we missed our calling. Having said that, the passion was real. No one can act that well. Right now, we have more important things to think about than sex. As to us? What will be will be."

Kelsey hugged and kissed her. "What do we do now?"

Bobbie stood up and paced a bit. "It's like this—you have no hope of getting your son back and I have no hope, period, without that money. So, it's all about the Benjamins. Thirty million cures a lot of ills."

"But, what about Del and Sonny? Not to mention the Mexican cartel whose money it is? I think I'm going to be sick."

"Sit down and take a deep breath. Let's take them one at a time. Del either killed or orchestrated the killing of at least three people. If we know that, somebody else has to be at least suspicious—meaning, he may have other problems. Sonny is a different cup of tea, but I saw the way he looked at me. If he doesn't shoot me on sight, I'll have a dog collar on him within an hour."

They laughed.

"I may have an idea that involves Sonny and may solve all of our problems—even the Mexicans. Thirty million is a big table. Now, why don't you make an appointment with a hairdresser and then we'll go shopping for new clothes."

Chapter Twenty-Six

Cleaning Up

The Pompeii

Vinny was waiting at the loading dock behind the hotel, with a laundry cart, when Sonny and Petey pulled up.

"You see the broad?"

"She's been upstairs for at least half an hour."

"Good. I'll knock on the door. You guys follow me and wait at the end of the hall. I'll signal you. You got the plastic bag?"

Vinny handed it to him. "Right here."

Sonny started to open the back door, but hesitated and turned to face Vinny and Petey. "The only way we survive this day is if you guys do exactly as I say. You got that?"

They both nodded.

"OK, let's do it."

They took the elevator to Johnny's floor. Sonny went to Johnny's room while Vinny and Petey took the cart to the end of the hall. Sonny knocked on the door and Suzy let him in. Johnny called out from the bedroom.

"Who is it? Get these things off me."

Sonny walked in. Johnny was nude and handcuffed to the bed. "What the fuck are you doin' here? Get these things off me. Where's Suzy?"

When Johnny saw the bag in Sonny's hands he tried to yank himself free, but to no avail. He screamed, "You rat fuck!"

Sonny straddled him. "Johnny, what's twenty-nine million divided by one?" He put the bag over Johnny's head and held it until he gave up the fight.

Sonny went back to the living room, where Suzy was pacing back and forth. "This cost you big time. This not part of job."

Sonny opened the door and waved to Vinny and Petey. They entered with the laundry cart.

Sonny walked over to Suzy and put his arm around her. "I told you I'd take care of you, didn't I?" He quickly brought his other arm up and put her in a strangle hold. She tried to resist, but Sonny was more than twice her size.

"Put her in the cart and take her to the car. Petey, find the handcuff key and get the cuffs off Johnny and then put his hand on his dick."

"Whoa, Sonny. I ain't touchin' his dick."

Sonny was enraged and lunged toward Petey, who quickly realized he fucked up. He held his hands up. "Sorry, Sonny—I just never done nothin' like that before. Which hand?"

When they were finished in the room, Vinny and Petey took the cart, with Suzy in it, to the elevator. Sonny took out his cell phone and dialed Joey Colletti in Chicago. Joey C., as he was known, answered his phone.

"Joey C. here."

"Joey, it's me, Sonny."

"Sonny, if you're callin' about Johnny, I didn't have nothing to do with that. The old man sent him."

"I'm callin' about Johnny, but it ain't about that. We got a problem out here."

"What kind of problem? You better not fuck with Johnny. You know that, I hope."

"Joey—I got no problem with Johnny. He and I had dinner last night and we were gonna have lunch today."

"Then what's the problem?"

"The problem is Johnny. He's dead."

Joey C. was silent for moment. "Sonny, I hope you didn't do nothin' stupid."

"I didn't, but Johnny did. You know about the oriental broad he sees out here?"

"I met her once. In fact Johnny introduced us. He loved that broad, Suzy something."

"Suzy Wrong. Well, the first thing he did when he arrived was hook up with her. She's one of them dominator tricks and Johnny got off on that shit."

"Go figure."

"Go figure is right, but he ain't the only one. You'd be surprised. She's one of the hottest tickets in town. Well, apparently he went back for seconds today and they got into some really kinky shit. You ever hear about guys jerking off with a plastic bag over their heads?"

"You gotta be shittin' me. I heard about that. They come right before they suffocate."

"Yeah, well—Johnny got it mixed up today and did it backward."

"Holy fuckola! This ain't good news. He's got a wife and a couple of daughters. The wife is a real pain in the ass, but this ain't good news."

"I hear ya. We're in luck a bit. There's a doctor's convention in town and a couple of the docs are down quite a bit at the tables. I'll get one of 'em to say it was a heart attack and send the body home before anybody can snoop around."

"Good—that's good. What about the broad?"

"I'll clean up."

"Good—there's no other way. Listen, Sonny, some of the guys may be a little suspicious—I mean, the timing and Johnny being sent out there about somethin' that involved you. I'm just sayin'. There's some shit goin' on here that you don't know about."

"Joey, Harry knows he was with the broad and it was Vinny who set 'em up—at Johnny's request. He never came here without seein' her. Everybody knows that."

"I'm just sayin'. Nobody trusts nobody right now. It's not like the old days when there was loyalty and you knew where people stood. It's all different these days."

"Everything is different these days. Where are you in all this?"

"Tryin' to keep my friggin' head down. I sit with my back to the wall and start my car by remote control. I'd suggest you do the same until this blows over."

"I gotta finish up here. You know how to find me."

A Motel in Northern Arizona, the Following Morning

Sandowski stretched and yawned as they got back in the car to continue their journey—a journey that was still a bit of a mystery to Sandoval. He looked at his younger sidekick. "You sleep OK?"

"I never sleep OK, but that's not my problem. I'm like mentally tired. You know what I mean?"

"Too well."

"So tell me— what're we doing? Where are we going?"

"Number one, we both had to get out of Dodge and I don't know when we can go back—if ever."

"I ain't goin' back. There's nothing there for me anymore. So what's number two?"

"Number two should be number one. The Devils put the hit on Davey, but somebody down here was involved in it."

"You got any clues?"

"It's got to be the cartel with help from one of the Feds."

Sandoval started laughing.

"What'd I say was so funny?"

"What's so funny? You accused me of goin' on a suicide mission when I sprayed a street corner of punks with a MAC. Now you're tellin' me you're planning on taking on a drug cartel and the Feds! You're totally insane!"

"I ain't doin' it alone."

Sandoval stared at him. "Let me guess—you think I'm with you?"

"Well, aren't you?"

Sandoval shook his head and gazed out the window. He turned with a smile. "I got nothing better to do."

They fist bumped and smiled.

At a separate motel not too many miles away, Sonny, Vinny, and Petey had just finished breakfast and were getting in their car to resume their journey to the same location, Apache Dunes. Sonny was driving, Vinny shotgun, and Petey in back. They turned onto the highway.

"Uncle Vince, can I borrow your phone?"

"What's wrong with yours?"

"I lost it. I mean, I didn't lose it. I found out where I left it, but I didn't get it before we left."

Sonny winced trying to figure out what he just said. Vinny turned in his seat, "Where'd you leave it?"

"Over at Sammy's place. We was watching a game and it must of slipped out of my pocket and got behind one of the cushions."

"Good thing Sammy found it."

"He didn't find it—I did."

Even Vinny winced at that one. "You lost me."

"I got an iPhone and they got this app where if you lose your phone, they can track it for you. It's like a GPA system."

"That's GPS."

All of a sudden the car swerved sharply as Sonny pulled off the side of the road. Vinny and Petey were both shaken up. Vinny looked over at Sonny. "What happened? You OK?"

Sonny put the car in park and turned to look at both of them. "Vinny, I know this is gonna be tough, but think for a minute about what Petey just said."

Vinny had a blank look on his face. Sonny beat his head on the steering wheel. "The broads—the broads we're trying to find. They got a cell phone and I got the number."

"Yeah, but how can you call and say you're the owner of the phone?"

"I can't moron, but Myra can."

"Sonny, no offense, but Myra is a Polish cleaning lady."

"Myra was goin' to med school in Poland, but she makes more money cleaning apartments in Vegas."

"I still don't get it. What if they ask for personal information?"

"Now think for a minute. What was it you were doin' for them?"

Vinny's light bulb was dim, but it eventually lit up. "The driver's licenses! They're in the apartment."

"Bingo! Now get Myra on the phone. Our luck is about to turn."

Sonny got back on the highway and fingered his St. Christopher medal. He looked in the mirror and smiled at Petey, who still hadn't pieced it all together.

Sonny's phone rang. He looked at the number. "It's Joey C."

"Joey, how ya doin'?"

"Where the hell are you?"

"In my car in the middle of nowhere."

"I hope you're not bein' wise. This ain't the time for it."

"Whatta ya mean, bein' wise. I told you—I'm on a highway in the middle of nowhere. What's up?"

"Don't you listen to the news? Listen to the news and call me back—right back."

Joey C. hung up. Sonny looked at the phone. Vinny asked, "What's up?"

"That's what I asked him. Joey said to listen to the news and call him back. Get CBS on the radio. The news is every thirty minutes. It'll be on the hour in about five minutes."

The CBS national news came on. "In a scene reminiscent of *The Godfather*, it appears that rival factions of the Chicago mob have gone to the mattresses. It all began yesterday with the death of high-ranking Chicago mobster Johnny Bellini in a Las Vegas hotel. Apparently, some of Bellini's associates regarded his death as suspicious. Last night the boss of the Chicago mob, Little Tony Mondelli, survived a botched assassination attempt by two of Bellini's soldiers as he was leaving a restaurant on Chicago's near north side. This morning, the two Bellini soldiers were found in the trunk of a car at O'Hare airport. Confidential sources have told police that Bellini and his associates had been planning a coup to overthrow Mondelli. Mondelli's condition has stabilized and he is expected to recover. Two persons of interest in the death of Bellini are missing."

A visibly shaken Sonny pulled off the highway again. "Petey, you take the wheel. I got some calls to make."

Sonny switched places with Petey. Petey pulled back on the highway as Sonny dialed Joey C.

"You hear the news?"

"I heard it. What the hell's goin' on?"

"That's what a lot of people wanna know and your name keeps comin' up."

"Me? What'd I do? I cleaned up Johnny's mess."

"Sonny, I tried to tell you yesterday that things were fucked up before Johnny died. Didn't I tell you that some people might be suspicious? Didn't I? Harry told the old man that you and your idiot sidekick are nowhere to be found and you tell me you're in nowhere. Excuse me—the middle of nowhere. How you think that looks? I'm supposed to tell you to come back to Chicago."

"You think I'm fucking nuts? I'm lyin' low until things settle down."

"I hope you know what you're doin'. They got ways of findin' people who don't wanna be found."

Sonny looked at his phone. "I gotta do what I gotta do. You OK?"

"Who knows? I told you—nobody trusts nobody right now. The thing is, the old man was dying anyhow. Nobody knows what these guys were thinkin'."

"Watch yourself. I'll be in touch."

Sonny hung up and looked at his phone again. "We gotta get rid of our phones and get those prepaid burners."

Sheriff's Office, Apache Dunes

Tom had just hung up the phone when Dylan and Jake walked in. Tom was smiling. Jake looked at him. "What's so funny?"

"That was Sandowski's boss. He wanted to alert me that Sandowski and another Chicago cop were driving down. He suggested we evacuate the town and short the municipal bonds."

They all laughed.

"I can't wait to meet them."

"His chief said it was only half in jest, but he will personally appreciate any courtesy we extend to them. He asked if I understood Sandowski's relationship with the undercover cop killed in Acapulco. I told him I did. I told him that I heard about the massacre of some Latin Devil gang members. He said, 'No comment.'"

"Did you hear the news today? They got a Mafia war goin' on in Chicago and it involves Vegas."

"*Capiche*."

Jake looked at Tom. "What's that supposed to mean?"

"It's a private joke."

"Whatever. I gotta cut out early. Ashley said she needed me at home."

Jake left and Dylan turned to Tom. "Is it me, or has Jake been acting funny recently?"

"I wondered if anybody else noticed. I did overhear him talking to Ashley about Dusty the other day."

"Dusty? They became best friends awfully quick, but that's women—I guess."

"You've got enough on your plate. I think Ashley may have had her fill of the desert."

"It's an acquired taste."

Las Brisas, Acapulco

Kelsey had her hair done and bought some new clothes. She looked like a movie star. "So, Bobbie, what's the plan?"

"If we need the bank numbers, and we do, we need to go back to the Dunes for them. No choice."

"What if I called Del and apologized and offered to split the money with him?"

"Let's see—he's been involved in at least two murders we know about and we tried to kill him. I'll take the other side of that bet."

"We need help. What about the mob guys? We didn't kill anybody and they were trying to rip us off too."

"It's better than Del and we might be able to pull it off."

Bobbie retrieved Sonny's cell number and dialed it. Sonny was in the car, still on the highway, when his phone rang. He looked at the number and his eyes got big. He yelled to Vinny, "Turn off the radio."

"What?"

"Turn off the fucking radio!"

Sonny answered the phone. "If it isn't Ma Barker. Was there something you forgot to steal?"

"Ouch. The truth is, we just got a call from our bank and they said the wire never went through. What's up with that?"

"The reason it never went through is that we were given the wrong numbers. Imagine that?"

"I think I know what happened. We've got more than one account and Kelsey musta got mixed up and gave you the wrong numbers."

"Let's say I just fell off the fuckin' banana boat and believe this bullshit—how you gonna make it right?"

"Sonny, that hurts my feelings. Truth is, I was kinda missing you. I like bad boys, but like they say—spare the rod and spoil the child. Do you feel like you got enough discipline when you were young, or could you use a bit more?"

Sonny squirmed in his seat.

"You there?"

"Talk to me—what is it you need this time?"

"Well … now that you mentioned it, there is something you can help me with."

"Why am I surprised?"

"How about I call you later and we arrange to meet somewhere. Where are you now?"

"On the highway not far from Apache Dunes."

"No way—that's perfect! I'll call you later. We have to arrange for a flight."

"You got the fifty g's?"

"I do and I think I forgot to say thank you."

Sonny just shook his head. "If you was a guy you wouldn't be able to walk—your balls would be too big. I got a problem with my phone. I'll call you at six."

Del's Mansion

Del was in a wheelchair on the patio when his phone rang.

"Del here."

"This is Carlos Garcia. I was told you wanted to talk to me. Is this phone cool?"

"The phone is cool, but I'd rather speak in person."

"This ain't no DEA trap is it?"

"This hasn't got anything to do with the DEA. It's a personal matter. I understand you lost something in the desert a few years ago and I might know who has it. Just being a good Samaritan, so to speak."

"Every time somebody does me a favor it ends up costin' me. Why the fuck do you care about me?"

"Who knows? I help you and maybe you can help me. Right now, everybody is losing."

"Check this out—I need a little bit more than that. We know somebody at Valley of the Sun bank was involved, but that narrowed it down to a couple hundred people. Does this person who has what belongs to me have any connection to the bank?"

"As a matter of fact, they do. It's an in-law connection. How about you come by my house? You know where I live?"

"I'll look for the biggest fucking house within five hundred miles and the only one with an observatory."

Carlos hung up and motioned one of his men over. "Julio, get Sherlock Holmes on the phone. Tell him to have his juvenile delinquents hack into the bank again and see if they can connect anyone by marriage to the Fed's wife. We got all her info. Tell him I want this NOW!"

"I thought we ruled her out?"

"We connected her to the doofus, Scooter. We couldn't connect her to the bank, but someone just made the connection for us."

Sandowski's Car, Nearing Apache Dunes

They saw a sign for The Cowboy Bar & Grill, five miles away—hot Italian beef and ice-cold Coors.

Sandowski picked up. "You see that sign?"

"I saw it—Italian beef and cold beer. What's wrong with that?"

"You suppose they got a clue how to make Italian beef out here?"

"I read a lot of people from Chicago moved out here. The Cubs have spring training here."

"That's right. Should we try it?"

"Gotta do it."

Chapter Twenty-Seven

Plan A

Cowboy Bar & Grill, Near Apache Dunes

Sandowski and Sandoval pulled into the gravel parking lot, which was full of Harleys and pickup trucks, some with rifles in the window racks.

Inside was dark and crowded, with cowboys playing pool as the jukebox blared country and western tunes. They made their way to the bar and found two empty seats. It seemed like all eyes were on them—which they were. Sandowski took a stool. Sandoval looked around. "Must not be any good dental plans in the area. Order for me, I gotta take a whiz."

"What'll you have?"

"Whatta you think? Italian beef and an ice cold Coors—just like the sign."

The bartender appeared to approach guardedly, while scanning the bar. A gigantic cowboy who was playing pool stared at Sandowski. Sandowski motioned to the bartender.

"Howdy, we'll have two Italian beefs and two Coors to start with."

The cowboy approached Sandowski with pool cue in hand. "This is a cowboy bar."

Sandowski looked around. "Yeah, I can see that."

Sandoval came out of the restroom and saw the cowboy looming over Sandowski. He reached in his back pocket and slipped brass knuckles on his right hand.

The cowboy persisted. "I said this bar is only for cowboys."

The activity in the bar stopped as everyone focused on the scene at the bar. The bartender stepped back from the counter.

The cowboy wasn't letting it go. "Are you a cowboy?"

The crowd laughed. The cowboy shuffled the cue from hand to hand.

Sandowski stared at him. "Do I look like a fucking cowboy?"

The cowboy was momentarily stymied as he tried to think of a comeback. "Why don't you and your little girlfriend get the fuck out of here while you can?"

Sandowski looked up at the cowboy as Sandoval approached. "That was a mistake."

In the blink of an eye, Sandoval had kicked the cowboy square in the nuts with his steel capped boots, broke his nose with a straight forward punch, and pounded his head on the edge of the pool table.

The crowd, at first in shock, started to approach, many with pool cues in their hands. Sandowski and Sandoval each reached under their shirts and drew their heat.

When the cowboy, dazed and bleeding profusely, started to stir, Sandowski shot at the light above the pool table, severing the chain. It crashed onto the cowboy, knocking him out for the second time. The noise was deafening and the crowd now ran for the exits, leaving the cowboy splayed out on the pool table.

The bartender peeked out from behind the bar. "I—I'm the owner and I don't want any trouble. Is this a robbery?"

Sandowski and Sandoval put their guns away and looked at him. "All we want are two Italian beefs and two cold beers—and no, we're not fucking cowboys."

"Coming up and on the house. I wish I had met you five years ago when I bought this place. I had high hopes for it, but this group just moved in and took over."

As the cowboys and cowgirls were scrambling to leave the parking lot, another car that had seen the highway sign was pulling in. Sonny parked the car as they watched the quick exodus. "Is it me, or does it appear the people are in a hurry to leave?"

Vinny was watching. "I hope they ain't closed. I have a taste for an Italian beef. Sonny, look—there's a car with Illinois plates."

Sonny pondered that for a moment. "No way somebody drove from Chicago today. Plus, no wise guy is drivin' a car like that. Just in case, let's be careful."

They entered the bar and let their eyes get adjusted. The bar was a mess—chairs overturned, tables full of glasses and bottles, and a giant cowboy passed out in a pool of blood on the pool table, with the light fixture on top of him. Two guys were sitting at the bar drinking beer and talking to the bartender.

Sonny called out, "You open for business?"

"Come on in. Take a seat at the bar."

"Did we miss the party?"

"Something like that."

Sonny gestured to the pool table. "Who's the ape?"

Sandowski looked over. "He's a tough guy—a cowboy."

"Looks like he met his match."

"You look for trouble long enough, you'll find it."

Sonny looked at Sandowski and Sandoval. "You guys don't look like cowboys."

"That's what he said."

Sonny held his hands up. "No offense. We just saw the sign and had a taste for an Italian beef."

"Same here."

"By the way, I noticed the Illinois plates. You guys from Illinois?"

"People are awfully inquisitive around here."

"Again, no offense. I used to be from there's all."

Sandowski nodded. "None taken. Everybody's got to be from someplace."

Sonny motioned to the bartender. "Can we get some Italian beefs and three cold beers—whatever's coldest."

"Comin' right up. The beef should be ready now."

The bartender served the beers and went to fetch the Italian beefs. After the first bite, Vinny called out to the bartender. "Ask the cook if he's got any seasoning back there."

"I'm the owner, cook, bartender, and janitor. I had a good cook, guy had retired from Chicago, but the cowboys ran him off."

"You mind if my nephew goes back there? He can fix the beef."

"Be my guest."

"Petey, do your magic." He looked over at Sandowski and Sandoval, "Hey guys—don't eat no more until Petey works on it."

Everyone pushed their sandwiches to the side, unimpressed with their first bites. Sonny addressed Sandowski. "I was listenin' to the news on the radio. They say there's a lot goin' down in Chicago."

Sandowski smirks. "That ain't exactly news."

"I mean the mob thing. Sounds like a war is goin' on."

"Good riddance. That doesn't concern us."

Just then, the front door opened and Tom and Dylan strode in with their batons out. When their eyes adjusted to the change of light, Tom walked over to Sonny and Vinny. "Well, well. Who do we have here?"

Sonny held up his hands. "We ain't doin' nothing wrong. We just stopped for a sandwich and a beer. Ask them guys and the owner."

Tom put his baton back on his belt. "No problem. This isn't my jurisdiction anyway. I'm just doin' a favor for the county sheriff. He asked me to check out a report of a brawl and shots being fired."

"How come you wasn't so friendly before?"

"I was having a bad day and you were looking for trouble. I hope you've given up on that."

"They're both dead. Who we gonna collect from?"

Tom now looked over at Sandowski and Sandoval and smiled. "Today, however, is a good day, because I'm meeting a new, old friend."

He walked over to Sandowski and Sandoval. They all smiled and Tom and Sandowski did a man hug. "Max, it's good to meet you finally. This must be Sandoval. This is Dylan."

"Cochise?"

"No, this is Dylan. He's Geronimo."

Max reached out his hand. "Geronimo, it's a pleasure to meet you. What happened to Cochise?"

Tom shook his head. "Funny you should ask. Apparently his wife decided she'd had enough of the desert. They put their house up for sale, said their goodbyes, and made a quick getaway. By the way, I've got the keys to the house and it's yours until it's sold and there's not much demand around here for high-end real estate."

The cowboy started to stir and the light fixture crashed to the floor. Sandoval looked at the baton on Tom's belt. "Can I borrow that for a second?"

Tom handed it to him and Sandoval casually strolled over and cold cocked the cowboy for the third time. Tom smiled. "His nick name was the Bear. Looks like he'll be hibernating for a while."

Petey emerged from the kitchen with a plateful of Italian beefs. He passed them around. "Try these."

Sonny took one bite and proclaimed, "Now this is Italian beef."

Sandoval agreed. "Look out Mr. Beef."

Sonny looked at Petey. "Where'd you learn to cook like this?"

"It's what I always wanted to do."

The bartender, seeing everyone devour their sandwiches, turned to Petey. "How'd you like to become my cook—my partner?"

Sonny and Vince looked at each other.

Sonny eyed Sandowski. "You haven't said anything."

Sandowski wiped some *au jus* off his chin. "I been too busy eating. This is great Italian beef, takin' everything into consideration." He gazed around the place. "The décor needs a little work."

Everyone laughed.

"I'd like to see what he could do given some time and proper ingredients. You ever make Gnocchi?"

Petey grinned from ear to ear. "With a special meat sauce and herbs my mother taught me and her mother taught her."

"You get some good food, a little lighting, and Sinatra on the jukebox and you got a winner here. Get rid of the name."

The owner was deep in thought with a gleam of hope in his eye.

Meanwhile, Tom gravitated back to Sonny and Vinny. "I didn't ask what you guys were doin' back in these parts, but you know the drill and these are my friends. If you wanna know what happens when you fuck with them, just ask Boo Boo there, if he ever comes to. *Capiche*?"

Sonny held his palms out. "*Capiche*."

He then interrupted the owner's daydream. "Were you serious about the offer to Petey?"

"I told you—they ran my cook off. I got two choices, as I see it. I can either put up with these scumbags, and barely make ends meet, or I can get a good chef and try to get a better clientele. You've got no idea how many people walk in the door and turn right around and leave."

Sonny stands up. "Vinny, Petey—let's go out to the car. We gotta talk."

They left their drinks on the bar and walked out to their car.

Tom motioned to Dylan. "Keep an eye on 'em."

Sandowski was curious. "Seems like you got a little history there. What's their story?"

"Like they say, it's a small world. We met when they were tryin' to find the gal who was killed with your Davey."

Sandowski's demeanor suddenly changed. Tom put his hands up. "They had nothing to do with the murders. They wanted her alive. They were tryin' to collect money her husband or, in their words, the dearly departed stiff owed them."

They all laughed.

Sandoval said, "So the stiff, stiffed 'em?"

They laughed even harder.

Sandowski looked at Tom. "So we might be on the same side?"

Tom took a deep breath. "The lines are real blurry on this one. With both the husband and wife out of the picture, the debt is history."

Dylan was at the window. He turned back to Tom. "What are they doing back here, then?"

Tom arched his eyebrows. "What, indeed?"

Sandoval walked over to the window and gazed out. "It's all over the radio about a mob war in Chicago that involves Vegas. Maybe they needed to get out of town."

"That's possible, but they don't appear to be in a hurry to me."

In the parking lot, Sonny, Vinny, and Petey were standing by their car. Sonny walked a few paces, as if thinking, and then turned back around to face them.

"OK, here's the deal and it ain't negotiable. Petey, you're staying here and accepting the offer—at least for a while. We'll get you new papers and some seed money. You're gonna have to get a new name."

Vinny looked concerned. "Sonny, is Petey in trouble?"

"If you call Johnny Bellini puttin' a hit on him trouble—then, yeah, he's got a problem."

"But Johnny's dead."

Sonny stared at Vinny. "If you recall—I was there."

Petey looked at Sonny sheepishly. "Sonny, when we was in the desert—"

Sonny cut him off. "I had to decide whether to kill you, and maybe Vinny, or Johnny Bellini—and I still ain't sure I made the right choice."

Vinny shifted nervously. "What about me, Sonny?"

"I think I'd talked Johnny out of the hit on you—at least for now. I told him I needed your help in findin' the broads, but I don't know who he talked to in Chicago. Vegas ain't an option for us right now and who knows who we can trust in Chicago. Joey said they wanted me to come home, but that don't sound like a good idea."

"What about the broads?"

"The broads and the money are our best hope until things get sorted out. Petey, you just fell in a pile of shit and came up smellin' like a rose. You keep your nose clean and—listen to me—you keep your mouth shut. You hear me?"

"No problem, Sonny. The truth is, I don't think I was really cut out to be a gangster."

"No shit. Now think of a new name."

Petey smiled caressing his necklace. "How about Christopher?"

Acapulco

Bobbie and Kelsey chartered a private plane to take them to Tucson where they rented a car and drove to their rendezvous with Sonny. Bobbie was driving and looked over at Kelsey. "You're being awfully quiet today."

"I just want you to get your money and get this over with."

Bobbie shook her head. "It's not my money. It's not your money. It was drug money, blood money, and it's sitting in a bank waiting for someone to claim it. It might as well be us."

Kelsey started crying. "I'm a terrible mother."

"No shit, but Del isn't exactly Ward Cleaver. Truth is—your son is in the best place he can be right now, with your parents."

"They did such a good job with me."

"There is that. Listen—don't expect me to feel sorry for you, but you and I are in something way over our heads and we need to focus on the here and now. Which is pretty fucked up, by the way." She laughed. "Our only hope of survival is a mobster who we ripped off."

Kelsey continued her pity party. "I've done such terrible things. We almost killed Del."

"The only mistake there was that we failed."

"How am I supposed to deal with what I've done?"

"There's a reason God put our eyes in the front of our heads—so we'd look forward and not back."

Bobbie took the exit ramp to a McDonald's parking lot.

She looked over at Kelsey. "Baby, I need you to get it together quick. That's Sonny's car and this is show time."

Bobbie parked next to Sonny's car. Bobbie and Kelsey got into Sonny's back seat. Sonny and Vinny were in the front.

Sonny looked at Bobbie. "Give me a good reason why I don't pop you right now."

"I'll give you thirty million if you give me a chance."

Sonny snorted. "This is like *déjà vu* all over again. The last time it cost me fifty grand."

Bobbie handed Sonny a package. "There's almost forty thousand there. We spent the rest."

"Ten grand in a couple of days? You ever hear of Motel 8 or Denny's?"

"You spoiled us in Vegas. We think we could get used to that."

Sonny looked at Kelsey. "Well, at least Harpo there got herself a new wardrobe. She decide to go straight?"

"She's having a bit of an identity crisis, but she's the one who knows where the money is."

"I'm all ears."

"The short version is that she was friends with a local fuck up, who happened to come into possession of the account number and codes for a numbered bank account that belonged to a Mexican drug cartel."

Sonny and Vinny looked at each other.

"He didn't know what he had and when he found out that Kelsey's brother-in-law was a banker, he asked for her help. It was through him she found out the bank was a bank in the Cayman Islands. She transferred the funds to a bank in Switzerland."

"What about the cartel?"

"The leader was killed."

"What happened to the fuck up?"

"He's not with us anymore either."

"Let me guess—he died in his sleep of natural causes?"

"Not exactly."

"How bad was it?"

"Think Spanish Inquisition."

Vinny looked puzzled and started to say something, but Sonny stopped him. "And—nobody knows about Miss America?"

"The cartel didn't, but her husband is the head DEA agent. He had an arrangement with the cartel and we had a little mishap, you could say."

"A little mishap with youse two could be a nuclear war."

"Not quite, but we did try to kill him."

Sonny was rubbing his temples. "Apparently you didn't try hard enough."

"Well, let's see—we bound and gagged him, beat him with a fireplace poker, turned on the gas, and blew the house up."

Sonny and Vinny were both stunned. "The Girl Scouts musta changed a lot since I was a kid."

Vinny jumped in. "The cookies are still good—especially the mint ones."

Everyone stared at Vinny. "What?"

Sonny just shook his head. "So you wasn't lyin' about the wire transfer? But, why'd you fuck us over with the bogus numbers?"

"It wasn't intentional. We thought her husband was dead. We still don't know how he survived. When we found out he was still alive, we freaked and took off, but didn't know where to go. I had your card, so we decided to go to Vegas and see if you would help us."

"You still ain't explained the bogus numbers."

"We were in such a panic to leave that Kelsey forgot to take the numbers with her. She had them hidden in the house. She didn't realize it until she was at the bank in Vegas and was afraid what you might do if we told you. I didn't know about it either."

Sonny exhaled. "Whew. So the husband is still alive and the numbers are at the house. Does he know about the money?"

"I'm afraid he does now, but he doesn't know where the numbers are."

"And the cartel?"

"He might have told them she has the money."

"So let me guess—you have a brilliant plan as to how we help you get the money and we all ride off in the sunset to live happily ever after."

"We have a plan."

"I can't wait."

"Like I said, he doesn't know where the numbers are—only she does. He may have survived, but, trust me, he's disabled and sure to have someone with him. If we can get him out of the house, I can get in and get the numbers."

"How do you plan to do that?"

"It's a bit complicated, but he didn't know about the money until the night we tried to kill him. Until then, he worshipped the ground she walked on."

"So you decided to whack him for kicks?"

"I said it was complicated. He killed his partner and had his partner's wife killed. She was a very close friend of ours. We think Kelsey was next."

"So, you think she can get him to meet somewhere to make things right?"

"You got a better idea?"

"I got no idea at all, which brings me to this—what the fuck do we got to do with all this?"

"We're thinking that you call him and say that she wants to meet somewhere to explain everything. He was the one, after all, who got her hooked on coke and she was wired the night we tried to kill him."

"And while he's out, you break into the house."

"He's got a security system worthy of Ft. Knox. He was paranoid of the cartel. He even has a safe room with video and audio monitors of the whole house. She has the entry code, but he shouldn't suspect anything if she's with him."

"What happens if it's a setup and he tries to whack her?"

Kelsey spoke for the first time. “I’ll take that risk.”

Sonny and Vinny were both shocked to hear her speak. “So, one of us drives you to the meet and one of us goes with you to the house?”

“Something like that. We are partners, right?”

“I don’t like it.”

“He doesn’t know you. If you call and it doesn’t seem right, we go to Plan B.”

“What’s Plan B?”

“We don’t have one.”

Chapter Twenty-Eight

Where's the Money?

Sheriff's Office, Apache Dunes

Tom was at his desk with a cup of coffee when Sandowski knocked on the open door and entered. Sandowski had shaved and looked well rested. Tom noticed. "I gotta say, the desert must sit well with you. You look a lot better than you did yesterday."

"I don't remember if I told you, but I've had a kind of asthma condition all my life. If my parents could have afforded it, we would have moved to the desert. I don't know if I've ever slept better."

"How about some coffee? Help yourself."

Sandowski poured himself a cup of coffee and sat down. He then took a flask out of his jacket and poured a bit in his coffee. He held the flask out for Tom. "Don't mind if I do. Thanks. Where's your bodyguard?"

Sandowski laughed. "I said I slept well. He was still asleep when I left and get this—in the hammock by the pool! He got in it last night and passed out. I'll tell you one thing—deputies in Chicago can't afford a house like that. What do they pay college football players these days?"

Tom laughed. "He got some insurance money when he blew out his knee, but the gal he married comes from money out east."

"Still and all—they can afford to just take off like that and put a for sale sign in the yard?"

Tom smiled. "I had two boys. Dylan we adopted after his parents died. Dylan brought Jake home one day and he never left. His momma was a mess and I doubt even she knew who his daddy was. They were both bright, but in different ways. Dylan inherited his daddy's brains. Jake is what they call street smart."

"So don't worry about Jake, huh?"

Tom laughed again. "No, I have a hunch that Jake is going to be just fine."

Homer, the deputy, knocked and entered. He handed Tom a message. "Sheriff, this just came across the wire. I thought you'd want to see it right away."

Tom read the message and then paused, as if deep in thought, before handing it to Sandowski. "Seems like a banker up in Tucson showed up for work this morning, but never made it into the bank. His car is in the lot with the keys and his briefcase inside."

"Any connection to the business at hand?"

"Only that the banker, one Mr. J.R. Blake, happens to be the brother-in-law of our DEA agent's wife, who's also missing. He's the guy Dylan and Jake went to Tucson to interview."

Sandowski whistled.

Homer cleared his throat to get their attention. "One more thing, Sheriff. The Apache kid, who Dylan has keeping an eye on things, just spotted two black Escalades heading this way from the north."

Sandowski looked at Tom. "The Mexicans?"

Tom furrowed his brow. "You wouldn't normally think so, coming from the north, but Tucson is north. Max—you believe in coincidences?"

"Never have."

"Why don't we go wake Sleeping Beauty and take him for some *huevos rancheros* at the Diner. We could have a long day ahead of us."

Tom and Sandowski walked out to Tom's Jeep in the parking lot. Sandowski's car was parked next to Tom's.

"Oh, Max, if you guys are comfortable at Jake's, why don't you take that for sale sign down for the time being?"

Sandowski popped his trunk and pulled out the sign. "You mean this one?"

They both laughed as they got in Tom's Jeep.

Del's Mansion

Ray answered the phone. It was Sonny calling for Del.

"Yeah?"

"Is this Del?"

"This is Ray. Who's calling?"

"I have a message for Del."

"What's the message?"

"Maybe you didn't hear me when I said the message was for Del. Tell him it's from his wife."

That got Ray's attention. "Hang on."

Ray hurried out to the patio and handed Del the phone. "Some guy says he has a message for you from your wife."

Del fumbled with the phone with his free hand. "This is Del. Who's this?"

"You don't know me. I'm just delivering a message from Kelsey."

"Why doesn't she just call me herself?"

"She was afraid there had been a little misunderstanding between you two and she was concerned you wouldn't listen to what she had to say."

Del looked at his casts. "If you call tryin' to kill me a little misunderstanding."

"I don't know about any of that, and according to Kelsey, it wasn't her idea. She says she was coked out of her mind and it was you who supplied the coke."

Del paused for a bit. "So, who are you—her agent?"

"Something like that."

"Where's her dyke girlfriend?"

"That's another mistake she blames on the drugs."

"So, let me get this straight. You sayin' she wants to apologize and go back to the storybook romance we had?"

"She ain't stupid. She said you both have issues and it just didn't work out. She just wants to part on better terms and she has something to offer that might take the sting out a little bit."

Del snorted. "The sting, as you say, would take a lot to ease the pain."

"She's aware of that."

"Why don't you tell her to drop by and we'll talk about it."

"Stoppin' by the house will bring back too many memories. She wants to meet you in a public place, one-on-one."

"Unfortunately, I can't go anywhere without assistance—due to that little misunderstanding you mentioned. So, I'll have someone with me."

"Then so will she."

"What makes you think she'll be safe, even in a public place?"

"She's worth a lot more alive than dead—and I mean a lot more."

Del paused again to think. "There's one little problem. I don't think it's a good idea for us to be seen together right now—for both our sakes. She knows where the Apache Wells are. Tell her I'll meet her there in an hour. One more thing—you never said what happened to the girlfriend."

"I guess she's lookin' for something. I hope, for her sake, she finds it."

"In case you aren't aware, I have the resources of a national organization at my disposal."

"We got something in common then."

Sonny hung up and Del looked at the phone, puzzled by that last comment.

Ray was looking out at the driveway. Two black Escalades pulled up and eight serious-looking Mexicans got out.

"Del, we got company. Two cars full of Mexicans."

"That must be Carlos. Let 'em in."

Ray wheeled Del into the living room and escorted the Mexicans inside. They quickly spread out around the room. Ray was nervous as he tried to keep track of them.

Del looked around. "Where's Carlos?"

The Alpha dog, Juan, replied. "Carlos will be a little late. Where's your wife?"

"Whoa, now. I didn't say it was my wife."

"Carlos say it's your wife. Where is she?"

Ray was visibly anxious, surrounded by the Mexicans.

Del tried to defuse the tension and buy some time. "Everybody calm down. Ray and I were just going to meet her when you showed up."

"Hold on, while I call Carlos."

Juan moved into the adjoining room and dialed Carlos' number. Carlos answered immediately. "*Jefe*, she's not here. He say they were going to meet her. He has another *gringo* with him."

Juan walked back into the living room with the phone at his ear. He looked at Ray. "You his bodyguard?"

Carlos' men laughed. Ray didn't answer.

"*Sí, Jefe. Comprende.*"

Juan put his phone away. He called over one of his men and whispered in his ear. He then approached Del. "Carlos said for us to take you to your meeting. Your *amigo* can stay here. Jesus, help him out to our car."

Ray started to move to help Del, but was blocked by two of Carlos' men. Four of the men lingered while the others struggled to get Del into the Escalade. Finally situated, but very uncomfortable, Del strained to see where Ray was. The remaining four men came out of the house and closed the door—no sign of Ray.

The two Escalades exited the subdivision just as Sonny was pulling in. He stopped the car and watched them speed away. Bobbie looked over at him. "What, you got a problem with something?"

"Either I'm mistaken or that was two carloads of bad guys."

"Toto, this isn't Kansas anymore. Hang around and we'll see more carloads of bad guys. They're the only ones who can afford to live out here. It's easy to tell good guys from the bad guys in the desert. The bad guys have all the money—them and the crooked Feds. Can you imagine smugglers and Feds having a block party? Welcome to Apache Dunes."

"Whatever. We got work to do. Let's get it over with."

They drove past Del's massive house and parked up the street. They got out, looked around, and approached the house from the pool area in the back. Sonny moved into the shadows with gun drawn as Bobbie rang the back doorbell. They waited anxiously, but no one answered. Sonny motioned for her to ring it again. Another minute passed and no one answered. Bobbie consulted the security card that Kelsey gave her and dialed the security code to open the door. Once inside, she started to enter the code to disarm the alarm system and realized it wasn't on. That didn't make sense to her and she paused for a moment, then heard a small dog bark from somewhere in the house.

She whispered to Sonny. "That's Kelsey's Peke, Tuffy. I'm surprised he's still alive. Follow me. We've gotta move fast—the wells aren't far from here."

They climbed the stairway to the second floor and started to enter the master bedroom when Tuffy came scrambling up the stairs. When Bobbie bent down to pet him they saw that Tuffy's paws were covered with fresh blood. Sonny pulled his gun again and Bobbie touched his arm. "Hold on a minute."

Bobbie opened one of the drawers of the bedside table and pulled out a .357 Magnum.

Sonny stared at her. "You know how to use that?"

"I wouldn't have lived this long if I didn't."

She checked the cylinder. Sonny motioned for her to be silent. He took the steps slowly, stopping to listen for any sound. When he reached the bottom, he motioned for Bobbie to follow. When they entered the living room, they found Ray face up in a pool of blood with his throat slit. Bobbie gasped and covered her mouth as Sonny hurried into the adjoining room and pulled out his phone. He dialed Vinny's number.

"Pick up dammit! Answer the fucking phone!"

When there was no answer, he stormed into the living room and yelled at Bobbie. "You two have been a curse since the day we met. If anything happens to Vinny I will personally kill you, and slowly!"

He found Bobbie on the floor, curled up into the fetal position and sobbing violently. He put his gun in his belt and smacked himself on the side of the head. He bent over and tried to figure out how to console her. Bobbie just waved him away. "Kill me. Please kill me."

Sonny stooped down and lifted her up. At first, she tried to get away, but then clung to him as she cried out of control. Sonny found himself holding her tight. "Hold on. Look, I'm sorry—this is all fucked up, but I ain't gonna let anybody hurt you. You hear me?"

Bobbie wiped her eyes with one hand, but made no effort to leave Sonny's embrace. "Sonny, I've never had anyone look after me—ever. You don't have to lie to me. I'll be all right."

"I ain't lyin' to you. Let's get the numbers and get the fuck out of here. Maybe Vinny's phone didn't have no service."

They went back upstairs to the master bedroom. Bobbie was looking through a group of books and found the one she was seeking. "I found it—Love Story."

"Smart move. I don't see no guy readin' that before bed."

They heard the Escalades return. They looked out the window and saw the Mexicans manhandle Kelsey and Del out of the car and into the house. Vinny was missing. Bobbie turned to Sonny. "Quick, I know how to get into the safe room."

Sonny followed her to what appeared to be the end of the corridor. Bobbie pressed a button that was obscured by paneling. The wall turned out to be a reinforced steel door that slid open silently. They entered and she closed the door and disabled the button. The inside of the room was windowless and soundproof. There was a state-of-the-art security panel with TV and audio monitors for every room in the house. The room was equipped with a generator, air system, refrigerator and freezer, toilet, shower, and bunk beds.

Sonny gazed around in awe. "What is this place? It looks like something out of a James Bond movie."

"Close. I told you that Del feared the cartels, so he invested in a safe room. No one can enter from the outside once the button is disabled. It's even bombproof."

"Too bad he didn't do something with the front door."

"He was never as smart as he thought he was."

The monitors had views of every room in the house and the patio and pool area.

They saw the Mexicans holding Del and Kelsey captive in the living room. Del and Kelsey were both shaken up after seeing Ray's body. Kelsey was now crying uncontrollably. Tuffy ran in, barking at the Mexicans. One of them grabbed him, slit his throat, and tossed him aside as if a rag doll. Bobbie spun around and grabbed her gun, but Sonny stopped her.

"We aint goin' anywhere until they leave. They don't know we're here and there are too many of them to fight. I wasn't too good at math, but I know eight is more than two."

They went back to the monitors and found the audio.

The Mexicans were spread out in the living room. Del was bound to his wheelchair and Kelsey was on the couch with her hands tied behind her back. The one called Juan faced her. "I gonna ask you again. Where's the money?"

Kelsey sobbed. "I told you—I told you. It was wired into a Swiss bank account. It hasn't been touched. It's all there—I swear. I'll give you the account number."

"We have the account number and we traced the money. Problem is—someone walked into the bank the other day and withdrew the money—all of the money."

Kelsey looked stunned. Upstairs, Bobbie was equally stunned and Sonny collapsed onto the bottom bunk.

"That—that can't be."

"So, I ask you one more time. Where is the money?"

"Why would I come here to give it to you, if it wasn't there?"

Juan appeared to ponder her comment when Del spoke up. "It had to be her fucking brother-in-law, the banker. I told Carlos about him."

Juan motioned to two of his men. They left the room. Del heard them open and close the front door.

The Diner, Apache Dunes

Tom, Sandowski, and Sandoval had just finished breakfast when Dylan joined them for coffee. Tom's cell phone rang.

"Tom here."

"It's me, Homer. I'm out at the Wells. We got a call about a dead body out here. I was in the area and got there right away. He ain't been dead for long—body was still warm."

"Any ID?"

"You ain't gonna believe this. It's one of them EYEtalians who was at the cemetery. First name Vincent. I can't pronounce the last name."

Tom stood up. "Homer, you meet us by the DEA agent's house. Park up the road past the house and wait for us—and be careful."

"That was my deputy. One of the Italians was just murdered at the Wells. My guess is the Garcia boys in the Escalades were involved. They're gonna be heavily armed. I've got vests, assault rifles, and plenty of ammo in my truck. I've been expecting something. You guys up for this?"

Sandowski smiled. "We were afraid we were gonna die of boredom."

Carlos' Escalade Heading to Apache Dunes

Carlos was on his way to Del's house when his cell phone rang. "*Hola*."

"Is this Carlos?"

"Who you think it is?"

"It's Carlos, the smart ass who's really a dumb ass."

"Wait—I know that voice. It's my old friend Cochise."

"Fuck you. We were never friends and this ain't a social call."

Carlos smiled. "Why didn't I see it? You and Dusty were in on this from the start and now you're calling to whatta ya call it—goat."

"First of all, it's gloat, asshole. Number two, Dusty and I didn't have anything to do with the money or the wire transfers, but we do now."

"How the fuck does that happen?"

"Shit happens."

"So what happens now? Finders keepers? You want to keep my money?"

"We found THE money, not your money. At best, you could argue that one third is yours, as it was your uncle's share. The rest belonged to two other scumbags—and guess what? They're all dead."

"And you being the nice guy you are, you want to give me my one third? How much would that be, by the way?"

"Let's just say I'm willing to make a deal. There's about thirty million US. After some expenses, I can wire you nine million today."

"Nine million isn't a third and what's to prevent me from hunting you down and getting the rest?"

"I'm impressed. I didn't know you could divide. The three million of expenses is for three separate million dollar contracts on you, if anything happens to Dusty or me. But wait—I'm not through. A law firm will have a copy of the wire and the bank statements. Anything happens to us and that info goes to the Sinaloa and Gulf cartels—and the Zetas."

"The fucking Zetas don't have nothing to do with this."

"You can explain it to them. I hear they're very reasonable."

Carlos started laughing. "Fucking Cochise, man! Everyone thought that Geronimo was the one with the brains. Where's he in all this?"

"You know him. He would have turned the money over to the authorities and they would have stolen it. He doesn't know anything yet—and he's not gonna be happy when he finds out."

"So, if I agree, you wire me the money and we go our separate ways."

"I'll see you at our fiftieth high school reunion—if you live that long."

Carlos was silent for a moment. "Call me back in an hour and I'll give you the wire instructions."

"Smart move."

"Cochise—one last question. That night in the desert, would you have let me die?"

"Carlos, if Dylan hadn't been there, we wouldn't be having this conversation."

"You are one cold motherfucker. You ever come over to my side, we'll partner up and take over the world."

"Carlos, you haven't been listening. This is retirement for me and I suggest you think about doin' the same. That's plenty of money."

Del's Mansion

Carlos' men had returned from the car with a cooler. They placed it on the end table. Juan walked over to the cooler. "We ask the banker, but he don't talk either."

Juan opened the cooler and held up J.R.'s head by the hair. His eyes were gouged out. Kelsey vomited and Del was shaking with fear.

"What about your girlfriend?"

"She never—she never knew about the money."

Upstairs, Bobbie cried as she heard Kelsey lie.

Kelsey had vomit all over herself. "Can I please go to the bathroom?"

Juan motioned and one of the men untied her and escorted her to the bathroom. She locked the door from the inside, went to the medicine cabinet, and got a razor blade. Bobbie saw this and lurched for the door, but Sonny forcefully restrained her.

Kelsey suspected Bobbie was in the safe room and looked directly at the hidden camera. She had a serene look on her face and appeared to send a kiss as she slashed her wrists.

Up the street, Tom, Sandowski, Sandoval, Dylan, and Homer were joined by two cars full of State Troopers. They dispersed to cover all entrances and exits of the house.

Juan's phone rang. It was Carlos.

"*Hola, Jefe.*" He paused. "*Sí, sí.* What about the *gringo* and his wife?" Another pause. "*Sí, sí.*"

Juan went in the adjoining room and motioned for the others to follow. He told them what to do. "Get the girl."

Jesus knocked on the bathroom door, but there was no answer. He forced it open and found the dead body. He called for Juan and showed him. Juan then casually walked over to Del and fired four bullets into his chest. He turned to the others. "*Ondolay, ondalay.* We're going home."

When most of them had left the house, Tom gave the signal and they were overwhelmed by a barrage of heavy gunfire. Four were killed immediately. Two were seriously wounded. No one could later recall if a warning had been given.

Bobbie and Sonny watched the monitors and followed Juan and Jesus up the stairs where they ducked into a closet in one of the guest bedrooms. They looked at each other, checked their weapons, and opened the safe room door. Sonny motioned to Bobbie. They took off their shoes and approached the closet on tiptoes. Sonny motioned one, two, three, and on the count of three they emptied their guns into the closet. When the din subsided, they heard voices downstairs. Bobbie reached over and took Sonny's pistol. She hurried back to the safe room, tossed the guns inside and closed the door or, more aptly, sealed the tomb. The guns wouldn't be found until the house was torn down and maybe not then.

Tom and Sandowski had entered the house and heard the gunfire. They approached the stairway and saw Sonny at the top of the stairs.

Tom looked surprised, but lowered his gun. "Would you look at who we have here?"

Bobbie seemed to appear out of nowhere. "Don't tell me—you must be Kelsey's friend?"

Sonny held his hands up. "We didn't do nothing. We were hiding."

"What was all the shooting just now?"

Bobbie shrugged. "There were two more gunmen. I think they committed suicide."

Chapter Twenty-Nine

You Never Know

Sheriff's Office, the Following Morning

Dylan had just learned about the money being taken from the Swiss bank by Dusty and Jake. He was pissed, and his anger wasn't assuaged by the smile on Tom's face.

"You knew!"

"I didn't know they'd be able to pull it off."

"Excuse me—why aren't you pissed too?"

"About what?"

Dylan stormed off to call Jake's cell. Jake answered. "I've been expecting your call."

"Jake—what the fuck? What the fuck? You—I can't believe—"

"Dylan, get a grip. What are you so upset about?"

"Why am I upset? It isn't—it's not your money, and what's up with Dusty?"

"Dylan, it's drug money. The government doesn't even know about it, and by the way, Scooter was killed over it and your parents were killed by a Garcia truck. You can afford to be high and mighty. You've got an Ivy League degree. Well, Dude, in case you forgot—I slept in my first bed when I stayed with you. It so happens that Ashley's family is made up of bankers and when Dusty told Ashley the story of the missing money, they made it kind of a game to try to find out what happened to it. It so happened that it wound up in Switzerland and that's when

Dusty came over to stay with her friend and scope it out. When they finally traced it, it was just sitting there waiting for somebody to take it and Dusty had all the information. It was way too easy."

"Yeah, well tell that to Carlos and his friends."

"Dylan, let me worry about Carlos."

"What are you gonna do now?"

"Ashley and Dusty have a mutual admiration society. We've found a place we all enjoy and plan to try it out and see what happens."

"So you, Ashley, Dusty, and her Swiss lover—what's his name—are going to live happily ever after?"

Jake was laughing uncontrollably.

"So, you think that's funny?"

"Geronimo, you were Dusty's first and only love. Andre is her gay artist friend—a great guy, by the way. Remember when you came back from the sailing trip and said that Dusty had changed, and I replied that we've all changed? Well, *compadre*—we think we know who we are and what we want to do, at least for now. Things are never gonna be exactly like they were. It was important for Dusty, and for me, to do this ourselves, as you were always carrying everybody. Now, it's not like we can't survive without you, it's just that we don't want to. We're going to lay low for a while, but I'll check in from time to time. Like Aunt Sue said, we'll keep the light on for you. Just don't wait too long."

"Jake—just be careful. Promise?"

"You too, brother."

Outside the office, Sonny and Bobbie pulled up in front. Tom walked out to their car. "I'm surprised you're still hanging around."

"I just wanted to tell you we're leavin' town, plus we haven't broken any laws, at least today."

"What about the broken taillights?"

"Are you fucking kidding me?"

Tom laughed. "I'm just messin' with you."

Sonny smiled. "I never know with you. I got a favor to ask. It ain't for me, it's for Petey—the kid who's the new cook. I don't want him to find out about his uncle. Petey's heart is a lot bigger than his brain. I'm gonna get him some new papers so nobody comes lookin' for him. He's gonna be Christopher from now on. You OK with that?"

"If he keeps his nose clean, he'll be fine here, but you two shouldn't hang around. This place is crawling with alphabets and they're all scratching their heads about a couple of missing guns. Seems the bullets that killed the Mexicans—the ones who committed suicide—don't match any of the guns they found and they've scoured the place. I don't suppose you two would know anything about that?"

Sonny and Bobbie looked at each other and shook their heads. "Go figure."

Tom thought he noticed a little sparkle in their eyes and smiled. "If I was you, I'd be on my way to wherever you're going and I don't want to know where that is. *Capiche*?"

Sonny smiled. "*Capiche*."

They had barely cleared the outskirts of Apache Dunes when Bobbie turned to Sonny. "I've brought you nothing but trouble. You can drop me off anywhere."

"I gave you my word that I was gonna take care of you."

"I'm not going to hold you to that."

"You don't know much about Sicilians. When we give our word, we mean it."

"That's sweet, but there's a couple of problems."

"What a surprise—you got problems. Stop the fuckin' presses."

"I'm serious. I'm not the kind of girl you take home to Momma. I've done some terrible things that I can't undo."

"News flash—my mother is long gone and neither of us are saints. I'm gonna tell you something I never told nobody."

"You never told anybody."

"That's what I said. The story was that my father was killed after the war. Maybe, but it don't matter cause I never knew him. My mother was a saint. She had five kids and not a penny to her name, yet she got us to America and made sure we had food to eat, clothes to wear, and a roof over our heads. I don't want to think what she had to do in those days and with no other family, but she did what she had to do and you remind me of her, in that way. You got a good heart and a good mind, but you been dealt a lousy hand in life and you gotta play the cards you're dealt."

"So you were poor, too?"

"Bobbie, if I hadn't been born a boy, I wouldn't have had anything to play with."

"Don't you have any other family?"

"I had an uncle, but he wound up in England after the war and we lost track of him."

"How'd he wind up in England?"

"When the Italian army in North Africa heard the British were close, my uncle and some others threw down their guns and ran toward the British lines. They all wanted to be Montgomery's cook. Apparently, one other guy was faster and my uncle became his sous chef and that's the last we heard of him."

"I forgot that the Italians fought in World War II."

"You weren't listening—they didn't. You said you had a couple of problems. What's the other one?"

"I've got twenty thousand that I didn't tell you about. I guess I owe you ten of that to make you whole on the fifty and that leaves me with just ten grand, period. That's all I have in the world. God's angry with me and He has good reason to be."

"Listen—I'm not what you call a real religious guy, but I do believe there's a God and more so the older I get. I'll tell you a little story. I was watchin' the football games one Sunday and surfing back and forth when the phone rang. I tossed the remote and got up to get the phone. When I sat back down, the channel had switched to a black bishop who was giving a sermon. At first I didn't change the channel because I was watchin' him put on his show, but then I realized I was listening to him. It was like he was speaking directly to me—like God working in strange ways, ya know? Anyway, he was tellin the story of a king who lost a battle for the first time and thought that God had abandoned him, but what really happened is that God saved his life, because, if he had won, two other kings, who he thought was allies, were gonna kill him and take over his kingdom. The bishop said the moral of the story is that sometimes what we think is defeat is just God telling us that we're goin' about something in the wrong way or with the wrong people. Now, your girlfriend was beautiful, but she was also seriously fucked up. That was no future for you."

"What about you and Vinny?"

"I loved Vinny and I'll miss him, but he was a dinosaur. All he knew was the mobbed-up Vegas of the old days, but those days are gone and they ain't comin' back. Most of the casinos are now owned by corporations, and that's a world that Vinny didn't fit into. There's still some rackets, but there's more money to be made by bein' legit. The old bosses, we call 'em mustaches, don't like to admit it, but they all got accountants and lawyers to tell them what to do. They're mostly legit—they just don't want to act like it. The real crooks are now the politicians."

"So let me ask you this. Are you gonna be welcomed back after all that has happened?"

"I'm about to find out."

Sonny handed Bobbie his phone. "Dial this number for me."

She dialed Joey C. in Chicago and handed the phone back to Sonny.

"Who's this?"

"Joey, it's Sonny."

"Sonny, where the fuck you been? I tried your number, but got some Mexican kid."

"I lost my phone and had to get a new one. What's up?"

"You been in a cave or something? You ain't talked to nobody in the last couple days?"

"Joey, you're the only person I talked to. How bad is it?"

"How bad is it? You mean you ain't heard?"

"I told you. I ain't heard nothin'."

"Well, you are one lucky motherfucker. The old man survived the hit from Bellini's guys and get this—the doctor taking the bullets out found a tumor that was the source of his problems!"

"You mean he ain't dyin'?"

"He'll have to do some treatments, but the doc says he should be fine. The old man thinks it's a miracle—maybe it is. He's whatta ya call it, born again."

"Where's that leave me?"

"Where's that leave you? They were afraid that Bellini's guys got you. I never said a word as I didn't know what the fuck was goin' on. They want you back runnin' things in Vegas. There's just a couple of problems."

"I keep hearin' that. What problems?"

"Sonny, I know you're tight with Vince, but he's missing and he was last seen with Bellini and the Asian broad. Bellini's dead and she's disappeared. I know, I know, but they don't know about her. Plus, Vince took fifty large from the casino. His idiot nephew is missing too. The old man wants 'em both dead and that ain't negotiable."

"Joey—listen to me and I don't want to have to repeat this. You listenin'?"

"I'm listenin'."

"That's where I been the last few days—tyin' up some loose ends. You ain't never gonna hear from Vinny or his nephew again."

"Sonny, that's gonna be good news back here. I don't know where Johnny and Vince went wrong, but I seen it happen before. When'll you be back in Vegas?"

"I'm not too far away, but I got an errand to run first. I'll be back tomorrow."

"OK, you call me if you need anything."

"What about the fifty large that Vinny took?"

"What fifty large? *Capiche*?"

"*Capiche*."

After Sonny hung up, Bobbie looked at him. "What errand?"

"Now that I know things are cool in Vegas, we're gonna stop for lunch at a restaurant up the road. You like Italian beef?"

"Who doesn't?"

"Good. Vinny's nephew, the one who was supposed to be tailin' you, is the new cook there. I gotta get him situated, so I'm gonna give him most of what's left of the fifty, help him find a nice place to live, get him a car, and stuff. We might need to spend the night."

Sonny looked at Bobbie and she smiled. "Sonny, you know what happens to bad boys."

Sonny squirmed. "Oh, one thing very, very important. Petey, or Christopher as he'll now be called, can't know about Vinny. You hear me? He can't know. The kids got a big heart and a small brain. We'll tell him that Vinny decided to go to Mexico until things settle down. You got that?"

"I got it. I can help with his house. I always wanted to be an interior decorator."

Sonny looked over at her. "I hope that place in Apache Dunes wasn't supposed to be your showroom—the one you blew up."

They laughed.

Campsite in the Desert Apache Dunes, That Night

Dylan was huddled by the campfire, still trying to sort out his conflicting thoughts. His motorcycle was parked nearby. He saw the light approaching and knew it would be Tom.

Tom parked his truck and retrieved a couple of blankets and two cold beers from the back. He walked over and handed Dylan a blanket and a beer.

"You knew where I would be."

"Of course. It's where your Daddy always came when he needed to think." Tom gazed around. "Probably where Geronimo came, too. I'm pretty sure they're both here right now. There's more beer in the cooler plus a couple of big ass Porterhouse steaks that Aunt Sue put her secret mesquite rub on and a couple of baked potatoes that just need to be warmed up. Oh, and I brought out a bottle of wine the Sports Illustrated writer sent me at Christmas. It's a Jordan Cabernet—supposed to be good."

Tom sat down and started to laugh.

"Please tell me what's funny about any of this?"

"Son, you gotta lighten up a bit. I was just thinkin about how things change. The desert is the only thing that remains the same. We used to come out here by horseback and cook hot dogs. Now you show up on a motorcycle and I came by truck and we have steak and a good bottle of wine."

Dylan finally cracked a smile and clinked bottles with Tom. Tom reached in his pocket and handed Dylan an envelope.

Dylan opened it. "What's this?"

"Looks to me like an airplane ticket—and first class at that."

"So you think I'm going?"

"You can do what you want, but this is the second time I'm gonna tell you that there's nothing here for you right now—particularly with Jake and Dusty over there. You got a passport?"

"Yeah, I got one in college. Everyone else had one."

Dylan walked over to the truck and brought back the cooler.

"You know I never wanted to leave in the first place."

"You seem to forget that you didn't have a choice. Seems like a long time ago."

"Well, I've got a choice now and I don't want to leave you and Aunt Sue. You saved me."

"Son, we saved Jake, for sure, but you were as much a blessing to us as we were to you."

"Aunt Sue always said that God works in strange ways. It was probably for the best that Jake blew out his knee and had to come home."

"Probably? If he'd made his second year he would have gone Hollywood and he wasn't prepared for that. It was only a matter of time."

"How'd he wind up with such a great wife?"

"It's like the song says, angels love bad men …"

Dylan joined in. "That's how it's always been."

They both laughed and clinked bottles again.

"How the hell did he pull this off?"

"There's different types of intelligence. Jake's a survivor and he had the best role model in the world. By the way, how'd you ever find the cave?"

Dylan laughed. "I've been waiting all these years for you to ask. You wanna see it? It's not far away."

"Maybe next time, but I do want to see it."

"So you think there'll be a next time? You think I'll be back?"

"Your daddy and I swore we'd never return, yet we wound up back here. There's something about the desert that brings you back—particularly you, Geronimo."

Dylan was pensive as he studied the ticket. "I know where Madrid is, vaguely, but where is Malaga?"

"I looked it up. It's on the southeast coast of Spain. You change planes in Madrid. They'll meet you at the airport in Malaga."

"One last thing that's been bothering me—what happened to the DEA guy? Everybody around here knew he was on the take. The government had to know, too. Why didn't he just disappear?"

Tom leaned back and gazed at the stars. "It's a bit complicated—what I've been able to figure out. He didn't create the situation; he merely took over from the previous guy, who did create it and who did just disappear, as far as I know. It's funny what happens to some people when they realize everything they fought for and believed in was a sham. Happened to a lot of guys who came back from Nam. They were never the same. My guess is he was dealing with that when cocaine hit and the money overwhelmed everybody. Hell, the government was dealing coke to pay for their secret wars. I don't think he was unhappy when Diablo died, but it was like having the proverbial tiger by the tail. What happens when you let go? His partner was a total fuck up and the partner's wife wasn't any better, but when you start eliminating your problems, it's sorta like tryin to dig yourself out of a hole. Now, I'm starving and you've got a big day ahead of you."

Dylan stood up. "Dad—did you hear me? Dad, thanks. I love you."

They embraced. "Thanks, Son. We love you, too."

Sheriff's Office, the Following Morning

Tom, Sandowski, and Sandoval were sharing Sandowski's flask with their coffee.

"You guys are welcome to stick around for a while. Jake ain't comin' back for a long, long time, and I can put you to work."

"We're in no hurry to leave. The air is like a tonic for me and it seems like we came in handy. Plus, I called my old chief and he said he's issued orders to shoot us on sight if we ever return."

They all laughed.

Homer knocked and entered with another wire and handed it to Tom. Tom read it and whistled.

Sandoval turned to Sandowski. "Looks like we're staying a while."

"One of Al Qaeda's top bombmakers had slipped into Mexico and was making his way north. A couple of CIA agents were tailing him. They found the agents' bodies this morning in the desert – decapitated. The bad guy has disappeared."

"Any chance he comes near here?"

"Odds are he's not far away from here, now."

"So this isn't Mayberry after all?"

"Sometimes I wish it was."

Sandowski turned to Sandoval. "Opie, you ready?"

"I got your fucking Opie!"

Sonny's Car on the Way to Vegas

They had spent most of yesterday getting Petey—scratch that, Christopher—situated. It's amazing how much you can get done in a day when you pay cash. He rewarded them with a veal Parm dinner that was out of this world. Sonny had never seen him this happy. They said their goodbyes in the morning and hopped in the car to complete their journey back to Vegas. For some reason it appeared that Sonny's neck was sore, as he kept rubbing it. Bobbie just smiled.

They were only an hour or so away when Sonny's phone rang. He picked it up without looking at the number. "Who's this?"

"Sonny, it's me, Joey. I meant to tell you something funny."

"It's been a long time since I heard anything funny."

"The guys were all sittin' around talkin' about things and, get this—the thing they say they're gonna miss the most is the Asian broad! They said, where you gonna find another fucking knockout who can use a whip and doesn't take no shit?" Joey laughed.

Sonny looked over at Bobbie who overheard the conversation and was smiling. "You just never know."

About the Author

The author's life experience took him from a small farm in Central Illinois literally around the world in an international business career. Apache Dunes is his first published novel and pays homage to two of his favorite authors, Elmore Leonard and Robert Crais. He resides in Chicago with his wife.

www.ingramcontent.com/pod-product-compliance
Lightning Source LLC
LaVergne TN
LVHW041108080826
845145LV00007B/1731

* 9 7 8 0 5 7 8 8 8 6 1 1 4 *